LOVE ON CALL

THE HEARTWOOD SERIES

MEG RILEY

CONTENT WARNINGS

Some details of the medical profession have been adjusted for your reading enjoyment.

To check content warnings for this book, scan the QR code below or visit megrileyauthor.com/books

CHAPTER 1
ALLY

"ALLY, you look like you're going to be sick," Lucia shouts over the buzz of people around us. She covers the microphone in front of her mouth so she doesn't deafen whoever is on the other end. Truth be told, I feel like I'm going to be sick. I let out a slow exhale to stop my stomach from churning. "What's that saying? You can dress her up, but you can't take her out? You're the epitome of it. Try to fix your face before the camera rolls, okay?"

I'm standing behind a set of tall double doors while two women I've never met fluff my face with makeup brushes. Lucia Delgado is the producer of *Stolen Love*, and she's irritatingly blunt when it comes to giving me feedback about how I read on camera. She hastily checks the clipboard she has balanced on her arm. She's a perfectionist to the point of being neurotic, but her attention to detail makes the network *a lot* of money, so everyone puts up with it. Today, Lucia wears a comfortable outfit consisting of black jeans and a black T-shirt. Her long dark hair is slicked back into a functional low ponytail. No one cares what Lucia looks like as long as she does her job and the production value is high.

I attempt to shape the corners of my mouth into something that resembles a smile, but the bile rising in the back of my throat is making it appear more like a grimace than anything else. The weight of my anxiety has been suffocating me in anticipation of this day. Fidgeting in place, I smooth out my white satin shift dress and rub a finger across my front teeth to make sure the newly applied lip gloss hasn't stained them. My dress clings to my back. I'm already sweating and the main event hasn't even started yet. This is not how I would have imagined my engagement party. Over-the-top weddings are not my jam. I had always envisioned an understated affair; a few close friends and family members in the loft of my favourite restaurant in Vancouver. But judging by the magnitude of our engagement party, this wedding will be anything but understated.

I glance over at my fiancé standing beside me. Nate Winslow is conventionally handsome. His build is tall and slender, and his suit is tailored to show it off. His cropped dirty-blond hair is gelled, and his striking blue eyes stand out against the teal colour of his tie. He is everything I could ever want in a husband, looks-wise at least. But we only met eight months ago on *Stolen Love,* and I wonder for a moment if I'm crazy for agreeing to marry a man that I hardly even know.

The room is spinning around me. Waiting for the towering double doors to open into a ballroom full of people gathered for my televised engagement party is enough to make me pass out.

It's one night, I remind myself. *Just one night and we can go back to our normal lives once some of this hype dies down.* I've been clear with Lucia, or as clear as I could manage. The engagement party would be my last official commitment to the show. She had already roped me into more events beyond what my contract had outlined, and I'd been kicking myself for not saying no sooner. But when Lucia mentioned how much our audience loved seeing Nate and me together, the thought of disappointing millions of viewers was enough to get me to agree to it.

"Places everyone!" Lucia shouts into the room instead of into her mic, forgetting to cover it this time, and I watch the entire room recoil as her voice comes over our headsets. The hair and makeup team back away from me, finally. I usually put my strawberry blond hair up in a ponytail, apply concealer to hide the night shift bags under my eyes, and wear my favourite tinted lip balm. My everyday appearance wasn't enough for the network, so they put together an entire team of professionals so that I'm primed, powdered, and glossed to where I am virtually unrecognizable.

Lucia starts a silent countdown to the doors opening, holding her hand in the air and counting down on her fingers. I glance at Nate again who is busy adjusting his tie. He's so calm and collected, like he does this every day. He looks down at me and winks an icy blue eye.

Lucia starts to back away from the doors, pulling one side open while her assistant pulls the other. My eyes struggle to adjust to the glaring lights as the doors open and the massive ballroom comes into view. The organizers have arranged tables around a spacious dance floor, adorning it with oversized floral arrangements in varying shades of pink. Everything around me glitters with the reflections cast from the chandeliers overhead. It's more lavish than I ever could have imagined.

The whole evening is like some kind of fever dream. Not even a year ago, I stood amidst a bustling labour and delivery unit, straightening out my baby pink scrubs instead of a white satin dress. Being a nurse was my dream job, a title that I was proud to have. I never intended to apply to the show, let alone get a call back from casting. Appearing on reality television was never a part of my five-year plan. As a general rule, I tend to avoid having too much attention on myself. But Spencer, my best friend since the eighth grade, saw an ad on Facebook that they were casting for it and suggested we apply. She had meant it as a joke, I think, and we both filled out the application forms one random Friday night, howling with laughter the whole time. We pulled out our most extravagant outfits and set up a camera on a tripod to film our audition tapes. I hadn't realized Spencer actually submitted them.

My audition tape was never to see the light of day, and now here I am, the top contestant and some sort of overnight celebrity. The reality of it all makes my head spin.

I'm aware of the cameras to my left and right, the crowd of people in front of me beckoning us into the room with their cheers. Their faces become clearer as my eyes adjust to the lights, and I realize that I don't even recognize half of them. Amongst the throng of other reality stars and celebrities, I spot the familiar flash of Spencer's fiery red hair and breathe a sigh of relief. Spencer and I met in homeroom, each looking like a deer in headlights as we walked into our first day of high school. I remember the day so vividly that I can almost smell my Lip Smackers lip balm. She had been wearing a One Direction T-shirt and we had instantly bonded over our obsession with Harry Styles. The obsession held up, too. Although, we had both fully planned on marrying him, so it's ironic that now we're here celebrating my engagement to another man. I make a mental note to find my best friend once all the commotion dies down. She always helps to ground me.

"Hold Nate's hand," Lucia says into the tiny earpiece that I was told to wear. This entire party is being televised live, the TV network wanting to leverage the way fans adore Nate and me on the show. I reach down for Nate's hand but my arm is stiff, and I'm aware of how robotic I look as I wrap my hand around his. "Pretend you like him, Ally."

Nate tugs on my hand, causing me to spin back towards him, and he leans down and plants a kiss right on my mouth. I don't even have time to close my eyes and lean into it. The room erupts in applause and cheering. Nate is completely unfazed by all of this, a showman by nature. He is used to putting on an act for other people, I realize.

Once we have satisfied Lucia's demand for a grand entrance, she leaves us alone to mingle with the guests. I don't recognize any of the people around me, including most of the people congratulating me on our 'fairy-tale' engagement.

About halfway through the night, Nate deserts me to schmooze with strangers, whom he no doubt thinks will help him advance his career. I glance around the room, scanning the crowd to find him. I am counting down the seconds until Lucia comes back on my headset to tell me to stand next to him. An engagement party for a couple who seemingly lack enthusiasm for one another doesn't make for compelling television.

That's the thing; I'm not even sure we're actually in love. Sure, Nate and I had some fun while we were filming the show. Of course we did; there were high-stakes games and strategies, and I have to admit that we complemented each other well. Out in the real world is another story. In real life, Nate Winslow is not the same kind, caring friend and partner I knew on set. I'm still trying to understand his strategy, although I have some ideas.

I spot Nate above the crowd and make my way towards him. He smiles his flashy grin as he sees me approaching and the sight of it makes me feel on edge. Something about his smile seems fake, like it doesn't quite reach his mischievous blue eyes.

"Hey, baby!" Nate greets me. I make a quick mental note to tell him later that he is never to call me baby. "We were just talking about you."

"All positive things, I hope." I try, and fail, to hide the hesitation in my voice. It shakes despite my best efforts.

"Of course." Nate gives me a *play along* look and places a hand on the small of my back. I try not to physically recoil. "Like how we're the ultimate power couple, and that's all down to how devastatingly hot you are." My laugh is nervous as I look around at the women in the conversation who are swooning at the comment.

"Hey lovebirds,"—Lucia's voice crackles in our earpieces—"it's time for the big speech."

Right. The speech. Where I have to stand in front of hundreds of people and make my smile somewhat believable. At least I don't have to say anything. The network wants to capitalize on the way the audience obsesses over how Nate 'worships' me. If only they could be a fly on the wall in our apartment where he rarely pays me any attention.

Nate doesn't hesitate before lifting his glass with one hand and tapping it with the spoon he was carrying in the other. A hush falls over the room, and all eyes turn to where Nate and I stand.

"Evening, everyone," Nate begins, that smarmy smile creeping over his face again, "thank you all so much for being here tonight. It means the world to us to have our closest friends and family in one room to celebrate our engagement."

Our closest friends? Where? The network didn't even invite my parents. They hired actors instead; my parents were too middle-class, I guess, and it ruined the illusion of the power couple they wanted. There's more than a good chance that my parents would have disregarded the invite, anyway.

"First off, I want to thank Nancy and Rob." It's Richard, actually. He could at least get their names right. "Ally's wonderful parents for accepting me into their family and giving me the gift of my life that is Ally Wells." Nate raises his glass and nods towards the two made-up middle-aged people smiling and waving and pretending to be my parents.

"Ally, my queen. My better half. My bride." I should feel more of a spark than I do when Nate speaks those words, but they sound so scripted coming out of his perfectly veneered mouth. "I could not have achieved the success I have today if it wasn't for you."

Yeah, you've helped forward your predatory career by giving yourself internet clout. I have to force back a visible eye roll.

"Not to mention, you let me live out my teenage fantasy of getting with a sexy nurse." Everyone laughs at the half-assed joke, except for me. And Spencer, I notice. Spencer and I make eye contact across the room and she raises her eyebrows, knowing how much I loathe when people reduce my career to nothing but a sex object. Nate would understand that about me, too, if he took some time to get to know me. My blood boils to the surface of my skin. I can't hold up the smile I have plastered on my face anymore.

"I can't do this," I whisper under my breath. I have no idea where I'm going with this or what I'm planning to do once the words have come out of my mouth. All I can say with any confidence at this moment is that I regret giving up the life I had for this. The show promised that I would find true love, but all it gave me was this polished, fake version. I would rather be single for the rest of my life than live in this sham of a fairy tale for one more second.

Nate's expression falls and the crowd murmurs, no doubt debating what could be going on between us.

"What?" Nate asks, his tone incredulous but harsh. He won't let me go that easily. I'm too integral to his success. My title as a nurse is supposed to make him appear more favourable, more real, to the public and his clients. Clients may not be the correct term. The people he bamboozles into handing over their failing businesses so he can restructure them into what I'm certain are pyramid schemes is a more apt description.

"I can't do this," I say, louder and feigning more confidence this time.

"Oh, you're doing this," Nate hisses through a tight-lipped smile. "Put on a smile, Ally. We're in love, remember?"

"I won't. I can't." I can't bring myself to say anything more. I'm pretty sure if I tried, I could puke in front of everyone. Although, that would be interesting for ratings.

Scanning the room to find Spencer, I notice her standing at the edge of the crowd, slack-jawed at the sudden outburst of courage I summoned. I have to grab Spencer and get out of here. I release Nate's hand—which is unexpectedly difficult due to his tight grip —and manoeuvre through the crowd to reach my best friend. Spencer will come up with a plan. She always does.

"What are you doing?" Spencer asks, her voice a familiar low and raspy pitch. She doesn't wait for my reply. "You know what? I don't care. Explain later. Let's go." Spencer grabs me by the wrist and pushes through people who appear shocked and confused, but they don't stop me. The film crew is trailing close behind, trying to capture all the drama. I don't look back at Nate, although I can guess he is red-faced and fuming about my unexpected departure.

My vision is spinning and I can barely comprehend what just happened. Thank God for Spencer, who doesn't hesitate to tell the film crew to "get the fuck out of her face" and asks the nearest server to direct us to the back exit of the event centre.

Spencer doesn't stop until both she and I are standing outside in the back alley, and once she does, she doesn't ask any questions except for one.

"Where do we need to go?"

"Can we go to your place?" It's only eight blocks from the event centre downtown, and I know no one can find me there. It's one perk of having a fiancé who never pays attention to anything I do. He would never guess where to search for me.

I say nothing until we are inside Spencer's familiar apartment. This little one-bedroom has always been a safe place for me, especially since the show started filming. It's a place where I can go under the radar and be incognito for a while. It's close enough to downtown but still tucked away from the prying paparazzi on a quiet little street in the west end. I appreciate it more than ever tonight when all I need is to collect my thoughts and process the mess I've made of my life.

I don't want to do anything except shower and scrub off the thick layer of makeup, throw on an old pair of Spencer's sweats, and pour myself a glass of wine. Once I've done all that, I flop onto Spencer's old worn couch, sitting across from her. I pull up a thick blanket around my shoulders, intertwining our legs beneath it. Spencer is looking across the couch at me, eagerly awaiting what I'm about to say, but it's still too early for me to try and explain. I don't know what just happened myself. I open my mouth to start, but failing to find the right words, I take another gulp of my wine instead.

"That bad, eh?"

"God, Spence, where do I even start?" I shake my head and peer up at the ceiling as if I'll find the answer written there.

"Maybe start by telling me why you ran away from your engagement party like it was your execution."

"I don't know. I was looking around at the extravagance of it all. Looking at all those people that I didn't even know, that don't even know me. Nate made his speech, and I looked to him, hoping to find familiarity and feel secure standing next to him."

"But you didn't," Spencer finishes.

"No. I mean, yes, exactly. I felt the opposite." I take another sip of my wine, cradling the glass in both hands as if it were a chalice of life-giving nectar. "He didn't even remember my dad's name. Not that they were even there to notice."

"I was saving that one to bug you about later," Spencer says with a soft chuckle. The sound eases some of the tension in my chest.

"God, he's such an arrogant prick. Do you know what he does for work?"

"Yeah, he's like some angel investor or something, right?"

"You could say that. He brags and brags that he's this philanthropist angel investor or something. But really, he uses Daddy's money to buy up the majority of failing businesses, and he strips them down and turns them into pyramid schemes—sorry, it's called multi-level marketing." This time, I don't hide my eye roll.

"Oh my God, what a slimy piece of shit!"

My phone pings from beneath the blanket I pulled around me. Fumbling around for it and trying not to spill my wine, I check the screen.

"Speaking of the slimy piece of shit." I turn the phone to show her the screen. There are messages pouring in from Nate, each one more vicious than the last.

NATE

Ally, where are you?????

> For fuck's sake, Ally. How could you humiliate me like that???

> Answer your goddamned phone.

> I swear to God, Ally, you made me look like a fool tonight, and you're going to regret it if you don't answer your phone.

> Ally, baby. Whatever I did, I'm sorry. Please pick up your phone so we can talk about this.

"Yeah, not a chance," I say after I read out the last one and throw my phone back down on the couch.

"So, what are you going to do? You can't avoid him forever, right?" I consider Spencer's words. I can't avoid Nate forever. Not with the show airing soon and the last few public appearances that the network scheduled for the release.

The network. Lucia.

As if on cue, my phone pings again. It's a voicemail. I play it out loud for Spencer to hear.

"You better have an explanation for this shit show you stirred up. I'm hoping that you and Nate had this planned as some publicity stunt or some shit. Otherwise, you bet your ass the network will be coming for you, and they will be ripping every penny they gave you for the show out of your social-climbing paws."

I look at Spencer, wide-eyed, silently pleading for her to come up with some fantastic idea for a way out of this.

"What am I supposed to do?"

"Girl, you are in deep." Spencer shakes her head and glances into her lap, thinking.

"I think I need to get out of town for a while," I admit.

"You think that's a good idea? Running away from all this?"

"I mean, what other choice do I have? And I'm not running— I need to let the dust settle here for a bit. I can handle the network, but Nate is going to find some way to drag me and my reputation through the mud in the most public way possible."

"You don't want to say to hell with what other people think and hold your head high? You could go back to your job at the hospital, try to get back to your normal life." Spencer is right; I should be able to hold my head high, but that's not me. Others' opinions matter to me. I've already disappointed enough people here. My parents when I quit my job and went on the show in the first place, my coworkers when I broke the news to them, and now Nate. I can't even confront Nate about the problems in our own relationship, let alone stand up to him now. Conflict is not my strong suit and I would be a quivering mess. Frankly, running away sounds rather nice at this point. I don't see another way.

"I can't go back to my old job. Everyone reacted like I was some superficial, vapid person looking for fame when I told them I was leaving to go on the show. To go back now that I've failed ... it would be humiliating."

"You don't owe anyone an explanation. It will all blow over." Spencer is right.

"I can't, Spence. I can't face all those judgmental stares and whispers behind my back. I can't return as the girl who abandoned everything for a reality show engagement that didn't work out. I need to disappear for a while."

Spencer sighs and looks at me with sympathetic eyes. "If that's what you need to do, let's make a plan. We'll figure out a way for you to leave with no one knowing, at least for now."

I breathe a sigh of relief. "Thanks, Spence. I don't know what I would do without you."

It feels as if the world is against me. First my parents, and now Nate. Having Spencer in my corner makes me feel like I might be able to get through this alive.

CHAPTER 2
MASON

"THERE'S my favourite piece of eye candy!" A white-haired elderly woman greets me as I enter the small exam room carrying her file. She's petite, though not frail, and always enjoys flirting with me. If I'm being honest, the days I get to see Mrs. Rose are always the highlight of my week.

"This is why you're my favourite patient, Alma. Don't tell the others." I caution her with a wink. Her blue eyes glimmer as she smiles, and all the creases in her face lift upward with it. I love treating my elderly clients. Some of them don't have any family around and their visit to the clinic is the most socialization they get. I make sure they enjoy it as much as I do. Though I admit, the friendly banter and personal conversation I like to carry with my patients is difficult to keep up with how pressed for time I am during my appointments.

"I better watch how much I flirt with you. I wouldn't want to go scaring away any eligible bachelorettes," she jokes.

"You're the most important woman in my life these days, Alma," I quip, landing a playful tap on her shoulder.

"Well, I hope not! There must be a special lady you look forward to going home to."

"It's funny that you think I go home," I say in a jovial tone as I flip through Alma's chart. But this time, I'm not joking. I've been sleeping in my office on a foldable cot since it became clear that if I wasn't available to handle emergencies, people could get hurt. Not to mention the fact there's rarely an opportunity for me to go back to my apartment for any length of time. I spend most of my time after work holed up in my office, finishing my charting and making sure referrals are in. If I want to maintain the level of care that the people of Heartwood expect since my father was in charge, I need to be here.

"How are you managing since your fall three weeks ago?" I ask, eager to change the subject. I'm referring to an incident that involved Mrs. Rose being knocked over by someone's dog on the street. It had escaped from the backyard, and Alma ended up with a broken arm and more than a few bruises, the faint hint of yellow and purple still obvious around her eye.

"Oh, I manage just fine ..." Her voice trails off as if what she said is not entirely truthful. I squint at her until she gives in and admits to what I am fearing. "It's hard for me to get around the house these days, and even harder to get out to do my grocery shopping." She points at the sling supporting her small and shaky arm. "I'm so tired since I fell, and it's even more exhausting doing everything with one hand."

"Is there anyone who can come and help you around the house?" I study the old woman's face, a deep line of concern forming between my brows.

"No, since Lonny died four years ago, I've been on my own. And now my kids have all left Heartwood. They wanted bigger and better things for themselves in the city, I guess." I hate the thought of Alma all alone in her house with no one to visit her. The image causes a deep ache in my chest. "My neighbour picks me up some eggs or milk on her way home if she can, but with her three young kids she's busy, and I don't want to burden her. Once all this has healed, I'll be back to my old spry and capable self in no time."

"Okay, well, I'll ask around and get you some help. In the meantime, we can take that sling off and give you your arm back." Alma shoots me an appreciative smile.

"You're doing a phenomenal job since you took over for your father," she offers. I shrug. "The whole town agrees. They notice how hard you work for them."

A lump forms in my throat as Alma speaks the words that I have been wanting to hear but can't make myself believe. I've barely kept my head above water for the last year. I never planned on coming back and taking over the clinic. In fact, I never planned on coming back to Heartwood at all. Once I finished my residency and fellowship in Ontario, I had hoped to stay there to work as an emergency physician at Toronto General. I wanted the accolades of working in a high-volume trauma centre. I wanted the adrenaline and the pay that came with working in a large centre.

Until my father reached out to me and shared the news of his Parkinson's diagnosis. I came back to help with the clinic. The situation was supposed to be temporary until we found a replacement to take over his practice, but his condition became worse by the day. His motor functioning rapidly declined, leaving me to pick up most of the slack. And by most of the slack, I was picking up all of it.

My younger brothers have been no help and wouldn't be able to help anyway, as none of them had wanted to follow in our father's footsteps like I did. Grady had always wanted to start his own business and now owns the bar in town. Hudson's dream is to make captain at the fire hall, and Jett. Jett is still a boy at heart, excelling in his ski lessons and now competing at a professional level. As the oldest of the four, I shoulder the brunt of the responsibility in the family.

By the time my father passed earlier this year, I had effectively taken over all the patient load, so it made sense to stay. The town of Heartwood relied heavily on the small outpost clinic, and I was determined to preserve my father's legacy. They also trusted me, being a Landry and all, more than they would have trusted a new doctor who was an outsider to the community.

"I appreciate you saying that, Alma. I'm afraid my father's shoes are proving to be difficult to fill," I say while my fingers fumble with the knot in Alma's sling.

"Nonsense, you're doing just fine," Alma reassures me, but I'm not so sure. I feel like I've been failing the clinic, especially after a patient died under my care a few months ago.

I finish assessing Alma's arm, checking her range of motion without the sling, and follow her back out to the waiting room, sending her off with a wave.

"Come and visit anytime, Alma. I mean it, don't wait until the pain is so bad you're having a hard time walking around the house." I place a gentle hand on the woman's shoulder. Alma nods her thanks and slowly makes her way out the clinic doors to a taxi waiting for her in the small parking lot in front of the clinic. I look around at the weeds pushing up through the cracks in the pavement.

She's my tenth patient of the afternoon and far from my last. Walk-in hours started after lunch, and these days, the waiting room overflows with people well before noon.

Today is no different, I note, sneaking back behind the reception area to pour myself a cup of coffee at the machine behind the desk. Winnie, the clinic's receptionist since before I could walk, always has a fresh pot brewed. I'll end up drinking it cold, as usual.

I glance around the waiting room. A group of children are playing with the toys strewn around the carpet in the corner. A mother is soothing her crying baby. A man is asleep, snoring away in one of the old leather seats by the window.

The clinic has seen better days, but I haven't had time to redecorate since taking it over from my father two years ago. The same leather-padded chairs are arranged in neat rows. A few old oak tables are scattered between them, with pamphlets laid out in neat piles. My patients never seem to mind that the clinic is outdated, although with the rate my patient load is growing, it may soon be time to expand the cramped seating area.

I pick the next chart out of the rack behind the reception desk and overhear Winnie engaged in a conversation Mr. Donovan, one of my regular patients.

"I'm so sorry, Reggie. There isn't time to get you in today." Winnie sounds exasperated. The increase in patient volumes has been affecting her too. I can see it in every new line that forms on her face, the dark circles that shadow her eyes.

I watch as the man's face falls. Reggie Donovan had known my father when they were young. Losing Jack Landry meant more to him than losing his doctor. No matter how hard I try, I can't shake the sensation that I'm letting everyone down, including myself.

"You can come by again tomorrow when the walk-in hours start, or I'm sure I can find you an appointment time later in the week." Winnie has been trying her hardest to make sure everyone gets seen, but there's only so much she can do within the clinic hours.

"Tomorrow isn't going to work. I would have to arrange transportation into Heartwood, and today was the only day that my son could drive me." The disappointment on Reggie's face is too much for me to take.

"Reggie! So good to see you," I interject in the conversation, extending a hand to him. "I have some time tomorrow morning in between house calls. How about I stop by the house and check you out?"

"Mason—" Winnie says, a warning glare casting over her face. Reggie's house isn't a quick stop in town; it's at least a thirty-minute drive into the valley. Which explains his transportation issues since Reggie has long since given up using a vehicle. He now relies on his family and friends in town when he needs them.

"It's not a problem. Tomorrow. Be there or be square, Reg." I raise my coffee mug towards him as I turn and stride back toward my office to prepare for my next patient.

As the last sliver of sunlight dips below the tree line, I flop into the shabby office chair in the back room of the clinic and stare at the pile of files stacked on my desk. I wipe a hand down my face, pull the first chart off the never-ending pile, and flip it open. The day of patients has wiped me out; I already stayed late to see each patient who came for walk-in hours and it will be close to midnight by the time I finish my charts. The work has to be done. Charts will continue to pile up, and I will continue to fall more and more behind. The place is less like a clinic these days and more like an emergency department, open twenty-four hours. If the responsibility of keeping it running didn't solely fall on me, I might find enjoyment in working here. I pull out the bottle of scotch that I keep stashed in the bottom drawer and pour myself a dram.

A noise in the hallway pulls my eyes away from the paperwork in front of me.

"Winnie?" I say, swivelling the chair around and tipping it back to look at her. "It's almost seven. I didn't realize you were still here." She's leaning on the door frame, arms crossed.

"I could say the same about you." A silence stretches out between us. Winnie is gearing up for one of her motherly lectures. There's a fight in her eyes. Even at thirty-two years old and a Doctor of Medicine later, she still wants to tell me how to live my life.

"Out with it," I grumble, cutting to the chase. I take an extra-long gulp of scotch hoping the burn in my throat will ease the cool sting of whatever is coming next. That she's getting ready to point out yet another way I'm failing.

"I'm getting worried about you, hun. You're burning the candle at both ends here. Sleeping in the clinic, working past the clinic hours. It's too much." I sense some hesitancy in Winnie's voice. It's not the first time she's brought this up, and during the last conversation that started similarly, I had responded in a less-than-gracious manner. In fact, this is the only thing Winnie and I ever fight about.

Winnie has been the receptionist at the clinic for decades. My father hired her when he opened the clinic; she's an old friend of my parents. With an extensive knowledge of the place, she knows every patient by name and is familiar with each of their family members. Having known me for just as long, she is family to me, too.

I was only ten years old when my mother died, and Winnie didn't hesitate to step in and be there for me. She took me to soccer practice when my father was busy at the clinic, held me when I had my heart broken for the first time, and took me shopping for my prom tux. She convinced me not to buy the white one with a hot pink shirt underneath and for that, I'm forever in her debt.

I grit my teeth against the harsh words I'm about to give her and think better of it. I can't hide the gruffness in my voice, letting Winnie know she needs to back off.

"There's no other choice, Winnie. The work has to get done, and I'm the only one who can do it." I hope that the finality in the statement means she'll drop the conversation, but I know Winnie better than that.

"Maybe it's time to hire some extra help around here." *Oof*. It's not the first time she's suggested it, but it still stings. People only hire extra help when they are incapable of handling things on their own, and that's not me.

"You know how I feel about this, Winnie. I made a promise to keep this clinic running the way Dad left it. I can't have other people coming in here and taking over. I need to do this myself."

"But the clinic isn't running, Mason." The hesitancy in Winnie's voice sounds more like desperation now. "Have you seen how long our waitlist is? Because I have. Do you realize how many people call here day in and day out asking for an appointment? I'm the one who has to break the news to them. That they'll be waiting months to get in. It's wearing me down. People are frustrated, I'm frustrated."

It's the first time I notice how tired Winnie looks. She still has her vivacious demeanour, her dark auburn pixie cut hair keeps her looking youthful, but new lines have formed around her eyes. I'm keenly aware of the reality that Winnie is reminding me of, and I feel it intensely. But I made a promise to my father to keep his legacy alive, to live up to his reputation. My father managed the clinic all by himself; I can't admit defeat or show signs of weakness.

It kills me though, to see Winnie like this, defeated and burnt out. I care about her; after all, she's like a mother to me. I hate seeing her this way, perhaps more than I hate the idea of this clinic changing, but I can handle this. I need to devise another solution, one that doesn't involve bringing someone new into the clinic.

It isn't stubbornness on my part; hiring someone new for the clinic would cause a commotion in the town. As much as Heartwood is growing and evolving as more people flock to the small town, there is still a vast majority of people who are resistant to change. I'm determined to maintain some of the charm of Heartwood. The clinic is a fixture that people rely on; they like having a doctor that they know, that they can trust.

"I'll consider it, Winnie. I can't promise anything, but I'll consider it." I hope Winnie doesn't detect the lie.

"That's what you said last time, Mason. And I'm tired of hearing the same empty promises over and over again." Her already petite frame becomes even shorter as her shoulders droop.

"It's not an empty promise, Winnie. I will consider it. But if my answer is still no, then you have to find a way to accept that." I'm about to turn back to my charts when Winnie drops a small stack of papers on my desk.

"While you're mulling it over, have a look through some of these resumes." She's tabbed some of them, the names highlighted to show the ones she considers the top contenders.

"What are these?" I know what they are. Winnie has gone over my head and looked for candidates for the clinic—candidates that I will ultimately refuse to hire. But I need her to say it.

"They're qualified and motivated people, Mason. Nurses who would jump at the chance to work in a clinic like yours." Winnie turns, walking back down the hall before leaving the clinic.

A nurse. Winnie wants me to hire a nurse. How is that going to help me, anyway? My eyes roamed over the resume that Winnie no doubt left on the top of the pile so I wouldn't miss it.

Ally Wells ... Registered Nurse ... Labour and delivery experience in a large urban hospital in Vancouver. Hasn't worked in over a year. Well, that rules her out.

I don't even bother looking through the rest. If this Ally Wells is the top contender, I don't care to know who came in second and third. I toss the pile of papers in the wastepaper basket and return to my charts.

I can handle this on my own. Every day is an uphill battle, with exhaustion weighing me down, but somehow, I still find a way to complete my tasks. I can do this until I come up with a better solution.

CHAPTER 3
ALLY

THE HEAT on the tarmac rises off the asphalt in pulsing waves. I shield my eyes from the sun, trying to take in my surroundings. It appears as if the tiny airport dropped from the sky, with only one runway cutting through a flat grassy expanse. The open field in which I am now standing is surrounded by a thick forest, stretching up the rocky mountainside until there's nothing but brown and grey rock. I crane my neck to take in the mountains looming around me on all sides. They are breathtaking, if not somewhat intimidating. The late summer heat means that the snow has completely melted, but I can imagine how stunning the rocks would be, blanketed in snow.

Heartwood is nestled in a deep valley, in the middle of the Rocky Mountains, on the border between British Columbia and Alberta. A world-renowned ski resort located two towns away, roughly an hour's drive from here, is the only reason anyone knows this place exists.

I had never heard of Heartwood until I started perusing online job postings, desperate for anything that would be my ticket out of Vancouver. I eventually stumbled upon a viable option, advertising for a registered nurse position in a rural outpost clinic, and I knew that this was my chance to get away.

I got a call back a few days later and accepted the job on the spot. The woman on the phone seemed friendly and kind and was very reassuring when I explained that I hadn't worked as a nurse for over a year. I wonder if my nursing skills will be like riding a bike, hoping that they will come back to me like muscle memory. First impressions are a strong suit of mine. People take to my bubbly and outgoing personality without much convincing. I'm determined to make a positive impression at the clinic, too.

Nate had told me he loved the fact that I was a nurse, that I cared so much about helping others. He liked how it looked to other people. I had intended to go back to my job after the wedding, once all the commotion had died down after filming, but Nate was adamant that I shouldn't.

"Let's ride this wave out, baby. Keep the momentum that we have from the show," he would say, trying to convince me to make social media my full-time job. Ironic that he always suggested dropping the nurse card every once in a while in a post. He expected me to give up everything that I had, but he never once returned the favour. His work always came first, and I was left in his wake.

He didn't take it well after I left him at the engagement party. The texts hadn't let up in the few days following the disastrous event. Every opportunity Nate got to publicly shame me, he did. His strategy got pettier and more vicious as the days went on. At first, he tried to garner sympathy, posting photos and videos of himself wallowing in his fancy high-rise apartment. Soon, he started calling me out, attacking my character and telling blatant lies. I found it hard to feel sorry for him with the backdrop of his floor-to-ceiling windows overlooking the downtown Vancouver skyline. His followers didn't have as hard a time as I did; they showed no mercy towards me in the comments.

I endured three weeks of a constant barrage of posts on Instagram and TikTok, most of them siding with Nate. Everyone had turned against me, including people who had acted like my friend to my face. They turned on me the moment I prioritized myself over anyone else. Luckily, Spencer had let me hide out in her apartment until I found this job and booked my flight.

Now, standing in the midday sun, I close my eyes and let the golden rays warm my skin. I inhale. The air smells like fresh pine and possibilities.

There's only one building that I can see; the squat, one-storey airport terminal sitting off the runway. The door on the side of the building is open, awaiting my arrival. I found myself alone on the small plane, prompting me to question whether I had selected an unusual flight time or if there truly existed a dearth of individuals with aspirations of visiting Heartwood. There are plenty of people leaving, though. As I enter the building, I notice enough people to fill the plane that I got off, all waiting to board.

The air is as stagnant inside as it is out, and many of the passengers waiting are fanning themselves with magazines they purchased from the little shop in the corner of the terminal. I wonder where they're going, if they are waiting in eager anticipation for whatever summer vacation destination they have planned. Or if any of them are running away from their lives like I am.

I make my way over to the old rusty luggage carousel as it creaks to life. It would be easier for them to bring my luggage to me, being the only passenger, but I wait for my bags to appear from the chute. I lean on one hip and pull out my phone, a habit when I'm waiting for something to happen. One notification, and it's from Spencer.

SPENCER

Let me know when you arrive. xx

Just landed! Waiting for my bags

I only have time to send a quick update when I notice the first of my bags come careening down. The first one makes its way past me and I heave it over the side while the next one comes out and bumps onto the conveyor belt. As I pull another bag over, I remember I have four more coming and realize I am going to need more luggage carts.

You wouldn't be able to tell that I was the sole passenger of the plane, with all the luggage making its way around the terminal. I don't even know why I bothered to bring all of my clothes with me; I bought most of them before going on *Stolen Love*, and judging by the weathered appearance of the airport already, I won't have a use for my fancy dinner dresses here in Heartwood. They are now just a painful reminder of that chapter of my life. Maybe one day I'll be able to reminisce on this time and laugh, but not today. Right now, all I feel is the sting of failure and the sour taste of false promises.

I push the two luggage carts piled high with my six suitcases and one garment bag full of ball gowns flopped on top over to the rental car desk. There's a cheerful and pink-cheeked woman sitting behind the counter, her eyes going wide as she looks up over her computer screen and sees me peeking over my mountain of luggage.

"Staying a while?" the woman says with a warm chuckle.

"I hope so." I give her a shy smile as her nails clack against her keyboard.

"Well then, welcome to Heartwood. Unfortunately, I only have one vehicle that will fit all those bags you've got." She turns in her seat and examines the big board behind her, searching for the right set of keys among the thirty or so pairs that hang from tiny gold hooks. "Ah, here we go."

She turns back to face me and hands me an old-looking set of keys, the only one with a rabbit foot for a keychain.

"It'll be the red truck at the end of that line of cars." She points down the row of cars in the lot outside the airport terminal.

I wheel the toppling luggage cart through the parking lot, sweat beading on my forehead in the heat.

This has to be a joke, I nearly say out loud as I reach the end of the row and examine the old red pickup truck. The side mirrors are off-kilter, and patches of the paint have peeled and rusted. I am not sure I trust that the old beater will turn on.

I eye the Jeep Wrangler sitting next to it. It's not new, none of the vehicles in this lot are new, but right now it's looking more reliable than the rust bucket I've been given. It's the kind with only two doors but has a hard top and plenty of space in the back for my luggage. I consider heading back to the airport and asking if I could take the Jeep instead, but I think better of it. The woman had been so friendly and kind to me that the thought of telling her I don't like the truck makes me queasy.

These are your first impressions here; don't want to ruffle any feathers. I huff a breath, readying myself to load the suitcases into the bed of the old truck.

I make the thirty-minute drive from the airport into the town of Heartwood. The truck, although it looks old and beat up, gets me around fine. I paid for a month's rental, which buys me some time to find another solution for transportation. The truck will do for now.

By the time I reach the main drag, winding through a couple of quiet streets, I've already seen most of the town. Houses spread out around the street which has a small grocery store, a pub and liquor store, some quaint and cozy restaurants, a bookstore, and a café, which will be my first stop. The flight was so short that they didn't have any snacks on board, and I was so eager to leave the city that I forgot to eat before I boarded. The growling in my stomach isn't letting me forget that fact.

I pull the truck up next to a similar one, only blue, and not as beat up. Putting the truck in park, I hop out and peer up at the wooden sign above the door, Thistle + Thorne.

The bell above the door jingles as I enter the café and the door shuts behind me. A friendly brunette with wavy hair cut in a short blunt bob waves from behind the espresso machine.

"Welcome!" She smiles, her eyes bright and cheerful. She goes back to the drink she's making, and the espresso machine hisses as she's obscured by a cloud of steam.

The café is warm and inviting, and not at all like the modern hipster coffee shops I'm used to back in Vancouver. No, this café could be someone's home. The furniture doesn't match but somehow still goes together. There are a few tables with an odd assortment of antique-looking wooden chairs, and some armchairs positioned strategically for conversation by the window. A bookshelf lines the wall on one side but doesn't only house books; it also stores a variety of board games. Pictures adorn the walls in mismatched frames. Some of them are wooden, and others are brass, but all of them contain paintings and artwork made by people in the town. I know this from the small cards in the corner of each one. It doesn't matter who made it; some are doodles done by children, and others are professional-level-looking photos.

I step up to the counter when the bell chimes again behind me. The café is quiet, but it's not because of a lack of customers. I skim over the menu, which is handwritten on a dusty old chalkboard. I'm so hungry that everything sounds appealing.

The brunette behind the bar continues making the coffee she was working on, pouring the steamed milk into a large ceramic mug and using careful motions to create a beautiful leaf pattern on top. A second barista comes out from the back room and greets me by the till.

"Hi there! What can I get for you?" He's young, in his late teens judging by the way he hasn't quite filled out his lanky frame, and his toothy smile full of braces.

"Is the only difference between the ham sandwich and the ham-on-rye the bread?" I ask, and the words coming out of my mouth make my mouth water.

"Uh, yeah. I guess so. And the ham-on-rye has Swiss cheese

instead of cheddar," he answers. I tap a finger on my chin, considering.

"Do they both have mustard?" I fucking hate mustard.

"The ham-on-rye has Dijon," the barista says, a hint of impatience in his tone.

"Can I get it without the mustard?" I ask.

The young barista opens his mouth to answer when I hear a short huff of breath from behind me. I turn to see a man waiting, arms crossed in front of him. I'm stunned by the sight of the most remarkably square and defined jawline, softened only by the shadow of stubble. A muscle twitches in his jaw, evidence of his insufferable impatience.

"Is there a problem?" I ask him. The soft, dark waves on his head bounce as he nods his head. His deep brown eyes are cutting right through me.

"Yeah, I'd like to get my coffee. Sometime today would be great," the man mutters back. His voice is deep and rumbles through my chest, warming it on the way through. He's tall and well-built, the rolled-up sleeves of his flannel button-down showing off his muscular forearms. I might even think him attractive if it wasn't for his abrupt and gruff attitude. But I have no time for rudeness. Manners and politeness go a long way in my world. It's a simple and effective method to ensure that those in my vicinity are at ease.

I shoot him a disapproving glare, but with my big blue eyes and bright features, I'm not as intimidating as I hope. I turn back to the barista to ask another question about the sandwiches, but the man cuts in front of me.

"She'll have the Thanksgiving turkey sandwich." He orders for me, and blood rushes to my cheeks in embarrassment and rage.

"You can't order for people just because you're in a hurry." My hand instinctively goes to my hip, a quirk that always makes me come across as a little more brazen than I feel.

"I can, and I did. You'll thank me later." The arrogant jerk has the audacity to wink at me. "It's the best sandwich on the menu, anyway." I make a sound that can only be described as a squeak.

"Play nice, Mason," the brunette behind the espresso machine warns. "He is right, though, the Thanksgiving sandwich is to die for."

I narrow my eyes at Mason before turning back to the kid behind the till to finish placing my order.

"Fine. I'll have that and a medium latte, two honeys." I ignore the man as he scoffs behind me.

"That'll be eleven fifty," Braces informs me. I reach into my wallet and pull out my credit card to pay. "Uh, sorry, our machine is down today. Cash only."

"Okay, no problem. I'll have to use some change." I rifle through my wallet, pulling out a few coins.

"Hurry it up, Honeybee." My shoulders tense at the voice behind me. This guy won't quit, and now a demeaning little nickname. Get real.

Mason reaches around me and smacks a ten-dollar bill down on the counter as I'm counting out enough loonies to pay for my order. My mouth falls open, but he smiles back, a stupid, arrogant smile.

I move a few paces over to the end of the counter and wait for my order, but his stare is still burning the back of my neck.

"You're welcome," he says behind me, and I ignore it. I refuse to spend any more of my time and energy on Mason.

He releases me from the grip of his gaze, and I hear him order a drip coffee, black. Typical. Anyone who drinks their coffee black seems to possess some kind of moral superiority complex. I make a silent prayer that the town is bigger than it seems on first impression because I am going to do whatever I can never to run into him again.

The woman behind the counter starts working on my order, expertly multitasking as she strikes up a conversation with me. It's a welcome distraction. At least most people in Heartwood seem friendly and polite. Mason seems to be the exception.

"I take it you're new around here." She looks at me with doe eyes from under feathery curtain bangs while the steamer hisses in the metal carafe.

"Uh, I am. How can you tell?" The woman raises her eyebrows at me like it's obvious.

"Well, for starters, you're much more put together than most people in this town." I glance down at my outfit. I'm not done up, but I do like to be polished, and I guess my white silk blouse and ballet flats don't scream small town. "And second, you haven't met our resident grump." The woman's eyes dart over to where Mr. I'm-better-than-everyone-because-I-drink-black-coffee is standing, paying for his order.

"Fair," I concede. "I just moved here. I'm starting a new job."

"Oh? It's not every day that people come here looking for work. There isn't much to do around here except for logging, and I would be willing to bet that you're no logger." The corners of her eyes crinkle as she giggles at her own joke. "What do you do?"

The woman turns to the panini grill and starts heating the Thanksgiving turkey sandwich as I pick up the latte she slid across the counter.

"I'm a nurse. I'll be starting at the clinic here," I say, and she whirls around, but she doesn't look back towards me. Her eyes bore a hole through Mason, who is still standing at the counter, placing the lid on his black coffee. His gaze is already fixed on me, though, creating this uncomfortable triangle of awkward staring.

"Ah. Well, that's a pleasant change ..." the barista says, her voice trailing off. She's still looking at Mason, who is still looking at me. The barista's glance shifts between us. What on earth is happening here? Is this the twilight zone? My eyes dart back and forth in time with hers.

As if shaking himself out of a trance, a low growl comes out of

Mason's throat as he turns on his heel and storms out of the café, leaving his still steaming coffee on the counter.

I don't know what has happened, but I can't bring myself to ask as I stand in front of the counter, slack-jawed.

"Don't mind him," the woman behind the counter says before I can even formulate a response. "Mason's a bit territorial and more than a bit protective of the town, especially with newcomers. He can come across as a bit standoffish, but he'll warm up to you in no time."

Ha. That's a good one, I think to myself, but outwardly I nod. There is no way I'll be spending enough time around this man for him to warm up to me. Not if I can help it. The whole point of me moving to Heartwood was to get away from pompous assholes that think they can speak for me. I've had enough of that with Nate; there's no way I'm going to befriend his Heartwood personality doppelgänger.

"In the meantime," the barista continues, "welcome to Heartwood. My name's Poppy Thorne. I own this place and the little plant shop next door." She gestures towards the archway that connects the two retail spaces, leading from the café to the little shop on the other side that is bursting at the seams with all varieties of plants. "Come in any time if Mason gets on your nerves." She chuckles as she passes me the Thanksgiving turkey sandwich in a to-go container.

The sandwich that Mason ordered for me.

CHAPTER 4
MASON

"I CAN'T BELIEVE you would go above my head like this," I hiss at Winnie across the reception desk. I'm trying to control the volume of my voice, but it comes out louder than I expect it to. I left my coffee on the counter at Thistle + Thorne and I don't even regret it. As soon as I heard that pretentious woman utter the words 'I'll be starting at the clinic,' I lost all sense of rational thought. Goddammit. I had let myself think she was *attractive.* The way those tight jeans hugged her curves, her full pink lips pursing at me. I paid for her order to be nice. Who the fuck carries change around?

"I didn't go above your head. I've been telling you straight to your face that we need to hire some more help around here. Last we talked, I showed you the resumes of the candidates I contacted." Winnie doesn't look up from the paperwork she's straightening out on the desk. For some reason, her nonchalance fuels my anger even more, that Winnie is just so unbothered by this betrayal.

"You just conveniently left out the part where you went ahead and hired someone without my approval. Last time we discussed this, I said there was no way I was hiring someone new for the clinic. I told you I can handle it," I mutter through gritted teeth.

"You've been saying that for the last three months, and it's only getting worse." Winnie taps the stack of papers on the desk to shuffle them into alignment before placing them in one of the patient's charts. "I didn't have another option."

"There was only one option, Winnie. Let me *handle it*." I growl. "You can't go around hiring people; this isn't your clinic." I hear the sting of the words as they leave my mouth. Winnie has just as much, if not more, of a claim to this place as I do. Just because she's been around longer, doesn't mean she can disrespect my authority. I don't need to be parented here.

"That's where you're wrong, Mason." Winnie clicks her tongue.

I bite back the snarky response I have ready on the tip of mine. I don't enjoy being patronized.

"Jack gave me some management power, including hiring power, before he transferred everything over to you."

I reel at the comment, which comes like a punch to the gut, the truth that they had both been hiding hitting me like a freight train. My father had given hiring power to Winnie. He had handed over the clinic to me before he passed, telling me he had faith in me and that he wouldn't entrust the clinic to anyone else. The words he uttered to me on his deathbed now have no actual weight; they've lost all meaning. All because he left out one crucial detail. He didn't trust me with his clinic, not fully. The only reason my father would have given Winnie hiring powers is if he knew deep down that I would fail miserably at managing the clinic on my own.

My chest feels like it's going to cave in and suffocate me. My father doubted me so much that he created a safety net without me knowing. Because I wouldn't be able to handle it. The great Jack Landry had predicted that this day would come. He anticipated I would fail.

"Don't take it personally, Mason," Winnie starts, but it's

impossible not to take something like this personally. She knows what a sensitive topic this is and how strained my relationship with my father had become. I resent my dad for so many things, but this tops it.

"How can I not—" I steel my voice against the crack that is about to threaten the tough exterior I work so hard to maintain. "How can I not take offence when my father, and now you too, are undermining my ability to run this place?"

"It's not about your ability to keep the clinic afloat, Mason. Your father knew you were facing challenges that he never had when he opened it. The town has almost doubled in size in the last two years." Winnie's expression softens into something that looks like pity, and it makes me want to scream. "You're not known for being willing to accept help when you need it. He knew how stubborn you can be. This was his way of making sure you didn't stick your head so far in the sand that you couldn't come back up for air."

"I don't accept help because I don't need it." My tone is clipped, and I know Winnie doesn't deserve this kind of treatment. This is my father's wrongdoing, although Winnie sure as hell didn't make it better. I survived med school, my mother's death, and now my father's too, with no help from anyone. I picked up the pieces and looked after my brothers at ten years old. What makes Winnie think I can't take care of the clinic myself too?

"It's not a weakness to accept help, Mason. And you may not agree with me, but I promise you, once you meet Ally, you'll be glad to have her around."

Ally Wells. Winnie's number one candidate and the number one ditz who can barely place a lunch order. If her ability to make clinical decisions is as good as her ability to pick a goddamned sandwich off a menu, I doubt she'll be any help at all.

"Did you at least consider consulting me about who I'd want to hire?" I know she tried to get my opinion, when she smacked the stack of resumes on my desk. But was that before or after she had already told Ally she had the job? "Instead, you go out and hire the first airhead that walks through the door that you think is *sweet*?"

"Ally has a good head on her shoulders."

"I don't care if she's Florence fucking Nightingale." My voice rises another decibel, and I force it lower, knowing I have to get control over it before I'm yelling at Winnie. As angry as I am, I've never raised my voice at her like this. "I don't want some uppity, big city nurse coming in here and waltzing around like she knows more about how to run the place than I do."

Winnie's eyes dart over my shoulder, prompting me to turn around and see Ally, standing in the doorway of the clinic.

"God help us ..." Winnie mutters under her breath, so muted that only I can hear it. If only I had controlled my volume earlier, I wouldn't be standing here like a jackass with my foot hanging out of my mouth.

I watch in horror as Ally's soft, plump lips form a shocked and confused kind of scowl. I have to give her some credit; she sure has her looks going for her. I hadn't noticed how blue her eyes were at the coffee shop. As she approaches me now, I notice how they sparkle with a thin circle of green around her pupils. If I wasn't so opposed to Ally and her very presence here, I might have let myself entertain the idea of asking her out. Her tight little body is begging me to throw her around and have a little fun. It's been a long while since I gave a girl a second thought.

A flutter ripples through my chest at the sight of how she's smiling at me now. Either that or it's nerves, as I envision the slap on the hand I'll be getting from Winnie later.

"Hi, I'm Ally. Ally Wells." She falters a bit as she goes to extend her hand. She's juggling an oversized tote in one hand and her *latte with two honeys* in the other. She shifts the paper to-go cup to her left hand, and I notice the massive rock she's sporting on her finger. I can't *not* notice it. The way the diamond shimmers in the light is almost blinding. She clumsily extends her hand to shake mine and I take it tentatively. It's small, soft, and delicate. If I were choosing a ring for it, I would go with something much more demure. Something elegant and classy.

From the way she's looking at me, I wonder if I've somehow won the dickhead lottery of the year. Maybe she didn't catch me shit talking back there. Returning her grin, I search her eyes for any sign that she already hates me for being so callous. The search ends abruptly.

"I'm the uppity nurse from the big city who has come to take over your clinic. The turkey sandwich was great, by the way." Ally finishes introducing herself, her voice cheerful, her smile never faltering. *And we're off to a great start.* Whatever. Who cares about Ally's opinion of me? Just because Winnie hired her, and apparently, she's here to stay, at least for the foreseeable future, does not mean that I have to enjoy it. Or be her friend, for that matter. She's a colleague and nothing more. I can be professional, keep our conversation to the bare minimum while we're at the clinic.

"I take it you two have already met," Winnie says, the corner of her mouth lifting into a mischievous grin.

I roll my eyes, dropping Ally's hand. She puts it back down at her side but doesn't appear awkward or taken aback. She's standing there staring at me, that infuriating little smile on her lips. I want to wipe it right off them. I want to do a lot of things to Ally that I don't care to admit.

CHAPTER 5
ALLY

THE WOMAN STANDING behind the reception desk, whom I assume to be Winnie Foster based on our phone conversation, stretches her arm over the counter towards me. I take her hand graciously. I've already ruined my first impression with Mason, for what reason I'm not sure, so I'm going to do whatever I can to not ruin the rapport I've already established with his receptionist.

Mason is still standing behind her, a snarl on his otherwise very handsome face. I get a sudden urge to tell him to smile more, but that would put me in even hotter water, and his stare already makes me feel like I'm being boiled alive.

"So lovely to meet you in person, dear." Winnie's smile is warm, her eyes a deep shade of brown to match the auburn colour of her short-cropped hair. She's shorter than me, but Winnie is the type of person whose personality extends far beyond themselves. She holds the exuberance of someone who lives life to the fullest and plans to squeeze out every drop.

"Likewise, Winnie." I do my best to plaster on my warmest smile, refusing to let Mason's foul mood ruin my day. I make a point of not making eye contact with him, but out of the corner of my eye, I can almost see steam coming out of his ears.

Get a life, I think to myself. If this is the kind of thing that Mason gets butt-hurt over, he must be the most miserable person alive.

"Don't pay attention to Dr. Landry. We're both so happy you're here," Winnie says, shooting Mason a withering look over her shoulder.

Doctor Landry. Mason Landry. Of course, black coffee guy would be the doctor, the only doctor at the clinic where I now work. The realization creeps over me that not only will I be unable to avoid Mason—Dr. Landry—as much as I would like, but I will be spending every day with him in this cramped clinic that only has three rooms for me to hide in.

Mason shrugs. "I'm not going to sit here and pretend like I want her here."

"That's enough, Mason." Winnie barks. "She is here now, and you will play nice." I like Winnie already. She has spunk. An awkward silence stretches out between them as Mason backs down. What is wrong with Mason that he has two women tell him to 'play nice' on the same day? Haven't I reached some unspoken, arrogant asshole quota for the year since leaving Nate? I don't think I have the mental or emotional stamina to face another one.

"Well, listen. I just stopped by to introduce myself and get the keys for the accommodation that was advertised," I cut in, hesitant but determined to keep some semblance of peace if this is going to work. I'm not yet convinced that it will.

Conflict with anyone is my worst nightmare, let alone with a colleague, let alone with my boss. It's the reason I came to Heartwood in the first place. To get away from Nate without having the uncomfortable conversations I've been dodging. I can't deal with confrontation. I become physically ill anytime I'm forced to speak up and say what's on my mind, especially if it goes against someone else. The sweating, the nausea, the racing heart can all be avoided by sucking it up and smoothing things over.

"Of course, I've got the keys for you," Winnie says, reaching into the top drawer of her desk and handing me a set of keys across the counter. "Mason can take you and show you where you'll be staying. It's only a block down the road, but it's a little tricky to find since it's kind of tucked in the trees."

Mason's face pales, a look of shock sweeping over his expression.

"The cabin. You're letting her stay in the cabin? You can't be serious, Winnie." Mason stammers, running his hand back through his thick waves of chestnut hair.

"That's what I said, Mason. Now show Ally where the cabin is and get her settled in. Make sure she has some firewood for tonight."

I don't know what Mason's connection to the cabin is, but I'm pretty sure that becoming the resident of it makes me enemy number one. If I wasn't already. The free accommodation was a perk that drew me to the job. The posting didn't specify what the accommodation was, so I didn't expect to walk into this. I'm trying to escape my own drama, and here I am, sticking my nose right into someone else's.

For a second, I consider leaving. I could get right back on that plane and slink back to Vancouver. This is not what I signed up for. But the only thing worse than having to work with Mason is crawling back with my tail between my legs and having to face Nate. And not just Nate, but everyone else there who watched the show and now thinks that it's well within their rights to comment on my personal life.

At least in Heartwood, there's a better chance of starting over with a clean slate. Maybe no one here even watches reality television. That's the dream. Regardless, there's at least two people here that seem happy that I'm here. I'll lean on Poppy and Winnie for now. Whatever it takes. I can't go back now.

CHAPTER 6
MASON

I still can't fathom how Winnie could offer the cabin to Ally without my permission. The cabin doesn't belong to her to give away. It isn't even mine to give away. The small wooden A-frame belonged to my father, and even though Jack Landry is gone, it still holds onto his essence. I haven't been here since the day after the funeral. I had tidied up and made sure no food was out to rot or attract wildlife, but other than that, I didn't want to spend any more time in the cabin than necessary.

And now Ally will be inhabiting the space, probably with her fiancé, changing everything around, no doubt. I can see her adding girly touches, pink throw pillows or some shit. Hanging pictures where photos of my family once hung. The notion makes me cringe and refuels my anger towards Winnie.

I volunteer to ride shotgun while Ally drives the beater of a rental truck they saddled her with so that she doesn't have to walk all her luggage over. The cabin is a short enough distance from the clinic that one could walk the route in under ten minutes. My parents had bought the property with the dream of renting it out as a vacation spot, but when Mom got sick, that dream went by the wayside. The cabin sat empty for years until my brothers and I were old enough to be independent. Then Dad moved in so he could be closer to the clinic. He liked to be within arm's reach in case of an emergency. As do I.

Winnie suggested I move in here, but the wound was still too fresh. I can't be around my father's things without the familiar sharp stab of grief reminding me he's no longer here.

Ally is sitting in the driver's seat waiting for my directions, which I give in curt one-word answers. The only way I can be professional right now is by keeping my damn mouth shut. I hear Winnie's voice in my head. *'If you don't have anything nice to say, don't say anything at all.'*

I point left toward the cul-de-sac. I can drive the short distance blindfolded, even though almost a year has passed since I dared venture onto the dead-end street. Hang a left out of the clinic parking lot, drive thirty seconds down the main road that leads toward the town square, another left, and then a right at the rusted metal mailbox.

Ally looks at me when I point toward a narrow opening in the trees at the end of the street. The familiar rusting metal mailbox hidden among the overgrown shrubs is the only indication that the space between the trees is, indeed, a driveway.

"Are you sure this is the right address?" Ally asks me.

"Been coming here my whole life, Honeybee," I say through gritted teeth. Ally turns the steering wheel and navigates the truck through the overgrown branches.

The opening is narrow, just wide enough for the old truck as the wheels bump down the gravel driveway. The click and screech of trees on the already rusted doors sets my teeth on edge like nails on a chalkboard. I make a mental note to come back and prune the branches. Not as a favour to Ally, but because the rental company won't be thrilled if this truck comes back scratched to shit. Not that it's in pristine condition to begin with. Who had the bright idea of giving her this old hunk of junk?

The driveway isn't long but provides just enough privacy, and my breath catches in my throat as the trees on either side open into a small clearing. The small wooden cabin sits in the centre, untouched and no different from how I left it. There's a porch at the front and a stone path that wraps around one side leading to a fire pit behind the cabin. My dad and I built the fire pit together out of large rocks we found down by the river and sat together in the fire's warmth, peering at the stars many nights. Just the two of us.

The memory is distant now, a slideshow of fuzzy images, but they are no less painful. It was replaced long ago with memories of feeling abandoned and neglected as the workload at the clinic became heavier. As he became more and more consumed by work.

"It's quaint." Ally points out as she puts the truck in park. I assume that by quaint she means dilapidated. I know the standards folks from the city have when it comes to their accommodations.

"There's a decent motel down the road towards town. I could take you over now." I spit out, hoping that Ally's snobbish taste might make her rethink taking up residency in the place that holds so much of my heart. I don't need her poking around where she doesn't belong. Ally wrinkles her nose, considering. She peers around at the trees before looking back at me.

"No, this will do just fine. I'm looking for a bit of a hideout if I'm being honest, and I like the privacy." My heart sinks. It was worth a shot. The next best thing I can hope for is Ally tiring of Heartwood and deciding to go home to the city.

"Is your fiancé moving in with you, too? The cabin might be a little tight." Ally's right eyebrow tilts up for a moment. I nod toward her hand resting on the steering wheel, looking at her ring. She lets her hand drop and fidgets with the rock, twirling the band holding the obnoxious diamond around her finger.

"No. He won't be coming to Heartwood with me." Her voice is almost sad, her eyes wistful. But she didn't deny that she has a fiancé. At least he can preoccupy her and keep her out of my hair. I shrug and fling open the passenger door which creaks and wobbles as if it might just fall off.

I reluctantly reach into the back of the old truck and heave a heavy suitcase over the side, dust clouding the air as it thuds onto the ground.

"Who gave you this rust bucket?" I say, referring to the environmental nightmare of a truck that is parked in the driveway. It looks like it's about to fall apart at any second.

"That was the only one they had left at the rental company when I landed," Ally says with a shrug.

"Bullshit. You should have asked for something else. Anything else would have been better than this. A horse and buggy would have been more reliable."

"I wanted to avoid causing an argument." My eyes roll back at her answer. Of course, Little Miss Perfect Ally didn't want to upset anyone. I unload the next suitcase.

"You don't need to help me with that," Ally protests, striding over to where I'm standing.

"I'll at least help you unload them, they're pretty heavy."

There's that nose wrinkle Ally does when I say something she doesn't like. It's almost endearing, and I think I'd like to say more things to annoy her, just so I can see it again. Ally is the kind of person I'd have fun toying with.

"I can manage just fine on my own, thank you very much." A fisted hand lands on her hip in defiance. *Also, kind of cute.* I shake my head. As much as I'd like to continue annoying her, I can't go thinking that she's cute in any way, shape, or form. Not if I'm going to get her to leave town and leave me alone.

"Do you think you brought enough suitcases?" I squint my eyes as the sun lowers in the sky right above the tree line.

"I'll have you know I uprooted my entire life to be here. This is my whole life packed into luggage." Ally waves an arm, gesturing at the pile of bags in the truck's bed. An entire life that doesn't include the fiancé for some reason. I notice a clear garment bag lays tucked in beside them and I pull it out next.

Swaths of sparkling fabrics fall as I lift it and I can make out a handful of floor-length gowns tucked into the bag.

"A little frilly for Heartwood, don't you think?" I lift my eyebrows at Ally. I'm forming a clearer picture of her, and the image is one that does not fit in here. I guess she'll last two weeks at most. That suits me just fine. The sooner she leaves Heartwood and the sooner she's no longer bothering me, the better.

"Well, I'm not planning on wearing them out to the grocery store." She wrinkles her nose again. "And those are none of your business." Ally reaches out and snatches the garment bag from my hand before collecting the bottoms of the dresses off the ground and storming off towards the cabin.

I pick up my pace and follow Ally toward the front door.

"I've got it," I say, reaching in front of her.

"No, thanks. I can handle it from here."

I hold up a gold key in front of Ally's face. "Not if you can't get in, now, can you?" I swing open the old screen door and wiggle the key into the lock. It's stiff since no one has used it in so long, but the key fits just as it always did, and the lock clicks as I turn it.

My chest tightens as I open the door and see the old familiar cabin. I half expect to see my dad sitting at the worn, traditional-style wooden table that sits in the middle of the space, coffee in hand. But the space is empty, except for Ally, who sweeps in like the place means nothing.

I catch a growl rising in my throat and stop it. I stalk back to the truck to get another suitcase. I can't set foot in the cabin, not with Ally here now. And screw her, by the way, for letting me think she was cute. She is not cute, barging into my life like this.

I haul a heavy bag out of the truck, the latch catching on the tailgate. Before I have a chance to catch it, the suitcase opens, the contents spilling onto the driveway.

"What the hell do you think you're doing?" Ally shouts,

waving her arms wildly and leaping down off the porch onto the gravel drive. I stand over the open suitcase, dumbfounded for a second, my mouth agape. It's not like I'm trying to spill all of her belongings on the ground, but as I look down at the contents of the bag, I realize why Ally is so panicked. I notice her cheeks redden as she examines what is lying before her on the gravel.

An assortment of brightly coloured tiny pieces of lace decorate the driveway. I can't help but picture Ally wearing them, her petite, lean frame with strips of lace accentuating the curves of her hips.

Ally stoops to pick them up and I meet her on the ground, kneeling to help.

"Please, don't. It's bad enough that you've now seen all my underwear. I don't want you touching it too." But as Ally makes to scoop up the lacy thongs, something even more intriguing falls out of the pile, rolling across the ground and stopping when it hits my foot.

A vibrator. Not just any vibrator—Ally's vibrator. It's a purple rabbit-style one, and bigger than I would imagine her enjoying. I shake off the thought. Ally lets out a shriek as I bend down to pick it up. If her face was red before, it's almost purple now. But damn, it makes her blue eyes glow almost iridescent.

"You don't have to be embarrassed that you own a vibrator, Honeybee." I can't resist visualizing her using it, and I feel my pants tighten around my waist. *Be professional,* I try to remind myself, but it's too late. The words are already tumbling out of my mouth before I can catch them. "It's also okay if you want to think about me while you're using it."

The corner of my mouth twitches up as I see the words land, and Ally's eyes go wide.

Not an appropriate thing for a boss to say to their new employee. I've never been someone's boss before, but I'll have to figure out how to navigate this whole boss-employee thing. Which could prove to be especially difficult given the way she looks. All I want is for Ally to wrinkle her nose and put her hand on her hip like she does. She doesn't, and I don't know how to interpret the disappointment that I feel. Instead, she snatches the vibrator out of my hand, puts the last remaining thongs back in their suitcase, and carts it in the cabin's direction, not stopping to make eye contact with me.

Taking extra caution to give them enough clearance over the tailgate this time, I finish unloading her suitcases and pile them on the driveway.

"You should go now." Ally is standing on the porch, arms crossed over her chest. I notice the way her hip juts out in her high-waisted jeans, the neckline of her blouse billowing open. *Prissy.*

I narrow my eyes in the orange sunlight now filtering through the tops of the trees. A moment passes between us as we stand there staring each other down. She's right. It's time for me to leave. I need to get far away from Ally if I have any hope of wiping my mind clean of the image of her in those lacy thongs, the fabric pushed to the side, making room for the vibrator. It's an image I will not, cannot, entertain.

The clinic is struggling enough as it is; it needs me to be clear-headed and focused, and envisioning Ally and that purple vibrator won't help with either. Two weeks. I give Ally two weeks tops. And if she's not gone on her own accord by then, I will see to it that she leaves.

"Sure. I gotta go help Winnie close up the clinic now." I turn to start my walk down the driveway and back to the clinic. A walk I know like the back of my hand.

CHAPTER 7
ALLY

"So, tell me all about it. How was the first week?" Spencer's velvety voice blasts from my phone speaker, the phone perched on the edge of the pedestal sink. I swipe on my favourite deep berry-coloured lip stain and examine myself in the small bathroom mirror as I rub my lips together.

The bathroom of the cabin is smaller than what I'm used to. Nate and I shared the one in his expensive downtown apartment. He had his own sink on the opposite end of the vanity, and the whole thing was big enough to host our engagement party. Nate's apartment was lavish but impersonal. All black-and-white marble and sterile fixtures. This bathroom is cozy and suits me fine. It has just enough space for a clawfoot tub and the little mirror above the sink has a hidden cabinet behind it for my toiletries.

"Between my new boss plotting my demise, and my vibrator falling out of my bag in front of him, I would say it's been a week," I reply. It's only been three days since I started at the clinic and I'm already second-guessing my decision to stay.

"What?!" Spencer shrieks into the phone. "Your vibrator? What happened?"

"Exactly what it sounds like. We both stood there staring at each other until I ran into the house," I explain.

"Oh my God. I would have died of embarrassment!" Spencer is trying to be empathetic, but she can't hide her laughter. I have to admit, although I did almost die of embarrassment, it will make for a pretty hilarious story one day, I'm sure. Today though, I see little humour in the situation. I'm too focused on tonight. I need to salvage whatever shred of a first impression is left. I take a sip of the wine I poured to take the edge off before my wild night out in Heartwood. If you could call any night out in Heartwood 'wild.' The town has a grand total of one bar, and it's the only business open late on any night of the week.

"And now you have to see him tonight?" Spencer asks.

"I think so. It sounds like the whole town goes to trivia night, or close to it. But who knows, maybe he's some anti-social recluse and he won't show."

"I'll be over here, manifesting that for you."

Spencer left for Amsterdam after she helped me get my life in order—if this could be called 'order.' I admire Spencer. She seems fearless, although Spencer's mom would use the term reckless. Spencer quit her corporate job on a whim and turned her life into one big, never-ending adventure, blogging and vlogging her way through foreign countries.

I stand back and examine my face in the mirror, deeming a simple makeup look sufficient for trivia night at The Whiskey Jack, the local pub in town. Winnie had invited me. She said it would be an opportunity to meet some people in town. I can only say that I know Winnie and Mason at this point, and I wouldn't call Mason a friend by any stretch. Although I'm also becoming more friendly with Poppy, as friendly as you can get with your barista. But she already has my morning coffee order down, which was more than I could say about Nate, and seeing her at the café on my way into the clinic always lifts my mood. I go into the clinic optimistic after seeing Poppy, a sentiment that is promptly ruined by Dr. Mason Landry, but that's beside the point.

"It would be more bearable if he didn't also hate my guts for some unknown reason," I mumble, leaning in towards the mirror to apply a final coat of mascara while I'm talking. Why is it that it's physically impossible to keep your mouth closed while applying mascara?

"Don't tell me I have to fly over there to beat someone up already, because I will," Spencer warns. "As soon as I'm back from Amsterdam."

"No, no, it's not that. It hasn't even been that bad. Everyone here is so lovely and welcoming ..." My voice trails off.

"Except ..." Spencer prompts.

"Except for Dr. Landry. Mason. Mason Landry." I'm rambling. It might be the notion of attending the town trivia night and meeting so many new people or the thought of seeing one person that sets me on edge. "I still don't know what to call him. He's like my boss, except he wasn't the one who hired me. Mason didn't even *want* to hire me."

"Well, that's a him problem, babe. Everyone loves Ally Wells." Spencer has always been my hype girl, and I'm thankful for her.

"Not Mason. He has this weird chip on his shoulder, like he doesn't want my help in the clinic. He's this grumpy shut-in of a person and it makes things so uncomfortable. When he is friendly with me, which is rare, I feel like it takes every ounce of effort."

I've successfully dodged him the last two days at the clinic. The first couple of days were spent learning the online system by sitting next to Winnie at the reception desk and greeting patients. I've finally started to get my bearings and earlier today Winnie had me taking patients into exam rooms to measure their vital signs and make sure they were ready to see Mason.

I've been nervous interacting with people in a clinical setting again. It's been so long since I have laid hands on a patient since leaving to film *Stolen Love*. Despite being somewhat sluggish in my clinical skills, I love talking to the people who come into the clinic. It's fulfilling. It's right.

That became clear the first time that I checked a patient's vital signs and realized that he was having severe chest pain and needed to be transported to the hospital. My heart swelled when I knew that I was able to help someone, a sensation I hadn't experienced in a long time. Being a television fiancée and Instagram personality was a superficial, empty business.

"Give him time," Spencer reassures me. "I'm sure he'll warm up to you soon enough."

That's what everyone keeps saying, but I'm still not convinced. It's hard to warm up to someone you refuse to talk to or even acknowledge. And Mason is the master of evasion.

"I'm hoping that tonight gives me a chance to gain some favour with the rest of the town before he influences their opinions of me."

"Have you talked to your mom yet?" Spencer changes the subject, but I don't respond. My mom is still a bit of a sore spot. "She messaged me the other day. To see how you were."

"Let her know that I'm fine." It's not that I don't love my parents. Sometimes I love them so much it hurts. That's what makes this whole situation worse. It's that every decision I've made in the last year has upset them, so every conversation with them feels strained. They weren't happy with my decision to go on the show, and they're even less happy about my decision to leave town. So, I choose not to address it.

I wrap up my conversation with Spencer and gulp down the remaining few sips of wine.

The entire contents of my suitcases are strewn about the floor. I tried on every single outfit I brought with me, including some of the gowns I brought. Nothing was working, and I decided that tonight was not the night to try out a new, adventurous style, so I've decided on an outfit that is always tried and true. My favourite pair of high-waisted, straight-cropped blue jeans that make my ass look incredible and a white puff sleeve top with a square neckline that shows off my smooth collar bone.

I throw my long strawberry blond hair into a relaxed bun and pull out a few strands that curl around my face. This is when I feel the most like myself, with some mascara and a bit of colour on my lips. Not the ten pounds of makeup that I would have layered on before filming. The concealer I am wearing still lets the freckles that I love so much peek through, and I appreciate them now more than ever after the makeup team completely covered them up for the better part of a year.

Giving myself one last look over, I throw my lip stain into my small black crossbody bag, slip my feet into my black strappy sandals, and head off down the street toward the pub.

I don't care if Mason has the lowest opinion of me, whether he does or doesn't want me here. At least that's what I try to convince myself. If I say it to myself enough, I might believe that it's true. I'm going to trivia night, I'm going to make some friends, and I'm going to make Heartwood my home.

WITH THE SUN dipping below the horizon, the mountains are cast in shadows, appearing as nothing but a dark outline against the sky. Despite the air starting to cool, I could really use a walk to calm my racing mind.

The Whiskey Jack comes into view as I make my way down the street towards the centre of town, sitting on the corner of the intersection of Main Street and First. The soft light from inside emphasizes it as the sole open establishment on the street. A cacophony of noise spills out onto the street corner as the heavy wooden door opens and shuts, and I can tell that the pub is already filling up for trivia night.

I can't thank Winnie enough for inviting me. Being included makes me feel like I'm settling in a little more. But I can't help the nerves at the idea of meeting so many new people, introducing myself, and hoping that no one recognizes me from the show. So far, it seems like the popularity of *Stolen Love* has not yet reached the sleepy little town of Heartwood, and for that, I'm grateful. This is my chance to create a new identity for myself, or rather, get back to my old identity from before I morphed into a person who I no longer recognized.

The pub is dimly lit, which gives it an inviting and cozy atmosphere, and there is hardly any room to move around as people form their teams for trivia and shuffle between the tables. The air smells of sticky dried beer and fry oil, but it's almost a nostalgic smell. I remember frequenting a very similar pub in my old neighbourhood with Spencer; that was before I went on the show. Since then, nights out have involved modern cocktail bars with minuscule glasses and garnishes that cost more than the liquor itself. Nate only wanted to go to the trendiest, hippest places, which also happened to be the most expensive. I like the pub here; it isn't pretentious and offers a space for people to come and connect rather than *network*.

As I survey the bar, I can see that most people are wearing jeans and some form of a T-shirt so casual that my crisp blouse is almost out of place. It's the most informal outfit I have since I had to revamp my entire wardrobe for filming. They asked for gowns and cocktail dresses, none of which felt like me, but I went along with it. That was the price of finding true love. I scoff at the thought. True love. Now I wonder if true love even exists if it can't happen on a curated set with the most romantic dates planned.

I scan the bar looking for a familiar face in the crowd. I'm always a bit awkward at these social events, especially when I don't know anyone. Not even a year of being put in the spotlight in front of thousands of viewers could change that. My hands are clamming up and my breath quickens.

I relax a little when I see Winnie at a half-booth tucked away in the back corner of the bar, waving me over. I relax even more when I realize Mason isn't here yet. I could get one more drink down before I have to face him and pretend that he doesn't rankle me.

Winnie pats the booth seat next to her as I approach the group. "We saved you a seat so you could be on our team," she proclaims as I assess who is seated at the table.

I recognize Poppy, thank God, and two other men that I haven't met yet. They each introduce themselves as Hudson and Jett Landry. Mason's brothers. That fact alone would have put them in my bad books if it wasn't for the warm greeting and friendly smiles they wear. They seem nothing like their broody and gruff brother. In fact, they're just the opposite.

"So, how's working for Dr. Dickbag?" Jett asks, taking a large swig of his beer, and trying not to choke as he stifles his laughter. At least it's not just me.

"I can't help but wonder if he's intentionally trying to make me leave." I don't want to badmouth my boss, but I won't lie either.

"That's my fault for hiring you without consulting him," Winnie admits. "I take full responsibility. He'll come around to the idea. Mason always does."

I nod, but I'm not so sure.

"It's busy in here. I've never seen a place so packed," I remark, diverting the conversation to a more neutral topic. We need at least four people to play in the trivia competition and our team is already complete. With any luck, Mason won't show at all.

"The whole town gets into trivia night. It's become a kind of staple. Grady started it about a year ago, and people look forward to it every month."

"Is it a different theme every time?" I wonder. Tonight's theme is Television Sensations, so I'm confident we can win, but otherwise, my trivia knowledge is limited.

"He changes it up every month, yeah," Poppy chimes in.

"Sometimes the theme is specific to a particular TV show, and people will binge-watch it and take notes. It's kind of intense."

"Your ears must have been ringing." Winnie looks over as a man approaches our table, a tray clenched under one bicep. He's freakishly handsome, in a rugged way. The sleeve of his slim-fitting black T-shirt accentuates the curve of his muscle, and I can make out tattoos that extend from the hem all the way down both arms. He's got an apron tied around his slim waist.

"Hey, Mama." He winks at Winnie with casual confidence. "What'll it be tonight, the usual?"

"You got it," Winnie says, turning to Ally. "Grady, this is Ally. Ally Wells."

Grady reminds me of all the guys that Spencer used to swoon over in high school, right down to his tattooed arms. Spencer has a type and her type hasn't had a great track record, but there's something personable about Grady already.

"Well, well, Wells," Grady says with a soft chuckle, laughing at his own joke. "The famous Ally Wells. It's a pleasure." He extends a hand to me, which I accept.

"I don't know about famous..." I hope he's referring to my unexpected arrival in Heartwood and not my brief stint as a reality star. I'm trying to keep it under wraps as much as possible. It would defeat the purpose of my fresh start.

"Anyone that my brother allows into the clinic is bound to be the talk of the town." Ah. The freakishly good-looking bartender is Mason's third brother. I never would have guessed. I can see a familiar resemblance in their faces, but it's their difference in personality that alarms me the most.

As if I somehow summoned him with my thoughts, Mason appears behind his brother, giving him a forceful clap on the back.

"Another killer turnout tonight, my man!" His tone is downright chipper as he draws his brother into a quick hug. But his expression falls flat as he surveys the table and his eyes meet mine. *So, it's just me that brings out the worst in him. Perfect.*

"Ally." He gives me a curt nod.

"Dr. Landry." If Mason wants to play it cool with me, so can I. He shimmies into an empty seat across from me as Grady takes the rest of our drink orders. I get my usual rosé.

I'm taking a generous sip of the cool, pink liquid and trying to avoid eye contact with Mason sitting across from me when the microphone screeches and Grady gets everyone's attention.

"All right, folks, what time is it?" he shouts.

"Trivia time!" Everyone cheers at once, the bar erupting with whoops and hollers. Grady is undeniably charming, and he knows how to rally a crowd.

"You all know the rules. No calling out answers, no collaborating with other teams, and no phones! Tonight's theme is television sensations, and the category is ..." Grady imitates a drumroll, and the rest of the bar taps whatever surface is in front of them. The entire bar vibrates with eager anticipation.

"Reality Stars!" My pulse quickens, the wine I just drank burning on its way back up. *Simmer down, Ally. He didn't say* Stolen Love. *There are tons of reality shows.* I bet half of the people here haven't even heard of *Stolen Love.*

The first few questions are straightforward about popular reality shows like *Survivor, Big Brother,* and *The Bachelor.* But after about a dozen of those, they get harder, the shows become more obscure, and the questions are about specific contestants. I look around the pub, watching the other teams furiously writing on their answer cards. I swear I can feel a bead of sweat forming on my temple. The fact that the entire town takes the time to study and brush up on their pop culture does nothing to quell the mounting anxiety and dread that the next question will be about me.

"Question fourteen ..." Grady pauses after announcing the next question each time, giving everyone the chance to quiet down to hear it. "On a new dating show called *Stolen Love ...*"

Oh God. This is it. So much for staying incognito. I slide down in my seat, burying my face in my wine glass and praying no one will catch on. "Only one of the male contestants came out of the show engaged. What was his name?"

I notice people in the pub giving each other questioning glances, mirroring shrugs across the tables. I might be out of the woods.

My team members murmur around me; no one has seen my show, and they are busy deliberating when I notice a familiar head of blond hair, a familiar polished smile, and flat grey-blue eyes standing over our table.

"Nate ..." I whisper, my past colliding with my present in one nausea-inducing moment.

"Nate! Let's put down Nate. That sounds right. I saw something about him on Insta once," Poppy shouts a little too loudly. Mason and his brothers shush her. She writes the answer down on our sheet before realizing that everyone is looking at the stranger standing behind us—a stranger to everyone but me.

I jump up from the table and push Nate backward, trying and failing in the crowded bar to get him away from our table, out of earshot of my new friends. Any success I had at keeping my reality star identity a secret will be long gone now, as my new friends take in the show in front of them, wide eyed and mouths agape.

"What are you doing here?" I hiss. He stands out like a sore thumb, even more than I do, with his ankle-length dress pants and loafers, tight-fitting dress shirt, and unzipped Patagonia vest. His douchebag uniform, complete with a silver Rolex on his wrist.

"I could ask you the same thing." Nate peers down his nose at the group seated around the corner booth. "You think you could abandon your commitments to *Stolen Love* so easily? You humiliated me." My head snaps back towards the group of onlookers. Yup. They definitely heard it. It's written all over their faces that they caught Nate's line about *Stolen Love*.

"How did you even find me? I didn't tell anyone where I was going."

"I have my ways of finding people, Ally. You must not know me very well at all."

"No, clearly I don't." I stare at Nate, holding his gaze until he breaks the silence.

"Well, this little stunt of yours, whatever it is, is over. Get your things, we're going home." Nate wraps a hand around my upper arm, a little too tightly, and tugs as if to take me with him.

My stomach drops. Nate can't possibly assume that I would go back to our life, a life that isn't mine anymore. The facade that he cares about me now is off-putting, considering how rarely he took my feelings into account when we were together. I pull my arm out of Nate's grasp. The movement causes a few people around us to glance over, wondering about the scene that is about to transpire between us.

To Mason's credit, and despite our rocky start, he stands up out of his chair and positions himself next to me. I feel his protective warmth behind me, and somehow his presence settles my nerves, a sense of safety washing over me.

"I'm sorry, Nate, but I think it's best if I stay here. At least for now. I just ... I don't want to inconvenience you by making you wait for me or anything." The words come out like a croak, and I hear my heartbeat thumping in my ears.

"Oh, you're coming back with me. Otherwise, there will be hell to pay, Ally. You made a commitment to me." My panic is rising, but it isn't from the adrenaline of standing up to Nate; it's about the thought of going back with him, going back to our relationship where I was nothing more than his shadow. I flip through my mental file cabinet of excuses that I use to escape conversations and come up short. I need to devise a plan, fast. Something that will convince him that my heart is no longer his, that I've moved on.

Nate is more likely to respect another man before he respects my wishes. I glance at Hudson and Jett, still seated at the booth. He won't buy it if I tell him I was dating one of the younger

Landry brothers, but he might believe the lie if I say I'm with the one man who stood up to come to my aid. Before I can second-guess myself, I twine my hand through Mason's.

"I've found someone else, Nate. I'm really sorry." I apologize again. Saying that I've found someone else is easier than telling Nate how I truly feel. Which is that I want nothing to do with him anymore. But I haven't thought through the fallout of what I've said. Mason's eyes widen at the gesture, realization washing over him at what I'm doing. The lie that I'm pulling him into. I match his expression, raising my eyebrows and willing him to play along. If he can put his contempt for me aside for one night, Nate will be out of my hair and out of my life.

"Someone else? You're joking. It's been a few weeks since you walked out of our engagement party." Nate glances between Mason and me, his eyes darting down to our hands. "You're still wearing your ring."

I twirl the ring around my finger with my thumb, a nervous habit that I've developed. I have to remember to get rid of this stupid ring as soon as I get home. I haven't wanted to get rid of it yet. There's a part of me that's still holding onto the idea of what Nate and I were at the start. What I hoped we could have been. My knuckles are white with the grip I have on Mason, praying he won't let go. Nate looks back at us, eyes narrowing.

"This isn't over, Allison." Nate spits out as he pushes his way back through the crowd and out through the doors of the pub.

CHAPTER 8
MASON

"WHAT THE FUCK, ALLY?" I yank Ally by the same arm Nate had in his grip moments earlier, tugging her into one of the tiny washrooms at the back of the pub. The toilet and the sink take up most of the space, not leaving much room for the two of us together. The door snaps shut behind us, and I take a moment to make sure it's locked.

Ally has already made a scene by roping me into this scheme of hers in front of everyone; I'm not about to make it worse by staging a fake public break-up, too. I won't hear the end of this as soon as word gets out around town.

Winnie is always trying to set me up, and she'll be all over this. She never misses an opportunity to mention how worried she is about how much time I invest in the clinic rather than making a 'real life' for myself. Her definition of a real life involves finding a woman and settling down. But this is my life. I grew up knowing that I aspired to be a doctor, like my father. Sure, this isn't exactly what I had imagined for myself, but sometimes you get dealt a shitty hand, and I am determined to make my dad proud. That can't happen if I'm not at the clinic keeping things running and making sure patients get seen.

I only hope I can convince Winnie and the others at our table to keep their mouths shut until I figure out what to do. If anyone else saw how Ally batted her eyelashes at me while she wrapped her fingers through mine, that would be it. Not only will it be an unwelcome distraction from all the work I have cut out for me, but I'll also lose my credibility as a doctor. I won't be the doctor dating *sweet and lovely* Ally, as everyone likes to think of her. I'll be the doctor who finally gave in to hiring a nurse, and then slept with her during her first week in the clinic.

Thankfully, everyone else in the bar seemed too invested in their trivia to notice when Nate stormed out. All I can do now is hope they won't think twice about how I was ready to fight him. It's not that I wanted to come to Ally's defence for her sake. Something about this Nate character made me want to crawl out of my skin. Maybe it was the vest he wore that screamed *finance bro*, or maybe it was the way he talked to Ally like she was his property.

I shut my eyes tight and pinch the bridge of my nose, considering the words I need to say to Ally. Gearing myself up, I mentally formulate the arguments for why this absolutely cannot happen. Number one, we are colleagues and nothing more. Number two, I do not have time for this type of childish bullshit. And number three, my eyes are lingering too long on Ally's soft, plump lips as she presses them together in a straight line.

She's standing so close that the soft puff of air she releases from her nose warms the space between us as she readies herself to fight back. She looks like a bull getting ready to charge.

"Do you realize what you just did?" I snap.

Something in Ally's expression changes, and she softens, her shoulders slumping like she's already tired when the fight hasn't even begun.

"Thanks for going along with it," is all she says in response. I've been preparing myself for more of an argument, so it takes a minute for me to rearrange my thoughts. What was the shift that I just saw in her? One minute, she was practically pawing at the ground like she was getting ready to charge, and the next, she looked defeated.

"Everyone in the bar wanted him to leave as much as you did, Honeybee." The nickname rolls off my tongue with less bite to it than it had before. Something about the way Nate knocked the wind right out of Ally's sails makes me want to be a little gentler with her.

Heat radiates between us. I can only assume it's my anger, coming to a simmer rather than the boil it had been earlier, but I'm still steaming, and I want answers.

"Who is that guy, anyway?"

Ally's eyes don't meet mine; instead, she looks off to the side over my shoulder, as if checking to make sure no one has walked through the door. As if she's afraid of who it might be. Again, I watch her shoulders slump as she comes up short of an explanation that's anything other than the truth.

"Nate," is all she offers.

"Yeah, so you mentioned earlier. You're going to give me more than that if I'm now supposed to start beating guys off you with a stick."

"I'm not asking you to do that, Mason. I panicked. I couldn't think of what else to do." Ally's voice has a hint of despair in it now. "I am not the most intimidating person, and Nate isn't easy to convince on the best of days."

"You never answered my question."

Ally sighs. The way her chest heaves so close to mine makes my cock twitch. It takes everything in me to keep my eyes trained on her face.

"Fine. Nate and I were together back in the city. We met on a dating show. I dumped him in a catastrophic and very public way. He's not a compassionate person, Mason. Why I was ever with him in the first place is a mystery to me, too. All I know is that I can't be with him now."

"Ah. That explains the panic on your face when Grady read the question about *Stolen Love*." I say, putting two and two together. Ally nods. Nate is the epitome of a guy I can picture going on a dating show. But was he ever invested in Ally? He sure seems to be invested in their relationship now, and something about that makes me see red. I'm not Ally's number one fan by any stretch, but anyone with half a brain could see that Ally deserves better than that sleazeball.

"And rather than tell him the truth, you come up with this excuse to get rid of him," I continue. It comes out like a question, but it's not. That's precisely what Ally is doing. Just like she can't bring herself to fight with me, she can't bring herself to fight with Nate. I would guess Ally isn't one to put up a fight with anyone.

"It was the best I could do." Ally shrugs. God, why does Ally have to be so cute when everything she does infuriates me? "Don't worry, Mason. He'll be gone soon, and you don't have to pretend to be my boyfriend all the time."

"Oh, I won't be pretending to be your boyfriend all the time. You've never lived in a small town like Heartwood. Everyone always knows everybody's business." And this kind of gossip would spread like wildfire. "I have enough problems right now trying to keep the clinic afloat and make sure nobody dies, Ally. The last thing I need is the rumour mill pumping out stories of how I'm now dating the hot new nurse." I catch the words as they come out of my mouth, and Ally looks up at me like a baby deer in headlights, her eyes wide. Her face shifts into a playful, shit-eating grin.

"You think I'm *hot*." She nudges my arm. "Here I assumed that Dr. Mason Landry had a heart of steel, unfeeling and cold. But you think I'm *hot*."

"Don't be twisting my words," I stammer.

"I'm not. Those were your exact words. I'm the hot new nurse."

"There is and never will be anything between us, Ally. There can't be. I need to have all my attention on the clinic."

"Oh, don't worry, Mason. I don't want anything from you. You're not my type." Ally winks at me, and even though I was the first to shut things down, whatever this is, the words sting. What is Ally's type? Nate?

"So, a doctor isn't enough for the uppity, Ally Wells." The words are harsher than I anticipated.

"No, just pompous assholes who go through life thinking they're better than everyone else." Ally pushes past me and puts a hand on the door, turning back to face me before she turns the lock. "I'm sorry. I need you to help me get rid of Nate. Can you do that for me?" This is the third time tonight that Ally has apologized for something she does not need to apologize for. Her need to smooth things over overtaking her clear disdain for me. She looks back at me with her big doe eyes, and I can't help but melt a little.

"Fine." Something about her makes me weak. "A week. That's all you get, and then what's-his-nuts better be gone."

Based on the way I'm feeling towards Ally at this moment, I'm hoping she will go with him. The thoughts I'm having about her now are not ones I should be thinking, and I'm worried they might morph into something irresistible if she stays.

After our conversation in the bathroom, I need to get outside. I need some air, and most of all, I need to get far away from Ally. It doesn't matter if I'm not coming back to finish the trivia game; Nate already screwed over our team when he showed up. They got distracted and missed about five questions. Fucking dick. I'm not the type of person to pass judgment on people I'm never going to see again, but something about Nate makes my blood boil. The smug look on his face was downright punchable, and even though as a doctor I've sworn an oath to do no harm, I sure want to harm Nate. The way he talked down to Ally, I can't stand for it. My father always taught me to be a gentleman, to stand up for people. Although I might have thought twice about my act of chivalry if I had known Ally was going to rope me into being her boyfriend.

I push through the crowded bar, not stopping to explain my unexpected departure to my brothers and my friends. For all they know, I got called to a clinic emergency or something. I make my way out to the street and take a deep breath of the cool night air. The quiet street is a welcome reprieve where I can hear my own thoughts. What a fucking disaster.

I waste no time walking back to the clinic, replaying the past twenty minutes in my mind and trying to make sense of what happened back there. More importantly, what's coming next? A week. I gave Ally a week of my time to get rid of her ex-fiancé. Now I have to make sure no one in town finds out about this, or it's game over. My reputation will be trash, and everything I've worked so hard for will be ruined.

When I get back to the clinic, it's dark except for the distant glow of the desk lamp I left on in my office at the end of the hall. My office has become my sanctuary at work, and is also serving as my bedroom. I've refused to move into the cabin like Winnie suggested; the memories in there are too painful to face every day. Not that I could now anyway, seeing how Ally had barged in and made herself right at home there.

Truthfully, I'm quite content on my cot in the office. Sure, it isn't ideal, but I go home to my apartment every so often to do laundry and sleep in a proper bed. Those days are becoming few and far between, I must admit. After the accident, there's been a crushing weight on my chest every time I think about going home or being too far away from the clinic. I failed in every way that mattered that day, and I am determined to never let it happen again.

The late summer heat is crushing in my office, so I slide the window open and let in the cool night air. It faces out into the field used as a helicopter pad, where an orange flag hangs limp on the still night. Crickets hum in the tall grass. I lift my shirt over my head and pull off the jeans I had on from the workday, getting ready to settle onto the cot for the night when a brown envelope on my desk catches my eye.

Winnie leaves my mail in a stack on the desk, but the familiar brown envelope almost never means anything good. I know that when I pick it up, I will see the stamp from the Ministry of Health in the upper left corner and my father's name in the centre of the envelope. Which reminds me, I still need to update the ministry and notify them that the clinic is now under my name.

I rip open the envelope and skim over the first few sentences.

To Dr. Jack Landry,

We regret to inform you that due to budgetary constraints and recent funding cuts, the Heartwood Medical Centre will undergo evaluation to determine its value to the community. With the growing demand for healthcare resources, the Ministry of Health is shifting towards a more centralized model for resource distribution by pooling resources to improve access at larger centres. A representative from the ministry will be in touch to discuss the next steps.

My vision blurs, forcing me to sit in my chair while I steady myself. The contents of the letter hit me like a sucker punch to the gut, and I'm struggling to find air in the stifling heat of my office. I knew the situation at the clinic was less than ideal, but I had no idea it was this desperate. If the clinic doesn't have funding from the government, there's no way it can stay open. I don't have the money to fund it myself, and the people of Heartwood would vehemently oppose a private clinic.

Is this the first letter of its kind? Or has this been an ongoing problem since my father had been in charge, another secret he failed to disclose on his deathbed? If this wasn't the first, then the letter is not a serious threat, or the clinic would have been closed by now. If it was the first notification of the threat to the clinic's funding, it would mean I am failing at more than just treating my patients. I would be responsible for the downfall of my father's life's work. His passion, his legacy.

I don't even want to consider the impact this could have on the town. Now more than ever, the people rely on the clinic and having somewhere they can go in a crisis. I know this firsthand. The number of times my pager beeps in a day is an acute reminder of how needed I am around here.

I set the letter down on my desk and lay on the cot, staring at the ceiling. I toss and turn a few times. Sleep is unattainable tonight, not only because of the stifling heat, but because my mind whirs with the events of the day.

First Ally, entangling me in some fake dating scheme like I'm the one that was cast on some silly game show and she's the host, toying with my heart. And now I'm facing the harsh reality that the government could rip the very thing I have poured my heart and soul into right out of my grasp.

I give up on the idea of sleep and consider how to fight this. I have to prove that Heartwood needs the medical centre. That they need me. There must be a way I can prove the clinic can manage the growing population and keep up with an increasing workload.

Unfortunately, the only way I can see that happening is by keeping Ally Wells around. Which means 'playing nice,' as Winnie and Poppy so kindly put it, and taking part in the facade of being her boyfriend. I just have to make sure that my fake feelings for Ally stay pretend and that whatever spark was between us tonight doesn't ruin my plans.

CHAPTER 9
ALLY

THE NEXT TWO days at the clinic drag on at a glacial pace. The place is bustling, as Winnie had mentioned it always is these days, but I can't shake off the rusty feeling every time I go to check on a patient. It makes everything take ten times longer than it should. My hands fumble with the stethoscope or the blood pressure cuff, and it's clear to me that my year away from nursing, spent in front of a camera or at various social events, has taken its toll.

I prepared myself for the challenge of returning to a nursing job, I've even worn my favourite set of lilac scrubs in hopes they would boost my confidence. But what I hadn't expected was the less-than-warm welcome from my counterpart at the clinic. The frosty demeanour I'm up against does nothing to quell my nerves. Every day my stomach ties up in knots.

Mason's been distant ever since trivia night, doing everything he can to keep me at arm's length. Despite agreeing to convince Nate we're dating, Mason seems determined to ensure the rest of the town doesn't perceive us the same way.

I can't blame him, though. In a town as small as this one, being a well-known fixture in the community must make you crave some semblance of privacy and want to avoid unnecessary attention. I empathize with the desire to escape the spotlight. It's not like I want to have a reputation in town for dating my boss a mere week after arriving, either.

At least, I reassure myself, Nate hasn't shown up at the clinic to harass me. Mason's only rule for our agreement is that he will refuse to play his part in public places. That includes his workplace —his domain.

So far, I've done a decent job of steering clear of him. It's easier to do when the desire to avoid each other is mutual. We've fallen into a routine, with me ushering his next patient into the exam room, conducting a quick check-up, and leaving their chart on the desk. By the time Mason arrives to see them, I've already slipped away, taking refuge behind the reception desk next to Winnie. Thankfully, Winnie has kept her thoughts to herself, but her side-long glances are anything but subtle whenever Mason sneaks behind us on his way to the staff room.

Despite the ever-increasing patient load, Mason has the clinic operated like a well-oiled machine, and he's become remarkably efficient in his appointments. I suspect that it's to the detriment of himself. Patients are in and out of the exam rooms in less than ten minutes. Winnie noted that my ability to conduct a basic assessment before Mason saw them improved the flow of the clinic. Mason has seen more patients in less time. I'd call that a win. A small one, but a win, nonetheless.

Mason dedicates most mornings to scheduled appointments, while afternoons on Tuesdays and Thursdays are reserved for walk-in hours—the busiest days of the week. On other days, Mason uses his afternoons for house calls. Most other physicians consider it an outdated practice. It's time-consuming and inefficient. However, when I asked him about it, his response was brief, as most of his responses are. He gave me a curt explanation that his father did it, so he would, too. Mason is a man of few words, and a scowl accompanies any utterance from him before he stalks off to his office at the back of the clinic.

I have yet to be allowed to accompany him on one of his house calls. He became defensive to the point of being almost rude when Winnie suggested I tag along. Something about his patients trusting him, not appreciating some random stranger invading their homes. I didn't press him further.

"I have you on the list to see Dr. Landry. If you could just go take a seat in the waiting room. It's going to be a bit of a wait today, unfortunately." Winnie is giving her spiel for the hundredth time today. The waiting room is full, and some people have taken to standing in whatever space they can find. Winnie has warned some newcomers that they are welcome to wait, but she can't guarantee that they'll get in. Besides the occasional glower and complaint from the odd wait-listed patient, I don't mind the bustling activity during walk-in hours; it makes the rest of my day fly by. It also offers a convenient excuse to avoid Mason until I can slip out the back door and retreat to the sanctuary of the cabin.

Picking up the next chart in the rack, I thumb through the pages, preparing to call the next person in. Before I can announce their name, the door's bell chimes, muted by a wail from the woman who enters.

"Help me, please! Please help her. Help my baby." The dark-haired woman approaches the desk. Her long locks are half-falling out of the haphazard bun on top of her head, and she's carrying a small bundle in her arms. My instincts kick in as I rush over to her, pulling back the swaddling blanket to get a look at the baby. My pulse quickens, adrenaline guiding my actions while keeping my thoughts sharp.

The baby is asleep, and as she squirms and wiggles, the tension in me releases. She couldn't be more than a few days old. She peers back up at me, and I notice that the corners of her eyes have a yellow tinge.

"Come on, Mama. Let's get you into a room and Dr. Landry will come and see you." After leading the woman with her baby to an empty exam room, she sits and I take some time to examine the baby and ask the woman a few questions.

"What concerns you about your baby?" I ask the mother, handing her a box of tissues from the counter in the corner.

"She's so jaundiced. She's sleepier than normal, and I'm so worried that she's not getting enough milk." Big gasps interrupt the woman's speech as her tears dry, leaving streaks on her reddened cheeks.

My heart aches for her. She reminds me of the women I cared for back when I worked in labour and delivery. My training tells me that this is the most vulnerable she has ever felt and that her emotional regulation is unpredictable. I rest a hand on her shoulder and crouch so I'm at eye level with her.

"Your baby is safe right now, Mama. She has some jaundice, which is expected for a baby her age. But she's breathing, and she's nice and awake, which gives us some time to get it all sorted." I reassure her before stepping out of the room to get Mason, who is occupied with a patient in the next room.

He is less than thrilled about being interrupted, the muscle flicking in his jaw as I can see him fighting his impulse to talk down to me in front of the patient he is examining. He groans under his breath as he follows me into the hall, where I explain the mother's concerns about her baby. I also try to garner some sympathy by emphasizing how distressed she is.

"Congratulations, Priya," Mason says, entering the small exam room, me in tow. He clicks the door shut behind him. He already knows the woman, and I realize he would have cared for her throughout her pregnancy. Women in the town come to Mason for prenatal care if they have no complications, but they go to the hospital in the next town over when they're ready to deliver. Mason tries to predict within a few days when that would be and ensures they're ready to make the hour-long drive when the time comes. With the steady influx of new people in town, especially young families, the logistics of this has become more and more challenging.

"We'll need to have you go to the hospital to have the baby's blood tested," Mason explains. I notice how Priya's face drops.

"I have no one that can take me." Priya's voice quakes, tears bubbling to the surface again. "It's too hard to go after the C-section. I only just got home yesterday. The drive is over an hour, and I haven't been cleared yet."

"Well, just hold on," I interrupt. Mason's dark brown eyes glare at me, almost black now; I know I will hear about this later. There is one thing that Mason hates more than being interrupted, which I've already done once, and that's being undermined in his own clinical practice. I don't care right now; Priya needs some support, and Mason isn't able to empathize with her. "Is she waking on her own to feed?" I ask.

"Most of the time. She's been waking every two to three hours. Sometimes I have to wake her, but once I do, she's fine."

"Ah, okay. Does she still take a whole feed?" I probe.

Priya nods. "I think so. She nurses until she goes back to sleep, and she seems like she's full."

"Good, that's fantastic. Is she having lots of diapers?" Priya takes a minute to consider my question.

"Yeah, I would say so," she answers, and I have all the information I need.

"Priya, I don't agree that you need to go all the way to the hospital."

Mason's eyes go wide and he cocks his head at me. The gesture is almost feline, a predator eyeing up his prey. Swallowing the urge to cower and back down takes all my force of will. I will smooth things over later, but right now, Priya is my priority. "It is safe to take your baby home as long as she continues to feed well and has a lot of wet diapers."

Priya's shoulders relax as she sighs.

"Promise that you'll bring her back at any sign of change. We can fit you into our house calls in the next couple of days to check up on you. Jaundice in newborns is normal, Priya. As long as they are waking up to feed and still wetting diapers, it's not an emergency. You're doing a great job."

I hold my breath as I wave off Priya and her baby, bracing for the impending reprimand from Mason as soon as I turn around. He stands there, leaning against the doorframe in the hall, arms crossed, ready for a fight that I'm reluctant to have.

"Don't start, Mason." I try to warn him, but it comes out as more of a plea.

"Don't start? You started this, Honeybee," he utters, enunciating every syllable of the nickname he's given me. "You started this when you made me look incompetent back there."

"All due respect, Doctor Landry"—I emphasize his title with a sharp edge—"if you spent more time with your patients educating them on these things, then that whole situation never would have happened." I regret the words as soon as they leave my mouth. My hands are shaking and sweaty. So much for smoothing things over. It's proving very difficult to avoid confrontation when every interaction with Mason is confrontational. I try to squeeze by Mason in the hallway, but he turns abruptly toward me and suddenly my back is up against the wall. The proximity of his broad chest has me pinned against the smooth surface of a poster reminding me to 'schedule my Pap smear today!' It's unnerving having Mason this close to me while being viscerally reminded of the existence of my vagina.

Mason is a whole head taller than I am, and he has to stoop to meet my eye level. Leaning down, he brings his face so close to mine I can feel his breath on my cheek. A warmth spreads through me that is akin to burning rage and humiliation, but the sensation moves low in my belly and settles between my thighs. Something about the way he's towering over me is turning me on, and I hate it.

"This is my practice." His voice is a low rumble and it sends a gooey warmth right through my core. "You may think you know more than me because you come from a large urban hospital, but you don't. I call the shots around here."

Whatever I had been feeling towards him, that spark ignited by his closeness, is snuffed out. My heart sinks. I took this job because I have something to offer. I have skills and knowledge, and I bring something valuable to the clinic. Mason either doesn't agree, or he's too stubborn and blind to notice. He just wants me to complete tasks that make his job easier and improve his performance. That type of man I'm accustomed to. It's all Nate wanted me for, too, to boost his public image.

"Fine." I put my hands up in surrender. "You call the shots." Mason's eyes flicker over to my left hand.

"You're not wearing your ring," Mason says, his brow furrowing as he interprets the significance of his observation. His gaze searches my face for confirmation of *why* I've decided to ditch the diamond, but I don't give him one. It's none of his business, anyway. Realizing the impasse, Mason turns away from me, stalking off towards his office.

I TIGHTEN the bow on my sneakers before heading out of the cabin and into the last golden rays of sunlight. A walk will do me good. The fresh air might help to clear out some of the frustration I have pent up towards Mason. My conversation with him earlier left me wound up, and it takes a minute of walking before my shoulders drop from beside my ears.

I'm still struggling to decide if I'm pissed off or turned on by the way he didn't even hesitate when he backed me up against the wall. The warmth of his breath on my cheek made an electric tingle zing down my spine. I doubt that's the reaction he was going for.

I can understand why he's angry; there's a knot of guilt forming in my stomach as I remember how I went over his head. It isn't my place to decide what's best for his patients. I'm pretty sure I've stepped outside of my scope in doing so, but if Mason had objected, he would have said something at the time, surely. Still, I don't deserve to have my hand pushed away in such a demeaning way. My self-assurance has grown stronger over the course of five years in the labour and delivery department. Newborn babies are kind of my thing.

I call the shots here. The words echo in my mind, a reminder that Mason doesn't see me as an equal, as a part of his team. I yearn for the opportunity to prove to him my true capabilities, beyond just menial tasks.

As I make my way down the sidewalk towards town, I can see the lights on at Thistle + Thorne, a cozy glow in the dim dusk light. Poppy would need to close the café soon; nothing stays open late in Heartwood. But we've become friendly over the last week, and I could use someone to talk to.

When I enter the café, the sound of the bell jingling overhead causes the brace-faced barista to peer over the espresso machine.

"Is Poppy in?" I ask him, and he nods, scurrying to the back room. Seconds later, Poppy emerges, and her face lights up when she spots me.

"Look who it is! The talk of the town," she says with a friendly smile.

"God, I hope not."

"You had to know that word would spread about you and Mason," she says, wagging a finger playfully. This is funny for her.

"Is Mason aware of this?" I ask, afraid of her answer.

"Oh no, no one would ever say anything to his face. No one is brave enough to do that." I huff a laugh in response. Right.

"Speaking of, when do you reckon Mason will 'warm up to me'?" I quote her from my first day in Heartwood. Poppy looks puzzled, and then I realize she hasn't been let in on the secret. I quickly come up with an excuse for now, until I decide to tell her that this is all just a ruse. "Even though we're ... dating now, he's still a possessive asshat at work." Poppy makes an exaggerated cringe face.

"Don't tell me he's giving you a hard time at the clinic."

"That would put it lightly. I'm about to head out on a *long* walk in the woods and possibly never return if that tells you how my first week has been."

"Hey, let me come with you. We don't have to discuss Mason, but I could use some fresh air, too."

"Don't you have to close up?" I glance around the café. There are a couple of tables that have empty coffee mugs and plates with scattered crumbs left on them.

"Eh, Ethan can handle it. There isn't much left to do."

Poppy and I set out towards the gravel path that connects the street to a trail winding all the way along the river. I breathe a sigh of relief, relishing in the crisp air. It's still warm with the last of the summer sun golden on my skin, but the air has the earthy smell that it's giving way to fall. A few yellow leaves scatter the pathway and crunch beneath our feet. We make our way along the wide gravel path, winding through the trees on the river's edge. The trail offers the perfect sanctuary after a long and frustrating day at work, and the swishing rush of the river drowns out my racing thoughts. We round the corner where the trail meets up with what used to be a trestle bridge. The pathway shows no more evidence that it was once a railway track other than the flat groomed terrain and the bridge.

Poppy doesn't ask any more questions about Mason, shifting her attention to my life before Heartwood. I tell her about my family, about my parents and Spencer. There's something about Poppy that is comfortable, and I indulge her in details about my life. How my parents weren't happy with my decision to go on *Stolen Love*, the way they judged me when I said I was moving to Heartwood. They couldn't accept that at this point in my life, I want to decide things for myself. Helicopter parents, I think, is the category that they would fall into. Their parenting style is one reason I haven't spoken to them since I left to film the show. It feels like forever ago now.

She just listens, nodding at the right times. Poppy may not relate to me at all, but she seems to understand why it's been hard for me to settle in here and why it's near impossible for me to stand up to Mason. I've never stood up to anyone before.

The hair on my arms raises at the sound of rustling leaves in the woods beside me.

"Did you hear that?" I ask Poppy, slowing my pace to ready myself for whatever is lurking in the trees.

"Uh, yeah ... dusk isn't the best time to be going out into the woods, Ally. Maybe we should turn around." Right as Poppy tugs at my arm, an enormous mass of black fur emerges from the bushes. The bear is only fifty feet away and is lumbering down the path toward us.

"Shit." My heart is pounding out of my chest. What are you supposed to do when you encounter a bear? I'm positive I've heard it somewhere. Make yourself look big and scream? Or are you supposed to play dead? No, I'm pretty sure that's for a grizzly, and this bear is black as night. Screw it. "Poppy, run!" I shout, breaking out into a sprint, turning down a path that I'm uncertain goes back towards town, but I can't second guess my decision now. Running is definitely the wrong thing to do, but I don't care; we have to get away from the bear. Poppy is close on my heels, and I chuckle to myself. This is an interesting reflection of how I handle most problems in life. By running away.

We're just about to the end of the trail where it opens to the sidewalk on Main Street. Turning back to see how much distance we've put between myself and the bear, Poppy and I slow to a speed walk as we come to the end of the path. I realize my mistake of not keeping my eyes ahead of me as I smack right into a solid wall of ... Nate.

Oh God. Running away from one problem and into another. *Classic Ally move.*

"Nate, right?" Poppy asks. She's trying to be polite. I haven't filled her in on all the reasons we need to avoid Nate at all costs.

"Let's just go, Poppy." I'm jittery from our close encounter with the bear. I don't have it in me to defend myself against a snake, too. I glance around, trying to find an escape. From here, we could cross the street and be back in the safety of the café in no time. I link my arm through Poppy's and try to steer her away from Nate. As I do, my foot slips off the edge of the curb, dragging my ankle downward followed by the rest of my body. I'm going down.

"Ally!" Poppy shouts, coming to my aid as I lay like a sack of shit in the street. It's humiliating enough just being in Nate's presence, now this. I can already tell that my ankle is throbbing and likely won't allow me to stand on it.

"My ankle ..." I try to push myself up onto one foot using my hands, but I crumple as soon as I put weight on my right leg. Poppy scoops my arm over her shoulder.

"Can you help me carry her?" she asks Nate. He's standing there staring at us like he's got two brain cells to rub together. "I need help to get her to the clinic."

"What? Poppy, no," I stammer. "I'm not going to the clinic."

"Why not?" She looks concerned.

"For one, I am trying to give Mason some space tonight." *And for the rest of time,* I think. "And two, it's his night off. He doesn't need me pestering him."

"Mason wouldn't hesitate to help you, Ally. He may be a bit of a jerk at work, but there's a reason he's dating you now. He cares about you, even if he has a funny way of showing it." I glance between Poppy and Nate. By the expression on Nate's face, I can see that he's registering who Mason is. The guy from Trivia Night. Heartwood's only physician. My *boyfriend.* A sneer forms on his lips like he's plotting, scheming.

"I agree." He pipes up, still not bothering to help Poppy hold me up. "We need to get you to a doctor. A visit to Mason is a *phenomenal* idea."

Poppy, sweet, innocent Poppy lights up, not understanding the snake pit she has just dragged us into. I'm just praying that Mason is still agreeable to the deal we made.

"Mason might not even be here," I say as we pull up to the clinic, testing any excuse to not have this interaction happen. Nate was such a *gem* and offered to drive us there in his rental Tesla. How'd he even manage to find a Tesla in Heartwood?

"Nonsense. Do you even know Mason? Of course he's here." Poppy waves off my comment. "If he's not, you can just give him a call and he'll come right away, I'm sure of it."

This is happening then. *Great.*

Nate has suddenly decided that he's the most chivalrous man on earth and rounds the car to help me out of the backseat. His touch makes me recoil, but I can't stand without some help. Poppy has gone ahead, holding her hand up to the glass to peer in the dark clinic. She must see some sign of life because she knocks frantically on the window. Mason emerges from the dark and unlocks the clinic door before he opens it, his eyes darting between the three of us. He furrows his brow. I give him a pleading look, hoping that he has somehow developed the power of hypnosis and can hear me sending him subliminal messages, begging him to play along.

"What's going on?" he asks, approaching the sedan to meet us.

"Ally fell and twisted her ankle. Nate brought us over so you could look at it." Mason's lip curls up into a sneer as he looks Nate up and down.

"Thanks, *buddy*," he says, his tone firm, a hint of condescension in his words. Mason slides his arm under mine and hoists me out of the car, taking the majority of my weight off my feet. "I can take it from here."

"No, I should stay with her. Make sure she's alright." There's a challenge in Nate's voice.

"Suit yourself." Mason has heard it, too, and he knows he can rise to it.

Mason ushers us all into the clinic and back to one of the exam rooms. He gently lifts me onto the table, his breath puffing softly into my ear. Nate is standing, arms crossed, in the corner of the tiny room, leering at Mason.

"Tell me what happened," Mason says, his voice morphing into the one he only ever uses with his patients.

"Nothing much. Twisted it off the curb," I explain, looking down at my ankle hanging off the exam table and refusing to make eye contact with Mason.

"She ate shit is more like it." Nate huffs.

"Thanks for the clarification," Mason says as he crouches low to manipulate my ankle, "but you can shut up now." The way he's turning it, it hurts, but I can tell it's already getting better. Not a break then.

"Well, I don't think it's broken," Mason says. I could have told him that. "But you are going to stay off it for a few days, and make sure to ice it." His tone is professional, almost reserved. Too reserved for a doting boyfriend whose girlfriend has just injured themselves. He's still crouched down by my foot, so I swing my uninjured foot and give him a kick in the shoulder while Nate and Poppy aren't looking. He gives me a *'what the hell was that for'* look and I try my best to make an exaggerated glance toward Nate, so he gets the hint. *Pretend you even remotely like me, asshole,* I scream in my head so maybe he can hear it.

"Thanks for helping me, *sweetie.*" If he hasn't clued in yet, then he needs a psychological evaluation.

"Oh, uh, yeah. Anytime, Honeybee. Can't let my girlfriend limp around with a sprained ankle." The look he's giving me says *'are you happy now?'* And I reply with a smug grin.

"Time to go, Ally," Nate says, indicating that he is the one who plans on getting me home. Fat chance.

"I'm going to stay here with Mason. He can drive me back." I deflect.

"I don't know, I have a lot of work to do tonight ..." Oh no, Mason is not doing this to me now.

"It's been a rough day. I could really use my *boyfriend* right about now." I give him my best and biggest puppy-dog eyes, making myself sick, but it works.

"Fine. I'll take you home later."

The explanation satisfies Poppy, and she's already halfway out of the exam room, Nate in tow.

"What the hell was that?" Mason says once we're alone.

"I'm sorry. I didn't know what to do." I'm flustered, trying to explain the situation as clearly as I can. "Poppy and I got chased by a bear, and then Nate was there, and I fell, and Poppy insisted we come." Colour rises to my face and his stare is making me feel hot, like he has me under an interrogation lamp.

"A bear? You got chased by a bear?" Mason's eyes are wide now. "Do you mean that literally, or are you being metaphorical and referring to Nate?"

"A real bear. I think I'd actually prefer getting chased by a bear than by Nate," I admit.

He sighs and shakes his head.

"How many people think we're dating now?"

I give him a sheepish look.

"I don't know. Poppy called me 'the talk of the town.'" I admit.

"Shit." Mason scrubs a hand over his lightly stubbled jawline, considering the situation we've gotten ourselves into. The situation *I* dragged him into.

"I'll tell her not to say anything about tonight. She'll understand," I offer.

"No. Don't do that," Mason says, almost defeated. "The more you try to counter the gossip, the more it fuels it, like fanning a flame. We just have to ignore it and go about our lives like this never happened. No more public displays of affection, understand?"

I do understand. It just makes my job of getting rid of Nate that much harder. But I nod anyway.

"Let's get you home." Mason's voice softens this time as he puts his hand out to help me off the exam table. The heat of his body is warm against me as he slides his arm under me and lifts me off the ground like I weigh nothing at all. I wish I could say that it does nothing to me. That I feel *nothing*. But that would be a blatant lie.

CHAPTER 10
MASON

THE CLINIC IS QUIET. Peaceful even. We somehow got through the morning of scheduled appointments on time today, meaning our lunch break feels like an actual lunch break. There's no one crying in the waiting room, no one pestering me about the wait time. And best of all, there's no Ally here flitting around and yammering to either me or Winnie. The girl seems to never stop talking. Today there's a bit of a reprieve. Ally hasn't been very mobile. Her ankle injury keeps her somewhat limited to the reception desk, so at least my office has been a haven.

Winnie offered to take Ally out for lunch "to get to know her better" and while it's nice to have the clinic to myself, it's the last thing *I* need. Winnie and Ally are already nightmarish when left to their own devices. They both seem to enjoy bossing me around, so I can only imagine how it will be once they join forces.

I survey the empty waiting room as I sip my coffee. There are some vases on the side tables with an assortment of flowers that weren't there before. The last thing that *a clinic* needs. What about people with allergies, Ally? I do a lap between the rows of chairs and gather the vases, stashing them in the staff room behind the reception desk even though there's limited counter space already.

The desk bell chimes, and I poke my head around the corner.

"Hey, Mason." Poppy is standing at the desk, holding a bouquet in a glass jar. Another fucking vase full of flowers.

"Poppy. Hi." Is Poppy here to ask me out on a date or something? She lifts the flowers as if that explains her reason for stopping by, which clarifies nothing for me.

"Delivery for Ally," she says. Of course. I reach out and take the bundle of flowers from her. They're beautiful, a generous number of large, fluffy pink petals interspersed with greenery.

"Thanks, Poppy. She's not in at the moment, but I'll put them behind the reception desk." I look at the card that's hanging off the vase, attached with a pink ribbon. *Whatever it takes, Al. —N.W.* Nate Winslow. On second thought, I won't put them on her desk. They can go straight in the trash.

"I have more. They're out in the car. Do you mind helping me bring them in?" I do mind. I mind very much.

"How many more?"

"A lot," Poppy says over her shoulder. She's wearing her dark brown bob in wild waves, that bounce as she walks out to the parking lot in front of the clinic.

I follow Poppy out to her car, a yellow Volkswagen bug that is full to the brim with those goddamned peonies. A groan escapes from me, and I see Poppy cringe. I'd rather stab my eyes out with a fork than have anything to do with this, but it's not Poppy's fault, and she can't be driving around with a hundred flowers in her car forever.

I gather an armful of bouquets and begrudgingly start helping Poppy bring them inside. They can live behind reception for now, but they are going the minute Ally gets back from lunch. She can take them to the cabin on her own, too. I don't care what she does with them, but they're not staying here.

"I'll just need you to sign for them." Poppy holds out a clipboard for me to sign. I'm in the middle of scrawling my signature across the page when the door to the clinic opens. Ally and Winnie come sauntering through, at least, Ally saunters as much as one with a sprained ankle can. They're laughing with each other like a couple of hyenas.

"I'm glad to see you ladies had a *delightful* time," I say with a hint of sarcasm. More than a hint, maybe.

"Mason, what's all this?" Winnie glances around at the piles of flowers all over the reception desk.

"This is a little extravagant for an apology, but okay, fine. I accept." Ally wanders behind the desk, picks a bouquet up and lifts it to her nose. "How did you know peonies are my favourite?" She flutters her eyelashes in an exaggerated swoon.

I bristle at the comment, a growl rising in my throat. Ally is treading too close to the line I drew about not mentioning our agreement in public. Even though I'm sure everyone knows by now.

"They're not from me," I grumble. The way Ally's mouth curves up into a smile indicates she knows exactly what she's doing, getting under my skin.

"Oh? Who sent them?" Ally searches the bouquet she's holding for a card.

"Three guesses and the first two don't count. You know what?" I throw my hands up in the air, a demonstration that I want nothing to do with this situation. "I don't care. Just get them out of here." I start down the hall towards my office. This is a colossal waste of my first decent lunch break in months.

"Are we going out on house calls today?" Ally calls after me, and I stop short, circling back.

"We"—I gesture between us—"aren't doing anything. Besides, you'll be too busy this afternoon getting these flowers the hell out of *my* clinic." I don't care if she takes five hours hobbling around on one foot to do it. Ally's cerulean eyes just about bulge right out of her beautiful face.

I don't care.

I storm back down the hall and into my office, slamming the door shut behind me.

"Word has it you found yourself a girlfriend, Mason?" My brother jeers at me from under raised eyebrows across the dinner table. "Took you long enough. Thirty-two years is a long time to have your virginity intact."

"Jett ..." Winnie warns. She's well-accustomed to our brotherly banter and playful teasing, but she draws the line when we're all together for Friday night dinner. It's her time to spend with us, and she prefers it when we pretend to like each other. Plus, it's been a while since the four of us have been under one roof like this. Between my work at the clinic and Jett being out of town training for his ski competitions, it's hard to find time when we can all sit down to dinner like this. The least Jett could do was hold off on being an asshat for one night.

I huff a half-hearted laugh in response to Jett's comment, stuffing my face with the last bite of food on my plate so I don't say something I'll regret. Arguing his point is only going to do the opposite of what I want, which is to steer the conversation away from my sex life. I'm no virgin, but I've also had a very dry spell for longer than I'm willing to discuss.

"Hey, I'm not the one airing my dirty laundry in front of the whole town at trivia, of all places."

"Enough, Jett." This time it's Grady that gives him the warning. I'm not one to bite when Jett starts his teasing. As the youngest of all of us, he's made it his personal duty to be a shit disturber most of the time. But he's trying to rile me up, and I no longer have the willpower to not say anything. Broadcasting my relationship with Ally, whatever it is at this point, wasn't something I chose. I'm still trying to decipher the terms of this fake boyfriend agreement myself. I swallow my bite and wash it down with a swig of beer.

"At least I have a relationship. I'm not going around banging snow bunnies and forgetting their names the next day." I'm not about to admit to them that this relationship isn't real. That fact will only add fuel to Jett's fire. *Real girlfriend's too much work for you?* I can already imagine the roasting.

"Not in front of Winnie," Hudson chimes in. Hudson is the peacemaker among us, and he takes his role seriously, no matter how impossible the task proves to be. Jett places his cutlery down on his plate and leans back in his chair. The way he brings his hands behind his head as he watches me makes me want to leap across the table at him. I love Jett as my baby brother, but man, that kid's got an ego on him. By the smirk on his face, I can tell that he's preparing another snarky quip, so I change the subject.

Standing up from my seat at the large oak dining table, I gather the empty plates and used cutlery from in front of Winnie, Grady, and Hudson. Jett can clear his own damn dishes.

"Thank you for a delicious dinner, Winnie." I lean down, balancing the plates in my hand, and give her a peck on the cheek. Winnie didn't have to step in to help my dad out after Mom passed away. But she did. And she accepted us, quirks and all, no matter how infuriating we can be.

Grady and Hudson stand up from the table and echo my gratitude, each giving her a quick hug on their way into the living room. The Friday night dinner tradition was born out of need. The original purpose was to give my dad a break from four rowdy boys to catch up on work or have some peace, but it has since turned into something we all look forward to.

Jett stands up last, bringing his plate to the sink where I've already started washing up. I'm surprised he even does that, although he drops it into the sink with a loud clatter before following the others into the living room.

They all mean well, but as the oldest, I've always been the most responsible of the group. I've never resented them for it. Scratch that. I resent Jett a little. More than anything, I envy the fact that they got to have a real childhood. None of them were old enough to remember Mom or the toll that her death took on Dad. None of them witnessed the way he changed, because they didn't experience the way he was before. Not like I did.

Winnie sits at the dining table, swirling her wine in her glass and surveying me as I sink my hands beneath the soapy water.

"Jett teases, but he's got a point." She takes a nonchalant sip from her glass as if what she just said won't irk the hell out of me.

"Don't say that too loud, Winnie. I don't think his head could get much bigger," I say between gritted teeth.

"What is this thing with Ally, anyway?" I don't look up from my task. I don't want to be having this conversation.

"It's nothing, Winnie. Nothing you need to worry about. This whole thing is my mess to clean up." A mess that I didn't make or even agree to make. I just got dragged into it against my will, and I have Ally to thank for that. My eyes roll thinking about Ally. She and Jett might make a compatible pair. They're both just as flaky and immature.

"It is my business if I'm going to be working at the clinic with her."

I can't argue with Winnie about that. She's the one who's going to be spending most of her time with Ally, not me. Not if I can help it.

"Don't worry about the clinic. I won't be making any grand displays of affection at work or anything. It's not real. I only agreed to play the part of her boyfriend so she can get rid of her ex-fiancé." I confide.

"The guy from trivia night? Who showed up flashing around his stupid Rolex like at any given moment someone could snap a picture of him and put it in GQ?"

"That's the one." Even just talking about Nate makes my blood pressure rise.

"Hm. I'm guessing he's the same one who sent all the flowers today. The ones *I* helped her move over to the cabin." I can see the gears turning in Winnie's head. "That's disappointing."

"Yeah, he is disappointing," I agree.

"That's not what I meant."

"You need to get your head checked, Winnie." I focus my gaze on the dish that I'm washing, and I realize I'm scrubbing so hard that I might break the plate. I ease up my grip. "I want nothing to do with Ally. Never will."

"Don't close yourself off just yet, Mason."

"You forget, I wasn't the one that wanted to bring her here in the first place."

"I haven't forgotten. You've reminded me, multiple times."

"I'm just saying." I place the last dish upside down on a towel next to the sink and turn to face Winnie. "She's not my cup of tea. Nor do I even have time to drink tea."

I don't know where I'm going with this analogy. The point is, there is no room in my life for a relationship. Not with the state of the clinic and my responsibilities to the town. I can't afford to divide my attention. Even if I wanted a relationship, Ally is the last person I want to get involved with. Someone who quits their job in healthcare to go on a reality show doesn't have much substance. There's no telling when she'll tire of her job at the clinic and dart off somewhere else.

"She's a sweet girl, and quite a looker. Don't tell me you haven't thought about her as more than a co-worker." I can't lie to Winnie, so I say nothing at all. The honest-to-God truth is that I have thought about it. Once, for about three seconds. The three seconds Ally stood in the driveway wrinkling her nose at me, when she put her hand on her hip in that stubborn, defiant way of hers. If I'm being transparent, once more when her vibrator fell out of her bag. Anyone would have gone there in their mind. It doesn't mean anything. Certainly not that I should jump into bed with her.

Just as quickly as I entertain the idea of Ally, I try to put her out of my head.

"Ally doesn't care about the things I care about; she would

never understand my commitment to the clinic, for one." I deflect.

"No? I think as a nurse, she would understand more than anyone."

"She quit her job as a nurse. She quit her job to go on reality television. I hardly think that qualifies her as a nurse. At least not one who takes her job seriously." I counter.

"I wouldn't count her out just yet. I think she's made of sterner stuff than you give her credit for."

"Even if that were the case—which it's not," I clarify. I wouldn't have Winnie going and getting the wrong idea. I'm already in too deep with Ally as it is, having agreed to be her fake boyfriend for the week. Is anything in her life genuine? "I just don't have the time or the space in my life to be getting involved with anyone. And even if I did, it would be a repeat of my father, neglecting his family to take care of someone else's."

"I just hate to see you close yourself off to the life that's out there for you, Mason." Winnie's voice sounds almost sad and it breaks my heart. There is no other way, and the sooner she realizes that, the better. Life outside of work doesn't exist for people like me. People who took an oath to help people, to save lives. Even without a relationship, I'm coming up short.

"People die." It comes out as a whisper. "People die when I'm not there."

Winnie furrows her brow, an almost pitying look sweeping over her face. It isn't pity but concern that shadows her expression.

"That wasn't your fault, Mason. There was nothing you could do."

I don't even know why I brought it up. Of course, it was my fault. I wasn't available when someone, a child, needed me the most.

The sound of the TV drifts from the living room adjacent to the kitchen and fills the silence that stretches between Winnie and me.

"Finding love takes guts, brains, and determination. Can these contestants strategize and woo the partner of their dreams? Let's find out, on Stolen Love ..."

You've gotta be kidding me. I'm trying to put Ally Wells out of my head. I don't want her in my living room, even if she is just on the screen. It's still too close for comfort.

I stomp through the kitchen and round the corner to see my three brothers fixated on the TV as the producers are interviewing Ally for her talking head segment. Seeing her on the show like this, she seems like a stranger. She's got about ten pounds of makeup on her face for one, but despite how made up she is, I can see that familiar sparkle in her eye.

"I've got my eye on one man here already. Nate gives me butter-flies. I can't tell if I'm smitten with him or just nervous around him, but he's exciting."

Ally talking about Nate that way after seeing how she behaved around him at the bar sets me on edge. Nate had her fooled right from the start. Something about watching this makes me feel like I'm infringing on her privacy. Ally avoided indulging me in the details of the show like the plague, so this feels like I'm breaching her trust. I don't care about Ally's feelings much, but I don't want to put myself in an awkward position the next time I see her at work.

Even as the thought crosses my mind, I can't help but feel a tugging in my chest for Ally. The way her smile dropped when she saw Nate enter the bar. The way her shoulders slumped as she backed down from our fight in the bathroom. Nate had done that to her. Nate had taken this bright, beautiful woman and made her a shell of herself. I won't condone glamourizing that type of behaviour and giving it any attention.

I cross the living room and hit the button on the side of the TV, and the screen goes dark.

"What the hell, Mason, we were just getting into that." Jett is the one to argue. Not surprising.

"We're not watching *Stolen Love.* Pick something else." The growl in my voice catches me off guard. Why am I getting so worked up over a stupid show?

"We want to get to know your girlfriend, man," Grady added.

"We are not watching this show. That's final." I flop down on the couch and keep my eyes fixed straight ahead at the now black screen.

"It's all good, Mason." Hudson gives me a soft smile. He's always been my favourite, although he could have more of a backbone sometimes. He picks up the remote and flicks through the list of top new releases on Netflix before everyone agrees to watch some new action movie. Everyone except for me. I'm more of a classic '90s rom-com guy. Something about Meg Ryan and Tom Hanks gets me every time. But I sit in silence and watch the opening scene. I've never admitted that I prefer romantic comedies to my brothers. It's a self-preservation tactic. I'd never live it down.

I yawn about halfway through the movie when my phone buzzes in my pocket and startles me awake. I pull it out, and Ally Wells' name lights up my screen. I can never get away from her, not at work, not at Winnie's, not even in my own thoughts. Ally Wells has been occupying every waking minute of my life since she arrived, and it's pissing me off.

I open her message.

ALLY

Sorry to pester.

Yeah, sure you are I think. Then, in another message,

ALLY

I'm out of firewood, and I'm kind of freezing
over here.

I shut off my phone screen and put it back in my pocket. Ally can figure out how to cut her own damn firewood. I remember her injured ankle from last night, the way she hobbled into the cabin when I dropped her off. Not an ankle that she should stand on to chop wood. Whatever. I'm sure she could figure out if she could stop being so prim for five minutes of her life. Ally is always well-groomed and put together. Sure, she doesn't wear the same amount of makeup as she wore for the show. That obviously isn't her preference. But she still comes to work in a matching set of colourful scrubs every day, her hair in that infuriatingly bouncy ponytail that just *screams* high-strung.

I glance out the window at the long shadows forming across Winnie's yard. The sun has set, and here in the valley of the mountains, that means it's about to get cold. As indifferent as I am towards Ally, I'm not a complete asshole. I hate the thought of *anyone* shivering in the dark, freezing. I may as well get this over with.

"I'm gonna have to cut this party short. I'm needed at the clinic." I stand up off the couch. Winnie has joined us in the living room, and she's staring right through to my soul. She can see through the lie. She has the same pager I do, and we both know it didn't go off. Winnie has an impeccable bullshit detector, and she also knows there's only one thing, one person, I would choose to lie about right now.

I shoot her a pleading look not to say anything. It's bad enough that my brothers are roasting me for how long it took me to find a girlfriend, let alone the fact that it's not even an actual relationship. I can only imagine what they would think if they knew that I'm jumping up the second she texts me, too. I can just hear Jett. The word *whipped* clangs through my head in his sneering voice.

I would go over to check on anyone if they were staying in the cabin with no firewood. This has nothing to do with the fact that it just happens to be Ally Wells.

CHAPTER 11
ALLY

Not ten minutes after I send the text to Mason, there's a knock at the door. My hand trembled as I hit send, and I threw my phone screen down on the couch as soon as I did. Mason Landry makes me feel like I'm in high school again, and he's the cool, detached, popular guy that I'm terrified to talk to. He's the guy that I would be convinced has no idea I even exist.

But here he is at my house, standing outside with an axe in hand in his plaid button-down and jeans. His hair is a bit mussed, but his waves are soft, and I have a strange urge to run my fingers through them. It's been difficult to maintain my cool around Mason since our heated interaction in the clinic. I should be angrier about it, having my hand slapped like a child. But all I can think about is feeling his breath on my neck.

Asking Mason to come to chop my firewood was not my first choice; it is in my best interest to avoid Mason outside of work altogether, but there's no other option. Fall is settling into the mountains now, and even on the warmest days of summer, the temperature drops rapidly after the sun sets. I was not prepared for the drastic change in temperature, and I'm still shivering in my long knit cardigan, sweatpants, and plush socks.

"I'll be out back chopping wood for a bit." Mason's voice is gruff and clipped. After his outburst at work, he's been more restrained around me. I should be grateful for it, but I'm not. I just want Mason to be himself, to let me see him for who he is.

"Okay." I feel exposed standing at the door in my sweats, so I tug the cardigan around me and cross my arms. "I can come out and get it when you're done," I say, offering to be of some help. But Mason is already halfway down the steps and walking around to the pile of wood leaning against the side of the cabin.

I close the door and wander back inside. My energy is jittery, and I don't quite know what to do with myself while I wait for Mason to finish, so I pace around in search of something that will pass the time. I need to do something that makes me seem indifferent to Mason's presence and like I haven't just been sitting around waiting for him to get back.

I sit on the couch and pick up my book from the coffee table. Reading a book would say casual-indifference-to-your-grumpy-but-super-attractive-boss, right? I stare at the page of the romance novel I was getting into for a few seconds.

Cock in hand, he strokes up and down his long pulsing shaft as he stares at her.

Nope. I slam the book shut. Thinking about cocks and shafts is the last thing I need.

I jump up from the couch and glance around the small living room before remembering that I have some dry goods in the pantry. I have enough that I could start some baking. Baking is not sexy. Baking does not turn me on. There's flour, cocoa, and sugar in the pantry, and I just loaded up the fridge with eggs and milk. I could make some brownies, and the heat from the oven warming would take the chill off the cabin.

The oven is preheating when I hear Mason's footsteps on the porch. He opens the door with one arm, a few pieces of firewood in the other.

"I can get it from the back. I don't want to take any more of your time," I offer.

Mason sets the firewood down next to the hearth. He stands up and looks at me, making my skin prickle with heat that isn't from the oven warming.

"Not a chance on that ankle of yours. Do you even know how to make a fire?" Mason runs his hand through his thick curls, just like I would have liked to do.

"That's rude to assume," I snap back. "I'm sure I can figure it out myself."

"So that's a no. I'm not trying to be insulting; you just don't seem like the kind of girl that would know how to build a fire."

"And what kind of girl would I be, exactly?" I unfold my arms from across my chest, letting Mason get a look at me before he makes his sure-to-be snappy and unfair judgment.

"You just seem a little ..." Mason hesitates, looking for the right words. "High maintenance." I scoff. High maintenance?

"Why, because I went on reality TV and now own several floor-length gowns, that makes me high maintenance?" I ask, laughing at myself.

"Well, yeah. Kind of." Mason shrugs. "You're more high maintenance than anyone else in this town." I can't argue. I do come across that way, even if that persona isn't me.

"You hardly know me, Mason Landry." I'm not about to admit to him that I can see his point.

"I know enough about you to bet that you'll let me stay and build you a fire." The corner of Mason's mouth lifts into a smirk, and I can't help but think it's the sexiest thing I have seen. I can't entertain that thought longer than I already have. Mason Landry is my *boss*. Never mind that he's also my fake boyfriend, the key word being *fake*. I clear my throat, readying myself to change the subject to distract myself from Mason's half-smile.

"Fine. If you insist. You can build me a fire." I turn on my heel and wander back into the kitchen, taking ginger steps on my still-sore ankle.

The silence between us is deafening, and I can't help but try to fill it. I hate small talk, but I hate awkward silence even more.

"So, what were you up to tonight that you could drop it and come over?" My question is intended innocently, but I realize what I have implied. That Mason would drop whatever he's doing to see me.

"I didn't drop everything to come over," Mason corrects me, as expected. "I was at Winnie's. My brothers and I have always gone over for Friday night dinner and a movie. This is the first time in a while that we've all been together for it."

"And you just got up and left? I could have managed over here. I've got extra blankets," I say. I hadn't realized that Mason and Winnie were so close, but it makes sense given that she has been working at the clinic for almost her entire career, which is longer than Mason has been alive. I don't bother asking why Winnie is filling in for his actual mother, making the boys dinner on Friday nights. I'm confident that he won't tell me, anyway. And now the gnawing guilt that Mason left in the middle of their movie night eats at me.

Mason continues stacking the logs in the fireplace and crumpling paper to place around them.

"They picked a movie I don't like."

Mason stands from the fire. It's roaring to life in the hearth behind him. I don't understand how he made it so quickly. There's a lot that I don't understand about Mason Landry. Here is this man who wields his power over me at work, but who drops what he's doing at a moment's notice to come and chop my firewood. I don't press him further; clearly, Mason Landry doesn't like to be put in a box.

"In that case, do you want to stay for some brownies? I just started making them," I ask without thinking. Something about

Mason being here in the cabin with me makes me wish he wouldn't leave. Not yet at least.

It's been lonely since I arrived in Heartwood. Living alone isn't something I'm used to. I've always lived either with my parents, with Nate, or, for a brief time, with Spencer. I hadn't realized how much I wanted another person around until now. The fact that it's Mason, that he probably wants nothing to do with me, doesn't matter. I just want someone to talk to for a little while longer.

He eyes the baking supplies I've pulled from the pantry and glances between me and the door, contemplating whether he has a better place to be.

"Sure."

"Wait, really?" My jaw drops in disbelief. I hadn't expected him to want to stay, and now I'm having a moment of panic realizing that I have to make more awkward conversation.

"Yeah. I've nothing going on. Besides, who's going to keep your fire going and make sure you don't freeze to death?"

"Uh, okay, great. They won't take long." I'm hoping that the careful measurement of each ingredient will be enough to keep my mind off Mason's butt in his jeans as he crouches low, stacking the logs in the fire.

I finish the batter, pour it into the pan that I place in the oven, and set the timer before limping back over to the couch, the fire warming the entire space.

"Your ankle is still bothering you." Mason points out.

"Thanks, Captain Obvious. It's only been a day since I, quote, 'ate shit.'" I wince as I take a seat on the couch and lift my leg up to rest it on the cushion. It's not as bad as it was when it first happened, but it's still sore when I've been on it for any length of time.

"Have you been staying off of it today?" he asks. He sounds as if he cares for a moment.

"Why, are you concerned I won't be at work on Monday?" Okay, that was a little snarky.

"Well, yeah. But I also care about my patients."

I wrinkle my nose at him and notice the corner of his mouth twitch. "I'm not your patient."

"You came to the clinic for an assessment yesterday, and you live in Heartwood, so yeah. That makes you my patient. Whether you like it or not, Honeybee." He comes over to take the seat next to me on the couch. "Can I look at it?"

I stare at him for a moment, weighing all the awkward scenarios that could come of having Mason Landry touching my feet.

"What? Do you have a foot fetish or something?" He gives me a withering stare. "Fine. If you must, you can look at my foot."

I lift my foot up onto the couch, and he gestures for me to place it in his lap, which I do. His hands are gentle as he peels my sock back, exposing my bare toes. This feels uncomfortably vulnerable. Somehow, having a man take off my socks is more intimate than having them take off my panties. His eyes widen as he sees the purple bruise that has formed under the knob of my ankle bone.

"This looks painful," he states. I shrug.

"It's not so bad. It looks worse than it is."

"You need to stay off of it."

"You need to stop telling me what to do," I snap back, but the grin on my face is giving me away. I'm not as feisty as my words would let on. Although, Mason makes me brazen somehow. It's a new sensation for me, and I don't quite know what to do with it.

"Doctor's orders." His eyes bore a hole through me as he gently moves my ankle to check my range of motion. I don't respond. Instead, we sit in silence while he continues rubbing a hand over my ankle, his soft yet calloused fingers sending goosebumps up my leg. I'm no doctor or physiotherapist, but as a nurse, I am almost certain that this is much longer than necessary for a standard musculoskeletal exam.

I am the first to break the silence, hoping that any conversation will make me feel less awkward. The shock of hearing my voice for the first time in a few seconds causes Mason to remove his hand from my foot. Which is what I thought I wanted, but somehow feels wrong. My foot is cold without the warmth of his hand.

"You said that Winnie is like a second mom to you. What's your family like?" As much as I hate small talk, I figure I may as well try to get to know this puzzling man. The man who keeps himself so closed off and guarded at work, but came running over at a moment's notice to chop my firewood, and caressed my foot in a way that made my insides melt. If we're going to work together for the foreseeable future, getting to know him may just help to ease whatever tension has been between us since I arrived.

"Neither of my parents are around anymore," Mason says, staring into the flames licking the logs in the hearth. "My mom passed when I was young, and my dad died just over a year ago."

"I'm sorry," I start, but I don't make eye contact for fear of ruining whatever it is causing Mason to open up to me.

"Don't be. They're old wounds now." He's cracking open the door, but the wall between us is very much still there. "To be honest, I resent my dad more than anything."

"Dr. Jack Landry, right?" Winnie had mentioned the late Dr. Landry a few times as she oriented me to the office. The town revered Jack; no one ever had anything negative to say about him. Whatever he did to cause such resentment in Mason must have been significant, but I don't pry.

"You got it. The great Dr. Landry."

"And now you're trying to fill his shoes." I'm piecing it all together. The reason that Mason walks around the clinic with a clenched jaw. He's trying to live up to the legacy that his father left.

"Mmhmm. Lucky for me, he left me an impossible task." His lips form a tight line. I'm well aware that the clinic is busier than ever, but I wouldn't describe the situation as impossible.

"How so?" I test the waters, seeing how much more Mason will indulge.

"You've seen it," Mason grumbles. "So many people have

moved to Heartwood in the last year; I don't know how I'm supposed to maintain the quality of care that my dad provided, that people around here expect."

The egg timer on top of the stove buzzes, and at the same moment, there's a hard knock on the door. I get up and walk over to the kitchen to take out the brownies before they burn. Mason, thankfully, gets up to answer the door.

"Hey, man," a familiar voice says as Mason opens it. The words are friendly, but the tone is not. I just about drop the pan of brownies on the floor.

"You shouldn't be here," Mason snaps. I'm taken aback by the sharpness in his voice, as if he's just as angry as I am that Nate has shown up here, at the cabin, my safe space. For a fake boyfriend, Mason's reaction is shockingly believable. Nate doesn't respond; he peers over Mason's shoulder toward me, approaching from the kitchen.

"I see you still haven't given up your little game, Ally." He sneers at Mason.

"It's not a game, Nate. Not everything in life is a game to be played." I saunter over to the door, attempting to come across as casually as possible, but my insides are a quivering mess. I cross my arms as I approach the doorway. Mason is standing next to me, propping it open. He doesn't back up to a friendly distance when I get close to him, and the knot in my stomach loosens a little. Our proximity tells a more convincing story of intimacy. We look like a couple. The warmth of his body so close to mine is oddly comforting and protective.

"I'm not playing, Ally. I just wanted to check in and see if you've decided to come home with me yet." The word 'yet' makes me cringe, as if the fuckface is so positive that the day is coming when I'll just drop everything and go back to him. It isn't even a question in his mind.

"I told you, I'm happy. I'm making a life for myself here." Mason's warm hand lands on the small of my back, and a tingle ripples all the way through me. The grounding feeling of it somehow makes me brave. "I think you should go."

It isn't the defiant clapback that I would have liked to say, but I hold my ground, and that's what matters. It's more than I would have said to him last week, and I have Mason to thank for that. Nate stands in the doorway in stunned silence. It's the most that I've ever spoken back to him. Throughout our entire relationship, which hasn't been that long in the grand scheme of things, it's always been Nate's way.

"You heard her, man. Ally's *mine* now." Mason's hand creeps up from my lower back to wrap around me. A flutter ripples through my abdomen and all the way into my chest. Those words coming from Mason make me feel more than I should allow. I can't help but notice Nate's eyes dart to where Mason's hand is resting on my hip, a flush of anger colouring his cheeks.

"Suit yourself. But if you change your mind, you know where to find me." Nate has informed me that he's staying in the only motel in town, as if he has anywhere else to say. His multiple unanswered text messages leave no question. "I'll be here for as long as it takes."

I swear there's a hint of a threat in his voice. Nate used to terrify me. After the show, I realized that beneath his doting, caring facade was something more sinister. He has money, he has resources, and he knows people in many places. He somehow tracked me down here in Heartwood. He's slimy and sneaky, and I realize at this moment that I don't trust him.

Mason keeps his arm wrapped around me as we stand on the porch, watching Nate stalk back to his black Tesla sedan parked in the driveway. I want to make sure that I see him leave. Nate looks back at us for a moment before getting into the car, and as he does, Mason turns and places a soft, comforting kiss on my temple, holding his lips there for a long and drawn-out moment. The warmth of his breath on my skin turns my insides to molten lava, bubbling to the surface and turning my cheeks a deep shade of pink.

I look up at Mason as the car bumps down the gravel drive.

"I thought your week as my boyfriend was up," I point out. Not that Mason has ever really committed to the part in the first place. I don't want to force him into it for any longer than he agreed to. Mason waves my comment out of the air.

"There's no harm in it; there was no one else around to see. Besides, I've known the guy for all of a week and have only encountered him twice, but I already hate his guts."

"Join the club." I roll my eyes and head back over to the couch.

"What made you stay with him, anyway? He doesn't seem like your type. I thought you didn't go for pompous assholes. Your words, not mine."

The question makes my heart pick up its pace. Mason and I have only just started to come to decent terms with each other, and I would rather not discuss Nate, the show, or any of my past that brought me here. He makes it glaringly obvious that he doesn't respect the fact that I quit my job for a reality show.

"Since you've got me pegged, tell me, what is my type?" I give him a quizzical look, dodging his original question. Mason likes to think that he already knows everything about me. "You?" The question is daring. I'm dipping my toe into waters that I shouldn't be going anywhere near. Mason stares at me dead in the eyes but doesn't say a word. "I think I'm ready for brownies." I clear my throat, changing the subject.

I hop up off the couch, as quickly as my ankle will allow, and I distract myself by cutting the brownies into even squares. Mason follows and accepts the brownie I'm holding out to him on a plate. His eyes roll back as he tastes it. I'd like to see his eyes roll back for a different reason.

"Perfection. Ten out of ten," Mason says, his mouth still full. "But you never answered my question. I don't know if you've ever been in a fake relationship, but in all the fake relationships *I've* been in, they're built on honesty and transparency."

He's joking. Mason doesn't let anyone close enough to even pretend, but his expression is sincere. He has a point. He opened up and shared aspects of his life he reserves for a select number of individuals. The least I can do is explain why I roped him into this whole scheme in the first place.

"Nate wasn't that bad at first. Have you seen the show I was on?" I figure Mason isn't a reality TV-watching type of guy, but who knows? Judging by his blank stare, I assume I'm right. "Never mind. Just don't watch it, please. It's kind of cringey. Anyway, Nate went all out on the show to woo me. It was called *Stolen Love*, and you had to compete with other contestants to win over the person you wanted to date. You could plan elaborate dates and whatnot. I guess I just fell for him because of the atmosphere, but it wasn't real life."

"And what about now? What happened that brought you all the way here?"

"Why I'm here is a whole other issue. That has less to do with Nate and more to do with me being a bit of a baby with confrontation." I laugh in a self-deprecating *my life is a complete mess, so if I don't laugh, I'm going to cry* kind of way. "Nate was just using me. He's not the most wholesome person. His job requires him to be liked, and that's difficult for him. I think he thought if he was with a nurse it would make him look better. I learned that I would never be important to him for any other reason. He was always occupied with work, and only wanted me when he had some client he wanted to impress." Mason nods as if he understands, but he still has confusion written on his face.

"So you came to Heartwood, of all places?"

"Like I said, a whole can of worms." I don't feel like delving into my own flaws. I have a strong aversion to confrontation, which leads me to go to great lengths to please others and make decisions based on their opinions. I could bitch about Nate all day, but revealing my own shortcomings is a little too vulnerable for our budding friendship.

CHAPTER 12
MASON

ALLY ASKED to join me on my house calls today. No, she insisted, following me out to my car and buzzing around me despite her injured ankle, blocking me from getting into the truck until she wore me down.

"You should stay back and ice that ankle of yours." I attempt to turn her around by her shoulder and send her back to the clinic, but she evades my grip.

"Oh, this old thing?" She pulls up the pant leg of her scrubs, revealing an ankle brace that appears a little too effective. "Found it in the back closet in the clinic. Winnie showed me where it was. It works like a charm." Winnie. I'll have to talk with Winnie about letting Ally snoop around the clinic later.

For someone who is a bit of a doormat, Ally is getting a little too comfortable standing up to me. As annoying as the little Honeybee is, I have to admit that this new side of her is refreshing. It's more respectable than the version of Ally that slumped over in defeat before an argument even began.

I don't regret bringing Ally along. The warmth I feel towards her after last night has a hold on me. I don't even know why I stayed. She just seemed a bit ... flat. I searched her eyes for that mischievous sparkle and came up short. I'm sure Nate showing up in town was the primary cause of that, but I can't help but worry that I may have also contributed. My cold, standoffish attitude to her at work wouldn't have helped.

Ally had transformed from this effervescent and hopeful woman to dejected and disheartened in a matter of a week since she's been here. As much as I didn't care to hang out with Ally, I also didn't want to leave her alone. That and I had no interest in going back to Winnies to be ridiculed by my brothers.

So I stayed. And Ally opened up like a flower blooming before me.

There's a new lightness in my chest today, a spring in my step that I haven't had in the entire year since my dad passed away. The only thing that's threatening to ruin my mood is the memory of Nate showing up unannounced. That smarmy asshole makes my skin crawl. I hadn't felt invested in helping Ally, but when Nate showed up, I fully committed to being her dream guy. I will be the best goddamn boyfriend Ally's ever had if it means Nate buggers off. He's so smug and arrogant, and I want him gone for my sake more than hers.

However agreeable I am this morning to her tagging along, apprehension washes over me as she sits beside me on the passenger side of my truck. I shift the gear stick into park on Mrs. Rose's driveway and look at Ally across the bench seat. House calls are important to me. Few doctors even do house calls now; they've long since switched to in-clinic visits only. But my father believed in meeting patients where they are, and I am determined to keep the parts of his practice that he valued.

I reserve house calls for elderly folks or people with mobility problems who have a hard time getting down to the clinic. And now Priya and her baby, whom Ally made the executive decision to include on our list today. My gut turns over on itself. Bringing Ally along with me today is nerve-racking. It's a privilege to be invited into someone's home. For many of my patients, they're vulnerable and protective about who they let in. Ally is still a stranger to Heartwood, not to mention I still don't trust that she's as invested in the clinic as she says she is. There's nothing to prove that this isn't just part of some publicity stunt.

"It might be best if you wait here for the first one," I suggest, but the look on Ally's face says loud and clear that she doesn't agree. Mrs. Rose is always friendly, and if anything, I'm certain that Ally will be well-received at this visit, but something in me still doesn't want Ally to be a part of this. Call me territorial, but I treat these house calls with great importance.

"You're joking, right?" Ally scoffs. "I didn't come out with you today to sit in the car, Mason. How am I supposed to see what you do if I don't come in?"

"You can imagine it when I tell you about it later."

"Here I thought we might be getting along. Dr. Dickbag is right," Ally mutters.

I purse my lips. Dr. Dickbag is the nickname Jett gave me when I got back from medical school. I should set them up. Ally wouldn't need me as her fake boyfriend anymore. She'd have a real one that is more on her immature level.

I don't care to be known as Dr. Dickbag, though, so I give in with a groan.

"Just let me do the talking, okay?" Ally is already getting out of the truck and on her way up to the house before I have time to give her any further instructions. I have to jog to catch up with her. I'm already getting annoyed by her enthusiasm.

Alma Rose's house is on a peaceful street a few minutes outside of town. She has a sprawling yard of coiffed grass, now turned a golden brown by the summer sun. Her garden is still bursting with colour, and I marvel for a second at her ability to maintain all of her flowers in her ripe old age.

Ally strides across the front porch and swings open the old wooden screen to knock on the door. A child shrieks from inside the house as Mrs. Rose opens the door, and a little face framed by fair curls peers out from behind her legs.

"Hi, Mason." I like that my patients call me by my first name; Dr. Landry was my father. "Don't mind my granddaughter, Annabelle. I'm babysitting her while my daughter goes to get my groceries. She's in town for the week. I see you brought a friend today." Alma smiles at Ally, and Ally extends her hand.

"Ally Wells, ma'am. I don't believe we've met. I'm the new nurse in the clinic."

Alma raises her eyebrows towards me.

"I'm glad you've opened up to some help around that place."

"I wouldn't go that far, Mrs. Rose." Ally chuckles. "He's not open to anything." The two women titter in unison like a couple of goddamned schoolgirls. Ally has known this woman for all of two minutes, and somehow, they've ganged up on me already. Ally has a way of doing that, pulling people into her orbit. I clear my throat.

"Let's get down to business, shall we?"

Alma gestures for us to come in, Annabelle running circles around Ally and me as we make our way into the kitchen. Alma sits down on a kitchen chair, and I pull the other chair out, positioning it across from her to examine the arm that she had fallen on. She isn't wearing her sling, but she's still favouring it, and I noticed how her hand trembles every time she lifts it.

"Alma, I understand it's difficult for you to go into the city, but I'd like to get you into a physiotherapist to see about this hand tremor. Your arm is quite weak from being in the sling for so long. I'm also worried there may be some lasting nerve damage from the fracture you had," I explain, gently moving her arm in various directions and studying Alma's expression for signs of discomfort. Ally is watching me and listening intently. Having her attention on me is oddly satisfying. I'm at a loss for what to make of it.

I finish up with Alma and write down the information for the physiotherapist in the next town over, promising to put in an urgent referral. I explain to her that there might be an opening while her daughter is in town, and perhaps she could take her.

A little hand tugs on the corner of my shirt. I turn and look down beside me at Annabelle. She has to be only three years old, and she smiles up at me, holding out a small plastic stethoscope. Her giggle is contagious as I lean down to let her listen to my heart and I find myself quickly being ushered over to the living room, her tiny hand dragging me by one finger. I'm aware of Ally's eyes on me, and it's a sensation I don't dislike.

Alma is already asking Ally a barrage of questions about how she ended up in Heartwood, how she is enjoying the town, and how she's getting on at the clinic. I'm relieved that Ally is getting on so well with her and that she's fitting in here. It bodes well for the clinic if Ally stays, since she might just be the key to securing more funding.

I crouch down on the floor next to Annabelle as she shrieks and dumps her doctor's kit all over the floor. I don't know what comes over me at that moment. Maybe it's the remnants of the playful mood I've been in since the morning, but I jump into the game of make-believe and play my part. Thanks to Ally, I've become adept at acting these days. House calls are a get in and get out type of deal, but today, I feel some of my tension loosen as Annabelle picks up the small toy blood pressure cuff and wraps it around my wrist, the only place it will fit.

Ally's gaze remains on my back as she answers all of Alma's questions, avoiding any of the questions that delve into her life in the city. I turn to look at her over my shoulder. There's a warmth in her stare as she offers me a coy smile, and I return it with one of my own. Annabelle was busy inflating the blood pressure cuff, using both hands to squeeze the bulb, and I let out an exaggerated "Ow!" She giggles, covering her mouth with her hand in a cartoonish way.

"Annabelle." She looks up at me with her big brown eyes, and my heart melts. "One day you could be a doctor, too. Or better yet, you could be a super smart nurse like Ally." The smile that spreads across Annabelle's face is my sweet demise as my insides turn to goo. I don't look over to see Ally, because I have a sneaking suspicion that the smile on her face would do me in for good.

"Is Ah-wee your wife?" Annabelle peers up at me, an innocent enough question, but I just about choke when she asks it. Ah-wee is far from my wife, but not as far as I would like. I hear Ah-wee—*Ally*—clear her throat behind us.

"We should get moving if we want to see our last patient of the day," Ally says, standing up from the chair and straightening out the scrubs she is wearing. I have long since given up the scrubs, opting for a pair of jeans and a flannel most days. No one in Heartwood cares much as long as I do the job well.

I pry myself away from my game with Annabelle, where she insists on taking my temperature multiple times "just to be sure."

Alma and Annabelle wave us off as we walked back to my truck.

"She was sure smitten with you," Ally says, climbing into the passenger seat and giving me a playful grin.

"Oh, older ladies can be positively feral around me." I wink, and Ally gives me a shove on my shoulder.

"Shut up. I was talking about Annabelle."

My phone rings from inside the cup holder breaking the playful energy that is pulsing between Ally and me. As the screen lights up, I can see that the call is from a strange number, not one that I have in my contacts. A feeling in my gut tells me I already know what the call will be about.

"Hold on a sec." I hold a finger up to Ally as I answer and get out of the truck. I won't have this conversation in front of her. It's bad enough that she knows I'm struggling to keep up with the patient load; I don't want her worrying that her job was on the line as well. Not when I'm hell-bent on making sure that this doesn't go any further anyhow.

Fuck, since when did I start caring about Ally Wells?

I hit the green button and answer the call I've been dreading since receiving the letter from the health ministry last week.

"Dr. Landry, my name's Simone Mitchell. I'm calling on behalf of the Ministry of Health. I'm sure you've been expecting my call," the woman says on the other end of the line.

"Dr. Landry was my father, you can call me Mason," I correct her, but I don't want to let on that I have, in fact, been expecting her call. I won't admit that it's all I've thought about all week. A ball of anxiety forms in my gut.

"Sure, Mason. I'm calling to discuss the future of the Heartwood Medical Centre. As you're aware, the ministry has funded it for the last few decades since your father opened it and applied." I am well aware. I let her continue.

"We've recently undergone some budget cuts, and that has meant evaluating our health services and doing some restructuring."

"By restructuring, you mean closing down the clinic." There's a beat of silence on the other end as Simone considers her next words.

"Nothing is set in stone yet. But we are looking into clinics that might be absorbed by larger health centres. Rural communities, like Heartwood, may be better served if patients travelled to a neighbouring town with more resources and relied on patient transport for emergencies."

"The nearest town is over an hour's drive." I can't believe what I'm hearing. Just the other day, Ally suggested a mother keep her jaundiced baby at home because she could not drive and had no one to take her. How are people like her supposed to manage? Or Alma? Heartwood Medical Centre is integral to the town.

"I understand, Mason. Nothing has been finalized at this time, so I would like to notify you that you have until the end of the month to show that Heartwood Medical Centre is necessary to the town and that it can meet the growing needs of the population. If you can improve services within your existing budget, we will consider keeping the clinic open and funded."

I end my conversation with Simone. She had offered me a chance, albeit a very slim one. I'm already struggling to see all of my patients, even with Ally here. How can I expect to overhaul the clinic and make it more efficient with just myself, Winnie, Ally, and the already mediocre budget I have?

Ally studies my expression as I climb back into the truck. I don't need Ally worrying, and I don't want to talk about how I'm failing at keeping my father's clinic open and running. I don't want to talk about anything.

"You're so serious all of a sudden." Ally points out, which does nothing to put me in a better mood. "Are you okay?"

"It's about nothing that concerns you, Honeybee," I grumble, turning over the key in the ignition. For the rest of the drive, we sit in silence. Ally gazes out the window at the passing trees. It kills me to keep this from her. We've been making some progress in the friendship department, and I feel like I just set us back further than where we started.

We still have two more house calls to get through this afternoon, including a visit to Priya and the baby to finish the day. I'm already preparing myself for the way Ally is going to shove it in my face that she was right about keeping Priya at home. She'll have some annoying little way of saying 'I told you so' and it won't do anything to help the foul mood I'm in.

By the time we get back to the clinic, Winnie has closed up. House call days are days that she can go home a little early, as long as she's finished filing the charts and prepping for the next day's appointments.

Ally walks around the reception desk and collects her things when I make my way out to the front, preparing to lock up behind her.

"So, how did you enjoy the house calls? Was it everything you ever dreamed of?" I'm teasing her, hoping that it lightens up the mood after I was the ultimate wet blanket on our otherwise decent day together.

"Actually, yeah. I think it's cool that you have such a close relationship with your patients." She's nonchalant in a disconnected way that I don't like. Ally throws her bag over her shoulder and follows me to the door.

"They only like me because I'm a Landry. They have high expectations of me, don't get me wrong."

"I don't think that's true. They seem to trust you." Ally turns to face me. God, she's pretty, even after a long day of work. Her hair falls out of the messy bun on her head in soft tendrils, and I'm tempted to tuck it behind her ear.

"I was thrilled to see Priya and the baby today. I'm so glad she's doing so much better."

"So am I." I glance down at my shoes and clear my throat, preparing myself for what I'm about to say next. It doesn't come easy. "You made the right call keeping them at home. It's easy to overthink things, and I forget that there are a lot of conditions that can just be monitored." As I look back up at Ally, she's beaming, her face lighting up at the small bit of recognition I just gave her. I wonder how often anyone has told her that her opinions are smart, that she has valuable ideas. Nate's tally would most likely be a whopping zero.

"By the way, I've been thinking a lot about Priya." Here it comes. It wasn't enough that I admitted she was right.

"I know, I know. You told me so. Don't go rubbing it in."

"You must have some low opinion of me to think I would shove that back in your face, Mason. All I care about is Priya's well-being. And the baby's." Ally turns again and continues walking out the door and into the parking lot. "Whatever."

My truck is parked outside, so I follow her.

"I'm sorry. I didn't mean to assume." *That's it, smooth things over. You need Ally, you idiot.*

"I just wonder if the new moms in town, or even moms-to-be, need some sort of prenatal or postnatal education sessions. Even just a social session, here at the clinic."

I consider her words. There isn't enough room in the budget for the clinic as it's operating now, let alone to introduce another program. Although, the timing is kind of perfect considering my phone call earlier. The program might offer a solution to a lot of my problems.

"I'm listening," is all I say, hoping that Ally has more of a concrete plan in that beautiful head of hers.

"You spend an awful lot of time doing education with people like Priya. If she had known before she had the baby that jaundice might be an issue, and what to look out for, she might not have needed to come into the clinic at all." Ally makes a valid point. "You said yourself that there are a lot of new families moving into town. A program like this might help to offload some of the unnecessary appointments and walk-in visits."

"There isn't a lot of money in the budget for something like this. We would have to organize it all and advertise it. It would be a lot to take on right now." I watch as Ally's face falls, and I hate myself for making it that way. "I'll think about it. And if you can come up with a way of getting some money together for it, I might just agree to it."

Her mouth quirks up in some sort of determined grin. I can't be sure what Ally has up her sleeve, but I'm beginning to see that I might just be a fool if I don't trust this woman.

CHAPTER 13
ALLY

I TAKE a deep inhale of the crisp morning air as I make my way into town. It's Saturday, and even though yesterday was utter mayhem at the clinic, I feel refreshed and inspired. Mason and I stayed late trying to see as many walk-in patients as we could manage between us, and then we stayed even later talking in his office.

Mason has been oddly cordial towards me since he let me come out on his house calls, which is puzzling considering how the day had ended. One phone call had been enough for him to almost completely shut down and shut me out for the rest of the afternoon. We went to the rest of the visits, hardly speaking a word to one another, and all he gave me was an abrupt nod when he dropped me off at the cabin in the evening. Whatever troubled him about that conversation seemed to dissipate, and Mason was downright *pleasant* at work yesterday.

Mason Landry is an enigma if there ever was one. We're in this sort of push and pull where he opens up to me one minute and gives me a small piece of himself before ripping it away in the next. Still, it was refreshing to see him let loose with Annabelle, even if his high spirits only lasted a short time. He seems at least fractionally more human to me now. Not to mention the fact that my ovaries violently exploded all over my insides watching him play with that sweet little girl.

I presented the idea of a fundraiser to him yesterday, navigating the eggshells I seem to walk on around him right now. How Mason receives new ideas and suggestions depends entirely on his mood. But the prenatal program is a good, no, *great* idea, and I'm not about to let him bulldoze me on this one. If money is the issue, it's an issue we can fix. Finding people who want to help and support the clinic is the easy part.

Mason was supportive as I presented my idea for a Harvest Festival. He agreed that the people of Heartwood would be all for it and even suggested we include a lumberjack competition to draw people in. We hashed out some of the loose plans and decided to hold it on the first day of fall. With September almost halfway over, the plan is ambitious and needs to be executed swiftly.

So it wasn't difficult to convince him that we need to get started on the planning today, and the first step is to canvas local business owners to see who might participate and make donations or offer services. I offered to do it myself, considering this was my idea, but he insisted it would play in our favour if we were both there. Don't ask me how having Grumpy McGee along for the ride is the best way to win people over.

Mason is already standing outside Thistle + Thorne as I approach him on the sidewalk. He's looking a lot brighter these days, and he's started to grow on me over the last week. We've been avoiding each other less and less at the clinic, and more impor-tantly, Mason has asked me for my opinion on various things, treatment options for patients and the like. I'm feeling more valued around the clinic, giving me a sense of fulfilment that I haven't had in a long time. I'm almost tempted to consider him a friend, but I don't want to get ahead of myself.

Mason greets me with a warm smile when he sees me approaching. It's his bright, genuine smile—the one that makes his eyes wrinkle in a way that makes my heart swell. I've been seeing it more and more recently. It always feels like I've achieved an impossible feat whenever Mason smiles because of me.

"I got you a coffee while I was waiting so we could get started." Mason turns around and picks up two cups off the little bistro table outside the café. "Splash of milk, two honeys, right?"

"Yeah, how did you—" I can't remember telling him my coffee order.

"You come in with one every day at work, and then you make several throughout the day. It was hard not to notice, Honeybee." I take my coffee from him. My fingers graze his, sending a jolt of electricity through my arm and straight to my chest. I get this strange urge to tell him not to pull his hand away, and to my surprise, he doesn't. He lets it linger a moment longer than I expect. I don't miss the way his gaze flicks down toward my hand, right where my engagement ring used to be, as if confirming that I have gotten rid of it for good.

"Where should we start?" I say, clearing my throat. Mason drops his hand to his side and shoves it into his pocket. "We've got a lot of ground to cover."

"I say we start right here, talk to Poppy. She isn't crazy busy at the moment. We can make our way down the street from there. That way, we'll be able to hit most businesses before lunch."

"I like your style, Dr. Landry."

Poppy is finishing up another customer's latte and passing it over the counter when we enter. Her face brightens when she spies us over the espresso machine.

"Back for more caffeine already? I might have to cut you off, Mason."

I like Poppy. We always chat while I grab my coffee on the way into the clinic. Now, I come to the café less for the coffee and more to hang out with her. Though every time I see her, I get a sickening feeling in my gut that I'm lying to her about Mason and me.

"No, now that Ally's here, we have something we want to talk to you about." Mason answers.

"Don't tell me we're going to have another brawl over the turkey sandwiches. I don't want to hire a security guard," Poppy says, waving her finger between us.

A blush spreads from my cheeks and down my neck. I've somehow forgotten all about that awkward encounter with Mason. He seems like a different person to me now.

"Hey, I stand by my judgment of the turkey sandwich," Mason argues.

"To be fair, now that I've tried all of them, I hate to admit it, but you were right. Although you didn't have to be such an ass about it," I tease.

"At least someone calls Mason out on his bullshit." Poppy and Mason have known each other since they were kids. They grew up together, although Poppy is a few years younger than him. I've pressed Poppy several times for more information about when I stop in for coffee, but she's never divulged any details. "Well, what can I do for ya?" She asks.

"We're trying to organize a fundraiser for the clinic," Mason starts, but gestures to me to follow up, seeing as I'm the one with all the ideas.

"It would be valuable if we could start running a prenatal program through the clinic, and we're wondering if you could help." I tell Poppy all about our plan to help educate the new moms in town and give them a place to come for extra support once they've had their babies. Poppy is thrilled by the idea of the Harvest Festival and doesn't hesitate to offer up her services. She'll take care of hot beverages and snacks, and she'll donate a prize to be raffled off. Two, actually. A basket full of coffee and tea, and the other will come from her adjoining plant shop.

"That went well. I think we're off to a great start," Mason says as we leave the café.

"Poppy likes you. I didn't think it would be a challenge to get her on board."

"At least someone likes me." Mason looks at me, his gaze burning through me.

"There's more than Poppy. I mean, there's Grady and Hudson. Who knows, maybe Jett? Possibly Winnie." I wink at Mason. "That's lots of people."

"They're family. They're kind of forced to like me." Mason chuckles. "What about you, Ally?"

I squint at him, lifting my hand to block my eyes from the sun.

"You're growing on me," I admit.

We finish canvassing for the day as the sun is making its descent in the sky. Overall, it's been a very successful day. Not only is catering covered, thanks to Grady, who volunteered the bar's kitchen to make mass amounts of burgers, but we also secured more raffle prizes and people willing to volunteer their services than we know what to do with.

"I think this deserves a celebratory drink," Mason suggests as we make our way back through town. He stops as we come back around to the Whiskey Jack.

"Er, I'm not sure. There's still a lot of work to do, Mason. I was going to go home and start getting all of this organized." I'm reluctant to accept an invitation to spend more time with Mason.

There's still so much I don't know about him, but the warmth that spreads from my core down my legs whenever I look at him isn't a coincidence anymore. I'm finding myself more and more attracted to Mason. It's dangerous territory getting involved with your boss, and I still have so much to figure out with Nate here; it would be like lighting the fuse on an atomic bomb. A fake relationship with this man is more than I can handle right now.

"We can do it together after; I'll help. Come on, one drink." Mason puts his hand between my shoulder blades as he reaches to open the bar's big wooden door. The sensation of it makes my toes curl.

"Fine. Just one, and then we should get back to work."

The bar is dark compared to the blinding sun outside, and it takes my eyes a minute to adjust. As soon as the inside of the bar comes into view, I spy Nate seated alone at the bar top.

"Mason, I think we should leave," I say, but it's too late. I've spoken loud enough for Nate to hear, and he whips his head around and spots me standing at the door. He slinks over to me like some villain from a Disney movie.

"Ally Wells. Care to join me for a date night?" My voice catches in my throat. I need Nate to leave already, but now I have no recourse. Mason gave me a week of his time as a fake boyfriend, and he already offered me another day. There's no way he will continue to play the role in such a public place. The rumours it would start would be inescapable. Why does his presence make me freeze like this? My mouth is full of cotton balls. I hate that I can't get over my fear of confronting him and tell him to get out of town.

Right when I feel like I'm ready to scream, I feel the familiar warmth of Mason's hand on my back again, and my nervous system settles. Crashing, violent waves become a gentle ripple in a calm pond.

"She's already on a date."

"Mason, you don't have to do this; we're in public," I whisper out the side of my mouth, hoping that Nate doesn't overhear.

"I know, and I don't care, Honeybee." Mason turns back to Nate. "I would leave now if I were you. You don't want to mess with the bouncer here." Mason nods toward Grady at the bar, whose biceps are flexing and tensing as he dries a glass. I can't help but smile at how such a domestic task makes Grady appear so tough and intimidating.

"You're actually with this moron." Nate spits. At least he's getting the hint.

"Yeah, she is with this moron, a moron that went to med school and runs his own practice," Mason retorts.

"Don't let him get under your skin, Mason," I warn. I'm worried that they might get into a full-on fistfight. Mason is easily ruffled, especially when his pride is attacked. Nate is a dirty fighter, too. He knows where to hit, and it's always below the belt.

I shoot Grady a pleading look, who has turned his attention from polishing glasses to the commotion that is going on over the bar top.

He strides over and puts himself between Nate and Mason. He has a foot on Nate and uses it to his advantage.

"Time to go, mate." Grady is a man of few words, but they sure pack a punch. Nate isn't about to mess with him, and he turns on his heels and stalks off.

"Thanks, Grady." I give him a sheepish smile.

"Don't sweat it. I'm glad you two are an item."

"Oh no, we are *not*—I mean, we're not together," I stammer, looking over at Mason. I need to stop this gossip train fast, but Grady isn't one to go talking, and there's no one else in the bar to overhear.

Grady gives me a skeptical expression and shrugs his shoulders, wandering back to his work behind the bar.

"Could have fooled me."

I CONVINCE Mason to leave the bar after our run-in with Nate. I don't want to be anywhere in public where he could continue harassing me, nor do I want any ideas of Mason and me being together to get around more than they already have. Mason doesn't object and suggests we head back to the clinic to continue our work on the Harvest Festival.

The clinic is dark when we arrive. No one has been here all day. Mason only comes in on weekends for emergencies, and luckily today, his pager has been quiet.

"We could have worked at the cabin." I walk into Mason's office, noticing the cot set up behind the door. The sleeping bag is rumpled and open like Mason had just been sleeping in it. I wonder how often he goes home to sleep, shower, or do something besides work. Nate spent a lot of late nights at the office, too. Although I'm not so sure Nate had been working. Mason throws the sleeping bag together and straightens it out as if he were making his bed.

"Would we have gotten much work done back at the cabin?" He turns to look at me. His stare is intense, motivated, although now I enjoy being at the centre of his focus. When Mason looks at me, I feel like I'm the only person on earth. I'm not sure whether he means to be suggestive or friendly, but I can only assume the latter.

"I'm thrilled with our progress today." I switch gears, back to a neutral topic of discussion. Mason runs his hand through the top of his hair, a move that makes me notice his inner bicep and a black tattoo. Unlike Grady, who wears his tattoos proudly, Mason keeps his covered most of the time, as if it serves as a personal reminder only for him.

From here, though, I can make out the shape of a bear, filled in with a scenic view of mountains that are the spitting image of the mountains around Heartwood. The sight of him in his fitted T-shirt makes my cheeks heat. Like he's allowing me into some intimate part of himself.

"Me too. I'm surprised at how much of an interest you've taken in the clinic."

"It's my job too now, you know." I lean against the desk as Mason walks around and pulls out the bottle of scotch he keeps stashed in the bottom drawer. He pours us both a glass before meeting me around the front of the big wooden desk.

"I guess I didn't expect you to care so much." I study his face.

"Why do you care so much? I mean, I know it was your father's clinic, but why the cot?" Mason stares into his glass, and I worry I pushed too far, asked too much.

"Sometimes the pressure to keep this place afloat is too much. My dad was a legend in this town, but he never had to manage with the workload that I have now." He swallows hard, and I study the way his Adam's apple bobs in his throat. I say nothing for fear that he might stop talking. "Heartwood has changed. Sure, to you it's still a small town, and don't get me wrong, it is. But it's also grown a lot, even in the last year."

I nod, still with my gaze fixed on Mason. I can't take my eyes off of him as he opens up to me. It's all I have wanted from him. For him to treat me like a partner in the clinic.

"With the way the economy is changing, there are many people moving out of big cities, seeking a simpler way of life. For some of them, that place is Heartwood. My caseload has almost doubled in the last year, and some days, it's like I'm failing at everything."

"So, you sleep here? Don't you have a place of your own, a life outside of this place?" I wave around, gesturing at the clinic.

"A life." Mason lets out a quick breath through his nose, a half-laugh. "You don't get one of those as a doctor. I learned the hard way that when you take your attention away for even a moment, people get hurt."

"You don't believe that, do you? That there is no doctor alive that doesn't live their own life outside of work?"

"I mean, I guess some can make it work, but not me. I don't get to have a life. Not when I'm responsible for the well-being of an entire town." I frown at his response. Is this why he is so cold to everyone around him? Because he doesn't want anyone to get too close? He is afraid that the moment someone gets close, he won't be able to juggle all of his responsibilities.

"You seemed lighter the last few days," I point out. "At the house calls and while we were out today. You seemed happier." I can't describe the shift that I've seen in him, but it's one that I like.

"Yeah, I guess it was nice to hang out with you the other night. I needed a laugh, to let off some steam, I guess."

"You need to let off steam. More often than you think," I say. Mason's eyes darken as he rises from his chair and comes closer to me.

"I enjoy letting off steam with you." His voice takes on a deeper, more husky, gravelly tone that I like. It rumbles low in my belly. I swallow my nerves.

"Thank you for defending me with Nate again today. It's the last time, I promise." Mason is standing so close to me now that I can see a faint hint of stubble coming in across his jaw.

"I don't understand why you don't tell him to get lost." His voice is still that low rumble.

"It's hard for me to speak up, especially to Nate, when I know it's going to start a fight that I can't win. I've always been this way; I hate making people upset or angry. It's easier for me to smooth things over and keep the peace."

"Running away, you mean." Mason doesn't soften the blow, and it stings for a moment. But he's right. "Some things don't have an easy way out, Ally."

"All I want to do is make people happy. It's why I became a nurse. I don't like to hurt people. I just want to fix everyone."

"Sometimes you have to do the hard thing, or else you end up sacrificing so much of yourself to make others happy." Mason is staring right through to my soul. Seeing parts of me I try to keep tucked away.

"Don't talk to me about unreasonable sacrifices, Mason." I glance over at the cot. Mason puts up his hands in surrender, but he doesn't move away from me. If anything, he has inched closer.

"I'm just saying. You don't have to try so hard to please everyone."

The tension between us is palpable, and I let my thoughts drift to the way Mason just licked his bottom lip.

"Nate isn't here; you don't need to be so nice to me," I remark, a playful wrinkle forming on my nose as I look up at him.

Mason doesn't flinch, his gaze unwavering as he meets mine, his eyes betraying a flicker of something I can't quite decipher, except for the unmistakable glance towards my lips.

"Do you think Nate is even buying this whole ruse?" His words hang in the air between us. "You're not exactly convincing as a head-over-heels girlfriend."

"Oh? And how could I be more convincing, Mason?"

"I don't know, pretend that you don't resent me? Don't flinch every time I get close to you?" How can I tell him that when I flinch it's because of the electricity between us, that I'm startled by the feelings he brings up in me?

"You mean like the way you pretended you wanted to kiss me the other night?" The memory of his lips on my temple creates a fluttering sensation in my chest.

"I wasn't pretending, Honeybee." His words hang between us, charged with an intensity that sends a shiver down my spine.

"You're drunk," I reply, my voice faltering as uncertainty dances in my mind.

"I haven't had any of this yet." Mason holds up his glass. The scotch in it is untouched.

Before I can process his response, before I can form another retort, Mason closes the distance between us, his lips capturing mine in a kiss that is both unexpected and electrifying. It's firm yet tender, a contradiction that leaves me breathless and wanting more.

He pulls away, his eyes searching mine for a reaction, but before he can gauge my response, I lean in, meeting his lips with a hunger I hadn't realized was there. This isn't just a kiss; it's a revelation, a collision of emotions and desires that threaten to consume us both.

The stubble on his jaw grazes my skin, adding a delicious friction to the sensation. Kissing Mason feels as I had imagined, and yet, it's so much more. It's prickly yet comfortable, intense yet reassuring. Our lips move in perfect sync, and I know that this isn't just about pretending anymore.

This is real, raw, and ours. I grip the back of Mason's head, pulling him deeper into our kiss. His hands trail down my back to my thighs as he hoists me onto the desk. I hear something clatter on the floor as I knock it off, but I don't care. I want Mason. I think I've wanted him since the moment I saw him in the café. I haven't been able to stop thinking about him. And now I'm certain that he wants me too. I know by the way he drives his tongue into my mouth, the way his hands greedily roam around my body.

Mason's phone dings inside his pocket. He ignores it, but something inside me can't. I remember the mysterious phone call from the other day, how I asked about it and he refused to tell me. There are still parts of himself that Mason hasn't let me into. There's still a part of me that is reluctant to believe that Mason will put me above his work, to prove to me I'm important to him in all the ways that I wasn't important to Nate. I pull away from his mouth despite every cell in my body, telling me to keep kissing him.

"This is a bad idea, Mason." I shake my head and look down at the floor between our feet. Anything to keep myself from looking up into his deep brown eyes. Because if I do, those eyes will be the end of my willpower. I can't kiss Mason Landry. My boss. My ex-fake-boyfriend. I never intended for this to become real. I'm not a serial dater, and I would be giving up on my goal of starting over if I walked out of Nate's arms and straight into Mason's.

"What are you saying? I'm good enough to be your fake boyfriend, but not a real one?" Something that looks like hurt flickers in his eyes. Maybe I'm imagining it. Mason was the one that imposed the strict boundaries on our relationship to begin with.

"What I'm saying, is that you're my boss, Mason. And my life is complicated right now. Your life is complicated right now. The feelings I get when I kiss you don't make things any less complicated. You and I both have a lot to figure out before we can ever entertain this." My mind goes straight to the phone call Mason took in secret, the way he wouldn't even look at the screen around me. I can't take any more secrets.

"So, what, I'm supposed to continue pretending to be your boyfriend? That kiss didn't feel pretend, Ally."

"No. You're not supposed to continue pretending to be my boyfriend. Your week was up days ago. You've already done enough for me. You can go back to being my boss, and I can go back to being the irritating nurse who gets on your nerves. We can be professional and never discuss this." I wave my hand between us. "Ever."

Mason's hands fall from where they were resting on my hips and he backs away, letting me pass him as I leave his office and head back to the cabin.

CHAPTER 14
MASON

I've got ten minutes before my next appointment. This will be the third one of the day, and it's not even nine. These days, Winnie has had to book appointments back-to-back all morning until noon, and sometimes later. It's the only way to fit everyone in, stay sharp and keep moving. After last night with Ally, that's proving to be a challenge, if not downright impossible. My mind is drifting, wandering back to the feeling of her mouth on mine. The way she looked up at me with her turquoise eyes. I was close enough to Ally last night to make out the smattering of freckles across her nose, and all I want to do is map them like a constellation.

We haven't spoken yet today, mainly because we've both been avoiding each other and it's awkward. We're back to this uncomfortable dance around the clinic. I was relieved when it seemed like we had moved past it. Now we're one step forward and four steps back. I can't say I'm not disappointed now. The possibility that our relationship would turn into something real was tempting, and now that door has shut for good.

It's not Ally's fault. Neither of us wants to address the moment we shared in my office. On my end, at least, the kiss was impulsive, a moment of weakness when I needed to keep my mind sharp. Ally was right to back off and shut it down before it went any further. Because it would have gone further. Her lips were intoxicating, and I found myself doing things I knew I would regret.

I can't afford any distractions right now, not if I'm going to keep up with this hectic workload *and* pull off a major fundraising event in the next few weeks. Ally is the most dangerous distraction of them all. As soon as I entertain the idea of her for a second, I'm fucked.

I scarf down a protein bar. I overslept today and got right to work when I woke up, not stopping to eat breakfast and now I can feel it. Finishing my last chart is my priority right now. There isn't much to write. Susan Hendrick brought in her oldest son, Charlie, for a rash he developed after eating a cake that one of his classmates had brought to school. Charlie is anaphylactic to nuts, and Susan jumps if he has so much as an itch. I can't blame her. Losing her youngest last year took a toll on her, as it did with everyone in town, including me.

I give her a prescription for an EpiPen refill and tear off a sticky note, slapping it on the front of the chart, scrawling 'allergy clinic' and placing it in the basket of charts needing referrals to be processed. Winnie will get to those later.

I've got my appointments down to somewhat of a science. Get in and find out the reason for the visit in two minutes or less. This is always the challenging part. All of my patients call me by my first name, many of them having known me since I was young. They like the small talk, though there's no time for small talk anymore. I've mastered the art of steering the conversation back to the purpose of the visit without coming across as rude or abrupt.

I do a focused exam, only looking at what's ailing them, nothing more. You learn that once you look around, you always find something that you're not prepared to deal with and then the appointment runs amok. If it's bothering them, they'll bring it up. That's my philosophy. Or at least it has to be my philosophy now.

At one point in my career, I wanted to make sure that I covered every base, left no stone unturned, and provided holistic care. It's just not possible now. I pick my battles. There is no way that I would get through the amount of appointments I do if I let everyone get off track.

Picking up the next chart in the pile to review for the next patient in the queue, I glance up at the door when I hear a soft knock. Ally wraps her knuckles against the door frame. I stare at her, waiting for her to state her business. She needs to get to the point. The longer she stands in my doorway, her full curved hip jutting out the way it does when she leans on one leg, the more I'm going to let my mind wander back to last night. I'm already getting semi-hard looking at her.

I'm so fucked.

"Sorry to interrupt," Ally says. "There's a woman here to see you."

"Mrs. Calhoun?" I ask, eyes skimming the chart in front of me. Anything to take my eyes off of Ally in her lilac scrubs. The ones that cinch in at her waist. "I know. I've got her chart and I'm just about to head in."

"No, no. She said she's not on the appointment list."

"Is it an emergency? Just tell her to wait for walk-in hours later today." I look back at the chart, glancing over the list of conditions that Mrs. Calhoun deals with. This won't be a short appointment.

"She said she's spoken with you on the phone already." My heart just about stops in my chest at Ally's words, but I don't look up.

Simone Mitchell has shown up unannounced at the clinic, and I can't show that I'm flustered by this. I'm not a religious man, but I might convert if I can pull this off without Ally finding out who she is and why she's here. "She's wearing a very put-together pantsuit, so I think she's here to talk business. Do you know who she might be?"

"Uh, yeah. I think I know who it is," I stammer, trying to

come up with a viable explanation. "She's an old colleague of my dad's. You can send her in."

It's not a lie. I'm certain that Simone and my father had spoken at least once. That he was aware of the impending collapse of the clinic. Another thing to add to my list of reasons I resent Jack Landry. I'm just hoping that my indifference to her being here in the clinic is enough to ensure that Ally doesn't ask any further questions. The last thing I need right now is for Ally to find out the real purpose of her visit. Or that her time in Heartwood could be cut short. I'm determined to find a solution before it comes to that, and now, with the fundraiser, I need Ally to be focused and determined to make it happen. It's our only shot at saving the clinic.

Ally returns with the woman in tow. She was accurate in her description. Simone is wearing a dark grey pantsuit that means business and her expression matches. She's got tight, dark curls cropped short that suits her sharper features.

My eyes shift over her shoulder, and I see Ally still standing right behind her. Before Simone can say anything, I usher her into my office.

"Ally, please prep Mrs. Calhoun, get a bit of a history, and find out why she's here. Tell her I'll be another ten minutes." Ally nods, accepting her task. I click my office door shut as quickly as I can, right as Simone speaks.

"Simone Mitchell," she says, extending her hand toward me. I take it. Her handshake is firm. She's not here to mess around. "We spoke on the phone."

I close my office door and gesture for Simone to sit in the old, worn armchair that faces my desk.

"I'm sure you're aware of why I'm here, Dr. Landry. Given our last conversation about the process and the state of the clinic." I give her a grim nod. "I've given your situation a lot of consideration, and before I write my report and recommendation to the Ministry of Health, I thought it would only be fair if I came to see it for myself. To get a better sense of things in person."

"I appreciate that." There's reservation in my voice. "How long are you planning on staying in Heartwood?" I need to know how long I need to keep Simone away from Ally, how long I need to lie to her.

"As long as I need to gather enough information and get an accurate understanding of what you do here, Dr. Landry." Not the answer that I was hoping for. With the Harvest Festival coming up, we won't have been able to make any meaningful changes. That's what Simone needs to see. She needs to witness firsthand how much the community cares about the clinic, how much it means to them. The only way to do that is by having her stay long enough to come to the festival. I hate myself for what I'm about to do, and I'm going to pay the price later.

"We're having a fundraising event next week for a new program that we're starting. You should stay until then." An entire week of trying to keep Ally and Simone apart.

"What kind of program?" Simone asks. That's all she cares about. How the clinic will provide better services for the community.

I explain the prenatal program to her, outlining the rough percentages of women who visit the clinic for routine check-ups for their babies. I detail how Ally will run it with her labour and delivery expertise and continue the program for women in their postpartum period. It's as much about education as it is about providing improved social support.

Simone nods, taking everything in. A tentative smile creeps across her face.

"It sounds like you have a solid plan for getting this clinic back on track, Dr. Landry. If this fundraiser is a success and you get this program off the ground, it could be the type of thing that would be very convincing to the ministry in favour of extending your funding."

I return her half-smile. I won't show my hand too early. This is a game that requires strategy. Simone will be looking for any reason to write us a negative report. After all, her job is to look for ways to save the government money.

I lift my wrist to check my watch. I'm already late for this appointment, which sets me back now for the entire rest of the day.

"I hate to cut this conversation short, but I need to be getting back to my patients," I say, standing from my desk and walking around to open the door.

"Of course. I'll give you a heads-up when I'm planning to stop by the clinic. I'll need to come and observe the function of the clinic a few times for an accurate report."

I'll find a reason for Ally to take the day off on those days.

"Sounds great, Simone." It does not sound great. It sounds the opposite of great. "Can you do me a favour and lie low around town while you're here? The town isn't privy to the situation yet, and I would hate to cause rumours to blow it all out of proportion."

Simone nods and turns on her heel, walking back out toward the waiting room. I release the breath I had been holding and grab Mrs. Calhoun's chart off my desk. I can't let this derail me. We've made a plan. We just need to execute it. But the idea of keeping this from Ally makes my stomach twist. I want nothing more than to hold Ally like I held her last night, to remove all the barriers between us. The image of her lips parting ever so slightly as I leaned in to kiss her is confirmation that she wanted it, too. This is for Ally's own good, I remind myself. She can't be worrying about the stability of her job when we have the opportunity to save it. We will save it.

THE WAITING room is empty now. I can't see it from where I'm sitting in my office, but there isn't the familiar din of patients chatting with one another. People in Heartwood wait without complaint despite the long wait times, though they mutter among themselves about how the situation at the clinic has gotten worse over the years. As much as I try to ignore it, it stings that it's gone downhill in the year that I've been in charge.

The overhead fluorescent lights are off, leaving only the dim light of the desk lamp Ally plugged in behind the reception desk. It's glowing at the end of the hall, the only sign that she's still here. She's stayed late every night this week, fuelled by her motivation to turn the funds from the Harvest Festival into something meaningful for the clinic. Ally has approached it with meticulous organization, writing and rewriting to-do lists, creating folders of permits that needed to be filled out to use the town square, lists of the best vendors, and maps showing where she'll station them.

I peruse the toppling pile of charts, papers falling out of each folder. It's a wonder that I've kept the clinic running for as long as I have. Ally offers the only real chance of making it last. My meeting with Simone earlier has only emphasized that fact.

I can hear the faint sound of her humming to herself while she works at her desk. People who hum while they work are one of my worst pet peeves. It sets my teeth on edge. It *did* set my teeth on edge. Before Ally.

When Ally hums, the sound is melodious, and it sends a warm ripple through my core. I'm not working late alone anymore like I used to, so many nights before.

"Can I come in?" Ally asks, hovering in the door frame of my office.

"I'm surprised you trust yourself to be alone with me in my office, Honeybee." The corner of my mouth lifts in a cheeky grin. I notice that Ally's mouth matches mine.

"Me? It's you that you need to be worried about. It's obvious that you can't resist me." I don't have a rebuttal ready. Ally is right. I'm defenceless around her. *Fucked. Whipped. All of the above.*

"I won't believe for one second that you hadn't thought about it, too." I remember the way Ally's hands roamed around my body until she used them to push me away. She wanted it. She wanted it as much as I did, maybe even more. Even though I've promised to keep things professional, I don't want her to forget it. Besides, bringing it up now makes Ally wrinkle her stupid cute little nose, and I've decided that teasing her has become my favourite activity.

My eyes trail down Ally's perfect body, stopping at the piece of paper she's holding in her hand. As if remembering why she came in here in the first place, Ally clears her throat and holds it up to show me.

"I need your help with the festival layout." I wave her over to my desk, and Ally obliges, coming to stand just behind me. She leans down over my shoulder to place the rough diagram she's drawn on my desk. As she leans down, her long strawberry hair cascades over her shoulder and tickles my neck. If Ally didn't make it clear how opposed she was to any sort of connection forming between us, I would think she was standing in such proximity on purpose. She has to know what she's doing to me, standing so close. "What did you have in mind for the Lumberjack Games? In order to submit a permit application, I need to draw up some plans, so it would be helpful to get an idea of where we need to set up the lumberjack competitions, the seating for the guests, and all that."

I nod and pretend that I'm studying the map, even though I can think of nothing other than the sweet smell of coconut that's radiating off of Ally.

"This is good. We can set the speed climb up over here, along the edge of the square," I say, pointing to where she's left an open space on the map. "And we can arrange the rest of the events in front." I can feel Ally's hair brush against my neck as she nods. She hasn't backed away from me. She's not as closed off to me as I thought.

"Okay great, thanks," she says, and I swivel my chair around so I'm facing her, her nose just about touching mine. Close enough that I wouldn't even have to crane my neck to reach up and kiss her again. A little social experiment to see where Ally and I stand. She doesn't budge. Ally holds my stare a moment longer than comfortable before backing away. So this is how it is now. She's going to be stubborn. Here I thought I was the stubborn one.

Fine by me. She can continue pretending that whatever connection we have is just for show. Nothing more than a fake display of affection to get rid of her ex. But something about her determination does something to me. A challenge. I want to make her crack.

"Do you want a ride home? It's dark outside." The sun set an hour ago, and Ally's been a little jumpy since her run-in with the bear on the trail.

Ally turns before she crosses the threshold of my office.

"I'm good, thanks. I'll brave the woods."

Damn Ally, for whatever she's doing to me right now. I say nothing in response before she pivots on her heel, and I watch her hips sway as she heads back down the hallway and out of the clinic. I don't find scrubs sexy. I *didn't* find scrubs sexy. Until Ally Wells.

It's been fifteen minutes since Ally left. I know because I checked the time that she walked out of my office. I get up from my desk, get in my truck, and make the short two-block drive before turning down the overgrown gravel driveway. I inch the truck forward towards the cabin just far enough that I can see a light on inside, proof that she's made it home safely. Then I drive back to the clinic.

CHAPTER 15
ALLY

IT'S ALMOST ten and there's still no sign of Mason at the clinic, which I've already learned is uncharacteristic of him. Winnie sits next to me at the reception desk, organizing a pile of charts that Mason will need to review for his first few appointments. It's thankfully thinner than other days.

"Mason's usually here by now," I point out. The slight eye roll from Winnie doesn't go unnoticed. "I mean, he sleeps here. He doesn't have an excuse for being late."

"He called me last night and told me to reschedule a few of his morning appointments," she explains. "So now I have to find time for them later in the week. Like that's so easy to do."

It's obvious that Mason has a massive weight on his shoulders from the ever-increasing demands of the clinic, but I wonder if he sees how much Winnie struggles, too. She's the one who breaks the news to patients day in and day out that they won't get an appointment anytime soon, the one that manages the chaotic schedule, and somehow keeps it all on track.

The bell above the door jingles but I don't lift my eyes from my work. I've tried to get ahead while Mason is out this morning, getting some paperwork done for referrals that will need to go in today. I only glance up from the chart that I have spread out in front of me when I hear a set of keys clang down on top of the desk. Staring at the keys, which are at eye level on top of the raised reception desk, Mason comes into focus, standing behind it.

"Give me your keys," he says. Not rude, but there's that demanding undertone to his voice. The one that causes a ripple of heat to cascade through me.

"Why?" I blink at him several times, and Mason narrows his eyes toward me. I thought we had connected over the last few days, but as Mason stands here, glaring at me and expecting me to just hand over my keys, I'm not so sure.

"I don't have time for this today. Just give me your damn keys, Honeybee," he says with a slight snarl, holding out his hand.

"Not until you tell me what you need them for." Mason lets out an annoyed sigh.

"I need your truck."

"You have your own truck. What do you want with that old beater?"

I inspect the set of keys sitting on the counter. What is Mason's game? Out of sheer curiosity, I reach down to pull my keys out of my purse and slide my set of keys across the counter toward him. My eyes narrow into a skeptical glare.

Mason doesn't say anything before he snatches the keys off the counter, turns on his heels and strides back toward the door. I get up and follow him.

"Where do you think you're going?" I shout after him. The few patients that have arrived early for their appointments glance up from their phones and magazines at the commotion.

Mason swings the door open, not bothering to hold it open for me. It just about smacks me in the face as it closes. I throw the door open again and increase my pace to a slight jog to catch up with him.

"I'm taking it back to the rental company," he shouts over his shoulder as he storms through the parking lot.

"How am I supposed to get around?" My voice is raising in pitch, almost a squeak now.

"What do you think the other keys are for?" I look down at the set of keys that I'm holding in my hand, only noticing the Jeep keychain dangling off the set now. There are a few other cars parked in the lot, but my eyes immediately land on the Jeep that had sat beside my hunk of junk at the airport. The one I didn't have the guts to go back and ask for.

"Is this what you were doing this morning? Why you blew off your patients?"

Mason whirls around and stops short. I almost run right into him. I have so much momentum in my stride. His finger is pointing into my face, almost touching my nose.

"I did not blow off my patients. I will find time to see them. This had to be done. That truck is a death trap, Ally. I can't have my girlfriend driving around in that thing."

"Fake girlfriend," I correct, although I thought of the two of us, Mason wouldn't be the one needing to be reminded. The rules of our agreement were imposed by him, after all.

"Right. Fake girlfriend. That's what I meant. It's a hazard to everyone else on the road. And you wouldn't do the responsible thing and demand a different vehicle."

I say nothing in response. Instead, I just stand in the parking lot in stunned silence. I'm still trying to wrap my head around whether *girlfriend* was a true slip of the tongue.

Mason stalks onto the street, heading towards the cabin to get my truck. I don't stop him. Whatever version of Mason this is, I don't hate it.

"LET'S GO, HONEYBEE," Mason shouts from the front door of the clinic. I've just finished making an afternoon tea to settle into the stack of referrals that grace my desk. The piling paperwork is endless, and Winnie is still working on rearranging the schedule to fit in the patients he neglected in favour of trading in my truck.

"Go where?" I round the corner, emerging from the alcove behind the reception desk.

"We've got house calls. You're driving."

"I—what?" I stammer. Since when was it expected that I would come with Mason on house calls?

"Figure you should take the new wheels out for a spin. Hurry it up. We're already late." Mason waves me over.

Winnie takes the stack of charts that are piled up on my half of our shared desk and nods towards Mason, urging me to go. The last time I spent a significant amount of time alone with Mason, we ended up making out on his desk, an incident I am hell-bent on not repeating. But Mason offering to bring me along on house calls, no, assuming that I will be coming on house calls is a massive step for him, for us, as colleagues.

"Okay, but really, what am I doing here?" I ask, climbing into the two-door Jeep.

Mason takes my phone out of my hand to punch in the directions. It's an address about twenty minutes outside of town. It appears to be smack in the middle of the woods.

"Your own house call. What do you think?" I've had enough of Mason's cryptic attitude today. I tolerated him demanding that I give him my keys without so much as an explanation but following him to some far-off house in the woods is another story. A thought occurs to me. If I didn't know Mason, I would have to wonder if he was leading me out to the woods so he could murder me or leave me for dead.

"My own? What do you mean, my own?"

"Consider it your official test and then you'll fly solo from here on out." Solo? Like go to people's houses on my own, solo?

"I'm not sure I … I'm not a doctor, Mason. I shouldn't be going out on house calls on my own."

"Bullshit, you're not a doctor, Ally. I mean, don't start prescribing medications or anything, but you know damn well as much as I do most of the time."

"I wouldn't say that …"

"There is such a thing as home-care nurses, isn't there?"

"Well, yeah. But house calls are your thing, Mason. Your dad's thing. I know how protective you are over that part of your practice."

"Times are changing, Honeybee. And I'm not so sure that the clinic will survive if I don't change with them." The words sound foreign coming out of Mason's mouth.

"Look at me, Mason," I ask, and he turns in the passenger seat to face me. "Follow my finger …" I hold up my finger as if I'm checking him for a head injury. He keeps his deep brown eyes glued to my finger for a moment before he blinks and gives his head a shake. He turns around to put on his seatbelt, and I miss having his eyes on me, so intent.

"I'm *fine*, Ally. Let's not make a big deal out of this. You still have to pass your first test, anyway."

I guess we're doing this. I manoeuvre the Jeep around the tight parking lot, and we head toward our destination.

The winding gravel road to get there seems to meander forever through the thick trees, and now I'm almost ninety percent certain that Mason is, in fact, bringing me out here to kill me. Or maybe it's not Mason sitting next to me in the car, but some demon-possessed version of him.

When we arrive, my first suspicion is confirmed: the house is secluded. This does nothing to rule out the murder theory, and I doubt a neighbour lives within ten kilometres.

The house is not modest by any means. Whoever lives here must have a hefty nest egg and spent it far away from civilization.

"Who lives here," I ask, pulling the Jeep into the long gravel drive, "a wealthy hermit?" The house looks like a cabin in every way except its size. It's at least three stories, the bottom level adorned with beautiful natural stone and raw wooden beams forming each of the three peaks. Smoke is billowing out of the stone chimney on the roof.

"Sort of, yeah. Reggie Donovan is an old friend of my dad's. He's a little ... eccentric," Mason says.

"Eccentric could mean a lot of things, Mason. Eccentric could be anything from a kazoo player who wears a lot of fun fedoras to a conspiracy theorist who wears a fedora made of tinfoil."

"Fedoras are non-negotiable in this scenario, huh?" The corner of Mason's mouth tilts up.

"They are the worst type of hat. Only the most eccentric people wear them." I quip.

"Noted. I'll make sure to wear one at work, just for you." Mason winks at me, and it makes the hair on the nape of my neck stand on end. "Reggie isn't that weird. He owned a multimillion-dollar tech company and sold it. Woke up one day and decided that technology has ruined society. Now he lives 'off-grid,' as he calls it," Mason clarifies, but it only leaves me with more questions than answers.

I peer up at the small mansion as we approach the front door. The entire roof is covered in solar panels.

A tall older man answers the door to greet us. I'm surprised he isn't carrying a shotgun or something, but he appears friendly. He's wearing a knit sweater, khaki dress pants, and honestly looks more put together than one would expect of a person who has chosen to live as a recluse.

"Reggie! So good to see you looking so well." Mason extends a hand and places it on Reggie's shoulder before remembering that I'm also here. "This is Ally. She's working at the clinic now." It's not a glowing review, but at least he has accepted that I am an employee of the clinic.

"I've heard a lot about Ally. For a man who tries not to involve myself with the outside world, I still find a way of staying current on town goings-on. Though I didn't think it could be done." Mason and I both wear the same blank stare. As if noticing, Reggie adds, "Getting Mason to settle down, I mean." He winks at us. Mason was not kidding when he said a story like this would spread like wildfire. Within a matter of two weeks, it has reached Reggie, a man who refuses to interact with normal society. Mason is going to love this.

Reggie backs away from the door, gesturing with his arm for us to come in.

The house is stunning, with all windows at the front in the expansive entryway. A grand staircase flanks one side, leading to a landing overlooking both this side of the entryway and the large living area on the other side. The wall above the natural stone fireplace features a mounted large taxidermy buck head.

We follow Reggie into the cozy but tidy living room.

"Whatever you gave me last time worked like a charm," Reggie says, taking a seat on the brown leather sofa.

"Don't tell me, Reggie. Ally is the one taking care of you today. Pretend like I'm not here." My face flushes. The thought of having Mason watch me as I work is unnerving, and I can already feel my hands shaking. I ask him some preliminary questions about his health history and any symptoms he's been experiencing in the last week before moving on to a basic physical exam. When I'm done, I remove the stethoscope from my ears and dangle it around my neck.

"What's your diagnosis?" Mason asks. He's perched on the arm of the couch, arms crossed.

"He seems ... fine. I can't find anything wrong with him."

"Perfect. You're right." I give Mason a quizzical stare. "I came to see him about a week ago when he had pneumonia. Reggie just finished his antibiotics, so I told him I'd come by to see him again, make sure it had cleared up. Glad to see that it has."

"You've already treated him." I muster my blankest expression. "Yes."

"So, this was a useless visit. Sorry, Reggie. Not useless for you. Just a waste of *my* time." Reggie gives me a *keep me out of this* look.

"Not useless. I wanted to know that you could identify when someone *doesn't* need to be seen in the clinic, just as much as when they do. You have no idea how many home-care nurses and family physicians just send everyone to the emergency department because they're jumpy and nervous about missing something," Mason explains. "Congratulations, you passed. But I knew you would." Condescending dick. I thought we had gotten past this delightful flavour of Mason's superiority complex.

I shoot him my most unimpressed stare. Maybe if I concentrate hard enough, I can shoot daggers out of my eyes.

I had no luck with the daggers, but I didn't speak to Mason for the rest of the visit. We finish up with Mr. Donovan and head back out to the car, my stride a quick and even clip.

"Care to fill me in on why you've given me the silent treatment?" Mason demands once we're back in the car.

"Why did you ask me to come out here, Mason? So you could give me some sort of useless test just to exert some control over me? You know, I could have been getting a lot of work done back at the clinic today. But no, you brought me on this futile little mission of yours, and now I'll have to stay late to make up for this. Not everyone wants to live at the clinic." I stick the key in the ignition but wait to turn it.

"I thought this was what you wanted. To be more involved in the clinic," Mason says, his tone incredulous.

"I want you to trust me, Mason. I want you to trust that I can handle myself." I turn the key and the engine whirrs. And whirrs. And nothing happens. "Shit." I turn it a few more times.

"Well, don't do that. You'll flood the engine."

"Gah! Just shut up!" I shout, exasperated.

"You left the headlights on, didn't you?" Mason props his elbow on the window sill and rests his head in his hand.

"It's the twenty-first century, what kind of vehicle doesn't have automatic headlights?" My voice raises an octave.

"One from the '90s."

Dammit. I left the fucking headlights on.

CHAPTER 16
MASON

"THIS IS YOUR FAULT, YOU KNOW." Ally is standing on Reggie's doorstep with her arms crossed, one hip jutted out. Her eyelids fall over her eyes in an affected glare, her pink lips twist in frustration. This is anything but my fault and Ally knows it. "You traded in my perfectly functional truck for a 1990 Wrangler with headlights that just *stay on*."

"Be fucking for real, Honeybee. I wasn't the one who left those headlights on and drained the battery." I snarl. I knock on Reggie Donovan's front door. Ally's standing behind me, but out of the corner of my eye, I can see that she's biting her bottom lip, bouncing on her heels.

"And *I* wasn't the one that decided to trek all the way to the middle of nowhere for no good reason." She huffs a breath out of a thin line that forms across her lips. Footsteps become audible inside the house, and Reggie answers the door. I smack Ally lightly on the arm so she can smarten up around my client and stop being a brat.

"Sorry to do this Reg, but is there any way we can get a ride back into town? My *darling* Ally here left the headlights on, and the battery is dead." I explain through gritted teeth.

"No can do, son. Don't have a vehicle here. You're welcome to come in and make some calls, though." I give him a nod. We go right through to the living room. Ally sits on the couch while I pace around the room, considering who to call first.

I dial the one and only person who could be available at a moment's notice and more than willing to help: Hudson.

"Hudson here," he answers. His voice always has a friendly lilt to it.

"Hey, I'm in a bit of a bind and wondering if you can help." I explain the situation and what I need from him: jumper cables or a lift into town to get my truck and jumper cables.

"Can't help you out today. We just got called out to a structure fire just outside of town. Some abandoned bed-and-breakfast. We'll be out there well into the evening." *No problem. No problem.* I end my conversation with Hudson and call Grady. Busy at the bar. His only other bartender called in sick, so he's stuck serving, and the place is as packed as it gets on trivia night. Jett? I don't bother calling Jett. I doubt he'll even answer.

Winnie. I try Winnie. She's playing bridge with her neighbours and she's on a winning streak with money on the table.

"Have you tried calling Poppy?" I ask Ally. She rolls her eyes at me. Still pissed then.

"Yep. No answer."

"Keep trying," I say, and Ally nods.

"You're more than welcome to stay here and find a way back to town in the morning," Reggie suggests. I look at Ally and try to invisibly shake my head. As soon as Reggie looks away, I'm mouthing the word *NO* in all caps. There's only one thing I want to do less than spend a night in the middle of nowhere with a man who doesn't believe in modern technology, and it's spending a night in the middle of nowhere with a pissed-off Ally Wells.

"That would be lovely, Reggie." Ally pastes on a smile and the most chipper voice she has, which, to be fair, is Ally's everyday voice. "We'll get out of your hair first thing tomorrow. Didn't Hudson say he could come by in the morning, my love?"

My molars grind together. "Yes, *sweetheart,* yes he did."

Reggie shows us upstairs to the room we can stay in. The *one* room. I point to the other two doors down the hall.

"What about those rooms?" I ask. Reggie quirks a bushy grey eyebrow and glances between Ally and I. Right. He thinks we're a couple in love.

"We aren't—" Ally starts, but Reggie interrupts her.

"Oh, you two haven't—say no more. Say no more." I notice Ally's face flush as she realizes what Reggie has implied. Ally and I are celibate. I stifle a laugh. If Ally and I were dating, there is no way we would be celibate. "Unfortunately, the other two rooms haven't been set up for guests at the moment."

Reggie walks down the hall and opens both of the doors for us to see. One room is full to the rafters with plants of all different species. The other has an overwhelming musty smell emanating into the hall. Ally covers her nose the moment he opens the door.

"This is where I harvest my mung beans," he says, very matter-of-fact. "Well. I'll let you two get settled in, and then you can join me downstairs. I'll fix you some supper. Oh, and just so you're aware, use the jug of water next to the sink for drinking. The water here is a little iffy. One sip and you'll be on the toilet for a week."

Ally's face turns a cute little shade of chartreuse next to me. Even nauseated, she looks cute. I close the door to the mung bean room to stop the stench from leaking into the hall. Reggie turns and heads back down the stairs as Ally and I retreat to the bedroom he has offered to us.

"I don't want to know what Reggie plans on making us for supper. Those mung beans are enough to put me off my meal," Ally says as I shut the door behind me. I take in the room. It's not small by any means. It's decorated in the same tasteful rustic cabin theme as the rest of the house, so the atmosphere is cozy. There's an ensuite to the right, with a jug of drinking water on the counter.

"It was your idea to stay," I say blandly. There is no way I'm going to let Ally forget about this. Not for a long time to come. That's assuming she'll be in my life for a long time to come.

"I didn't know about the mung bean situation when I agreed to it. You'd think for someone with this much money, he would at least spring for potable water." I say as I mime a gag

"Off-grid, remember? Reggie mentioned once that he doesn't appreciate the government adding fluoride to his water." I recall.

"Fluoride in the water seems a hell of a lot better than having the shits for a week," Ally says, and I can't disagree.

ALLY and I head downstairs to join Reggie in the large open kitchen. I'm surprised that the aroma coming from the stove is mouth-watering. Reggie turns as we enter, a tea towel thrown over his shoulder.

"Make yourselves comfortable. There's wine on the table. I made it myself. The grape crops weren't as good this year with the cold snap we had in the spring, so it might be a little tart."

I pour Ally a glass and hand it to her before pouring myself one. She takes a sip, more than a sip. A gulp. And the expression on her face makes me glad that Reggie has his back turned. She looks like she stuck an entire lemon rind in her mouth. Her lips pucker as she cringes. Even when she's tasting something foul, Ally's lips make me wonder what they would feel like around my cock. It twitches at the image playing out in my mind.

I close my eyes and plead with the universe for something half-edible as Reggie wanders over and puts a plate down in front of us. I peek one eye open and am relieved to see a delicious plate of pasta with a beautiful red sauce and fresh basil.

"Reggie, this looks ... amazing." Ally croons.

"Made it all myself. Right down to the wheat. Well, my chickens made the eggs. But they came straight from the coop."

"If the wine is any indication of how good this will be …" Ally says. She sounds sincere but based on her reaction to the taste of it, her statement is ironic. I give her a kick under the table and a look that says *behave*.

Despite our skepticism, the pasta is, in fact, *delicious*. I have a hard time holding back a moan as I take the first bite. The sauce is made from fresh garden tomatoes and herbs and the result is incredible. Maybe there's something to this *off-grid* thing.

We finish up dinner, and Ally and I excuse ourselves so as not to impose on whatever plans Reggie has, foraging for more food, or spinning his own yarn. Who knows what the man does in his spare time.

"Did you hear from anyone about a ride?" Ally asks as she trails behind me on the staircase leading to our guest suite. I shake my head no.

"If I had heard about a ride, we wouldn't still be here, would we?" Ally clicks her tongue in response to my snark as we retreat to the privacy of our room.

"It's a good thing Reggie's under the impression that we're saving ourselves for marriage. He would have thought we were boning up here for sure," she says once the door is fully closed.

"*Boning?* Jesus, Ally," I say. But I do want to *bone* Ally. How long has it been since I've had sex, anyway? Too long, and the erection that the word *boning* on Ally's lips has given me is a harsh reminder of that.

"Would you prefer I said *making love?*" Ally bats her eyelashes.

"I'd prefer we weren't talking about this." I need to change the subject before my erection becomes visible under my jeans. *Picture something unsexy. Ally with an enormous piece of spinach in her teeth.* It does nothing to suppress the arousal that's about to make itself known. I would pick a piece of spinach out of her teeth just to be near her. God, what is wrong with me?

"Hey, you didn't exactly pipe up to clarify that we aren't a couple."

"Wouldn't that ruin the illusion for Nate?" I cock my head toward her.

"I guess. But be honest, when is Nate going to cross paths with Reggie and talk to him long enough to learn the truth?" Ally is right. Truthfully, I don't mind being Ally's fake boyfriend anymore. I wouldn't mind being more.

"It's a little early for bed. What does Reggie do all day with no TV, no phones, no nothing?" Ally says, throwing her hands up.

"I'm sure he just sits around and reads," I say, my statement clearly sparking an idea in Ally's mind as she raises her hand.

"I brought my book! I've been meaning to finish it." Ally jumps up and heads over to her bag that she dropped by the door earlier.

"What am I supposed to do?" I ask. "Sit here and watch you read?"

"I don't care. Be a big boy and occupy yourself. Go on your phone or something. Don't you have TikTok?" I shake my head. I'm not one for social media. Never cared for it. There's no service and no Wi-Fi here, anyway.

"Why don't you read to me?" I suggest. Ally's eyes go wide as she reaches around in her bag for her book. "Do you not know how to read aloud?"

"No, it's not that ..." Ally puts the book away, her freckled cheeks turn a deep shade of red as she says suddenly. "Nevermind. I don't want to read."

"Oh, come on, Honeybee. Show me your book." I go over to where she's standing and pull the book out of her bag. The cover has a shirtless man on the front, and I now know why Ally is reluctant to show it to me. My mouth twists into a cheeky grin. "Read to me, Ally," I demand, shoving the book at her. I want to see how Ally pretends there isn't a spark between us while she's reading me an erotic novel.

"Fine. But you asked for it. Remember that," Ally says, taking the book and walking back over to the bed. The singular queen bed. For us both to sleep in. I lay next to her, head propped in one hand, a shit-eating grin on my face, waiting for Ally to begin. She opens the book and glances up at me a few times.

"Go on, I'm listening."

She starts, and it's simultaneously better and worse than I was expecting. It's so much more explicit than I anticipated. So much for killing my boner.

"*She's slick and wet underneath me. My cock is pulsing with need as I take it in my hand and guide it into her crease.*" Ally's stare is boring a hole through the page, and I'm surprised the entire book hasn't burst into flame from the heat in her eyes. Good. *Lean into the heat, Honeybee.*

"*I push into her. In and out. In and out.* God, what type of horrible writing is this? Do I need a play-by-play of every thrust?" Ally says with a giggle that loosens the tension between us. "*She shudders, her walls clenching around me. 'Good girl, come for me.'*" Ally's breath does a nearly imperceptible hitch. *Nearly* imperceptible. "I should stop," she says, looking up at me.

Her face is hot and flushed, and she's breathing deeper than before, her chest heaving. She's right. She should stop. Trying to make Ally crack and admit there's something between us has been a fun little game. But she said no, and I'm not one to cross boundaries.

"I'm going to get some shut-eye. You should, too. Hudson will be here early to pick us up before work," I say, shuffling down on the bed to make myself more comfortable. I don't dare stand up from the bed right now. I have my hard length concealed in my pants the way I'm lying, but it would be very apparent the second I stood up. Ally nods and goes into the ensuite. I hear the tap run for a while. I assume she's splashing cold water on her face. Like I need to.

I shut my eyes when I hear the bathroom door open.

"Are you not going to get under the covers?" Ally asks.

"Um. No. You can have the covers." Being under the blankets with Ally is too tempting. I don't trust myself. And I have a newfound resolve to be respectful. Very new, as of like, ten seconds ago.

"Don't be ridiculous, Mason. You can sleep under the covers."

"If you insist. But don't blame me if you can't keep your hands off me and we wake up spooning." I climb underneath, not bothering to take off my clothes. If I'm going to sleep under the covers, I'll need to keep my pants on.

"You would be the little spoon, right?" Ally teases, her blue eyes shimmering as she gives me a playful jab with her finger. What I wouldn't give to be Ally's little spoon ... but I don't admit it.

"In your dreams, Honeybee." I quip instead.

"Can you turn around?" Ally asks. "I don't want to sleep in my scrubs and I'd rather you not look."

I do as she asks and turn over to face the wall, but the mirror leaning in the corner of the room gives me a sliver of a glimpse of the lace underwear Ally has on before she slips under the covers. The very weight of Ally in the bed next to me sends a warmth right through my bones. It's comforting in a way that I haven't felt in a long time, if ever. Something inside me slackens and sinks into the mattress a little more than before she laid down.

I shift over to my back and stare up at the vaulted ceiling, hands crossed over my chest. I'm trying to think of anything but Ally lying next to me in her bra and thong. Trying not to imagine what it would be like to take them off. I'm still determined to get Ally to admit that she feels this, too, but doing it while we're lying next to each other in bed just seems unfair and a bit sleazy.

"I'll sleep better tonight, although we're stuck in a stranger's house. At least, a stranger to me," Ally says into the dark of the room. "I won't have to worry about Nate finding me here."

I turn to face her. Despite the night enveloping the room now,

I can see the outline of her face close to mine. She blinks her long eyelashes, eyelids heavy.

"Is that something you worry about?" I ask.

"Sometimes. More so now, since he showed up the other night when you were over. Thank God you were there, too. Now, I kind of toss and turn, playing out scenarios in my head, planning out what I would say if he showed up and I was alone."

Ally's statement makes me realize that she's afraid of Nate, and the thought makes me seethe with rage. How much control must he have had over her life to make her afraid like this?

"Do you want me to come and stay at the cabin with you? Because I would." Ally's breathing is becoming slower.

"No, you don't need to do that, Mason. I know how you like to be at the clinic. Thanks, though." Her voice trails off, becoming sleepier.

"I mean it, Honeybee. I will ruin him the second he does anything to you."

She doesn't respond, so I don't know if she's heard me or not. I toss and turn for a while before falling asleep next to her.

CHAPTER 17
ALLY

Sometime in the small hours of the night, I'm awoken by Mason thrashing in the bed. I emerge from the fog of sleep and hear him muttering something. He's not awake, not aware of what he's saying. I can just make it out, the word no, and something about *not letting him die*. His skin is clammy with sweat when I move closer to him, and he's still thrashing from side to side. I bring my hands to his head and hold him close to my chest, stroking his hair, his face, the rough stubble on his jaw scratching my hand. His dark waves have fallen over his face and are stuck to his forehead. I gently comb them back with my fingers. Mason's thrashing subsides as he comes to.

"It's just a dream," I whisper, reorienting him back to reality. "You're safe, Mason. It's just a dream."

"I let him die." His voice is just a whimper and his body shudders as he releases his tears.

"It's okay, it's not real." I run my hand through his hair, a gentle way of bringing him out of his sleep. On instinct, I plant my lips on his temple. "It's not real."

"It was real. It happened. I let him die." I can't tell if Mason is awake or still stuck in that place between a dream and reality. I know Mason has seen some horrific things in his career, and the trauma still haunts him.

"It's okay. I'm right here, Mason." The reminder of my presence makes me wonder how many nights Mason wakes up like this alone. An ache sits heavy in my chest. For as long as I live, I never want Mason to wake up alone.

I lean down and brush my lips across his mouth. I would do anything in this moment to take away whatever's tormenting him in his dreams. His cheeks are wet with tears, but his sobs no longer wrack his body. His lips return my kiss. It's gentler this time, softer than our kiss the other night in the office, and not as hurried. Our lips move lazily together as if they too are half in and out of sleep.

Mason wraps his arms around me and pulls me down so my head comes to rest just below his chin, and he drifts back off to sleep. His breath evens out, peaceful and rhythmic, and I lay awake in the dark listening to it for some time.

HUDSON SHOWS up as expected at seven, jumps the battery in the Jeep, and we're on our way home. Mason and I sit in silence for the drive back to the cabin, neither of us quite knowing how to address the events of the previous night. I can't be sure that Mason even remembers me kissing him. Perhaps it's best if he didn't. We could forget about it and carry on with our day, pretending nothing ever happened.

The memory of his lips meeting mine sends a jolt of electricity down my spine. It's a feeling that confirms the worst. I'm never going to forget about that kiss. The way his mouth was salty with the tears that rolled down his cheek. How his body softened into mine as he kissed me back. He held me in his arms for the rest of the night until we both awoke this morning and untangled our limbs from each other.

He gives me the day off work and says I did overtime last night. A pit forms in my stomach. Mason could have given me the day off to avoid me, to avoid talking about last night. The air between us isn't tense, it isn't cold, but it is … distant, restrained. I can't quite put my finger on it. It's for the best. I don't regret kissing Mason last night, but I'm definitely giving him mixed signals. I told him that I didn't want to cross the line between a fake and real relationship, so I need to hold firm on that.

I start the shower as soon as I get home. There's a part of me that doesn't want to shower, even though I need to. Mason's earthy smell is still on my skin, and something about the spicy pine scent makes me want to savour it, linger in it.

Later that evening, Poppy sits on a bar stool at my little kitchen island, watching me cook dinner for her, chin propped in her hands. I've started to enjoy her company more and more and the way she's sitting here in the cabin now, there's an ease between us.

"How did everything go last night? Did you end up getting home?" she asks as she takes a sip of the wine I just poured for her. I'm cooking my favourite curry recipe for her and the smell of the spices fills the cabin, making my mouth water. Reggie gave me a bag of fresh tomatoes before we left which I've used in the sauce and it's divine.

I'm glad to have a friend in town that I can invite over for a girls' night, though my heart aches thinking about Spencer. The time change between here and Amsterdam has really impeded our regular phone calls, and I feel like there's a piece of my heart missing. But Poppy has been gracious and sweet. A pang of guilt stabs through my gut when I remember that I've been lying to her about Mason and me. I've been lying to everyone in Heartwood. It didn't bother me so much before, but as I've grown closer to Poppy and Winnie, and started to think of Heartwood as my home, I hate the deception.

"This morning, yeah. Hudson came and picked us up," I explain.

"So, you spent the night in a secluded house in the woods? Sounds romantic." Poppy swoons. I can't keep this secret from her anymore. Not if I'm going to make genuine friendships. I can trust Poppy, I'm sure I can. She tends to keep to herself, and she doesn't strike me as the type to stir up drama.

"Less romantic than you'd imagine," I start.

"Oh, does Mason snore?" Poppy giggles, bringing her hand to cover her red-painted lips. The colour is striking against her pale skin and dark features. "I bet he snores."

"No, Poppy. He doesn't snore." *He's actually really nice to sleep next to.* "We're just … not together."

"What? Like, you haven't had *the talk* yet? The 'defining the relationship' talk? I mean, it's still early days."

"No, I mean, we're not dating at all." Poppy blinks her big doe eyes at me, trying to comprehend, so I take the moment to fill her in on the events of the last few days, explaining why we aren't as lovey-dovey as she assumed. I feel like I'm telling my child that mommy and daddy are divorcing. She's bummed. The pout that forms on her lips shows it, but she takes it in stride.

"Well, how are things going at the clinic? Now I need to know everything." She takes a long sip of her wine. "I assumed he would have been nice to you at work. I have to try to wrap my mind around this."

"It's gotten better. Dr. Dickbag has been … less of a … dickbag." Poppy snorts at the name and just about chokes on her wine.

"Dr. Dickbag is a fitting name. I'm going to write that on his to-go cup the next time he comes in for a coffee."

"Don't!" I shriek, laughter erupting from me as the rice I'm cooking boils over on the stove. "Shit!" I move it from the burner and regain control of the situation. "But seriously, don't. I'm making some decent headway with him. We've graduated from a fake couple to, I don't know, friends?" I scrunch my face like I'm waiting for Poppy to say that's the most ridiculous thing she's ever heard.

I leave out the part about Mason kissing me in the clinic, and about me kissing him while we shared a bed last night. We both agreed that kissing is impulsive and that it should never happen again. Well, I told Mason it should never happen again. The way his shoulders had sagged when I pulled away from him in his office told a different story on his end. One that is difficult for me to make sense of. Not to mention the tension between us last night that buzzed with electrifying energy. The way his hips shifted as I read my smutty book aloud gave me a glimpse in my periphery of his length, hardening in his jeans.

I also leave out the part about him taking a private meeting with some stuffy pantsuit in his office. The way he pushed me out of the office before shutting the door made the hair on my arms stand on end. How he dodged all of my questions about it afterward. He was being shifty, and it reminded me of Nate. Explaining what Mason and I are now, it's impossible. So, *friends* will do for now.

"Mason is just overprotective of that clinic. He sees that you fit in well here, and you have something to offer."

"Thanks, Pops." The nickname slid out before it registered, but I see how it makes Poppy smile. "I hope he does. I want to make a go of this. I love being able to make a real difference for people."

"Why did you leave your labour and delivery job in Vancouver, anyway?" Poppy's chestnut bob swishes as she cocks her head to the side.

"It was for the show. And then Nate didn't agree with me when I said I wanted to go back to work. Our schedule was so busy with social events after filming, and networking events for his job."

"So, he got to carry on building his own career after filming, but you didn't?" She scoffs.

"No, I mean. It wasn't like that. His business was struggling. Clients were unhappy, and he was having a hard time bringing in new business. He got a couple of scathing complaints to the Better Business Bureau and was drawing all kinds of unwanted attention. It made sense that I would help him out. He said it was good for business having me at networking events because I'm friendly and I'm social."

"Sounds like he was using you."

"Oh, he was. He is. He's still hoping that I'll go back to the city with him. It won't reflect well on him if I don't."

"So, you told him you were dating Mason to avoid the confrontation," she says, everything clicking into place. I nod.

"Mason gave me a week to convince Nate to leave. I've already overstepped that deadline."

"What are you going to do?" Poppy asks, her dark, round eyes wide. She's beautiful in a doll-like way.

"You tell me." I shrug. "I am doubtful that Mason will extend our agreement."

"He's just wary. The last time he got involved with someone, it didn't end well, like catastrophic, and the whole town found out about it," Poppy explains. I take a long pull of my wine. Kissing Mason last night didn't feel like kissing someone who has sworn off relationships. Not with the way he kissed me back.

"Well, we're colleagues, nothing more. I'll figure out how to get rid of Nate on my own. For now, I just need to focus on the Harvest Festival." I turn back to the stove to finish off the curry and reach into the cupboard to pull down two heavy pottery soup bowls.

"The Harvest Festival is an incredible idea, by the way. I've heard multiple customers talking about it in line at the café. The whole town is buzzing about it."

"Speaking of which, I need Mason's help tomorrow. Do you think he'll be busy?" I ask.

"Ha!" Poppy laughs, throwing her head back. "Mason, busy on a Saturday? I'm pretty sure that man just sits in his office and stares at his pager, waiting for it to go off."

"Fair point." I finish scooping out the chicken curry, ladling it over rice, and I pass the steaming bowl of food over to Poppy.

"This looks amazing, Ally." She picks it up and carries it over to the couch.

I finish serving out my own portion and pick up my phone to text Mason before joining Poppy over in the living area.

ALLY

Can you swing by the cabin tomorrow? I need some help with something for the Harvest Festival.

A few seconds later, I see the blue dots indicating Mason is typing. Does he just sit at his phone and wait for me to text him, too?

MASON

As long as you can keep your lips off of me.

Sorry, too soon?

Two can play at this game. If he's trying to get me to reconsider where we stand with each other, he's going to have to do better than that.

ALLY

You can't stop thinking about it, can you?

MASON

I can't stop thinking about the way your mouth would feel wrapped around my cock.

Jesus Christ. What's he trying to do to me? I glance over at

Poppy sitting in front of the TV, flicking through the limited channels to find something for us to watch. She's distracted enough that she won't notice the way my face is burning.

ALLY

Is this your idea of keeping things professional?

I watch as the little blue dots appear on the screen and disappear. A message comes through a few moments later, but it's not a dirty one.

MASON

Only kidding.

Back to being colleagues, I guess. I'd like to say that I'm relieved that Mason is joking, but I'm aware of the warm wetness soaking into my panties at the idea of his cock alone. It's a thought that's going to be difficult to get out of my head. *Thanks a lot Dr. Dickbag.* I'm about to shut off my phone and forget about the favour I was about to ask him. Fake relationship aside, having him over here tomorrow is not the brightest idea if we're going to remain collegial.

MASON

When should I come over?

ALLY

Bright and early. Unless you're too busy.

MASON

I'm never too busy for you, Honeybee.

I click my phone off and leave it on the counter. Mason and I are colleagues. More than that, he's my boss. Mason and I need to keep things professional. Even though the kiss that we shared has been keeping me up at night. Based on Mason's text, he's been thinking about it, too.

Poppy and I finish dinner, and she heads home for the night.

She'll be up early to open the café, and I need to collect myself in time for tomorrow. It didn't matter what Poppy and I talked about after I got that text from Mason; I couldn't get the image of him out of my head.

My mouth. His cock.

I pace around the cabin, trying to squash the urgent need that's coursing through me. If I don't do something about this now, I won't be able to face Mason tomorrow. Not when there won't be anything to prevent me from giving in. He'll be here, at the cabin. With no one else around.

Fuck it. I shake my head as I stride over to my nightstand and pull out my purple rabbit vibrator, the one that Mason had held in his hand the day we met. *It's also okay if you want to think about me while you're using it.*

So much for putting the idea of him out of my head. As hard as I can try to be professional around him, there's no point in trying to keep my thoughts about him platonic. My saving grace is that nothing will actually happen between us. Mason won't let it. I won't let it. I don't need to be second best to a man who only cares about work anymore. But that doesn't have to stop me from imagining the way Mason would feel inside of me.

I lay back on the bed, pulling off my sweats. I don't bother taking off my thong. This won't take long. I push it over to the side, giving me access to my opening. I'm swollen and wet already. Flicking on the vibrator, I work it up and down my slit, letting my eyes roll back at the sensation. No one has to know the kind of thoughts I allow myself to have in private.

The curtains on the front windows are open, dusk falling over the trees outside. The light inside the cabin makes me visible to the outside world. Anyone could walk up to the cabin and see me lying here, legs spread wide open on the bed. Anyone, including Mason.

I don't bother getting up to close them.

CHAPTER 18
MASON

I PULL up to the cabin bright and early, as promised. Ally never told me what the plan was for today, but I guess if I can be cryptic, then so can she. She's already waiting for me outside when I pull into the gravel drive, and the sight of her standing on the porch, leaning on the railing in her denim cut-offs and loose-fitting tank top, makes my chest seize. All I keep thinking about since yesterday is that damn kiss. Not the one at the clinic, although that one was hot as hell until Ally decided to be the responsible one. No, my mind has been stuck on the way Ally held me as she kissed me to wake me up from my nightmare.

I've had the same nightmare almost every night for the past year. Every time, I wake up shaking and sweating, trying to convince myself that it hasn't happened again. That nobody else has died. Two nights ago was the first time I'd been woken from my nightmare by a soothing embrace and comforting words spoken in a hushed voice. It was the first time I fell back into a deep slumber, one that wasn't plagued with dreams.

"I thought I'd repay you for the coffee you got me yesterday. It's no latte from Poppy, but it's the best I can do with black coffee," Ally says as she hands me of my dad's old mugs and the sight of it makes my heart ache for a second. Ever since Ally moved into the cabin, memories have been flooding back to me about my dad. It hasn't been as difficult as I thought it would be. In fact, remembering him the way he was at the cabin has been pushing out the more painful ones, and I've wondered if keeping his legacy alive is about more than the clinic.

I take the cup of coffee, giving Ally a quick nod of thanks, and I survey the yard. She's gathered all kinds of painting supplies, but what she intends on doing with them is a mystery.

"Put me in, coach. What are we doing?" I say, gesturing to the supplies. She's set up my dad's old workhorses and placed a sheet of plywood overtop forming a makeshift table. Small cans of colourful paint dot the yard.

"We're painting signs for the festival! Everything else is just about in order for tomorrow, so now we need decorations." Ally sets about explaining all the signs we need to paint today, and we have our work cut out for us. There will be one directing patrons over to the food carts, one indicating where there will be booths with games, the raffle tent, and a few more decorative ones. Ally has cut out pumpkins and sunflowers, as the theme is fall harvest and she's leaning into it.

I quickly learn that I am not nearly as adept at painting as Ally is. My lines are a little sloppy, and somehow, my colour choices are a little off. I'm standing back, surveying Ally as she finishes up the sign she's working on, and I can't help but notice how steady her hand is. Her fingers wrap firmly around the wooden handle of the brush, making long, clean strokes.

"What do you think?" I hold up my sign to show Ally and she scrunches her face in the prettiest little grimace. "Don't give me that look. I'm trying my best over here."

I set down the sign and go over to where Ally is standing. Her painting is gorgeous. The details that she's added to the pumpkins make them appear real. She has a real creative eye. I make an exaggerated point of looking down my nose at it, like I'm some art critic in the Louvre.

"Stay in the lines next time, Honeybee." I nudge her and she whips around to face me, still holding the brush she was working with. Red paint flies off the end of the bristles and lands on my face. Ally's mouth hangs open when she realizes what just happened, but her eyes twinkle as she tries to cover her laugh.

"I'm sorry, I didn't mean to do that, I promise." But her apology doesn't land through her laughter, and I'm already picking up my brush covered with yellow paint and flicking it towards her.

Ally shrieks and makes to run away from me but I catch her, grabbing her around the waist and spinning her around in mid-air.

"Asshole!" Ally cries, and somehow this time, I know that she's kidding. It's been a while she would have called me that and meant it. I turn Ally around to face me, my arms still wrapped around her waist, holding her close. I tell myself that this is playful. The kiss in my office was a mistake. Letting ourselves inch closer to that line the other night at Reggie's was a mistake. We're friends now, although I can't help but enjoy having Ally's tight body next to mine.

"You have something on your face. Let me get that for you," I say with a wink, lifting my hand as if to wipe away the yellow paint on her face. Ally is standing there, peering up at me with her big turquoise eyes. There's still red paint on my hand, and when I swipe it across her forehead, it mixes with the yellow, creating a streak that resembles a sunset. A sunset over an endless ocean of blue.

"Beautiful," I say, the words almost a whisper. I see Ally's throat bob as she swallows hard. I reach my hand up to her face, this time to brush a lock of hair behind her ear, but Ally turns away, breaking the spell of the moment.

"We should get these paintings under the porch," she whispers, yanking me out of my stupor. "I see some clouds rolling in and I don't want them to get ruined." Despite the way she kissed me at Reggie's, Ally is still trying to keep a healthy distance between us.

A few grey clouds are gathering overhead and a cool breeze wafts between us. Our bodies are practically steaming in the chill of the air. Ally's right about pulling the signs undercover, and about pulling back from me. I help her move the last of the signs under the cover of the porch as Ally turns to look at me. We're almost at the finish line now. A finish line that will either make us or break us, and the latter is enough for me to restrain myself around Ally. No distractions.

"That's our work done for the day," she says, and I'm hoping she isn't implying that I should leave. For all of my previous judgements of Ally, she's proving me wrong about her. When I'm with her now, I'm at ease. She has no lofty expectations. She holds no prior judgements or opinions on my reputation as a physician. When I'm around Ally, I'm just *me*.

"Let me make you some dinner, or a drink, or something for your hard work today," she offers. Dinner between friends. Dinner is safe, right?

"I have a better idea. Why don't you wash the paint off and I'll meet you back out here." Ally glances up at the sky, wondering what I could be planning with the clouds looming. It's not supposed to rain today, based on the weather report, and after the last few days, I'm craving a night to unwind and forget about the clinic for a while. My pager better behave tonight. I consider turning it off for a moment, but I know I can't.

Ally nods and retreats inside the cabin. Of the two of us, she got the brunt of the paint war. I walked away with only a few splatters.

I wander around to the back of the cabin and open the creaky door of the old wooden shed. My mind wanders to Ally in the shower, hot and steamy, the water running off the peaks of her perfect tits. It's all I can do not to get in with her. But the way she turned away from me moments before is all that I need to know. Nothing more is going to happen between us. Whatever we shared last night, whatever part of Ally opened up to me as she held me, is sealed shut once again. I still can't even make sense of how I got here. One minute, I was strategizing how to get Ally to leave, and now, I not only want her around the clinic, but I'm imagining kissing her again, her body naked and wet in the shower. My cock pulses and hardens at the image.

Standing in the doorway of the shed, my heart just about cracks in two as I skim over my dad's collection of tools, dusty and untouched. There's a generous supply of old camping, fishing, and hunting gear. Not that anyone has used it recently.

Dad had stopped being able to take my brothers and me out camping a long time ago. This version of my dad, the one that spent so much time outdoors, that part of him meant something, too. He was more than just Heartwood's physician, the founder of the Heartwood Medical Centre. Maybe I can be more, too.

I pull an old tent and two sleeping bags out onto the lawn by the fire pit. We've had this tent since I was a kid, and at this point, I could put it up with my eyes closed. I've set it up and positioned a log as a backrest next to a roaring fire by the time Ally re-emerges from the cabin. She's thrown her hair up into a messy bun and she's fresh-faced, just a faint pink shine on her full lips.

"What is all this?" Ally smiles and when she does, it seems as if her entire face sparkles.

"A camp-out. It's something that I used to do with my dad. Or are you too high-maintenance for camping?" I tease.

"I'll have you know, Mason Landry, that I love the outdoors. I'm just surprised. Don't you want to get back to the clinic tonight?" She's right, I often spend my nights in the clinic, there's never not something to catch up on. Ally has noted my routine, and I try not to think about how that fact tugs on my heart. The line keeping Ally and me from crossing into dangerous territory is becoming blurrier by the second.

"Not tonight. A night off from the clinic won't kill me," I say, waving her over to take a seat on the blanket I've spread out in front of the fire. She settles in next to me and leans back against the log I rolled over. Ally maintains a comfortable distance from me, although the space between us feels taut, like I'm being drawn toward her.

"You deserve that—a night off, a life outside of the clinic." Ally stares into the flames, licking at the logs in front of us. "What was your dad like?" she asks.

The question comes out of nowhere, and I'm stunned for a minute. I make a point not to talk about my father. But something about the way Ally has asked with genuine curiosity makes me want to share him with her.

"Jack Landry," I say, pushing air out through pursed lips, "was a legend in Heartwood. He *is* a legend. Everyone who knew him loved him. Being a dad was all he ever wanted, apart from becoming a doctor. And then he got four sons, which was like his wildest dream come true. He would take us out hunting and fishing and camping all the time when we were young. We could never go too far, so he was always available at the clinic, but we didn't care to notice. We just ate it all up. Those days were short-lived," I explain. "You know, this was where he lived. In the cabin."

I hadn't planned on telling Ally about the cabin's history. One, it was too painful to talk about, and two, I never wanted Ally to feel guilty about moving in here. But she deserves to know now, and I want her to know about this part of me, the part of me that still has fond memories of my dad before I came to resent him.

Ally fixes her eyes on me as she shakes her head slowly.

"I'm sorry. Winnie didn't tell me. I never would have—" I cut her off before she can say anything more. The last thing I want is for her to apologize for something she had no control over.

"You don't need to apologize, Honeybee. I actually like seeing the cabin being lived in. It's nice that it feels like a home again." I turn and look at the small wooden building in the middle of the forest.

"What changed? Between you and your father, I mean." She must have sensed in my tone earlier that things weren't always that good where my dad was concerned.

"He wasn't the same after my mom died. It broke him, you know. He believed that if he tried hard enough, he could save everyone. When my mom was diagnosed with cancer, too far gone for treatment, he couldn't save her, and he felt like he failed at the one thing he dedicated his life to. He doubled down on his work at the clinic and left us behind in his wake."

Ally reaches down and places her hands on mine. When I look up, my eyes meet hers, the rims of them sparkling and watery.

"So the apple doesn't fall far from the tree." She lets out a shaky laugh, and the sound of it does wonders to ease the tension in the air. But Ally is more accurate in her assessment of me than she realizes.

"I never thought I would turn out like my dad. I tried my best not to. But he left me this shit hole of a situation that I can't seem to dig my way out of." I wave my hand in the direction of said shit hole, the clinic.

"You don't have to dig yourself out of it. We're doing it together. At least, I want to do this together." Ally places her hand on her chest as if swearing an oath, a promise to me that she will devote herself to the clinic like I have.

"Forgive me if I don't work well with others. I've always been alone in this. God knows my brothers aren't any help. It's like I'm the only one who cares. About Dad, about the clinic, about any of it."

"I care about it," Ally whispers, and I decide to risk looking up into her eyes. This is treacherous, allowing myself to feel the things that I'm used to pushing aside. Anytime I have ever allowed these feelings for a woman to creep in, the harsh reminder that the clinic is my one and only priority makes me back away, run for dear life.

Ally is different. Ally cares about the same thing I care about. *I only care about Priya's well-being. And the baby.* Her words live in my mind, proof that Ally understands the call we answer to serve our patients. This thought alone is what brings my defences crashing down. Ally could be a partner in this. Not someone who takes time away from the things I care about and value, but who adds the passion and fire I am craving. Ally is everything that my life has been lacking.

"You're the first person in a long time to walk into my life and make me feel less alone, Ally. You're the first person who hasn't pitied me for the life I've given up for this clinic. Who hasn't either lectured me or praised me for working myself to the bone and then just stood back to watch as I drown."

The urge to reach up and grab her, pull her towards me, is so strong I might have to sit on my hands. But I need to hear it from her. I need some confirmation from her that she's willing to take the leap, too. No more pulling back. No more second-guessing.

Ally is the first to reach up and cup my cheek in her hand, her thumb brushing back and forth on my rough jaw.

"Say you feel this, Ally. Say you want it, and I'll give you everything," I whisper.

"I want *you*. Mason Landry. Not Dr. Mason Landry. Just *you*," she says. Those are the words I've been waiting to hear, the ones I've been baiting Ally to say. She's admitted it. She's admitted that she's just as fucked as I am, and I love it.

The warm glow of the evening sun creates a golden aura around her hair. She looks angelic as the features on her face soften. Her walls have come down, and I take this as my cue to do what has been consuming every part of my thoughts ever since I saw Ally for the first time in the café. Ever since *I* kissed her in my office, my body has been demanding more. Ever since *Ally* kissed me, my heart has been reaching for her.

I bring my mouth to hers and kiss her, this time ignoring the gentle caresses of her tongue and driving mine into her mouth with more need, more desire than I've ever dared. This moment is the only one that matters. Where I am kissing Ally, and holding Ally, and my biggest concern is the clothing that I want to rip off her perfect body. The rest I can deal with when the time comes. *If* the time comes.

Ally's kiss is reassuring, telling me that my feelings are important, my desires are important. She matches my need, grabbing at the buttons of my flannel, fumbling with them as she undoes them. I bring my hand up to grip the back of her hair, tilting her head back to gain access to the long column of her neck.

She has my shirt unbuttoned now, and she is running her hands down my chest, my abs, making her way to my belt buckle. My belt is tight, being stretched taut by my growing erection, and I'm impatient for her to undo it. I need her to release me, unleash me. I've been bound up for far too long. The physical need for Ally is palpable now, and when I look into her eyes, I can see she needs me just as much.

She's unbuckled my belt, but she's taking her sweet time with my pants. Ally looks me in the eye as she rubs her hand up and down along the outline of my cock through the fabric of my jeans. I bite my bottom lip to keep myself from exploding just from her touch.

"Should we go inside?" Ally whispers to me, her hand still between my legs.

"We're doing this right here and right now, Honeybee," I say, my voice dropping in pitch as I bring my hands up to cradle her face.

"What if someone shows up? What if Nate shows up?" she asks. The sound of that dipshit's name on Ally's lips makes me almost feral. The testosterone coursing through my veins doesn't help.

"Then he can watch." My voice is low and raspy as I add, "And don't ever say his name while you have my cock in your hand again."

"Jealous?" The corner of her mouth quirks up. She's such a fucking tease.

"I don't need to be jealous of him. But when we're together like this, I want to be the only one on your mind."

My hands roam around Ally's body, landing on her soft, curved hips as I pick her up and shift her so she's lying on the blanket I had spread out on the ground. I have Ally right where I want her, and my hand explores the soft bit of skin that's exposed beneath the hem of her tank top. As I lean over her, perched on one elbow, I lift her shirt to expose her soft, round tits, taking my time to trace lazy circles around her hardened nipples. Her back arches in response to the sensation, and she gazes back to watch me admire her.

I lean down so that my lips graze the shell of her ear.

"Tell me what you want from me." I rasp, goosebumps forming along her arms.

"You know what I want." Ally lifts her head to bury her face in my neck, trailing her lips along the edge of my jaw.

"Say it again. Say what you need from me." This is Ally's weakness, the place that she never dares to let herself go. But I've seen glimpses of the subtle strength within this woman, and I need more. If I can be a safe space for her to say what she needs, maybe she'll be able to do it in other areas of her life, too.

"What about '*I call the shots*?'" Ally mimics my show of dominance from the other day.

"That was then," I say, interrupting myself to plant soft kisses down Ally's neck. "Now, Honeybee, I'm all yours. I'm at your mercy. Do what you want with me, Ally Wells. Do your worst." I rasp, swallowing a moan.

"I want *you*, Mason. I want *all* of you." She moans, arching her back as I nip at her collarbone. I'm still allowing my hands to roam —rolling her nipple between my fingers. Ally lets out a breathy moan as I flick it and let my hand trail lower.

"I'm going to need specific instructions," I say with a playful wink, "Use your words."

I'm enjoying toying with Ally as usual, but watching her hips squirm and shift as my hand makes its way to the waistband of her leggings gives me a different satisfaction. Ally looks down at where it's landed, her eyes pleading.

"I want you to fuck me, Mason. I want every inch of your cock filling me." There's that bold side of Ally that I've been craving. I slide my fingers into her pants, finding the contours of her slit through the lacy thong she has on. I've been thinking about those lacy thongs ever since I saw them strewn about the driveway.

"That's my girl," I murmur, and the corner of Ally's mouth lifts into a grin. The words slipped out before I could catch them, and although a part of me wishes I could stuff them back in, the look on Ally's face washes away any ounce of regret. *My girl.*

I remove my hand from her pants just long enough to push down my own, feeling the sweet relief of releasing my pulsing cock from the restrictive denim. Ally's eyes widen at the size. Her reaction is unexpected, but, judging by the size of her vibrator, I don't think this will be a problem.

"Are you sure you want every inch?" I check in with her, smirking slightly. Ally nods, biting down on her bottom lip, and I just about come at the sight.

"Every inch." She whispers. "Just go slow." I'm used to going slow. The size of my cock has been off-putting for some women in the past. But here's Ally, not only willing to take it—but *wanting* it.

I don't waste any time pulling Ally's leggings off. Seeing her in the flesh is better than anything I could have conjured up in my mind. She's already wet, and I can feel it soaking through the thin fabric of her thong. I pull a condom out of my back pocket and rip the package open with my teeth. I roll it on and lay back on the blanket, pulling Ally on top of me. She lets me remove the last shreds of her clothing, lifting her tank top up and over her head, and I take in every inch of her naked body. She's all lean curves, her skin smooth and fair save for a smattering of freckles where the sun kisses her.

This is every man's wet dream, having a gorgeous woman straddling them naked in the open air in the woods, the heat of a campfire keeping us warm. I position Ally's hips so she's lined up on top of me, holding her weight so I can ease her onto my length and control the depth so as not to overwhelm her.

I nudge my tip into her opening, and ever so slowly, edge myself in. Ally lets out a guttural moan as I fill her, stretch her. Hearing her breath hitch sharply, I pause.

"God, you feel like heaven," I whisper, waiting for her to ease herself down as far as she can handle.

"*More*," Ally says with a soft cry, and I oblige, pushing up into her another couple of inches.

"Are you okay?" I ask, checking in with her.

Ally nods, her eyes pleading for even more. I lift her hips up and back, bringing myself out right to the tip, a little tease before driving into her until she's seated on top of me.

"Say it, Honeybee. Say what you need."

Ally responds by lifting her hips, flicking them up and back in a smooth, rhythmic motion.

"I want to ride you. And I want to watch you come undone as I fuck you."

"That's my girl," I say again. This time my words are confident, deliberate, and I don't question them. I push her up so she's sitting tall, giving me access to the parts of her I know she wants touched. I rest my hand on her hip, wrapping my thumb around to make tight, soft circles around her clit. Ally bites down on her lip to muffle the cry that would have erupted from her.

I make the circles smaller and quicker as she moves her hips in time with my finger. Her breath is ragged. She's close to her edge, so I don't dare change what I'm doing until her walls constrict around me. The tightness of it brings me closer to my release, but I fight the urge to come. I want her to have everything she wants and deserves first. I want to give Ally all of me.

I thought I was falling for the version of Ally that's bold and strong, but I'm mistaken. This is my new favourite version of Ally, the one that only I can make crumble.

Ally shudders as she falls forward on me, everything in her body succumbing to the pleasure wracking her. The movement of her hips slows but doesn't stop, and I can feel my full release pumping into her. A loud clap of thunder erupts in the sky as I climax, and it covers the sound of my groan.

Ally and I lay here a moment, her small frame curled up on my chest, my length still buried to the hilt inside of her. All of the tension that wound me tight unravelled. I hold her close, wrapping my arms around her and trailing my lips along the curve where her neck meets her shoulder.

A raindrop lands on Ally's back, and I watch it run down the length of her spine.

One raindrop turns into several, which turn into a downpour as the sky opens up on us. Ally pulls back and looks at me, hair wet and sticking to her face.

Ally throws her head back and laughs. "Should we go inside now?"

CHAPTER 19
ALLY

I CHANGE into dry clothes and sit on the couch warming myself up by the fire, waiting for Mason to emerge from the shower. He still had some speckles of paint left on his face when we came back inside. I pick up my phone and send Spencer a text. She won't see it until the morning, but I can't wait to update her on this turn of events.

ALLY

Dr. Dickbag ... more like Dr. Big Dick.

I decide to add an eggplant emoji so I get the message across. Spencer is going to scream—I wish I was there to see her face.

ALLY

P.S. If you ever want to move to Heartwood, remind me to introduce you to Dr. Big Dick's brother.

I lock my phone as I hear the door to the bathroom creak open.

I thought Mason was hot when I was riding on top of him, but as he walks out of the bathroom the sight of him in nothing but a towel is making me weak in the knees all over again. His body is still glistening as he dries his hair with a hand towel, leaving his damp waves mussed. Just asking for me to bury my hands in them, pull on them.

I'm drenched again just looking at him now and remembering the feeling of having him so deep inside me. A shiver runs through my body, thinking about his words in my ear. *That's my girl.*

Since when did Mason think of me as *his?* Sometime in the last few weeks, Mason has shifted from someone who wanted nothing to do with me to a man who puts me at the centre of his universe while he fucks me.

"You're looking at me like you want to eat me for dinner." Mason laughs.

"Maybe I do," I say. Mason walks over to where I'm seated, the look on his face intense as he whips the towel off from around his waist.

"I prefer to be enjoyed as a dessert." He chuckles, and my heart melts inside my chest. No matter how serious Mason could be in one moment, his sense of humour peeks through his tough exterior. It's one reason that my heart is softening towards him.

Mason leans over me on the couch, the position making it impossible for me to ignore what is hanging between his legs. Mason is huge. Like, *huge.* I can't wrap my mind around how I took it all or how good it felt.

He kisses me, and he effortlessly summons the slickness between my legs with a flick of his tongue on mine. Mason has crept into my heart, unbeknownst to me. That asshole from the café has drawn me into his deep brown eyes and shown me what lay beneath the surface. He's letting me see *him.* Beneath the mask that he wears for everyone around him, Mason has a heart of solid gold. He feels deeply, he loves deeply, and if I lived a thousand lifetimes, I wouldn't forget what it felt like to be loved by him.

The thing is, Mason sees me, too. He sees a strength in me I didn't know was there, and he knows how to coax it out of me. He gives me space to speak my mind. His little trick of making me tell him what I wanted from him was clever, and now I'm craving the high I got from my boldness again.

"Are you going to keep making me tell you what I want?" I bat my eyelashes at him.

"As hot as that was, it's my turn now." Mason shifts his body from where he leaned over me and kneels on the floor, turning to face me. He leans into me between my legs, and I place my hands on either side of his face, drawing him into a deep kiss.

"And what is that, Dr. Landry?" The flesh between my legs swells almost to the point of pain, needing the relief of Mason inside of me again.

Mason takes his time answering me, and my breath catches in my throat as he lowers his head, kissing and licking a teasing trail down my belly.

"I want to watch your pussy as you come." He rips my pants off again, gripping my thighs, spreading me open, and baring me to him. The ache between my legs is unbearable now as he grabs a handful of my ass and pulls me towards the edge of the couch.

Mason is drawing this out as his eyes take in my body, and it's excruciating.

"You're perfect, Ally," Mason murmurs as he kisses the insides of my thigh, starting at my knee and trailing higher. A shiver runs through me at the way his stubbled jaw brushes the fleshy part of my thigh.

"Wait," I say, pushing him away from me, confusion crossing his face. I twist myself over on the couch to reach the drawer of the side table and feel around inside until I find a small bullet vibrator.

"Jesus, how many vibrators do you have hidden around here?"

"I don't know what to tell you, Mason, I like good vibes." I flick it on and move it down between my legs.

"What are you doing?" Mason asks, looking up at me from

where he's perched by my crotch. I'm still spread eagle in front of him.

"I always use a vibrator." I hesitate. "I like some action ... on the outside, too." I don't have to tell him this. Mason already knows how I liked my clit played with. I don't bother telling him it's because Nate refused to pleasure me with his mouth, how I would make use of the vibrator while he pumped his fingers inside of me.

"Wait, did Nate make you ...?" Realization dawns on Mason's face.

"Yeah, don't most guys hate ... doing this?" I cover my face with my hands to hide the blush creeping across my cheeks. I just gave myself away that I've never known the feeling of a man's tongue on me.

"I am not most guys." Mason grabs the vibrator out of my hand and tosses it aside. "You're all mine today, and I want nothing more than to taste your sweet honey on my tongue."

My heart skips a beat.

His deep brown eyes peer up into mine, never breaking contact as his tongue connects with my slit, pushing into it slowly, relishing it. Mason closes his lips around my apex, taking a long, deep suck on my clit.

"*Fuck, Mason.*" Is this what I've been missing out on all this time? His soft, wet tongue makes smooth, languid circles and my whole body shudders. I just about lose myself to him as he inserts a finger, followed by another, into my opening. His mouth is still working on my sensitive bundle of nerves as his fingers glide in and out. Mason must have *aced* his anatomy class in med school.

This is all I need from Mason, to be at the centre of his attention, even just for a moment. To be all that exists for him right now. Not the clinic. Not the rest of his responsibilities. All I need is for him to put it all aside and be with me.

A warm tingle spreads from the concentrated spot between my legs to the rest of my body, right through my limbs, down to my fingers and my toes. Right as I think that the pleasure is going to take over, erupting through my muscles, Mason removes his mouth. He does exactly what he said he wanted to do and fixes his eyes on my pussy as he slides his fingers in, my walls contracting around them. He brings me down off the cliff for a moment, curling his fingers within me, hitting the spot on my front wall that keeps my orgasm building.

Mason reaches his hand up and under my shirt, flicking his finger over my nipple, the waves of sensation from multiple points of contact on my body making me squirm and shake.

He doesn't take his fingers off my nipple as he goes back to swirling his tongue around my clit, flicking it in a quick, pulsing rhythm.

The pleasure winds tight within me and all of my muscles clench at once, a sudden burst of sensation as my hips buck against Mason's mouth. It rolls through me like waves crashing on the shore repeatedly as Mason flicks my sensitive nipple while he drives his fingers deeper. I let out a loud cry as the final wave crashes over me, my body clenching and releasing over and over.

Mason removes himself from me and comes up to rest next to me on the couch. I close my eyes, letting the afterglow of the earth-shattering orgasm envelop me as he brings my head to his chest and buries his face in my hair.

"Ally, I ..." Mason starts to speak, but his voice trails off as his phone vibrates on the old wooden coffee table in front of us. I can't help but notice the name that comes up on the screen. *Simone Mitchell.* Is that who's been calling all week? Some other woman? It would certainly explain the secrecy. My heart pounds in my ears.

"Sorry, I need to get this," Mason says, getting up and pulling on his jeans as he heads outside onto the porch. What is Mason hiding? He can't have another woman in his life, not with the amount of time he spends at the clinic. I'm pretty sure I've seen him every day this week, and anytime he isn't with me, he's at the clinic. Unless he's not. Doubt creeps over me and I'm suddenly nauseated. I've only just considered that maybe Mason is worth more of my time and energy than I initially thought. Now I'm not so sure.

I can see a pattern taking shape the same way it did with Nate. The mistrust, the racing thoughts. I had no proof that Nate cheated, but I never trusted him once we finished filming the show. He was always full of secrets, including who he was at his core. Nate had used me for my status as a nurse, whatever status that was. He needed me to make the public think he was a much kinder person than he actually is. Having a nurse's favour was one way to do that.

Mason is quick with this call, and he comes back into the cabin with a smile on his face that doesn't quite reach his eyes.

"Hey, I just realized that tonight is movie night. I kind of snubbed Winnie, but I promised her I would watch a movie with you to make up for it." Mason is trying to evade talking about whatever the call was about and whoever was on the other end. I know it wasn't Winnie.

"Sure, your pick." I'm still riding the high of having Mason thrust into me until my vision went black, so I don't press it. Yet. Although Mason makes me feel more brave, this is a confrontation I'm not ready for. Not when I've only just accepted my feelings for him.

I slip into my leggings and hoodie again and settle back onto the couch, wrapping a thick wool blanket around my shoulders.

"One of my favourites tonight. *You've Got Mail*." Mason surveys the shelf of movies next to the fireplace, pulling out a plastic box containing a DVD. No one has upgraded the cabin to Netflix yet. I give him a quizzical expression.

"*You've Got Mail*? Really? You wouldn't rather watch like, *The Godfather* or something?"

"Nah. Those movies are overrated. Give me a rom-com any day." Mason pops the disc into the player.

"You don't strike me as a rom-com kinda guy," I say. Mason Landry is always surprising me.

"Oh yeah, big rom-com guy. I'm a sucker for Meg Ryan and Tom Hanks. There's enough sadness in the world, I don't need to watch anything that doesn't make me feel good. Love stories are heartwarming. They give me hope, even if they aren't realistic." Mason shrugs and clicks the movie on and before he sinks into the couch beside me. "But keep this to yourself, Honeybee. My brothers would have a heyday with it."

I smile for a second as I rest my head on his shoulder. The thought of being the one person in the world who knows about Mason Landry's love for romance is comforting. But I know that there's more to him that I have yet to uncover.

I don't quite relax into him. There is still something unspoken between us nagging at me from the back of my mind. But I try to enjoy the movie with the knowledge that our relationship is much more comfortable than it was before, whatever it may be.

"Don't you think it's odd," I say, part way through the movie, "that people like this movie so much, but it's basically about two people cheating on their partners?" Mason cocks his head to the side, considering what I've just said.

"I wouldn't say they're cheating. They build a friendship, but not much more than that. Not right away," he argues.

"Hm." I wonder what Mason's definition of loyalty is. Of honesty. I wonder if we have different definitions.

"It's kind of nice. They both part with their previous relationships on good terms. It shows that we can always choose to change the path of our lives. That you can leave something behind if it isn't serving you anymore, and it doesn't have to be a big fight." I don't have to ask what Mason is implying about my life choices.

"I agree. I left my past life behind me when I came here." I left a lot of things behind when I left the city, not just my life as a reality star, but all my friends and family, too.

"Did you though? Because it seems like someone didn't quite get the message." Mason gives me a knowing stare.

"I know. I need to tell Nate to leave me alone. No excuses, just the truth. It's just not that easy for me." I look down at my hands, folded in my lap.

"It seems straightforward to me."

"You're a man. It's easier to say what needs to be said as a man. You don't have to think twice about it."

"That's not quite true." Mason's denial of my statement leaves me wondering if there's more that is going unsaid between us than I realize.

"I was always taught that as a woman, I'm not supposed to ruffle any feathers. I watched my mom always being the one to smooth things over when someone was unhappy or when an awkward situation arose and someone was uncomfortable. I guess I've taken that responsibility on, too."

"That seems exhausting," Mason says.

"It is. It is exhausting trying to make everyone around you happy all the time."

"And impossible. Not without giving up on your own wants and needs, and that seems like a pretty miserable life to me."

"Isn't that what you do? Ignore your own wants and needs for the clinic?" My comment strikes a nerve with Mason as it lands and I see him flinch.

"That's not the same, Ally. I don't have a choice. I'm not ignoring anything. I'm doing what I have to do. You don't know what kind of horrible things can happen if I'm not invested." Mason's gaze drops to his lap as a shadow envelops his face. What kind of trauma does Mason have hidden away?

"Like what, Mason?" I ask, dipping my head to meet his eyes.

"It's nothing, Honeybee. Nothing you need to concern your-self with. It's my mess and I am the only one that has to deal with the consequences now." I don't want to overstep by asking for any more details. Mason isn't a sharer and pushing more would also push my luck with him.

I settle back into the couch beside him, and we turn back to the movie that's been on in the background.

Outside the cabin, the wind and rain have whipped up into a frenzy. Inside, Joe Fox is about to meet Kathleen Kelly in the park and reveal his true identity. Kathleen is quick to forgive Joe. I just hope I can forgive Mason for whatever he's still keeping from me.

CHAPTER 20
MASON

I leave Ally sleeping at the cabin this morning. She hardly moves when I get up and place a gentle peck on her forehead. She somehow looks beautiful, even with her messy bun half falling out and her mouth hanging open. I feel a squeezing in my chest as I look at her, this stunning woman who has swept into my life and turned it upside down in the best way possible.

It takes all my effort to get out of bed and leave her this morning, but I have important business to attend to if the surprise that I have planned for her for the Harvest Festival is going to go off without a hitch. It has to go off without a hitch.

Ally has devoted all of her free time to this fundraiser, to the clinic, to me. If there's anything I can do for her in return, it's giving her a show at the Lumberjack Games.

I can hear the muffled shouts and banter between my brothers all the way out in the hallway of my apartment as I make my way up to the top floor of the old three-storey walk-up and pull out my keys to unlock the door. The walls of this building have always been thin, but they seem like paper with my two brothers staying here. I have to remember to apologize to the neighbours once Jett leaves for the ski season. He's been staying in the apartment since he's been on his off-season through the summer, and Hudson has made himself right at home in my room since I'm rarely here anymore. God only knows what these two idiots get up to while I'm at work all day.

They're wrapped up in a very serious video game; a back country skiing game that Jett is dominating. Jett dominates at all things ski-related, including video games. It's in his blood, both on the slopes and not.

I'm greeted at the door by a wet snout and a wagging tail.

"Hey, Rubs." I reach down and pat Ruby, Hudson's rust-coloured golden retriever, as she leans into my legs. She's a sweet girl, and the only girl that Hudson will entrust his heart to at this point. "Don't you have a job, Hudson?" I quip, looking over at them both sitting on the couch, *my couch,* and noting how Jett's presence does nothing but disrupt our routines.

Hudson is driven and a hard worker. He spends his days as a project manager at a local construction company while working on-call at the fire hall. His theory is that knowing how to build homes helps him understand how they'll burn. It's sound enough logic. Hudson applies himself to both of his jobs with a profound dedication that I admire. We both inherited our work ethic from Dad. But whenever Jett comes around, he pulls my younger brother into his bullshit, and they do nothing but slack off. Which only adds to the list of reasons my brother Jett annoys the living shit out of me. At twenty-nine, you'd think he'd have grown the hell up a little by now.

"Not much happening around town today, with the festival and all. I gave the boys the day off from working on our job site so they could go. You're welcome, by the way." Hudson doesn't look up, and I can see him chewing on his bottom lip, his tell when he's focusing on something. I know that what he's just told me is significant. He's been managing the build of a new hotel going in just outside of town, and it's not a small project.

The conversation distracts him enough that I watch as Jett's skier crosses the finish line and Hudson leans back on the couch and groans. Jett jumps up off the couch, whooping and shouting. Sore winner.

"Don't you get sick of skiing all the time? It's not enough to spend all day every day in the winter competing. You've got to play this dumb game in your off-season, too?"

"Pow is life, brother." Jett flashes me a grin as he throws up a *hang loose* sign. I roll my eyes so hard they just about fall right out of my face. Ruby jumps up on the couch and nuzzles her face into his hand, demanding that he pet her. At least someone gets along with Jett. Then again, Ruby would get along with a serial killer if they'll pet her.

"Whatever. You're *both* coming to the festival later, right?" I point a finger at Jett. Hudson will be there, there's no doubt about that, but Jett better at least make an appearance, or there will be hell to pay. The entire purpose of the event is to support the clinic. Our dad's clinic. They never cared much about it, though. Not the way I do.

"Absolutely, my man," Jett exclaims. "I want to be there when Hudson has to bring the fire truck around and rescue you from the top of the pole like a scared little kitty cat."

I ignore the comment even as Jett wanders over to where I'm standing in the kitchen and lands a hard smack right in the middle of my back.

"You're doing the speed climb, eh?" Hudson asks with a skeptical tone. "It's been years, dude. You sure you can make it?"

"Yeah, it's for a good cause. And I want to see Ally's face when she sees what I've been planning this whole time." Hudson is right, though, it has been years since I've done a speed climb. Over a decade, to be exact. I was the best in town as a teen, winning all the local competitions, even going to a few provincial championships. My lean build was not short on muscle, which made it easier for me to haul myself up the ninety-foot poles. I've practiced a couple of times, and it didn't take long for me to find my rhythm again.

Not to mention the fact that I've hand-selected my competition, a few of the loggers in town that have never competed but agreed to do it for the cause.

I came back to the apartment to get all my gear, which I've kept shoved away in my storage locker, and to have some peace so I can get in the right mindset to compete. Neither of which is a simple task with these two ding dongs in my space.

"Things are getting pretty serious between you two." Hudson says. It's an innocent observation. Ally and I haven't discussed the new terms of our relationship, but serious is not a word that I would use to describe it—yet. I'm still only her fake boyfriend. If we're going to put 'actual' boyfriend on the table, well, I don't know where she would even fit into my life. I want her in it, and that's enough for now.

I shrug, all of my uncertain emotions wrapped up in one gesture. "Yeah, I guess so."

"You sure you have enough room on your plate for a relationship?" That's the million-dollar question right there. Hudson has genuine concern on his face. His intentions are always so good. So I refrain from getting snarky in defence. I don't have an answer for him.

"I don't. That's the problem. But neither does she, so we'll figure it out."

"It doesn't matter," Jett pipes up. *Here we go.* "Mason will shit the bed with Ally, just like all the other girls he's dumped because he's married to that clinic." I grind my teeth together, the muscle in my jaw flinches. This isn't helping with the calm and focused mindset that I need to be in for the race. Jett opens the fridge behind me and grabs a beer. It's not even ten in the morning. *Work hard, play hard* is Jett's motto. Although I'm not sure he ever works at all. He pops the lid off, not registering the bite in his previous comment. It's just his usual pot-stirring crap.

"Just let me know when it happens so I can be there for Ally to help her pick up the pieces," he says, leaning in next to my face with a shit-eating grin before taking an exaggerated sip of his beer next to my ear. My jaw clenches. Jett is trying to get under my skin, but the thought of him going after Ally makes me want to turn around and scream. Only one word comes to mind—

Mine.

"Fuck off, Jett." I won't let him rile me today. I stuff my rage down before I give myself the opportunity to react because I'm positive if I did, I would punch Jett right in the throat. And I need my hand in one piece for the speed climb.

I walk out of the kitchen and grab the keys to my storage locker from the hook by the door. I can tell by how Jett whines *'what?'* behind me that Hudson is staring daggers into him.

CHAPTER 21
ALLY

I WAKE up to an empty bed and my heart drops for a second before I roll over and find a hand scrawled note on the pillow next to mine.

On a top-secret mission...see you at the festival. xo.

I smile to myself, thinking about Mason and his muscular hands writing out an x and an o. Mason Landry is a softie, much to my surprise, and I'm not complaining.

My phone vibrates on the nightstand, and when I pick it up to see who's calling, I just about leap out of bed with excitement when I see Spencer's name on the screen.

"Look who finally returned my calls," I say, my tone more light-hearted than my words. I always understand when Spencer is too busy to talk, and there are never any hard feelings toward my best friend.

"Not my fault you call me at outrageous times. I couldn't *not* call you back after that text you sent. I need to know what the fuck is going on with *your boss*." She just about shouts into the phone.

"Jesus, Spence, I'm still waking up over here." I rub my eyes, my vision clearing.

"Well holy shit, Ally. Last time we talked, you were adamant that Mason was off limits."

"He was off limits. I mean, he's still off-limits. He's still my boss. And my fake boyfriend? I don't know what we are."

"How do *you* feel about it?" I consider her question. I don't know how I feel about Mason, but something that feels like optimism blooms in my chest. Which is more than I could say three weeks ago when we met at Thistle + Thorne. I want to see where it goes, if only because I have a dangerous amount of curiosity. From what I've seen so far, I know we could be great together. If our sexual chemistry is any indication, we could be downright explosive. My breath catches as my heart flips over in my chest just thinking about the last twenty-four hours with Mason.

"I feel … good." I don't have a better word to explain how I feel yet. Good. Grounded. Solid.

"Tell me something I don't know. You just got railed by Dr. Big Dick. Of course you feel *good*." Spencer cackles on the other end of the line, and I can't help but laugh with her. I'd be content getting railed by Mason for the rest of my life. That's a terrifying thought. There's no way Mason has even entertained the idea of an actual relationship, let alone allowed his mind to go down the path of *forever*.

"I don't know. Mason has surprised me. He isn't who I thought he was. He's sensitive, and kind—"

"—and has a massive dong," Spencer cuts in. "Speaking of, is this something that runs in the family?"

"Get your head out of the gutter, you perv." I giggle. "And how could I know that? Come to Heartwood, and I'll introduce you."

"Deal. Listen, I gotta run here. Hot date with some Dutch guy, I'll tell you later." I'm not surprised that Spencer has found herself a guy in Amsterdam already. People love Spencer wherever she goes.

"Be safe, Spence." I wish her well on her date—which, let's be honest, is more of a hook-up—and click off my phone. My heart dances in my chest thinking about today, about the Harvest Festival, about talking to Spencer, and about Mason. Giddy. I feel giddy. I stare up at the ceiling and smile to myself. Today is going to be a great day.

"WHATEVER HAPPENED to that guy from the bar?" Poppy asks, arranging potted plants on little stands around her booth. It's still early, but I wanted to get down to the town square as soon as possible to make sure that it looks perfect for the Harvest Festival.

I take a long sip from the coffee Poppy poured me from the large metal carafe at her coffee stand, trying to avoid the question for as long as I can. I look around, surveying the town square, which has been completely transformed. The festival hasn't opened yet, so I take the moment to appreciate the quietness before the chaos. Poppy's booth is in amongst other vendors from the town. Next to the row of booths with Poppy's tent, I can see Grady setting up the grill to prepare it for the first few visitors getting lunch.

The signs that Mason and I painted are on display, along with scattered hay bales, pumpkins, and sunflowers. The Lumberjack Games have all been erected in the centre of the square, a smattering of logs and tools dotting the grass. That idea had been Mason's contribution, and it had been a tremendous hit. Tickets to the festival sold out in a day. I turn back to Poppy and fiddle with a potted plant that she left on the table.

"Nate. He's still hanging around," I admit. "He seems to think that if he just holds out for long enough, I'm going to reconsider and go back to the city with him."

"And are you? Considering it, I mean?" Poppy looks up at me

with raised eyebrows. She doesn't know the full history between Nate and me. I've alluded to some of it on our morning coffee dates before I go to work and while Poppy opens up the café. But I've left some details of my relationship with Nate hidden. I want a new beginning, and that can't happen if everyone already holds preconceived ideas about me. Despite Nate's best efforts, I've tried my best to keep these parts of my life separate.

"No. God, no." I shake my head and make a face like I've just tasted something awful. I have no plans to leave Heartwood now. Especially not with recent developments with Mason. Whatever we are, whatever our relationship is now, I'd be lying if I said I wasn't at least curious to see where it goes. I like the version of Mason that I've come to know over the last couple of weeks. The feeling that I get when I'm with him confirms that there are fewer feelings between Nate and me than originally suspected. I look at Nate, and my heart does nothing. In fact, I think it retreats so far inside my chest it becomes fused to my spine. Mason, though. When I look at Mason, it jumps up and down like a kid in a candy store. There's only one name for that feeling, and I don't want to say it out loud. Not until I have a better idea of where Mason stands.

"Well good, because we enjoy having you here." Poppy is referring to the town, but then she corrects herself. "I enjoy having you here."

I give her a warm smile. I enjoy being here, too. Heartwood had started as a temporary hideout, a place to get away from prying eyes and B-list celebrity gossip. The reality show turned my life into something I was not expecting. Truth be told, I wasn't expecting to feel as at home as I have in Heartwood, either. I've been able to do the job that I love, helping people and feeling valuable again. It also helps that a smoking hot doctor is fucking me every day and night and that I might be falling for him. There's no place else I would rather be than here in Heartwood.

"Ally!" I whip my head around at the sound of my name. I'm

hoping it's Mason. I haven't seen him yet and with the first few festival goers showing up, I'm getting impatient for him to arrive. But the voice that I hear is smoother, the way a snake is smooth, and my heart sinks when I turn and see Nate walking toward me instead. He always seems to show up whenever I'm talking about him. It's as if I could summon him like a demon from the underworld. I shudder at the sight of him. Of course, he's wearing a tailored suit. To a Harvest Festival. Like a stuck-up prick. I plaster on a blank expression.

"Nate." My friendly tone changes as he approaches. Poppy looks away and down at her plants as if they're about to tell her some fascinating gossip, trying to seem disinterested in my and Nate's conversation. Although I know Poppy, and her face gives her away that she's still eavesdropping.

"The place looks great." The comment comes out flat, like it's just a necessary part of the conversation. It doesn't matter how Nate would have said it; his compliments never sound genuine. I nod in thanks anyway. I put a lot of hard work into the festival and it clearly paid off if Nate is noticing. If only Mason were here to appreciate it with me. I quickly survey the festival grounds over Nate's shoulder to see if I can spot him.

"What can I do for you, Nate?" My tone is impatient.

"I've got two plane tickets, Al. One with your name on it." He holds them up.

I bristle at the nickname. I hate when he calls me that. It makes me sound like a Muppet. I huff a long sigh and glance around me. Mason isn't here yet. Why isn't Mason here yet? The festival is about to start and I could use my fake boyfriend, or, real boyfriend? I'm not sure, but I need him right about now.

"Well, you wasted your money on that one."

"Money is no object in this case, Al." He flashes me a sleazy grin and the sight of it makes me nauseated. "I've let you have your fun and play your little game, but once you're done with this little charity case, you need to make your decision."

My stomach flip-flops. I need to give him a definitive answer, one that he may not even accept.

"Once the fundraiser is over." It's only just starting, and the schedule has it running into the early evening. I can buy myself some time, if not to come up with a better plan, but to delay the inevitable confrontation that's making my hands clam up. Where is Mason? What good is a fake boyfriend anyway if you can't sic him on your ex?

"End of the day today. Oh, and by the way, Lucia is here, too. Apparently, she wants to help me with my case to bring you home. Something about a contract with the network that you are also in breach of." Oh God. I had forgotten that the network also wouldn't let me go without a fight. I've done my research, though, which is what Nate hasn't considered. He's always been one to underestimate me, and I know that the network doesn't have the hold on me he thinks they do.

"Let me enjoy the day, Nate. I'll come and find you after the festival. We can talk then." Nate shoves his hands down in his pockets, a smug look crossing his face.

"Oh, we will talk, Ally. You can be sure of that. There will be no more delaying this."

I set my coffee down and help Poppy with arranging her flowers, anything to make myself appear occupied so that Nate leaves. From the corner of my eye, I can appreciate his scowling face, swivelling on his heel and stalking off. Poppy and I make eye contact across the display table. My eyebrows raise as my eyes flick down toward the ground. I shake my head. I don't want to discuss the interaction. I'm going to push it out of my head for as long as possible and do my best to enjoy the hard work that I've put into the event.

It looks like the entire town has shown up; hoards of people file in through the archway at the entrance that I had decorated with fall flowers and pumpkins earlier, gathering around the field in the centre of the square. Hay bales are positioned all the way around in a semi-circle to provide seating for the Lumberjack Games. In the centre of the circle, logs stand upright for the speed climb, stumps are ready for the chainsaw carving, and a tree trunk as big as my car is lying horizontal for the sawing competition.

"Welcome to the first-ever Heartwood Harvest Festival!" The announcer's booming voice comes over the loudspeaker. "In about ten minutes, the Lumberjack Games will begin, so get your snacks and settle in for a jaw-dropping, heart-pounding, nail-biting show!"

Mason is still nowhere to be found, and I feel the blood rush to my cheeks, heating my face. I put in all of this hard work, and so has he, and the festival is starting without him. I look around the town square one last time before wandering over to the food tent to greet the festival guests as they wait for Grady to pile burgers and hot dogs on their plates.

"Hey, Grady, the burgers look delish." Grady looks up from behind the grill as he places a patty on a woman's plate. "You haven't seen Mason yet, have you?"

Grady shakes his head no, but doesn't take his eyes off the patties he's flipping. He's turned into a burger grilling machine. The smell of the meat cooking is making my mouth water.

My smile widens as I spot Winnie approaching the tent. She's looking festive in a floppy straw hat decorated with sunflowers similar to the ones placed around the square. She looks like sunshine, and she might know Mason's whereabouts. Perhaps an urgent matter came up at the clinic, though I'm doubtful, considering the whole town seems to be here.

"Careful, Winnie! Poppy might try to sell you at her booth wearing that hat!" Winnie throws her arms around me.

"This is amazing, Ally!" Winnie squeals. "I can't believe you did all of this for the clinic. This is so special, thank you." She squeezes my arms as she pulls out of our hug. Her eyes are watery, glimmering with genuine gratitude.

"My pleasure, Winnie. It's my clinic too now, thanks to you." I glance over Winnie's shoulder. "I just wish Mason was here. Have you seen him yet?"

"I'm sure he'll turn up, love. He wouldn't miss this for the world." Behind Winnie, I can hear the crowd in the square cheer as the Lumberjack Games begin.

"Let's hear it for our first competitors of the day for the ninety-foot speed climb ..." the announcer shouts, and the crowd erupts in applause. I wander over to where people are taking their seats and find an empty spot on one of the hay bales at the very back of the semi-circle. People around me are murmuring, buzzing with anticipation.

The announcer lists off the names of the people competing, none of whom I recognize, but they all seem to be locals in the town based on the shouts and hollers from people in the crowd. I'm not surprised that I don't know many of them; most of the loggers are out of town for weeks on end. I turn around on my hay bale, craning my neck to scan the crowd for Mason as the announcer gets ready to announce the last name on the roster.

"And last ... but certainly not least ... your very own ... Doctor Mason Landry!"

What the hell? I whirl around to where the competitors are all lined up to take their places, only to see Mason striding out of the crowd and taking his place by one of the tall vertical logs. My mouth flops open in disbelief. Mason. Mason is competing in the Lumberjack Games. I have to say it multiple times to get myself to believe it. Mason is competing in the speed climb. Nope. This is still surreal. Mason, who spends all day and all night at the clinic, is going to shimmy his way up a ninety-foot pole, strapped on by a thin harness.

My heart thuds in my throat. What the hell is he thinking? He could seriously injure himself. Has he ever even practiced or done this before in his life?

There's still time before the air horn blows, and I weigh the merit of running up there and stopping him. But the crowd whoops and hollers louder than ever. Mason is beloved here, and I'm starting to see why. He cares so deeply about the town, and now I can see that he cares about me, too. He's been planning this surprise for the last two weeks. How he's kept it from me, I don't know. But Mason keeps other things under lock and key, so I can't be shocked.

Trust. I trust Mason. Whatever he's keeping from me, be it his hidden identity as a burly lumberjack, or something worse, I trust him.

I can't help the smile that spreads across my face and I join in on the cheering, just about jumping right off my hay bale as I wave my arms. Mason has such a charming energy about him up there, as he waves to the crowd. I notice his eyes scanning the faces, and they meet mine for a moment as he winks at me. The butterflies roll around in my stomach as I watch him steady himself, concentrating on the task he has ahead of him. He pushes his sleeves up, pulls on a pair of heavy work gloves, and takes a moment to double- and triple-check the clips around his belt. The way he handles the rope in his hands is sure, confident. He's done this before.

The announcer instructs the competitors to take their positions. I hold my breath for Mason. He's a doctor, an intellectual man. I have the urge to close my eyes as the crowd holds a collective breath, waiting for the race to start. I have to force myself to watch.

The sound of an air horn goes off, signalling the start of the race, and I watch as Mason nimbly clips his harness onto the safety cable. It's not like Mason lacks muscle by any means, but he's lighter and leaner than the rest of the competitors, and it gives him a speed advantage. I realize my jaw has dropped as I watch Mason scale the log, his movements quick and precise, his muscular legs propelling him farther and farther up. He has the lead now, but another man is gaining on him.

A flush spreads from my cheeks down my neck as I watch him climb faster and faster. Higher and higher. The height alone would paralyze me. I can't help but notice the way the harness cuts in under his firm ass, accentuating the muscle that's flexing beneath his jeans. My whole body feels like an inferno watching him up there. Maybe it's the harness or the way his flannel shirt sleeves are bunched around his thick forearms. I have a feeling it's neither, but the fact that Mason has done this for me. That he has kept this surprise up his sleeve just for me.

The entire crowd is fixated on the race as Mason puts more distance between himself and the other competitors. I bookmark all the questions I have for him so I can ask him later.

A shout erupts from my body as I watch Mason reach the top, just ahead of the others. It has taken him less than half a minute to get to the top, and he whips the rope dangling from the bell at the top, signalling his victory.

"Ladies and gentlemen, your winner ... Mason Landry!"

Mason stops for a moment at the top of the log, holding onto the rope he has secured around the trunk and turning back to wave at the crowd below before he starts his descent. The joy on his face is palpable and even from a distance, I can tell Mason is looking at me. I feel my heart skip a beat. His gaze on me sends a shiver down my spine, even from this distance, warming me through to my core.

The game concludes, and all the competitors swiftly slide down the logs. People from the crowd disperse and wander over to browse at the vendor tents as the next competition is being set up.

It doesn't take long for me to find Mason. He's already beelining towards me, having marked where I sat from on top of the log. The smile he wears is contagious, and I'm beaming by the time he reaches me.

Before I can speak, Mason strides over to me and pulls me into a hug, wrapping his arms around my waist and lifting me off the ground. I let out a sound somewhere between a giggle and a shriek as I feel his powerful arms sweeping me into the air. Mason takes one second to pull away from me, only to plant a warm, wet kiss on my lips. Heat radiates off of him from the exertion of his climb, his hair sticking to his sweaty forehead. I don't care. All I care about is Mason's mouth on mine. I kiss him back, both of my hands holding the sides of his face, smiling into his mouth.

Until I feel about a hundred pairs of eyes on us and I'm pulled out of my heady trance.

"Mason, everyone is looking." I glance around at the people around us, staring. Mason lowers me to the ground, but he doesn't remove his hands from my waist.

"I don't care if people see us, Ally. Not anymore. I told you I don't want a fake relationship, and I don't want a secret one either."

"You're just on a winner's high," I say, a mischievous grin taking over my lips.

"I'm on a high, Honeybee. But it's not from winning."

I kiss him again, and I know deep down the answer to the question I've had for the last few days. We're not fake dating anymore; this is real. And the whole town of Heartwood now knows it.

As Mason places me back down on the ground, I'm literally and figuratively brought back down to earth. Nate is standing on the edges of the crowd, watching our very public display of affection. He looks so smug, standing there with his arms crossed like I'm his and he's just waiting for me to wake up from a dream. I remember the conversation that I need to have with him after the festival has wound down to a close. That's real, too. It will be easier now, sure. I'm no longer lying about my feelings for Mason, or what we are. But now that Lucia is here, I have another challenge to face.

That's a later problem. Right now, I want to celebrate— Mason's win, the festival's success, and love.

"Come with me. I have a surprise for you, too," I whisper into Mason's ear as I take him by the hand and lead him away from the crowd. I want a moment alone with him to soak all of this in before I have to face my other reality.

CHAPTER 22
MASON

I FOLLOW Ally away from the festivities. The sound of the laughter and cheering from the crowd, the whirr of chainsaws from the log carving competition, grows distant and muted. Ally only stops to pick up a wicker basket and an old blanket she had left tucked out of sight under the table at Poppy's booth.

Poppy raises her eyebrows at us as Ally ducks under the table to look for it. The whole town got to see the show we put on after I won the log climb, so I guess the cat's out of the bag now. Judging by the adorable wink Ally gives her in return, they'll spend a lot of time discussing me over their morning coffees on Ally's way to work. If there even is a work for Ally to go to. The thought of which makes my stomach churn. We're not out of the woods yet, as successful as the fundraiser has been. There's no guarantee the Ministry of Health will be impressed by the fundraiser or the prenatal program.

The town knowing about Ally and I is the least of my concerns now. Now that my feelings for Ally are real, I say let them talk about us all they want. The rumour mill won't be spinning *false* stories about us, at least. This will help our case convince Nate he's no longer welcome in town. I know he was watching when I picked Ally up and swung her around after my climb. I saw him out of the corner of my eye, lurking on the outskirts of the festivities. I'd be lying if I said I didn't linger a little longer in our kiss because of him.

Ally and I head across the field and down the block of houses toward the path leading to the river. I don't question where she is taking me. No matter where Ally goes, I will follow. To the ends of the earth. She could be leading me into the fiery pits of hell, and I wouldn't question it. Her strawberry blond ponytail bounces and sways across her shoulders. I have the sudden urge to pull on it. An image of me fucking her from behind, her firm ass in full view, flashes in my mind. It doesn't matter how sweet and lovely Ally looks right now. I want to do dirty things to her.

Ally stops as we come upon a clearing in the trees right on the river's edge. It's secluded enough we can no longer see the town square. They can no longer see us either, I note.

"Here?" I ask her. Did Ally somehow know this was the very spot I used to come fishing with my dad? That this spot already means so much to me?

"Yeah, is this okay? I found it the other day while I was on my run. I sat here for a while watching the river, and it was so peaceful." She answers my question and the one I hadn't yet spoken out loud. Ally understands me on a level I can't explain. A level that needs no words. I nod back at her, a lump forming in my throat.

This place where my dad brought me as a kid has felt empty since he died. Little by little, Ally is transforming the parts of my heart I had closed off, not wanting to feel the pain of loss and grief. First the cabin, now this. It's like these places around town that held so many memories were dry and barren, and now Ally has swept in and started planting flowers in the dirt. Sitting here with Ally now, I want to fill the places I closed my heart off to with new memories. Memories of Ally and me.

Crickets chirp in the grass in the heat of the last summer evening. The low-hanging sun is turning everything a glowing shade of gold, highlighting the edges of the trees overhead and shimmering on the river. I close my eyes to feel the warmth on my face, inhaling the scent of the pines. It won't be long until winter is in full swing. Everyone in Heartwood knows to take full advantage of the summer sun when it's here.

Ally sets the basket down and spreads the old, tattered picnic blanket on the ground. She wastes no time sitting down and pats the blanket next to her, beckoning me to join her. As I sit, she hands me a wine glass, which she had pulled out of the basket, along with a bottle of bubbly rosé. *Kind of a girly choice*, I think. But that's just Ally, feminine and sweet, and I'm done judging her. I love that she loves rosé. I love her matching pastel scrubs, the way she hums, the way she wrinkles her nose. I love that she's soft and warm and kind. The things I once found irritating about her are the very things that make Ally beautiful and uniquely *her*.

More than anything, I love sharing Heartwood with her.

"You planned this?" I ask, wrapping my arm over her shoulder and bringing the wine glass to my mouth. The clear, pink-tinged liquid is refreshing in the late summer heat. And it's damn good, too. *No wonder women love this stuff,* I think to myself, taking another long pull. *Why have I been drinking scotch for so long?*

"I figured we would have something to celebrate. Although I didn't think it would be your win at the speed climb." Ally laughs as she looks up at me from where she's sitting in the crook of my arm. "Where did you learn to do that, by the way? And why have you kept 'Lumberjack Mason' hidden from me until now?"

I shrug. Lumberjack Mason is an identity I haven't revealed to anyone for many years. It holds so many feelings from my teenage years I haven't been willing to talk about. Until now. I want to let Ally in. I want her to see all of me. The good and the bad.

"Growing up in Heartwood, it was that or take up skiing. My brothers chose to ski, although only Jett has kept at it. I chose ... lumberjacking. I used to chop all the wood for our house growing up. I was the only one around to do it if Dad was busy at the clinic, and if I didn't, my brothers and I would freeze at night. But also because it allowed me to release a lot of the pent-up angst and rage I felt as a teenager. I was always angry. About my mom's death, my father never being around, and the responsibility I took on looking after my brothers. All of it. When the first Lumberjack Games came to town, the summer I was about to go into grade twelve, I thought it was the coolest thing I had ever seen. So, I started practicing. I hauled some old logs out into the yard and started chopping them into somewhat recognizable carvings. I started climbing, and I was hooked. It was a distraction from all the bullshit my dad was putting us through, if anything. It gave me an outlet. Something that was all mine."

Ally is still gazing up at me with awe and wonder in her eyes, like she's meeting me for the first time. In some ways, she is meeting *me* for the first time. This is the most I have opened up to anyone in my adult life. It's a look I could get used to, and I wonder what else I can surprise her with to recreate the moment.

I turn my eyes off towards the mountains at what looks like the end of the river, where it veers off in a sudden turn and disappears into the surrounding trees. There is one secret I've kept from Ally that could destroy her. If the fundraiser isn't enough to keep the clinic open and funded, I'll have to break it to her that her hard work was for nothing. Worse, that she no longer has a job and I've been keeping this from her all this time. There will be nothing left keeping her here in Heartwood, not even me, once I drop that on her.

Much to my relief, Simone hung back at the festival and made herself scarce, like I asked. I spotted her once, lingering on the edge of the crowd watching the games, and was relieved to see she changed out of that dreadful pantsuit. Everyone in Heartwood would have spotted her from a mile away and known there was something out of the ordinary going on.

"I personally love Lumberjack Mason, and his butt looked

phenomenal in that harness, I might add." Ally smirks at me, that damned sparkle in her eye.

I set down my wine glass and shift on the blanket so I'm facing Ally. I dip my head and graze my lips up her neck until they meet the soft pink shell of her ear.

"Just you wait until you see me in nothing *but* the harness." I breathe. Ally shivers, the warmth of my breath causing goose-bumps to form on her arms despite the late afternoon heat.

I lay her down on the blanket and shift myself onto my forearm so I'm leaning over her, staring into her big turquoise eyes. They draw me in like so many times before, but here, reflecting the colour of the icy blue river, I just about drown. She searches my face, waiting for me to say the words sitting right on the tip of my tongue.

I love Ally. I'm in love with Ally. I know that now. There's still something inside me that isn't allowing the words to come out. I will forever belong to her once I do. Ally deserves more of me than I'm able to give. She deserves all of me, not a half-assed love. I can't give her all of me yet, not when the clinic is still in peril.

If Ally can figure out a way to trust me for now, I will find a way to let her in. Once the clinic is more settled and we're on the other side of this mess with Simone and the Ministry of Health. It just can't happen before I've secured my father's legacy.

"It means the world to me that you did all of this, Ally. The whole festival, it couldn't have turned out any better. You are remarkable," I say, leaning my forehead on hers.

"Aren't you glad you kept me around?" Ally replies, the corner of her mouth lifting into a cheeky grin.

"More than you know, Honeybee." I just hope this fundraiser allows me to keep her around for good. I press my lips against hers again, and she opens them, her tongue finding mine. I could kiss this woman forever. She breaks my trance, leaning back to look at me.

"I never met your father, but I've heard a lot, and knowing you

... He would be so proud of you, Mason." The words make the lump in my throat impossible to swallow, and there's a sharp stinging behind my eyes. "You work so hard, you care so much about others. All I want is for you to extend some kindness to yourself sometimes."

Ally is right. I see it now. Unfortunately, in my line of work, having a life is easier said than done. I'm more willing to try than I was a month ago, and that's saying something.

My lips find hers again. I can't say how I'm feeling, but at the very least, I can try to show Ally how much she means to me. Ally wraps her hand around the back of my head, twining her fingers through my hair and pulling me deeper into our kiss. I trail my mouth across her cheek and nip at her earlobe, appreciating the soft moan that escapes Ally's lips. That moan spurs me on, and I kiss her neck more hungrily in response, running my hand up and underneath the T-shirt sticking to her body from the day's sweat. Ally still smells so damn good, and I inhale her coconut scent as she throws her head back to give me more access to her neck.

I find her pebbled nipple under her bra and roll it between my fingers. It's a move that, by now, I know Ally likes. Ally's hips shift and squirm on the old picnic blanket, and her reaction to it makes me rock hard in an instant. I have the urge to be far from the festival, away from anyone who might see us, throwing Ally back onto her bed to admire her body without the nuisance of clothing. The trees around us offer some privacy, and I'm tempted to do all the things I'm craving to Ally right here, right now. I'm not above a little public indecency. Not when it comes to Ally.

"Mason! Thank God I've found you." The sound of Winnie's voice just about makes me jump out of my skin. I'm expecting her to have a smug grin on her face, the *I told you so* look of someone who has been begging me to get with Ally ever since she moved here. But her face is telling a different story. There's a look of panic shadowing her face that creates a heavy pit in my gut. It's Winnie's bad news face.

"Winnie, what—" I can't even get the words out before she cuts me off mid-sentence.

"I've tried paging you multiple times. There's an emergency back at the fair, the chainsaw carving ..." Winnie's words are clipped, and her breath is ragged, no doubt from running around the festival grounds trying to find me. And here I am, once again distracted by a woman, shirking my responsibilities to the town.

I fumble and jump up off the picnic blanket, patting around my jeans, feeling for my pager and finding only empty pockets. It must have fallen during the log climb. There's no time to worry about it now. My heart races and bile burns the back of my throat as the memory of the last time this happened comes crashing back. Last time, I had neglected my responsibility to the clinic for a date, and someone had died. Not just anyone, not that any death means less. But having a child die is a different trauma. No, this can't be happening again. I won't let this happen again.

I attempt to regain my composure and let out a deep breath, counting backward from five in my head. It's a trick I learned during medical school to compartmentalize my fear, let the adrenaline be helpful rather than a hindrance, and regain my focus. But my breath shakes as I force out another exhale.

"Where am I needed, Winnie?"

"The clinic," Winnie shouts over her shoulder. She's already making a beeline back toward the town square. I move so I can catch up with her stride.

Ally rises to her feet, about to follow Winnie and me.

"Tell me how I can help." Ally is close to my heel. I whirl back around, holding out my hand to stop her, and Ally just about crashes into me. I grip her by the shoulders and hold her back, away from me. Having her any closer would threaten all of my logic.

"Please stay here. Enjoy the end of the festival." This is something I need to handle myself. I've failed the clinic and the town one too many times. I will not have a repeat of the last catastrophe, and this time it's on me to take care of it. The clinic, Heartwood, is my responsibility, and I need to prove once and for all I can take care of it. My father never would have let anything come in the way of his duty to protect and serve his town. Sometimes to his own detriment, sometimes to the detriment of his family. But that's the job.

Ally has been a distraction, and the erection I'm still trying to get rid of is evidence of that. I need to have all of my wits about me right now, so Ally needs to be far away from me.

"Please let me help, Mason. You can't do everything on your own. I thought you had realized by now." Ally is pleading, but all I hear is time ticking by while someone might bleed out. A chainsaw accident. There won't be much time.

"I said *no*, Ally." My voice sounds like the version of me from three weeks ago, the version of me I'm no longer proud of. *I call the shots.* "I need to do this myself. You wouldn't understand, but it needs to be me. No distractions." I break inside at the words tumbling out of my mouth, at the hurt flashing across Ally's face. She wants to be valued, to be seen for her intelligence and skills. I do value her. Ally doesn't realize how integral she is to the clinic. To me. But this isn't the time. I know that drawing this line between us may be the end of whatever we had. It doesn't matter, not anymore.

This is a sign I need to re-prioritize. This is confirmation I don't have room in my life for anything but service to the town. People get hurt unless I'm all in.

I don't turn back to look at Ally, knowing her expression is going to break me even more. I was going to tell her I loved her. That isn't an insignificant thing. It isn't something I want to walk away from, but I have to. Other people's safety depends on me, undistracted by trivial things like a relationship with a woman. Even though deep down, I also know this is not just any relationship, and Ally is not just any woman.

CHAPTER 23
ALLY

I STAND BY THE RIVERSIDE, my mind in a haze, transfixed by the sight of Mason's retreating figure. A mix of confusion and sadness swirls within me as I watch Mason fade into the distance. Mason has turned down my offer to help and let me in yet again. A part of me wants to scream at him for being so stubborn as he walks away. I want to shout from where I stand on our picnic blanket that he'll drive himself into the ground the more he refuses any help. Sure, he gave me some insight as to what made him this way yesterday, the expectations he has created in his mind around how his father would run the clinic if he were still alive. The pressure he has placed on himself sounds crushing and exhausting.

Still, something isn't adding up. I'm not so sure the pressure he feels from running his dad's clinic is the sole culprit. The nightmares, the subtle hinting about people getting hurt. There's more to the story he is refusing to acknowledge. And then there are the secretive phone calls. Whether it's all connected, I can't say. But there's more to the story here that Mason is willing to divulge, and I can't put my finger on it.

The longer I stand here, my bewilderment at Mason's sudden departure morphs into anger. My blood pressure rises in my veins until my heartbeat is thumping in my ears. Mason is being child-ish. But something else within me *sags*, like sails after the wind has died down, leaving me directionless. My heart fell when Mason dismissed me, and an expanse between us opened up into a cavernous void that may never come close to closing again.

Mason not only rebuffed my offer to help, but I also got the sense he closed a door on whatever part of himself had been soft-ening towards me. The part of him that had stared into my eyes just moments before on the grass, ready to submit to the feelings growing within him. His eyes had shown it the moment before he walked away. The Mason Landry, who had just been holding me, kissing me with need and urgency, was no longer there.

I bend down to scoop up the picnic basket and gather the blanket, slinging it over my arm. Pieces of grass cling to its worn threads, but I don't stop to shake it out. This place will now forever bear the memory of Mason and me and the moment I swore he was going to tell me he loved me. His lips had parted, so close to forming the words I wanted to hear. The words I have been screaming in my heart, whether or not I was ready to admit them. The words that would forever alter the course of our rela-tionship.

Mason has demons hidden in the back of the closet that aren't going away overnight. I may never have another opportunity to hear those words again. And worse, I doubt they will ever mean the same thing coming from anyone else.

I want to blame Winnie for interrupting, but that would be misplaced. Mason could have responded in any manner of different ways. But saying I would be a distraction when all I ever tried to be is helpful?

At least now I know what real longing feels like. The feelings I have for Mason blossomed into something I've never felt before, confirmation that Nate will never be the one to give me what I need. Even at the height of our relationship's success, I never expe-rienced the warmth and undeniable pull towards Nate the way I do with Mason. The network had carefully curated our relationship to the point where we had been duped into thinking what we had was love. It was a staged reality to please other people, not me. Not even Nate. My feelings for Mason are messy, but they're real.

I have to face Nate now. It's time. Releasing a pronounced sigh, I give myself a moment to fold up the hurt Mason had caused, and carefully place it on the shelf at the top of my mind. I will pull it out later, unfold it and examine it from all angles, process what just happened when I have the time. Today, though, I know what I need to do. I walk back towards the festival grounds, my steps even and sure, a newfound sense of purpose and determination within me. However bittersweet it may be.

The crowd is dispersing now, heading back to their homes as the Lumberjack Games wrap up. A few contestants walk away with their trophies. There was no monetary prize, of course, but none of them had cared. The loggers had been more than willing to take part in the cause to help Mason. He doesn't allow himself to see how willing people are to help, how much they appreciate him.

A brief pain tugs in my gut and I stuff it down before it overtakes me, dragging me under the surface. I'm blinking back the tears that form on my lashes as I see a woman approaching me from across the field. She's walking with purposeful strides, standing out against the rest of the crowd who are leisurely wandering home. As she draws nearer, I recognize her as the woman from the clinic, the woman who came to speak with Mason. The woman who prompted all the secrecy from him, too. I can't place her name.

"Hi, I saw you earlier talking to Dr. Landry." She cuts to the chase. "I wanted to congratulate him on the success of the Harvest Festival, but I can't find him."

I stare back at the woman and blink, trying to make sense of who she is and what her connection is to Mason. The woman registers the confusion on my face and extends her hand.

"I'm so sorry. How rude. Simone Mitchell. We met the other day at the clinic." *Simone Mitchell.* At once my brain makes a million connections. Simone from the clinic. Simone who lit up Mason's phone screen. The call he had refused to take in front of me. Was it just the one, or had all the other secretive calls been from Simone as well?

"Dr. Landry should be proud of this event. It'll be tough to convince the ministry to extend their funding for the clinic, but this fundraiser may show them how important it is to the town."

"I'm sorry, extend funding?" I stammer, struggling to get the words past the lump forming in the back of my throat. If this is what Mason has been keeping from me, it's sounding so much worse than I expected. A cheater I can deal with, kick them to the curb and forget about them. But if Mason has been using me for his own gain, to keep the clinic open, knowing how deep the wound is ... My head spins.

"Again, I apologize. I assumed Mason informed you when he hired you. Isn't that why he hired you?" My mind is reeling. How long had he known about this? Mason hadn't hired me. He hadn't even wanted me here. No wonder. He was about to lose the clinic. When had he decided I was *useful* to him? My eyes sting, threatening more tears. Winnie must have hired me as a last-ditch effort to save it, and here they both were, using me to their own ends. Simone continues when she realizes I'm not going to say anything. Words are useless.

"The government is trying to restructure healthcare delivery, which means amalgamating services in rural communities and removing services that are no longer keeping up with growing demands. Funds will be funnelled into larger, central health centres."

Realization dawns on me. Mason has been so standoffish towards me, but the more the phone calls from this Simone poured in, the more eager he was to pretend to be my boyfriend, to help me, to get close to me. I have to consider that the connection we had was all part of his plan to keep me around. My heart thuds in my ears, making them ring and the edges of my vision blur.

The sting of betrayal replaces the disappointment from before, and it takes over me, morphing into a burning rage. I realize I still haven't answered Simone. By the look on the woman's face, she's understood the weight of her words, the shock she inflicted on me. Simone's expression softens from determination into one of ... pity. She places a hand on my shoulder and it makes me recoil.

"Just so you know, what you did for the clinic today gives it a chance. It's a slim chance, mind you. The Ministry of Health is tough to convince, especially with funding issues. The prenatal program is just what they want to see as innovative approaches to health promotion."

"At least this wasn't for nothing," I mutter, stalking away from Simone. I know it's not her fault, but I won't stand here and continue to listen to how much of a difference I *could* have made. Not when the person standing in the way of lasting change for the clinic was Mason.

The clinic has a *slim* chance. How much longer would I even have a job in Heartwood? If the clinic goes under, there's nothing left for me here.

As I turn to leave, my gaze catches on a familiar smarmy smile that makes me want to rage even harder. In the wake of my conversation with Simone, I had forgotten all about who I had intended to speak with. All the hurt and anger is simmering just below the surface, and right now, Nate seems like the perfect target for me to let off some of the pressure before I explode.

"Do you want to get your doctor-boyfriend before you talk to me? Or have you finally grown up enough to have a conversation?" Nate smirks and I want to punch it right off his goddamned face. Enough is enough. I'm so sick and tired of being used by everyone around me. Mason was different, or so I thought. He had made me feel like I was important, like I offered something that mattered. And I did. I *do*. Simone said so herself. But rather than including me in the conversation, in seeing me as a partner, he saw me for the doormat I am. Mason took advantage of me like everyone else in my life.

"You need to get out of my face, Nate, and go home." I go to push past him and keep walking but he follows. He's either not getting the message because he's stupid or he doesn't care. I would put money on the latter. Nate has always had ulterior motives. He takes and takes, always the boundary pusher.

"Not until you face the music and realize this is not where you belong, Ally." I whipped around to face him.

"Since you have me all figured out, where do you think I belong, Nate?" I ask the question I already had the answer to this morning, but now I'm not so sure. This morning I was convinced that where I belong is Heartwood, working at the clinic alongside Mason. How did all of that change within such a short time?

Nate towers over me, which used to make my insides flutter, but now all I feel is his intimidating presence, and I wish I could meet his eye level when I dress him down. At this moment, I hate myself for my short stature, the way it makes me seem like a cartoon character, stomping my little feet and shaking my fists.

"With me. Back in the city. Playing the power couple from *Stolen Love*. You're the woman everyone envies for being with me." The universe revolves around Nate Winslow. He reaches into the breast pocket of his suit jacket and pulls out two plane tickets, waving them around. "Your choice, Ally." Is it, though? It doesn't seem like it.

"He's right, Ally." Lucia strides up behind him. *Great.* As if confronting one self-absorbed narcissist isn't hard enough, Lucia is likely going to wield my contract as a threat. Maybe Nate should hook up with Lucia. They're two peas in a disgusting, rotten pod. "You and Nate are something special, and the world wants more of it."

"I don't care what the world wants, Lucia. I've fulfilled my obligation to you, to the show." Lucia doesn't have a leg to stand on where my contract is concerned. I looked into it in the weeks I spent planning my getaway. The contract only stipulated my obligation to complete the filming of the show. Anything beyond those ten episodes was just a perk for the network. I had agreed to the televised engagement party because I thought I was going to marry Nate. I got swept up in the hype, the attention we were getting from the audience.

"You could have so much more, Ally. Do you see what you could be? Instead of working in some rinky-dink clinic in nowheresville?" Lucia's sleek, dark ponytail swishes from side to side as she gestures around her.

That's the comment. That's what sets me off. The spark that lights the fuse. To hell with their opinion of me. I love Heartwood, and the people here.

"You may think Heartwood is a 'rinky-dink' town, Lucia. These people treat me with kindness and welcome me with open arms." *Well, except one person,* I think, and a stabbing pain shoots across my chest. Heartache. That person is the reason I have to leave the town I now consider my home. "Which is far more than I can say about you two. All you care about is your bottom line, Lucia. It's all about how much money you can make for the network by exploiting people who will follow along with your schemes." People like me. I turn toward Nate and my eyes feel like they're glowing red.

"And Nate, you're no better, using everyone in your path to get ahead. You never would have paid me any attention if you didn't think I could save your injured reputation, which you deserve, by the way. It's about time people see you for who you are. Leave. Me. Alone." I don't give either of them the chance to rebuke my arguments before I snatch the plane tickets out of Nate's hand. The date on them is for today. I take the one with my name on it and tear it in two.

Shoving his ticket into his chest, I push past Nate and head back toward the cabin to pack my things. I need to leave Heartwood on my own terms before getting laid off makes the decision for me. Before Mason has to break the news to me that my job no longer exists because the clinic has closed for good. But there is no way I'm leaving with Nate. I don't look back as I walk away. I don't give two shits about Nate or Lucia.

I don't give two shits about anyone.

CHAPTER 24
MASON

THE RHYTHMIC BEAT of the helicopter blade pounds in my ears. Wind kicks up dirt and dust from the field behind the clinic, flattening the long shimmering grass in a circle around me. The sun has set on the field, darkness enveloping the clinic now. I look up and see the first smattering of stars in the sky. The pilot of the helicopter looks down at me as the machine hovers in the air. We give each other a curt nod, a mutual appreciation for each other's efforts. The first response is always a team effort, and it's apparent to all here today that Allan Green could have had a different outcome had we not all responded with machine-like efficiency. It's a grim reminder of the call that I am here to serve. People's lives depend on it.

It was a gruesome call, though chainsaw incidents are never a walk in the park. Everyone in Heartwood is aware of the potential dangers of the trade. But for something like this to happen at the fundraiser, in front of a crowd of onlookers, on a day that should bring hope to the clinic and the community, makes something inside me feel heavy.

I never would have wished for something like this to happen, but a strange feeling of relief washes over me. Simone saw it all.

Unless she's an unfeeling cyborg, which is entirely possible, she can't deny that my presence today made all the difference for Allan. Had he been forced to make the hour-long drive to the nearest hospital, the outcome could have been unimaginable.

I shudder, shoving the image to the back of my mind. There are more than a few memories haunting me from back there. This will likely be one of them. I've become adept at keeping things neatly tucked away in tidy little boxes. Until today.

I tried every strategy in the book to lock away the look on Ally's face when I left her by the river. Breathing techniques, counting backward, visualizing putting it to the far reaches of my mind. That look is burned on the inside of my eyelids, and it makes them sting. I told her I didn't need her help, didn't want it. And worse, that she would be a *distraction.*

Winnie is waiting for me by the back door of the clinic, wringing her hands together and clearly holding in a breath.

"He'll be okay, Winnie." She's known Allan for decades, as have many people in town. That's one of the downfalls of working in a rural community. Everyone knows everyone, and when tragedy hits one person, it hits the whole town. "His hand may not be, but he'll live. And he'll adapt."

"Poor man." She shakes her head, suddenly looking worn and tired. "He'll never make a living the same way again." I put my arm on Winnie's shoulder as we regard the helicopter until it's out of sight, heading down the valley towards Calgary.

"If I know the people of Heartwood, he'll be taken care of. He won't be on his own." I lightly turn to Winnie and guide her back into the clinic. "Go home and get some rest, Winnie."

"What about you, Mason? Go on home to Ally."

I shake my head. I have a lot of charting to take care of, and it will take me a while with my mind elsewhere. I also have a feeling that I am the last person that Ally would want to see right now.

Winnie turns to face me in the dimly lit hallway of the clinic.

"Are you okay?" Winnie has always cared about me like her

own son, but she skirts around questions like these, knowing how uncomfortable I am talking about them.

"I will be, Winnie. It's not the first time I've seen a partial amputation, and I'm sure it won't be the last." My lips tighten into a straight line, an acceptance of a grim truth.

"Will you stop pretending like you don't know what I'm talking about?" Part of compartmentalizing for me is not indulging in conversations about whatever it is I'm trying to forget. In this case, it isn't Mr. Green's partially amputated hand. It's Ally. The thought that will plague me most if I let it.

"I burned some bridges today. Like severely charred, never to be crossed again." I slash my hand through the air. Done deal.

"Are you so sure? Personally, I've never seen a girl look that concerned who wouldn't be willing to at least talk things out."

"You don't know Ally, then. I hit her right where it hurts today, Winnie." All Ally wants is for someone to appreciate her worth, to see her for how brilliant and capable she is. I did see it. I saw it so clearly, and in a moment where it mattered, I rejected it. I rejected her.

"I love you, Mason. And I only want the best for you." I steel myself for the motherly lecture that's coming. Whatever Winnie is about to say, I won't like it. No sentence starts like that if it isn't followed up by a gut punch. It's Winnie's version of *no offence, but* … "But you're a fucking idiot if you don't at least try. I would be failing you, I would be failing your mother, if I let you walk away from this."

I stifle a laugh that bubbles up at the sound of Winnie cursing. Winnie rarely curses, except in particular circumstances, and only when she means business.

"It's a lost cause, Winnie. Even if she forgave me, you know as well as I do that a relationship doesn't have a place in my life. Today was proof of that. I was too distracted by my own feelings that I wasn't available when I was needed. I need to be practical here. I just need to let Ally go. It's better for the both of us, for the clinic, if I do." I turn my back on Winnie, about to head into my office to wallow. I just need to be alone right now.

"That's bullshit, Mason." Winnie is not ready to give up. She's only just getting started. She's practically pulling on boxing gloves. "That's bullshit and you know it. More than anyone, Ally understands the responsibility you have to the town, and here she is, offering to help you carry this load that you refuse to let anyone in your life share. Here she is, offering to take on some of it to give you more space in your life for joy, for happiness. That's love, Mason. Life will never be easy, but it can be easier when you choose to go through it with someone else."

I don't respond. I go into my office and close the door on Winnie, feeling yet again like a piece of shit. Winnie doesn't deserve this kind of treatment, but I'm not in the mood right now. I already feel like trash for hurting Ally today; what's one more shitty thing as a mark against me? God, I need a drink.

I pull out the glasses I keep in my drawer, the ones that I had pulled out when I shared a drink in here with Ally. Something stabs at my side as I see a remnant of pink lip gloss on the rim. I slam the drawer shut, not daring to look at it.

The problem isn't that I don't want love or someone to share my life with. I've wanted a fairy-tale love since I was young. Since I saw how much my father loved my mom. Since I started watching classic romantic comedies and dreamt of that kind of story for myself one day. As much as I hate to admit it, I'm a complete and utter sap. I turn to mush at a love story.

The problem is that it will never be my story. Not now that I've taken over the clinic. Not now that I've made an oath to serve Heartwood. I can't have any distractions in my life, someone who wouldn't understand working late hours, having to drop everything at a moment's notice.

But Ally does. She understands certain things take precedence. How many nights did she stay late with me? Ally poured herself into this clinic, putting in endless hours just to raise money for a program that would help the clinic and help the town. How had I been so blind? Ally not only shares my passion and care about the clinic, she cares about me.

I gulp down the scotch I poured, shuddering as the liquid burns my throat on the way down. I know now that I need to let Ally in to see all of me. Even the parts of myself that I would rather keep hidden.

Tomorrow.

Tomorrow morning I will go to the cabin first thing and explain everything to Ally. I will tell her how much I appreciate her and how badly I need her in my life. How I am a better man because of her, and I will never stop trying to be better for her.

Tomorrow. Tonight, we both need time to cool off.

CHAPTER 25
ALLY

I ROLL over in the early morning light. The cabin is quiet. My eyes are puffy from crying, and they're dry. So dry. Last night, I think I cried my very last tear, ever.

I blink my eyes a few times to focus and the pile of suitcases by the front door comes into view. After I hastily booked a flight back to the city, I spent the rest of the evening packing everything that I had brought with me. I sat on the floor, an entire bottle of wine in my system, belting out angsty songs from my teenage years between sobs. I had only ever intended for this to be a one-way trip, but here we are.

I reach over and pick up my phone off the nightstand. There's an unread text message from Spencer that I click open. I texted her last night, though the memory of typing out the message is foggy.

> Not feeling so good about Dr. Dickbag anymore. Coming home tomorrow.

SPENCER

> Lucky for you, I just got back last night. I'll be at the airport to pick you up. Send me your flight info. xx

I text her the flight number and decide to get up and get myself somewhat cleaned up. It's nearing eight o'clock. I have two hours before my flight. Two hours before I can leave Heartwood and try to forget that any of this ever happened. Until I land in Vancouver, the city that I was trying to escape in the first place. So much for my clean slate.

The air is just warming up by the time I'm heading out the door. I didn't take the time to put on any makeup. I hardly even brushed through my hair, throwing it into a pile at the back of my head held together by a large claw clip. I'm wearing my old hoodie and leggings. I can't be bothered to put on anything nicer. No one will even see me today. I'm doubtful that I'll see Mason. He'll be so absorbed in the clinic this morning that he won't even register that I haven't shown up for work. The plan is to get to the airport, beeline straight to Spencer's car once she picks me up, and head back to her apartment to hide under a pile of covers for the next week.

I haul the last of six suitcases into the back of the Jeep that Mason had forced on me. I have to say it has served me much better than the old rattle trap I got. Resentment quickly replaces my sadness thinking of him.

If Mason doesn't want my help, so be it. I'm done being used and then tossed aside once I'm no longer needed. God, does it hurt, though. It's been a long time since I felt this invested because I care, like my life's work means something. And now, it doesn't mean anything because the clinic could be shut down, anyway. It doesn't matter what I do because that ship had already left the harbour when I arrived.

Mason kept it from me. All this time, all the vulnerable moments we've shared, and Mason had forgotten to tell me that my job, my entire livelihood, was in jeopardy. I moved my entire life here, made friends and connections, and he's prepared to just let me have it all taken away.

Tires crunch on the driveway behind me and squeal to a stop. I wipe the remnants of tears from my face as the dust cloud settles, and Mason emerges from his truck. What is this asshole doing here? I just want to leave in peace and never turn back.

Mason walks over to the Jeep and eyes the pile of suitcases in the back.

"You're leaving?" Mason says as he approaches. It's worded like a question, but he says it more like a statement. "I say something you don't like, and you just decide to run away again?" Mason shakes his head, incredulous. His tone isn't mean, but it strikes a chord with me. Maybe it bothers me so much because I know there's a grain of truth in it. And maybe it's cowardly, but I don't care at this point. "Ally, I'm sorry. I'm so sorry I didn't let you help me yesterday. I thought I needed to handle it on my own. I thought I could handle it on my own."

"You need me to help you stop the clinic from shutting down, is what you mean." A look of shock crosses Mason's expression as I spit out the words. "Yeah. I met Simone. She told me all about the clinic. When were you going to tell me I moved my entire life here for nothing?"

"Ally, I—" Mason stammers. I know the excuse he would give. He didn't bring me here, Winnie did, and blah-dee-fucking-blah. He'll sound like every other guy when they try to weasel their way out of a mess. The old *we were never official* plot. Mason stops, realizing that I'm beyond listening to explanations. It hurts too much, being pushed out over and over again and only wanted when I'm needed for his own benefit.

I'm struggling to hold back tears, and I can hear my voice wobble. "I think I could have gotten over the fact that you repeatedly denied my offers to help you. At least, I'd like to think we could have talked about it and I could have gotten it through your thick skull that you *need* people, a partner, a team, whatever. You can't do this alone. And it's not a weakness, accepting help, Mason. It's a strength. But what I can't get over is the fact that you used me once you found out about the funding being pulled. You didn't want me here when I first started, but you sure did once you thought I would help you convince the government to line your pockets again."

"I never told you, Ally, because I wouldn't have told any of my employees. I never even told Winnie about the ministry funding. It wasn't your problem to deal with. I am the boss, and I was taking care of it. I believed in you, too. I believed that the Harvest Festival, the prenatal program, would work," he pleads.

"Save it, Mason." I don't want whatever explanation he has to give me, anyway. Looking at Mason now, hearing him speak his side would cause me to second-guess my decision to leave. I love him, and I would give him a chance if I heard him out. How many chances had I given Nate? Too many to count. He took those chances and ran with them, give an inch, and they'll take a mile.

"So what, you're going to go running back to Vancouver and back to Nate?" That was a low blow. My eyes sting as I fail miserably to contain my tears, which are now lining my eyelashes. I try to blink them away, but a singular tear runs down my cheek and gives me away. "Shit. I didn't mean—"

I cut Mason off again.

"Well, you said it. And if running away is leaving a place that I know I'm not appreciated, then fine. Yes. I'm running away." I don't bother clarifying that there is no way in hell that I would go back to Nate. I won't coddle Mason anymore. Let him wonder if I've chosen someone else. Mason made his bed when he showed me I wasn't a priority to him. He can put on his big boy pants and deal with it.

"I appreciate you, Ally. More than you realize. The whole town does. I've been a fool not to make sure you know every single day how much I value you."

"Do you value me? Or do you value how much work I've poured into your crumbling clinic?" I cross my arms over my chest, guarding my heart behind my ribs. "Because those are two very different things."

"You, Ally. It's you. I want you, I need you." Mason is saying what I want to hear. Unfortunately, his actions over the last few weeks speak louder.

"I don't buy it, Mason. I won't buy it until you start showing me that you prioritize me. No, that you prioritize *yourself* enough to let people into your life, to live your life for you instead of for everyone else around you." I walk around the side of the truck and reach for the driver's door handle, but Mason cuts in front of me, just as I did a few weeks earlier, convincing him to let me work with him. I'm tired of trying to convince him.

"Tell me what I need to do to show you that I'm ready. That I care about you more than anything else? Tell me, and I'll do it." Mason's eyes are pleading and my chest heaves as I prepare to say the words that will sever this thing between Mason and me for good.

"You'll let me go." I see the words land on Mason, the way they crash into his chest like a wrecking ball, pushing him backward, away from me.

"Is that what you want, Ally? Be honest with yourself. Is that what you want?" Mason is holding my stare intensely. "If you can stand here and tell me you want me to leave with your whole heart, I will. I can respect your wishes, unlike Nate. But I don't think you do, Ally. I think you know that this thing between us is something more. I think you know that this has never been fake. It was never fake for me. Maybe it's more than you bargained for, moving to Heartwood. But isn't it worth staying and fighting for? Fight for *something*, Ally. For once in your life, fight for something."

My breath catches in my throat. Fighting isn't my style. What about fairy-tale romance? You don't have to fight for things that are meant to be. Mason should understand that. His beloved '90s rom-coms are the epitome of the relationship we both deserve.

"It's too late, Mason. You could have told me what we were up against. I would have had your back. This whole time, I was on your team. You were just too pig-headed to realize that this was even a team sport," I say. My eyes refuse to meet his.

"Okay." He puts his hands up in surrender, hearing me. "Loud and clear, Honeybee."

The way he says my nickname this time, with a hint of melancholy, cracks my heart in two. But if he will not prioritize me in his life or make enough space for me, then this is how it needs to be. The least he can do is respect my need to be far away from him right now.

I climb up into the driver's seat, and Mason shuts the door for me. Our eyes meet through the window for a moment, only a moment, before mine flick away. Any longer and my decision to leave would become murky, my footing less solid in my choice. This is how it needs to be, at least for now. I've spent too long trying to bend and fit into a box that other people have made for me. A box that allows them to use me to their own ends.

Besides, what's left for me in Heartwood now? Even if the clinic survived, I can't say that I would choose to go back to the status quo of working for Mason, of never feeling like I quite measure up.

I manoeuvre the Jeep in a tight turn, driving over the front lawn and steering it away from a dumbfounded Mason. I don't look in the rear-view mirror as I continue on down the drive. I don't look back because I know what I would find there. My heart, standing in the driveway, completely and utterly broken. Just as I am.

I don't stop the car until I've passed the colourful 'Welcome to Heartwood' sign, and it's no longer in view in my mirror. I've held myself together by a thread, and it's only once I'm outside of the city limits that I pull the Jeep over to the side of the road and come undone. I allow the sobs to consume me until I can no longer draw in air. It took every ounce of effort to go against what my heart wanted and leave. I wanted to hear Mason out. To give him a chance. That's my problem, though. I want to give everyone the benefit of the doubt, and until I stop assuming that everyone has good intentions, I'm going to bleed myself dry of empathy.

Going back to Vancouver is my only option. It's the only option that allows me to take back control, to choose what happens to me, where I go, and what I do. To not let other people make those decisions for me. When had I started allowing other people—men—to dictate what my life looks like?

Mason had been the exception. At least that's what I thought. He had seen me for who I am and had realized the potential I have to make a real difference. But he had withheld a key piece of information that would have changed the trajectory of my life. I never would have uprooted my entire life and moved to Heartwood for some dead-end job. Heartwood was supposed to be my clean slate, my fresh start. I didn't know that it had already been sullied before I even arrived, doomed to be a repeat of the same patterns I've already lived through.

When the final sob leaves my body, and I am able to come back up for air, I turn the car back on and finish the drive to the airport, where I board the plane and head back to Vancouver.

THE MORNING AIR is still fresh as I walk back to the clinic, dew still gathering on the tips of the grass. I left my truck in the drive. I thought I needed the walk to clear my head, but the time it takes to walk back over to the clinic is time I spend fixating on my interaction with Ally.

Ally is gone. My insides drop as if I have just crested the peak of a rollercoaster, and now I am plummeting toward the ground. It isn't the exciting adrenaline-filled rush, though. It is a dreadful realization that the best thing to have walked into my life in years just turned around and walked right out of it. The worst part is that this was all my doing, and I suspect I won't forgive myself for it for a long time.

The cabin will need to be cleaned and locked up now that Ally is no longer residing in it. It will be the last time I come back to the cabin for a while, I resolve. Facing the emptiness of the cabin now is a thought that causes my chest to seize. Maybe I'll sell it. It would go for a pretty penny with all the tourists flocking here looking for a vacation spot. Someone will tear it down and put a more modern home in its place. It's probably for the best. I didn't even want to look back at it as I made my way down the drive. So much for Ally turning it into a home again. The thought clangs around inside the hollow cavern of my heart.

My mind races with questions that I don't have answers to. Is Ally right? Have I just seen her as the solution to my problem? A feeling in my gut tells me no. I know enough to know that the way my heart pulls toward her, the way I yearn to be near her, is love. But I also can't say I wasn't relieved when Ally offered me a solution to a problem that had been plaguing me, that she didn't offer me a sense of relief where the clinic was concerned. Still, it had never crossed my mind to *use* her, to take advantage of her offer to help. I kept the information from her to protect her feelings, and instead, it was the very thing that broke her. That was my mistake. Sweet, soft Ally doesn't need protecting. She has a strength within her that is subtle, but steadfast. Easy to underestimate but fierce if you take the time to appreciate it. Ally is strong *because* of her gentle, kind nature. Not despite it.

I gaze up at the sky, where the sun is just beginning to rise, painting the horizon with streaks of golden light. At this moment, I can't shake the feeling that a significant chapter in my life is ending. Not just Ally, but the clinic as well. It's like the dawn of a new day is also signalling the end of these important parts of my life. The uncertainty of the future weighs on me, and I can't help but fear that my sky will remain cloudy for a while. Without Ally, my life feels as shadowed as a misty morning, with no sunlight piercing through the haze.

I round the corner onto the main road, the clinic coming into view. It's late enough in the morning now that the sun has risen above the treetops, illuminating the front of the building. And the woman that I am least eager to see waiting here for me.

Simone shifts on her feet in the soft morning light. Sometime between the festival and now, she has changed back into her stuffy-looking pantsuit. She has her back turned to me, and she's holding her hand cupped around her face, peering through the glass door into the clinic. She's been here less than two weeks, and she's already figured out that I spend every waking minute in this goddamned building. This is the first impression that I give, apparently. Workaholic. No wonder Ally didn't feel appreciated or wanted.

Seeing Simone here now makes my already foul mood escalate into something almost feral. Whatever gratitude I felt towards her earlier is gone. She isn't responsible for Ally leaving, I know, but had she never shown up here, I might have been able to fix my mess with Ally before it escalated to this point. I growl beneath my breath, stuffing it down and plastering a smile on my face to replace the sneer. If I still have a sliver of a chance at saving the clinic, I won't ruin it now by being a dick.

"Can I help you?" I say in my most chipper tone, although it's fake, and the sound reminds me of the dickwad, Nate. Simone whirls around to face me.

"Just the man I was looking for. I'm on my way back to Calgary, so I thought I would stop by on the off chance you'd be here."

"There's a good chance I'm here, but I had some business to attend to." Business that makes my heart feel like it's shattering into thousands of shards, never to be repaired again. *Get a hold of yourself,* I scold myself. I am not this person. I am not the person who wallows. I compartmentalize. I tuck my feelings into tidy boxes. It was how I got through middle school after my mom died without completely losing it. It was how I got through high school when I became the man of the household without ever signing up for the role. It was how I got through the last year as I took over a failing practice and failed along with it when Noah died.

"I wanted to congratulate you on the success of the fundraiser yesterday. Even though it came to an abrupt and traumatic end. Please send my best to ..." Simone's voice trails off, waiting for me to fill in the blank.

"Allan. Allan Green," I say, and she smiles. It's as warm a smile as she's capable of, probably. Government android. I shouldn't say that. Simone is giving this place a chance. Besides, I appreciate her effort. It's a smile that says she's secretly rooting for me, for the clinic, despite her job description and requirement to remain neutral and objective.

"Yes, Allan. I hope he'll be okay." She sounds almost robotic. Maybe she is a government android. I wouldn't feel so bad about passing judgment. "At any rate, between the fundraiser drawing such a crowd, and the ... incident, I think I have a fairly convincing report. In your favour, of course."

"I wish I could take credit, but the Harvest Festival wasn't my idea. Neither was the prenatal program. I was just along for the ride." I can't bring myself to utter Ally's name for fear that it will make me break, and looking weak is the last thing I need in front of Simone.

"Well, it was a great success. I think I have a lot of evidence to include in my report that will be very favourable for the clinic. You should have a decision by the end of next week."

My mouth tightens into a thin smile, the corners barely lifted. I'm grateful for all that Simone has done. She didn't have to come all the way out here. She could have written the clinic off and never given it a second look. But I also know that without Ally here to enjoy this with me, the victory is meaningless. Somehow, the very thing I have been working so hard for this whole time just feels empty without her to share it with.

The clinic has a chance of survival. But without Ally, where does that leave me? I will resume my life as it was. I'll go back to sleeping in my office, trying to keep up with my patients, my house calls, and my pager. I will pick up my life exactly where I left off, barely keeping my head above water.

I fight the sinking feeling in my chest, but it overtakes me anyway. Life won't be the same now. Not now that I've had Ally in it. The moment I opened my heart to her, bared my soul to her, I changed. She took the vulnerable pieces I gave her and handled them with care, and my DNA was altered in a permanent way. I've experienced what it was like, no matter how much I tried to shut it out and reject it, to have a partner to face the hardships of this career with. Someone to shoulder even a small part of the burden. Someone to comfort me when the traumas of this job come back to haunt me in my dreams. Someone to laugh with, to share even a sliver of joy with. I've experienced life with Ally, and now I want nothing less.

CHAPTER 27
ALLY

I spot the flash of red hair at the arrivals gate instantly. Other passengers flood the area around the baggage claim, bags thudding on the ground as they drop them to hug their loved ones who have waited for them. I do the same, beelining for my best friend. I throw my large tote bag on the floor and throw my arms around Spencer's neck. If anyone can pick me up right now, it's Spencer.

She wraps her arms around me, our hug lasting longer than most friends would, but Spencer is more like my sister at this point. I bury my face in her long, thick red hair and blink back the tears of relief that are threatening to spill just being in her presence.

I pull back out of the hug and look at Spencer. A part of me feels like a wounded puppy coming home with my tail between my legs, but I find no judgment in her eyes.

"Hey asshole, you were supposed to be the one picking me up at the airport." Oh God, I'd forgotten that Spencer only got back from Amsterdam last night and that I had agreed to be her ride. That was before the show, before everything went to shit. And now here I am making her pick me up, and jet lagged no less.

"Oh my God, Spence! I'm so sorry. You must be exhausted!" I

hold my friend out at arm's length to get a good look at her. Somehow, Spencer looks perfect in her straight ankle-length jeans and slouchy sweater that hangs off of one shoulder. Spencer always looks stylish and put together, even when she's nine hours ahead and just finished a whole day of travel.

"Shut up. There's no way I wouldn't be here." Spencer picks up my large brown leather tote from the ground and swings it over her shoulder. She nods toward the baggage carousel that is squeaking as it groans to life. The first bag makes its journey around, a few bags falling on the conveyor belt. "Grab your shit. We're getting brunch."

I feel the tightly wound spring that has been squeezing my insides the whole plane ride home uncoil and loosen. I'm back with my friend, and I can relax. Spencer has always been my safe place.

I stand next to the baggage carousel and watch as my six suitcases fall one by one onto the conveyor belt.

"How many bags do you have, Wells?" Spencer's jaw hangs open.

"I moved my entire life to Heartwood, Spence. I wasn't planning on being home anytime soon." I shrug and try to shake off the sting of the mention of Heartwood.

"Good luck fitting those in my car." Spencer swivels and heads toward the exit with an arrow pointing to short-term parking. I follow, pushing my baggage cart, making sure that none fall on the way.

Spencer has brought her tiny little Toyota Corolla from the early '90s, and fitting my suitcases in the back is like an impossible game of Tetris. She got the car as a hand-me-down when we were teenagers, and she's has never upgraded. It works fine to get from point A to point B when Spencer isn't travelling, which is rare. It just isn't ideal for jamming six suitcases into it. I manage to get all of my suitcases in the trunk and the backseat, with my seat pushed almost all the way forward, and I take a moment to thank the universe for giving me short legs.

We don't have too far to go; it's about a twenty-minute ride from the airport to our favourite brunch spot downtown, only a few blocks away from Spencer's apartment.

I gaze out the window as we cross the Granville Street Bridge, admiring the city skyline, the way the sun shimmers off the windows of the high-rises, how the buildings crop up out of nowhere against the backdrop of the North Shore Mountains.

I close my eyes and let the sun warm my face. As beautiful as this city is, Vancouver feels foreign to me now. It's like my favourite old T-shirt from when I was a teenager, still the same comfortable feel, but it doesn't quite fit the same as I remember. It's not home anymore. I don't know where I can call home. Heartwood had become that place for me. Now, Heartwood is a place I want to shove into the far reaches of my mind and never think about again. That includes Mason.

I feel my chest hollow out, sucking my breath in like a vacuum, into the void. No matter how hard I try, I can never forget Mason. That's what terrifies me.

We take our usual table in the corner by the window, where we used to sit and people-watch as we sipped our lattes on a Sunday morning. I have no interest in people-watching today, and I'm going to need something stronger than a latte. As if reading my mind, Spencer pipes up when the server comes around to our table.

"We'll do the bottomless mimosas, easy on the orange juice, please." God bless Spencer. The lanky server shakes his head and chuckles but happily obliges and heads over to the bar to get our drinks. Spencer just stares at me, waiting. I'm relieved that she hasn't started bombarding me with questions, but it also leaves me wondering where to even begin telling her about the shitstorm that has become my life.

"You never told me how your date was with Hot Dutch Guy?" I say, trying to delay the inevitable questions about Mason.

"It was fine. He was cute. Dating European guys is weird, man. They're so forward. So direct. Dating Canadian guys is so much more fun. You never know what they're thinking."

"That's called playing mind games, Spence." I tap a finger on my temple. "And most people don't like it in their relationships," I add.

"One guy straight up asked me if I would put out after our date. Not in those exact words, mind you. They're very eloquent, even when they're trying to get in your pants." I laugh so hard I snort, thinking about how brazen someone would have to be to rankle Spencer.

"I don't think that's a problem with European guys. I think that's a problem with men. The species as a whole."

"Hey, when did this conversation become about me and my sex life?" Spencer scolds. "First things first. Who do I need to fight? Because I will. I have enough travel points to book a flight to Heartwood tomorrow and I will cut. A. Bitch." Spencer makes a gesture with her finger as if she's slashing her own throat, eyes wide as if she's a psychopathic serial killer and she's out for blood. It might appear menacing if you didn't know Spencer.

I shoot Spencer a withering look. I've mentally written Mason's name in my burn book, but he doesn't deserve the lashing that Spencer would give him, that's certain.

"Settle down, Firecracker." I use the nickname I gave Spencer as a teen when we were just getting to know each other, when it became apparent that Spencer's personality matched the fiery shock of red hair on her head. "No one is going to get cut."

"Then there better be a reason my best friend has come running home. Not that I'm complaining. For very selfish reasons, I'm happy you're here."

I start from the beginning, filling Spencer in on all the details I wasn't able to tell her over the phone when the time difference and dates with hot Dutch guys came between us. I leave nothing out, except for a few specific details about our sexual encounters that I'm not ready to talk about yet. In all my past relationships, Spencer was privy to all the gory details, but these still feel too raw to put out in the open. Mason was the first person who truly saw me for all of my insecurities and flaws. He gave me the space to grow, to use my voice. The wounds of losing him need more time to heal before I can revisit them.

Spencer listens and nods along, adding a few well-timed '*What-the-actual-fuck*'s. When I finish my story, we sit in silence once again, neither of us quite knowing what to say.

"I know you don't want me to fight Mason, but I am going to be making a voodoo doll and needle the *shit* out of that thing when I get home." I let out a laugh and have to cover my mouth with my hand to stop myself from spitting my stiff mimosa all over the table. Although the wound is still fresh, there's a certain catharsis in letting it all out and having Spencer on my side.

"Honestly, Spence, I am just ready to put this all in the past and move on." That's a lie, and I recognize it instantly. I don't want to move on from Mason, but I have no choice. What's done is done, and it's my only option now.

"How do you feel being back in the same city as Nate?" The question stumps me momentarily, and I let a breath out from between pursed lips. I had carefully considered the idea of returning to Vancouver, where my reputation as the winner of *Stolen Love* precedes me wherever I go. But the thought of running into Nate ... I have to turn it over in my head and examine it from all angles. Where can I go in Vancouver where I don't risk bumping into him? By the end of our engagement, we ran in a lot of the same circles, visited a lot of the same places.

Would I run into him in our old neighbourhood? Would he find out I had come back and try to get in touch with me again? My mind reels, weighing out every scenario. I don't want Nate knowing I'm back. He is such a self-centred prick; he would assume that I came back for him. I have too much to worry about right now without adding him to the mix.

"I guess I'm just going to lie low for a while. I'll have to find a place to live, and make sure it's nowhere near Nate's usual haunts." For now, avoiding him will be easy. Brunch at the mom-and-pop café tucked in the west end is one thing, but the idea of making any public appearances makes my skin itch.

"Your Mom would love it if you moved home," Spencer offers, her face cringing, knowing that the suggestion will not land well. I glare at her across the table. Spencer adores my parents. She has since we were young. Her parents had been absent for most of her life, there but never available. When we met, Spencer commented frequently about how my mom would ask about my day while she made me an after-school snack. I thought all moms did that, and frankly, her constant interrogations got under my skin. Spencer's jealousy was short-lived when she realized my parents would take her under their wing and give her the sense of belonging she had always craved. I'm fairly certain that she talks to my mother more than I do at this point.

"Nice try. I've given up a lot of my pride over the last few months, but that's a low I just wouldn't recover from. Moving back in with my parents at the ripe old age of twenty-nine isn't where I imagined myself."

"You can't ignore her forever, Ally. Besides, she'll be thrilled that you're back."

"Thrilled that I failed at both of the endeavours she opposed right from the start." I take a long sip of my mimosa, which is ninety percent Prosecco, thanks to Spencer. She's right. I've missed my mom since I've been away, I haven't quite come to terms with crawling home yet. Not after our last interaction where both of my parents blew up. *This is not the life that we had set up for you, Ally.* Like my life was theirs to control, not mine.

"She cares about you. She wants the best for you. You can't blame her for worrying." I nod, but I don't continue the conversation. Spencer knows better than to push the subject. "Well, if you aren't going home, does that mean you'll stay with me?" Spencer's face lights up as she clasps her hands under her chin and bats her eyelashes at me, a silent plea. I don't want to put a damper on her excitement, but I waffle at the suggestion.

"Err ... I don't know, Spence. You've already done so much for me, I don't want to impose on your life any more than I already have."

Spencer waves a hand in front of her face.

"Pfft, it's no biggie. Besides, I need someone to look after the place while I'm travelling. And we're sisters. It's no imposition." I give Spencer a sheepish smile.

"Only if you're positive. And please tell me to get the fuck out the minute, the second, you start to get annoyed by me."

"That'll be a problem because you're literally the most annoying person I've ever met. But it's okay. You owe me," Spencer says with a wink. As much as I know Spencer is joking, I do owe her. Big time. Her apartment is still the perfect hideout, away from the public eye, and away from Nate.

"Hey, I know how you can pay me back," she says in a singsong voice as if she's about to ask a favour of me. She knows I'm not going to like it. "There's an event I have to go to tomorrow night if you want to come with. I get a plus one, and I'm pathetically single. Be my date?"

I hesitate. Attending a big event with Spencer, who has almost a million followers on social media, isn't my definition of lying low. Any event that Spencer is invited to will have a lot of attention on it. Sensing my hesitation, she reaches over the table and places her hand on my arm.

"Come on, come with me, please? It will do you good to get out and about. No one from the show will be there; it's just a bunch of travel bloggers, and the reality dating world rarely crosses over with ours." I consider it. It would be an opportunity for me to take my mind off of Mason, and I could avoid cameras if I was motivated enough. Spencer is right; who from that crowd would recognize me, anyway?

"Okay, okay. You've convinced me. I'll come." I give in, rolling my eyes. My expression shifts as I muster my blankest expression. "On one condition: if this is a date, I expect you to put out when we get home."

Spencer shoves my shoulder across the table, nearly knocking over the pitcher of mimosas, and we both burst out in a fit of laughter.

"Pervert."

CHAPTER 28
MASON

.

MY EYES GLAZE over as I watch my brother serve his customers from my seat at the bar. I swirl the ice cubes in my water and wish that it was something stronger. Anything. I would even take a glass of Ally's bubbly rosé right now. That stuff was damn delicious, though I could never admit that to anyone but her. The memory of it makes my chest tighten, and I take a swig of my water to loosen it. I'm still on the clock. There's rarely a time when I'm off the clock now.

The Harvest Festival had been a huge success—the town thought so, Simone thought so. Hell, the Ministry of Health thought so, and I have money in the bank to prove it. Whatever Simone had written in her report had been enough to convince them to extend funding for another year and increase our yearly budget. The amount that they promised over the next year was astounding, enough to hire another nurse for the clinic. Now, I suppose, I'll have to hire two. Despite seeing the words in writing, that everything I've been working for has paid off, the success hasn't sunk in for me yet. There's still something lacking, something missing, and unfortunately, I don't think I can get it back now.

I thought that this would feel better, keeping the clinic running, keeping my dad's legacy alive. The pinnacle of everything I've worked for since I came back to Heartwood and took over the clinic. Here it is, handed to me with a giant bow on it. This victory, a triumph against all odds. So why do I feel like I've royally fucked up?

The blond woman seated with her boyfriend in the back booth throws her head back as she laughs at something Grady just said. Grady always has such suave and charm with his customers. He has an ease about him I wish I inherited. He got Mom's magnetism, I got Dad's gruff demeanour. Although people saw his gruffness as charming, whereas most people just think I'm rude.

The woman turns back to her boyfriend and leans her head against his shoulder. They're seated together on the same side of the booth, the same seat Ally had occupied the night she roped me into being her fake boyfriend. The couple is looking out over the rest of the bar like they own the entire world. I'm certain that's how they feel, too. I felt that way with Ally. Like I owned the entire universe, and Ally was my co-conspirator, making everything in our world come together for our higher good.

Get it together, you sap, I scold myself. Wallowing about Ally will not bring her back. Wanting her to come back now would be another colossal mistake, now that she had made up her mind and chose Nate. She wouldn't have up and left, gone back to Vancouver, if she had no intention of being with Nate. The scumbag would never leave her alone. She's made her choice, and now she'll have to live with it.

"Looking glum there, brother." Grady walks around the bar and starts preparing the couple's drink orders. He tilts a frosted glass against the beer tap and pours, a perfect head of foam forming on top. My mouth waters at the sight of it.

I grunt at my brother in return. Grady and I know each other inside and out, and he can tell when something is amiss even before I speak. The closeness I have with Grady feels too vulnerable today; I'm not prepared to talk about the thoughts that are plaguing me. Why I even came to the bar knowing that Grady would see right through me is beyond me. I consider for a moment that there's a part of me that wants to be seen, wants to be heard and understood. Ally has been the only person besides Grady that saw beneath the surface. She saw the mess that I keep hidden, the ugliness that lives in my mind, and she never shied away from it.

"I would have thought you'd be celebrating today, since getting the news about the clinic," Grady says, returning from dropping off the couple's drinks on the table. He picks up a glass from the sink behind the bar and dries it, not once looking at it but staring me down instead. I huff a laugh, realizing that I'm officially one of those sad, pathetic people who wallow alone at the bar and pour his heart out to the bartender. I wonder how often Grady does this for other people, if he lives up to the gruff-but-caring bartender stereotype.

"I keep thinking I should be happier, wondering when some sort of satisfaction or accomplishment will set in." I remember Ally's words from the other day, and the truth of them sinks into my bones as I repeat them. "Dad would be so proud right now, and that's all I've ever wanted."

"Until a month ago." Grady's gaze is now focused intently on the glass like he has just said something that would land like an atomic bomb and he's avoiding looking at the blast. A month ago. Not when Ally and I shared our first public kiss at the Harvest Festival. A month ago, when she first arrived in Heartwood.

Is it that obvious to everyone else? Has everyone else seen plain as day my feelings for Ally from day one? Jesus. Try as I might to keep my feelings locked up tight, to portray to everyone around me I'm not to be messed with, when Ally is involved, all that goes to shit.

"What happened a month ago?" It's obvious what my brother is getting at, I'm not a complete idiot, but I want to hear him say it. I won't offer my feelings up that easily.

"You can't be that fucking dense, Mason." Grady looks like he's about to throw the glass right at my head. "A five-foot-nothin' strawberry blond bombshell with cute little freckles and a hell of a smile. Ring a bell?

"Ally?" I try to play dumb. I don't want to talk about Ally yet. "That was just a ruse. It wasn't real. Ally needed her conniving ex to get out of town, and I played the part. Probably a little too well." Grady's expression and the way he's lifting one eyebrow say he isn't buying it. There's no way I can't pass off our kiss after the Lumberjack Games as fraudulent.

"Everyone in town saw the way you melted whenever Ally was around. Your feelings for her were never fake, Mason, and you know it."

I scoff and shrug off the comment.

"It's a moot point now. Ally's gone back to Vancouver, and I have to focus on the clinic." Ally was a fun distraction, but it couldn't have gone on for much longer, anyway. The incident at the Harvest Festival was proof of that. I had a reason, and a good one at that, for shutting myself off to the idea of love for so long. I can't have both. It's a sad reality, but it's better that I've come to terms with it and accepted it now. I can't be a doctor and have a life outside of work. My father had tried and failed and left his family in the lurch. I refuse to do that to Ally. She would always have taken second priority to the clinic, and she deserves more than that. She deserves the moon, but I'm not going to be the one who can give it to her.

"You're not Dad, Mason," Grady says, as if he can see right through me and is rifling through my thoughts. "Dad tried to be everything for everyone, except the people that mattered to him. It's impossible to save everyone without sacrificing parts of yourself. You could learn from Dad instead of trying to be like him and realize that all you need to be is everything to *you*."

It doesn't elude me that Grady never mentioned prioritizing

Ally. He's talking about prioritizing myself. What would it even look like to prioritize my own needs?

Ally had a peculiar way of nudging me out of my comfort zone, of shedding the weight that caused me to be so stubborn and serious all the goddamned time. It never took away from my ability to do my job. In fact, it made me *better*. The morning after that first night at the cabin with her, I found myself more vibrant, more engaged.

I played with Mrs. Rose's granddaughter, something I never would have done with any of the children that visited the clinic. Whether that change of attitude was down to having a night off, or a night off *with Ally*, I can't say. What I know is that I had never considered taking time for myself before Ally came waltzing into my life.

Ally had made me a more well-rounded person. She had seen me for who I am, without the clinic as my entire identity. Embracing this newfound identity feels impossible to do without her, but I'll have to try. Ally is gone, and she has shown no intention of wanting to come back. She hasn't reached out once since she left, and she seemed pretty determined to move on with her life the last time I saw her. If there was something I could do to convince her to come back to Heartwood, I would do it.

Bleep. Bleep. I reach down to my pocket as my pager chimes, a jarring sound in an otherwise hushed bar, and interrupts my thoughts. The message that displays across the screen causes my pulse to quicken, my heart to thumping in my ears.

Clinic STAT.

Winnie hardly ever used the medical lingo that I'm used to, save for when she needs to get my attention and emphasize the urgency of a situation. That's what worries me about her message coming through now. My brow furrows as I stare at the text, not bothering to lift my eyes as I slide my glass across the bar toward Grady.

"Put my drink on my tab," I mutter, though all I've had to drink is water. My mind has checked out; it's already elsewhere, trying to parse through a mental list of scenarios I might encounter at the clinic and strategizing my first course of action. *Check for a pulse, secure the airway, look at breathing.* It's a script that I memorized years ago, one that allows me to go into autopilot and respond in an organized and systematic manner rather than succumbing to the adrenaline rush that threatens to derail my focus.

I let the heavy wooden door of the bar swing closed behind me as I take swift strides toward my truck. The tires screech as I stomp the gas pedal onto the floor and make a sharp turn in the clinic's direction.

Winnie is standing outside the clinic, awaiting my arrival. She has her coat wrapped around her as she braces herself against the wind and the rain that's rolling in, coming down almost sideways now. The rapid weather changes are the first sign of fall in the mountains, the yearly storms a harbinger of the harsh winter to come.

Concern shadows her face. More than concern. I recognize the wide-eyed look she is wearing as fear and a pit forms in the bottom of my stomach. Winnie has been around the clinic much longer than I have. Though she doesn't have official medical training, she offers a second set of hands when needed. Winnie has seen enough throughout her career to know when a situation is cause for concern.

"It's Mrs. Hendrick's boy Charlie." Winnie doesn't waste another second informing me who I'm about to see as I throw open the clinic door. She doesn't need to say more to warn me, either. The face of the Hendricks' youngest son, Noah, is still etched into my mind, on my heart. A face that I can never unsee as the life left his eyes. The last thing anyone needs is a repeat of that fateful, deadly day. Before Winnie can brief me, I'm pushing past her through the front door, and she takes the moment she has to catch me up.

"He's had an allergic reaction. He's anaphylactic to nuts. Usually his EpiPen is enough to keep him from going into shock, but today it doesn't seem to be working." I roll up my sleeves as I cross the waiting room, heading for the first exam room where I can see Charlie sitting on the chair. I can see his chest heaving with every breath, even from out in the hall.

"Go get me the epinephrine kit, Winnie, and supplies to start an IV. He's going to need a line and we don't have much time," I instruct her.

Winnie doesn't hesitate before she scurries off toward the supply room tucked behind the reception desk to gather what I've asked her to.

I examine the small boy, talking him through every step and explaining what is about to happen. His mother, Susan, whom I've known since high school, is standing by with tears in her eyes. Charlie's breathing is ragged and laboured, his lips puffy and swollen. As I lift my stethoscope up to listen to his lungs, I can only hear minimal air moving. They're tight and wheezy, never a good sign. I wrap a blood pressure cuff around his arm. It's blotchy, a mix of pale skin with red, angry-looking spots. Hives on top of pale, poorly circulated skin.

His blood pressure takes forever to read, and when the numbers finally display on the screen, it's worse than I had anticipated.

Winnie returns and hands me the IV supplies and the epinephrine kit, which I take from her first.

"I'm going to need you to mobilize the helicopter; he's going into shock, and he'll need to be transported to the children's hospital." Winnie's mouth forms a thin, grim line.

Outside, the wind howls, and Winnie and I stand in the door for a moment, a silent understanding between us that this situation is dire. The helicopter is the fastest way to the hospital, but its ability to fly in inclement weather is less than ideal. Winnie nods once before retreating to the reception desk to make the necessary phone calls.

I get to work administering another dose of epinephrine, starting an IV, and hanging a clear bag of fluid. Colour returns to Charlie's face, but I know that it'll only be a matter of time before the symptoms return. His condition is severe, and the epinephrine injections that he's had already can only do so much. His blood pressure is improving with the fluid, but not by much. I take a moment to make an epinephrine infusion, which will keep his blood pressure more stable until he arrives at the children's hospital. My hands tremble as I draw the medication out of the vial. Anything I do here is only a temporary fix until we can get the patients to a higher level of care.

"The helicopter is on its way," Winnie informs me from where she's standing just outside the exam room. "They aren't far away, they were about to make a stop at the ski resort but dispatch sent them here instead, They can fly in, but the storm is only just ramping up, so it may be a challenge to get him out."

"We're going to find a way. I can only do so much for him here, and if his allergic reaction continues to progress despite the epinephrine, we're in trouble ..." My voice trails off.

"You can help him, right?" Susan's voice is panicked, the words are the same ones she cried as I struggled to save Noah.

"We'll do everything we can, Susan. First, we need to focus on getting him to the children's hospital," I explain. "The epinephrine I gave him is buying us some time, but he needs to be closely monitored for a little while."

"Go with him, Mason. Please." I can see tears welling in her eyes.

"Susan, I don't know if—" I glance towards Winnie, who is giving me a warning glare, as Winnie does.

"You have to. I can't leave Lainey alone, and I doubt they'll let me bring her." Susan gestures to a toddler sitting in the corner of the exam room. Her white-blond hair is tied up in two curly pigtails and she's playing with a baby doll, blissfully unaware of the tension in the room.

"Isn't your husband around to come and get her?" I suggest, but Susan shakes her head.

"He's out on tour, logging over two hours from here this time." Her voice quakes. "You have to go with him," she repeats. "I don't want him to be alone if ..."

I don't even want to go down the road of imagining the worst, but it's impossible. The clinic, this exam room. The very expression on Susan's face is a stark reminder of what could happen. Not even a year ago, Susan's eldest son had lain in this very exam room when he had died. There was nothing I could have done for him. This time is different, I tell myself, and I'm determined to make sure that it stays that way.

It feels like hours pass, but it's only been about twenty minutes. I've stabilized Charlie for now, with fluids and the epinephrine infusion, but he'll need more care than what I can offer. I hear the familiar beat of the helicopter rotor hovering over the clinic roof before making its landing in the field out back. Winnie runs to meet the crew at the back door, holding it open as they roll the stretcher through.

"If you don't mind, I'd like to come with him," I say to the flight nurse. She's wearing navy blue flight coveralls and has her dark hair slicked back into a low bun. I've always thought the flight crew looked like they belonged in the military, but she smiles at me sweetly.

"That's not necessary. We can take it from here. He'll be at the children's hospital in no time." She tries to dismiss me.

"You don't understand. I need to come. I need to make sure he's okay." I won't let him go alone. I refuse to let Susan down. She's been a constant in Heartwood, and my heart already shattered for her once as I held her while she sobbed on the worst day of her life.

"Are you sure about this, Mason? The storm is getting worse, and I would worry about you being up there if you didn't need to be." The centre of Winnie's brows furrows with worry.

"Don't worry, Winnie. I've been up in the helicopter with patients many times before. Today is no different." I worry that today is, in fact, different. The trees around the helicopter pad out back bow with the force of the wind. The pilot said that it's only the surrounding area affected at the moment, and it isn't severe enough yet to prevent take-off. I just pray that we can stay ahead of it.

"Call Hudson, Winnie. Tell him I'm taking a patient to Calgary. He'll be able to cover any other emergencies if something comes up," I instruct Winnie. It's not an ideal solution. Ideally, I wouldn't be leaving town at all. Hudson has enough first-response training, having been with the fire hall for almost ten years now, that he can handle anything that might arise while I'm away. At least for a little while.

The crew straps Charlie onto the stretcher and loads him up into the helicopter. The flight crew climbs aboard, and I hoist myself in after them. I turn and look out the window as the helicopter leaves the ground to see Winnie standing in the back door of the clinic, her face fraught with concern. It doesn't help the sticky, drowning fear that I'm barely holding back. I gulp it down, bring my focus back to the task at hand. Charlie needs me. Susan Hendrick needs me. And I need to make sure that everyone is okay.

CHAPTER 29
ALLY

My stomach twists into knots as Spencer and I approach the event venue. I've been to what feels like a million public events, most of them televised, and yet tonight my palms are clammy, my neck is flushed, and I feel like if I open my mouth to speak, I might vomit.

I've only been gone for a month, but I'm different now, changed. Maybe not *changed*, but I've rediscovered the parts of myself that I had somehow lost in my effort to live my life for other people. Heartwood reminded me of who I am, and I'm not Ally Wells, reality TV personality, anymore. I'm not even Ally Wells, labour and delivery nurse. I'm just *Ally Wells.*

Being here at this event feels strange, uncomfortable. My dress is tight and restrictive, and my heels are digging in where they shouldn't. I'm here as Spencer's guest at a travel blogger event where I expect to not know anyone, and I'm hoping that people won't recognize me. There's no staying anonymous at one of these functions, but I can try my best to remain elusive. Out of the way of any cameras that might be here. If word got out that I'm back in Vancouver and Nate caught wind, avoiding him would be impossible. He would come after me.

I made a pointed effort not to check social media while I was in Heartwood. The whole point of moving there was to have a break from it all. The reality of what happened hit me like a ton of bricks as soon as I got back to the city and opened my apps. I hesitantly scrolled through Instagram, looking for any mention of my name or Nate's. It was like some form of sick, self-inflicted torture, but I decided if I was going to come back to the city, I better have some idea what I'm in for.

At first, people were highly critical of my exit from the engagement party. The comment sections were chock full of women swooning over Nate and fawning over the fact that I 'broke his precious heart.' Precious is one way of putting it. Though, after a couple of weeks, the comments about me being 'a selfish, callous bitch' subsided, and any slander against me was replaced with wild theories about the whole scheme being a publicity stunt. What's more entertaining than a live engagement and wedding? A live breakup.

Once I was satisfied with my recon, or self-flogging session, I set all my accounts to private, deleted over half of my followers, and deleted the apps right off of my phone. An immediate weight was lifted off my shoulders. It was liberating, being free of other people's opinions of me.

"Are you okay?" Spencer turns to me, her inquiry sincere, pulling me out of my thoughts. "We can go home if you're not ready for it." No matter how cheeky Spencer and I can be with each other, Spencer cares for me, and I appreciate her considering my feelings. I entwine my arm through hers.

"As long as we stick together, I'll be fine. It's been a while since I've been in the public eye like this." We stride up to the trendy bar, our heels clacking on the pavement. The man standing at the door recognizes us both and waves us through, not bothering to check that our names are on the list. He's the first person to recognize me. There will be more.

My skin prickles as eyes turn towards me, trailing Spencer and me as we make our way to the bar. Conversations hush around us as people watch me move through the crowd. This was a terrible idea. What the hell was I thinking? But I'm here for Spencer, and I have to face the music, eventually. I can't help but wish that it was Mason standing next to me. I could use his firm hand on the small of my back to ground me, to give me courage. I try to summon that version of myself now and fail. My hand shakes as I reach out for the drink that the bartender slid across the bar after Spencer ordered for me. God, I feel like a fish out of water. I can barely even speak.

"Ally Wells?" I spin around at the sound of my name being screeched by a woman I don't recognize as if we were old high school besties. The confusion on my face must be obvious because Spencer steps in to introduce us.

"Ally, this is Emily Harris. We connected through Instagram and have met at a few events." The way Spencer raises her eyebrows at me as she makes our introductions indicates that she and Emily aren't as buddy-buddy as she made it seem. Another clout chaser. I internally roll my eyes. I know the type well. The kind of person who would capitalize on any connection, no matter how small, to get ahead.

"It's Ally Wells in the flesh, at our little travel influencer event." Emily looks starstruck. I never considered myself a celebrity by any means, and I will not start playing the part now. Not now that I've resolved to leave that part of myself behind for good.

But that was the Heartwood Ally. Would Vancouver Ally still be so decided? Would being back in the city suck me back into the lifestyle I wanted to shake? It seems like it already has in a small way. Even agreeing to attend another publicized event is proof that I'm not as resolved in my newfound identity after all.

"Spencer is my best friend, so I'm here to support her." I emphasize 'best friend,' hoping Emily will understand that it's an exclusive club of just the two of us. I glance over Emily's shoulder and notice a group of her friends coming over to join us. They're eager and giddy, and I have a feeling it has something to do with me. Great.

"Ladies, I was just chatting with Ally here. She's here with Spencer Sinclair." The following barrage of questions that come flying at me leaves me stunned. I feel like I'm dodging bullets left and right. They want all the details about why I left, and whether Nate and I are back together now that I'm back in the city.

"I guess I needed a break, away from all the hype," I answer. "And no, Nate and I will not be getting back together." I see their collective shoulders droop at the response, but I don't miss the glint in their eyes at the idea that Nate is now confirmed to be single. Nausea roils through my gut. I swallow down the bile rising in my throat as one of Emily's friends pipes up.

"What a clever publicity stunt, the runaway bride." The comment should offend me, that people would assume I would be so conniving. But the tone of the woman's voice makes her sound more envious than anything, and it's just kind of sad. "You must have gained so many followers on Insta now."

"I would give my left tit for a following like that." Another one of Emily's friends pipes up. I notice that yet another one of the women is holding her phone up, trying and failing to be discreet, as if she were taking pictures of me.

"Oh my God, imagine if Nate showed up here." She drops her phone back into the clutch she's carrying. "We would all be famous just for being here."

"Ally, can we take pictures with you for our stories?" Before I can respond, the tall blond is holding her phone up, readying herself to get a selfie.

"I don't really want pictures right now, sorry. I'm kind of trying to lie low since I got back." The woman pouts and gives me a sad puppy dog face that looks kind of punchable. "And for the record, Nate's a piece of shit." I try to warn them about him. While I'm doubtful that I could ever be friends with these women, I would never want one of them getting caught up with Nate. No one should endure that, no matter how many tits they would give to be with him. But the women aren't listening to me. They've already shifted their attention to someone else, some other big Instagram influencer that has walked through the door. I'm not who they want me to be anymore, a preening, attention-seeking celebrity, so they've lost interest. I would be more put off by their vapid and fickle attitude if I wasn't thoroughly relieved to not have to discuss my ex and my very public love life.

I swivel back around towards Spencer and focus intently on the drink in my hand that I'll need more of if I'm going to endure the rest of the evening.

"Uh ... Ally?" I notice Spencer's eyes dart over my shoulder, to where the women are still fawning over the newcomer.

"No. Fucking. Way!" One of them shrieks with excitement, prompting me to glance back briefly, only long enough to catch a glimpse of whoever walked in. And then my head snaps back in a double take.

God, it really is like Nate can be *conjured*. Next time I get close enough to him, I should check to see if he has little horns peeking out of his hair. Scratch that, I never plan on getting that close to him again. I lift my hand to shield my face so I can angle myself away from him and hope that he doesn't notice me.

It's too late, he's already walking towards me. Damn this sparkly, sequin-covered dress that I wore. It makes me look like a freaking disco ball. I thought it was pretty for a night out down-town, but now I realize that I stick out like a sore thumb. A sore thumb that Nate is careening towards.

"Ally, my *darling*." I shudder at the mere sound of his voice. The ice in my glass clinks as my hands tremble. Not with the same nervous jitters that I used to get around Nate. They're trembling with *rage*. I whirl to face him and steel my expression, refusing to give him the satisfaction of knowing how he affects me.

The words are lining up on the tip of my tongue, readying to tell him he can slink back to hell where he came from. I can't be convinced that he doesn't emerge from the netherworld when his name is said three times. How did he find out where I'd be? Spencer's bestie Emily, or one of her little girly pops, must have tipped someone off. Nate cuts me off before I can say anything, and it becomes clear why he's shown up here. The reality is worse than I could have imagined.

"Al. Baby. We've had our differences, and it hasn't always been easy for us. I'm so grateful that you came back to Vancouver *for me*." People whisper around us, and I notice a camera flash out of the corner of my eye.

Fuck my life.

Nate must have noticed too, because he increases the volume of his voice so that he is audible to whoever is filming. "Thank you for giving me another chance, for giving *us* another chance."

I'm hardly able to make sense of the words he's saying. All I know is that they're manipulative and wrong and he's hoping that I'll be *good little Ally* and won't want to make a scene.

"Let's try this again, shall we?" Nate looks around at the crowd and garners some sympathetic laughter from the ones who are in on the joke. And then Nate is lowering himself. Down onto one knee. Nate is getting down on one knee. Nate is getting down on one knee and pulling a small ring box out of the breast pocket of his sport coat. My pulse quickens, and the room spins around me.

"Can we do the damn thing, Ally?" *Puke.* I lift my hand to my mouth to stop myself from gagging and projectile vomiting all over him.

"Absolutely ... fucking not Nate." I square my shoulders to maintain my newfound confidence, but tears sting my eyes. This is all too much. I thought I walked away from this life, this drama, and I want no part of it anymore.

"Please give me another chance, Ally. I'm *begging* you." The glint in Nate's eyes is not loving. Not kind. Spencer approaches from behind me.

"You are a vile piece of human garbage, Nate." I spit out at him.

"Walk away, Ally. Don't give him any more of your energy." She tugs my arm and guides me away from Nate. From another public disaster of a failed engagement. I never should have agreed to come with Spencer tonight. I never should have come back to Vancouver. Heartwood gave me everything I could ever want, and I was happy there. Like truly, from the tips of my hair to the soles of my feet, down to my bones, happy. I was doing the job that I love, helping others, making a real difference. I made friends who cared about *me*, a community that supported each other.

Spencer links her arm through mine this time, steering me back through the crowd and out onto the bustling sidewalk, into the crisp night air.

I pull my jacket tighter around my shoulders as Spencer and I exit the bar onto the street. Fall is in full swing here, but the temperature in Vancouver doesn't drop at night the same way it did in the mountains. Still, a shiver runs through me. We wander a few blocks through the downtown core without saying a word and found a quiet spot to sit and gaze out at the calm water in Coal Harbour. I breathe in the salty evening air. We sit in silence for another couple of minutes, listening to the gentle lapping of the waves, the boats softly knocking against the docks in the marina.

"I'm so tired, Spence." I'm the first to speak once I'm ready to articulate what I'm feeling. Even so, the only word I can think of is *tired*. I'm weary. I've given so much of myself to something that hasn't panned out yet again. "Maybe I should give up, lie down like the doormat that I am and let people walk all over me."

"You don't mean that."

"I do. Everything has gone to shit, Spence. Where am I supposed to go from here? I had it all figured out when I left Nate. I wanted to throw up both middle fingers as I left that stupid engagement party. *Fuck you, Nate*." I raise both hands, my middle fingers pointing towards the marina. It's dark and empty, except for the boats.

"Hey, fuck you too, lady!" someone shouts across the water. Oops. Maybe not empty. Spencer barks out a laugh.

"Sorry, continue," she says between giggles. But I continue like she asked.

"What do I do? I meet a guy, not just any guy either. Like an idiot, I fall for *my boss* and let him pull the same bullshit. He used me, just like Nate did." I shake my head, letting my words sink in. It's the first time I've spoken out loud about all that has happened in the last month. "I wish I could be the type of person who didn't care at all. Like what would happen if I put myself first for once?"

"That's fucking stupid, Ally." Spencer turns to look at me, dead in my eyes. I recoil, taken aback by her brashness. Spencer is feisty, but she rarely calls me out like this. To be fair, I'm normally not a complete fucking mess of a human being, so it tracks. The passion in Spencer's voice as she uttered the word *stupid* was enough to catch me off guard. I'm listening now. "The best part about you is that you *care*."

Well, that's not where I expected this to go.

"The well of your heart is bottomless. You are empathetic and kind. You are intuitive. You choose to see the best in people, to give people the benefit of the doubt even when they clearly don't deserve it. People like you are so rare, so special. That's not something to shut away because you got hurt."

I blink away the tears that are collecting on my bottom lashes. I look out over the harbour; the moon is high now and shimmers, the light broken by a few ripples in the still water.

"The world is full of shitty people, Spence. It's full of people who see me as a target, someone that they can take advantage of."

"Now you're talking lies." Spencer waves the air like what I said left a stench. "Sure, there are assholes in the world. But there are a lot of good people, too. What about your friends that you made back in Heartwood? Winnie, Poppy, Grady." Spencer counts the names on her fingers. "I would bet that Mason was one of those people too; you were just too hurt to see it, and you blamed him for something that your ex did. You were looking for it, waiting for him to prove to you he was 'just like all the other guys.'"

Spencer makes exaggerated air quotes with her fingers.

"Mason lied to me. While I poured my heart and soul into that clinic, he stood back and watched, knowing that every day I spent pouring my heart into the fundraiser that it might all be for nothing. I can't forget about that."

Spencer shakes her head. "After all this, coming back to the city, having Nate propose to you for internet fame, you still can't see it, can you?" I give Spencer a quizzical look, my brows lowering, forming a line between them. "That." She points back in the direction we came from, back towards the bar. "That is what it looks like when people use you, Ally. Mason put all his faith in you, believing that you could do what he couldn't. That's not the definition of taking advantage of someone. Sure, could he have been more honest? Yeah. Do I still want to punch him in the throat for the way he kept it from you? Of fucking course I do. But can you try to understand it? To see where Mason was coming from?"

Spencer has a point. I wouldn't forgive him that easily, but after everything that I knew and loved about Mason, I have to consider that he might not have been using me in the same way that Nate did. Not with malicious intent, anyway. "I'm not saying you should forgive him overnight, but it might help you move on if you can understand why he did the things he did."

Trying to understand isn't what I feel like doing right now, although I know Spencer is right. Even if I can't forgive Mason yet, I can admit that I've been unfair to him, knowing the pressure he was under. I try, and fail, to stifle the pain in my chest before it rips the air out of my lungs. Spencer pulls my head into her lap, and I let the tears come from all the pain and anger that have built up in me over the last few months. Longer. Over my life. For every day that I changed myself to please others.

I mourn for the girl that burned so bright for others to the point of extinguishing her own flame. It seems impossible now to accept that part of myself and find a middle ground, where I can be kind and caring without sacrificing myself. Without making compromises on my own boundaries.

I lay on Spencer's lap for a while; I'm not sure how long. I could lie here forever if it meant I didn't have to face my reality. My phone chimes in my purse, bringing me back to the present moment.

It's Winnie. I sniffle and use the back of my sleeve to wipe the tears from my cheeks, leaving them sticky and tight.

"Winnie, it's nice to hear from you." I try to make my voice sound at least somewhat more chipper than I feel. I don't care how I sound to Winnie over the phone, although I don't particularly want anyone to know that I've been sobbing into my best friend's crotch for the last ten minutes over Mason.

"We miss you, hun." God, it's good to hear Winnie's voice. It confirms for me that the last month in Heartwood wasn't a fever dream. I lived it. I met people I would never forget about, that I hope would never forget about me. "But I have a more urgent matter to talk about."

My heart thumps in my ears. Urgent is never a good word when it comes from Winnie. She's laid-back, carefree, and doesn't get her feathers ruffled over much. My gut clenches. If Winnie is calling me, she's calling about Mason. I say nothing; anything I'd say would be a waste of time, and I need to know why Winnie is calling like yesterday.

"Mason went out in the helicopter with a patient, and he hasn't called yet. He usually calls as soon as they land. There was a dreadful storm rolling in when they left. Has he called you?"

He has not called me. I'm the last person Mason would want

to talk to, and I'm far from a person who he would choose to call before Winnie.

"No. Do you think he's okay?"

"I ... I don't know. It isn't like him not to follow through." Winnie's voice shakes, and it doesn't help the nerves that are buzzing inside me.

"Why was he out on the helicopter in the first place? What happened?" It's also unlike Mason to be so careless. To leave the town unattended in the storm. Whatever it was must have been something awful.

"It was Susan Hendrick's boy, Charlie. You know what happened to Noah, Susan's oldest." Winnie says it as a statement. Like it's a given that Mason had shared that piece of information with me. *Joke's on you, Winnie. Mason told me fuck all, apparently.* "It triggered something in him. He's never been the same since Noah died, and tonight terrified him."

Noah. A memory flashes across my mind, the night at Reggie's. Mason wasn't saying *no* in his sleep, he was saying *Noah*. I couldn't place it at the time.

"I let him die." Mason had been so distraught. A child had died, and Mason blamed himself. My eyes sting again. I'm too emotional to deal with this right now. I rub the spot between my eyebrows to quell the burning in the bridge of my nose.

"Uh, okay, well, if you hear from him, will you call me right away? I'll see if I can find anything out in the meantime."

"Will do."

I click off my phone, stunned and becoming more and more anxious by the minute, speaking a mile a minute to fill Spencer in.

Spencer wastes no time scouring the internet for any news she can find about the storm. All I can do is sit next to her and bite my nails, my leg shaking involuntarily. What more can I do except hope and pray that Mason is okay, and this is all just some big misunderstanding, like he's an idiot and forgot to charge his phone or something? A thought niggles at the back of my mind. He would have found a way to call Winnie, even if he had to use a phone at the hospital.

"Here," Spencer says, turning her phone so I can see the screen. It's a post from someone in Calgary with a video attached. The sound is loud and fuzzy, the high winds in the video distorting the audio, and the image quality is poor and dark. But I can make out the outline of a helicopter wobbling in the sky. The text reads something like 'Medi-vac heli came in for a crash landing. Hope everyone's okay.' I can only skim it before my vision goes blurry with panic.

I can't bear the thought of anything terrible happening to Mason. Not when we left things on such tenuous terms. Whatever Mason had intentionally done, or unintentionally done, it doesn't matter now. I would do anything to know that Mason is safe.

My next thought hits me like a gut punch. There's a chance that Mason isn't safe. Spencer's words clang around in my head. He believed in me, he trusted in my ability to save the clinic against all odds. He knew I would do it. I don't want to be someone who closes themselves off to love. I still want to care and love and pour my heart out. Spencer is right. It's who I am at my core. I want to be more discerning about the people I give myself to. I want to set boundaries so that I can care about and love myself, too.

Mason has some explaining to do, sure. But I hate the wall that I erected between us, the lie I told myself to protect myself—that I don't love him with every part of me.

"I have to go to Calgary." It's all I need to say to Spencer. My friend nods, understanding, and turns back to her phone to look for the next flight out of Vancouver.

CHAPTER 30
MASON

"Hold on back there!" The helicopter pilot shouts into the headsets, his voice sounds distant over the crack of thunder that seems like it's right next to us in the clouds. The cabin of the small aircraft shudders. "We need to make a rapid descent to get out of these storm clouds!"

I'm useless back here as the flight crew secures everything a little tighter, including the stretcher where Charlie is laying.

The helicopter sways, fighting against the wind. The floor drops out from beneath me, my stomach lurching up into my throat as we drop what feels like two hundred feet. An alarm blares in the cabin up front, warning the pilot about the rapid descent. The sudden drop was necessary to get us out of the turbulent cloud cover that had enveloped us faster than expected, but I can't quell the nausea as my gut roils.

This is it. This is where I die. And on my tombstone, it will read, *this asshole should have listened to Winnie.* She'll carve it into the stone herself.

The gusts still rock the helicopter, but overall, the jarring bumps have settled out down here at a lower altitude. We're almost out of the mountains, and the stretch of the flight across open prairies should be smoother.

"What's the ETA on touchdown?" The flight nurse, the one with the slicked back bun, shouts into her mouthpiece.

"Not long now. Another thirty-five minutes or so."

I notice the nurse's expression shift, her mouth forming a tight line as she looks over at Charlie. The epinephrine infusion is helping with his blood pressure, but his breathing has become more laboured. His eyes are wide, and he has a look of panic on his boyish face. I've learned through my years in medicine that a patient looking panicked is an ominous sign. People can often sense when things are going sideways before healthcare professionals do.

"We're almost there, Charlie. Hang in there a little longer," the nurse says, pulling her stethoscope from around her neck to listen to his lungs. Her mouth forms that same grim expression.

"Is my mom coming to the hospital?" The question comes out as a broken rasp as Charlie rests his head back on the stretcher and closes his eyes.

"Charlie? Stay with me, Charlie," the nurse says, giving his shoulder a shake. "We're losing his airway!" She shouts to her partner through her mouthpiece, who places a mask over Charlie's little face and starts pumping air into his lungs, helping him breathe.

"Prepare the intubation supplies." He instructs her. "We're going to need to intubate before his airway swells shut."

Patient transport isn't my area of expertise, but anyone can figure out that inserting a breathing tube is a risky decision in flight.

"Are you sure we can't make it to the hospital? We're only about twenty minutes out now," the nurse says as she opens a kit containing an array of tubes and equipment that would help Charlie breathe.

"Not if you want him to survive," the partner says, a bleak truth. The nurse nods.

"How can I help?" I ask. I fidget in my seat, not quite knowing what to do with my hands. This was my bread and butter in Toronto, for the brief period that I worked in the emergency department. Now I'm frozen, unsure how to help or if I would end up being in the way.

"Keep talking to him, Dr. Landry. We're taking care of it." It's a menial task, when I could help in more meaningful ways. I'm a trained physician, and this nurse and respiratory therapist are barking orders at me. To be fair, I haven't had to intubate a patient in years, let alone a child, and this crew does it day in and day out. But it makes me wonder how many times I barked orders at Ally when she was only trying to help?

I lean down next to Charlie so I can speak into his ear.

"Everything's going to be okay, Charlie. You're safe. We've got you, buddy." My voice quakes. "We're going to put you to sleep now, so we can help you breathe, alright? And when you wake up, Mom's going to be at the hospital with Lainey, and you'll be okay." I don't know if he can hear me, who exactly I'm trying to convince.

First Noah, and now Charlie. If Susan lost both of her boys, it would be the end of my career. For no other reason than I wouldn't be able to endure one more day.

The nurse pushes a few syringes of medications through the IV that I had inserted earlier. All of Charlie's muscles relax, the paralytic drugs taking over. The tube is placed in mere seconds, the ventilator beeping to life and taking over Charlie's breathing. I release a breath of my own. Charlie is stable for now.

"Another rocky descent coming!" the pilot announces over our headsets.

Rocky is putting it lightly. Next to the children's hospital, the helicopter pad is coming into view, but the storm has caught up with us as we slow to come in for a landing. The small aircraft struggles against the gusts, swaying side to side as the pilot attempts to line us up with the fifty-foot concrete pad. I can picture us making it all this way, only to plummet to our deaths during landing. The statistic that most aircraft crash during take-off and landing comes to mind and I try to shove the knowledge out of my head. The thought that replaces it is Ally.

Ally. If I die here today, I will have never gotten the chance to tell her how much she means to me. And worse, the last words I would have spoken to her were bitter ones. I called her a *distraction.* I told her she was useless to me when she was anything but.

The stretcher bumps and sways as the pilot tries to gain control for landing. The final slam onto the pad breaks the landing gear, and we come to a screeching halt. Metal making contact with concrete. Without thinking, I lunge across Charlie, trying to anchor him against the turbulence. The impact pitches me forward, and I use my outstretched arm to break my fall. A searing pain jolts through my arm, dull and electric all at once, as bone crunches against bone.

I grit my teeth against the pain, pushing it aside. Charlie is the priority right now. The epinephrine drip that I started helped to slow the progression of Charlie's shock, but his airway had continued to swell, coming dangerously close to closing completely. He would need to be admitted to the paediatric intensive care unit. Maybe for days.

I watch as the flight crew wheels the stretcher past the triage desk, a team of doctors and nurses waiting to meet Charlie on the other side of the double doors separating the waiting room from the treatment area. The triage nurse gives me a curt nod, and I return it as I watch her eyes move from my face to the arm that I'm bracing against my abdomen. She has the look of a nurse who has worked so many years that at this point, she may as well have X-ray vision. She gives me a knowing glance and waves me over to her desk.

"You're a little old to be coming to the children's hospital, but considering the day you've had, we'll get you in for an X-ray." She holds out her hand for my healthcare card, which I don't have on me since we left in such a hurry. I pat around my jacket pocket and jeans looking for my phone, since I always have a picture of the card, but I come up short. It must have fallen when I lurched forward in the helicopter.

My stomach sinks when I realize how worried Winnie will be waiting by the phone. I answer a few quick questions from the triage nurse and before I know it, she's completed my registration and is ushering me down the hall towards the radiology department.

The X-ray is quick, but I wouldn't say painless. The tech moves my arm around to get the right angle, and each time he does, my bones crunch on each other. It takes everything in me not to be sick.

I can't say how long it will take me to get the results of the X-ray, not that I need them. I could have told the doctor that it was broken the moment I fell, and the searing pain just about blinded me. The triage nurse already did me a favour getting me in for imaging right away, but I sure as hell am not about to skip in front of a child to see the doctor. I consider asking to read the X-ray myself. We haven't had access to imaging for so long that my X-ray reading abilities are a little rusty. I wouldn't trust myself to find an abnormality unless my arm was obviously deformed, and you could tell by looking at it across the room.

That leaves me here, sitting on an old vinyl chair in the hallway, left alone to consider my thoughts, and the one at the forefront is Winnie. She would be sitting at the clinic, waiting for my call, the image of which makes my stomach clench.

My arm is throbbing like a bitch, but it's better now since the triage nurse secured it in a sling, so I get up from the chair and make my way over to the nursing station. Two nurses are sitting behind the desk, clacking away on the computers.

"Can I get a pain killer or something? Some Tylenol?" I ask to no one in particular. The nurse who answers me is young, probably in her early twenties, and she's wearing a similar set of scrubs to the ones Ally liked, just in a dark navy as opposed to the pastel ones Ally prefers. Her expression isn't friendly. How she landed a job in a children's hospital is beyond me.

"Do you want a popsicle and a prize, too?" She jeers as she saunters over to the medication cart and pulls out a couple of pills.

"Actually, yeah. A popsicle would be amazing. Thanks." Nurse Crabby points over to the fridge across the hall from the desk.

"Help yourself." Which I do.

"You mind if I use the phone?" I ask, licking my popsicle, and the other nurse looks up at me this time, taking a second to register what I've requested. Saying nothing, she hands me the receiver over the desk, followed by the phone base so I can dial the number. She turns back to her charting, and I flash her an exaggerated smile.

"Thank you *so* much," I say as I punch in the numbers to the clinic by memory. The other end of the line rings and rings, over and over, until finally Winnie's voice comes over the speaker to let me know I can leave a message.

I hang up and dial her cell and the phone clicks after only a couple of rings.

"Remind me to stock the fridge in the clinic with popsicles when I get back." Not for the kids. For me.

"Mason! Thank God you're alright." The wind of the sigh she releases nearly blows right through the phone. "I've been so worried. There's been a video circulating on the internet saying that the helicopter crashed."

"Well, it wasn't a smooth landing, but I wouldn't say we crashed. I'm waiting for the result of the X-ray, but I think I fucked my arm up pretty bad. I'm at the hospital now. They had to intubate Charlie en route, but he'll be alright, and so will I."

"I'll let Susan know right away about Charlie. She's going to drive to the hospital as soon as the road conditions are safer," Winnie says, adding, "and Ally will be so relieved that you're mostly in one piece."

"Why would Ally be relieved? Winnie, tell me you didn't call her." This was the last thing Ally needed, to be reminded of me when she's trying to move on. I'm trying to move on too, and failing miserably. Her name on my lips makes my heart flutter. Logically speaking, I shouldn't want to hear about Ally, but every fibre of my being does. I want to know everything about her; I want to feel the tiniest thread connecting us, even if it is only through word of mouth.

"Of course, I did, Mason. I called everyone that you might have been in touch with." I can't blame Winnie. It makes sense. But I also have nothing to say in response that won't fuel an argument.

"Don't get mad at me, Mason. It's on you for whatever happened between you and the sweet girl," Winnie scolds.

"Fuck me, I almost died today. Go easy." I fire back, earning a hostile glare from the nurse behind the desk. Children's hospital. Right.

"Maybe a near-death experience is what you needed."

"You want me to be on the brink of dying? I never took you for a sociopath," I snap back.

"Just saying. You were due for a wake-up call," she says, clucking her tongue.

"You're sick, Winnie."

But she's not lying. I was a piece of shit to Ally when all she did was try to help. It's no wonder she left and wants nothing to do with me anymore. She confided in me, told me about how giving she is, how people take advantage of her. I turned around and did the same thing too, in a way. Even if it wasn't intentional. It didn't matter. I didn't consider how my actions would affect Ally, and that was mistake number one. It was a mistake I fear I won't be able to undo at this point.

It's so like me, too. I dedicate myself to this clinic, to my work, and I think that makes me a good and selfless person, but it doesn't. It's a way of avoiding the discomfort that I'm afraid of.

I'm afraid to admit that I can't do it on my own, as Dad did. I pour myself into my job so that I can say that I'm doing it on my own, but at what cost? I push away everyone who cares about me. Even Winnie thinks I'm a piece of shit at this point. I have nothing in my life that means anything other than work. Ally meant something, she meant everything, and I pushed her away.

"Tell me how to fix it, Winnie, and I'll do it. But it's going to take a lot more than an apology at this point."

"Show her she matters to you. Show her you have room for a partner in your life. That you want to share some of your responsibilities with her. That's all she wanted," Winnie says it like it's easy. Like I can snap my fingers and have the solution right in front of me.

A partner. I can't imagine what having a partner would even look like.

I've always believed in this narrative that I can't have both things; a successful career as a doctor and a real life. Now I'm wondering if that's true, or if I was just too damned proud to let anyone in to help me, to take some of my burden. Ally tried. She was willing to help me and not let me feel like I was lesser because of it. Ally understood the weight that I carry and was willing to carry it, too. She made me better, opened me up to new ideas and experiences. She let me have *fun*.

Someone taps me on the shoulder and I look over to see the flight nurse holding my phone out to me. The screen is cracked.

"I gotta go, Winnie. I'll be home later. I'll text you when I get in, but don't wait up." I click the receiver down and take my phone from the nurse.

"We found it when we were cleaning up," she says before walking away again.

"Thanks," I call after her.

I click on my phone to make sure that it still works, and it's in perfect working order. A little too good. I have an unopened text from Jett. Probably to say something snarky about me causing a plane crash.

JETT

> Sorry about you and Ally, buddy. She was too good for you, anyway.

It started off with a decent sentiment, at least. I see that he's also sent a link for an Instagram post I open. I haven't used Instagram in ages, but Jett is always on social media, reading all the comments about how *hot* all the snow bunnies think he is. I bet he runs his own fan account.

The post is from some woman, *@emharrisxo*, that I've never heard of before. But I recognize the person she's filming. I would recognize those long strawberry waves anywhere. My chest seizes. Ally is stunning, a shimmering ray of light in a sparkly champagne mini dress, her lean legs on full display and looking toned in her strappy heels.

Unfortunately, I also make out the person who is down on one knee in front of her. I watch in horror as he pulls out a ring box, the diamond inside so massive it's visible from across the room. And Ally, the woman who was, just a few weeks ago, forcing me into a relationship so she could get rid of this guy, raises her hand to her mouth in shock.

The word she utters is almost inaudible, but the shape of her lips forms the word *absolutely,* and I shut off the phone. I can't watch another second of the woman I love agreeing to marry someone else. Not someone else. *Nate.* The sleazeball that took advantage of her.

I want to hate Ally for it. I want to let my rage bubble up for her turning around and leaving after everything we shared. Nate is a piece of shit, but he's a piece of shit that dropped everything to find her in Heartwood, who pursued her with such fierce determination. I can't blame Ally for seeing the appeal in that. For choosing that over the small morsels of attention she had to fight to get with me.

CHAPTER 31
ALLY

THE FLIGHT over the Rockies and the descent into Calgary were harrowing. Multiple bags fell out of the overhead compartments, and I had to pry my fingers from the armrests when we landed. If that was the flight in on a commercial jet, I don't even want to imagine what it was like for Mason in a helicopter. Nausea roils in my gut as I consider what might have happened to Mason up there, what might have happened before I got the chance to make things right with him. To kiss him just one more time.

The pilot's voice crackles over the speaker as people unbuckle their seat belts. *"Welcome to Calgary. We apologize for the bumpy ride. For anyone with connecting flights, be sure to check the board for any delays. The storm seems to have affected many flights leaving Calgary International Airport tonight. Stay safe out there, folks."*

I only wish Mason would have heeded that warning. If I wasn't so worried about him, I'd be absolutely fuming at his recklessness. I can't let myself go down that road, not yet. Not until I see him with my own two eyes and confirm that he has both feet safely on the ground.

Spencer unloads both of our bags from the overhead bin. She had insisted on coming with me the moment I said I was going.

She also insisted on using her travel points for the flight and a rental car. I look over at Spencer, my heart swelling with gratitude. This entire experience would be nerve-racking without her. I owed her before, but now I can't think of anything that will repay this.

We unload off the plane as quickly as we can and rush through the airport, walking at a near jogging pace. The place packed with stranded travellers. People mill around in the terminal, displaying obvious outbursts of frustration over the number of delayed flights. Some have given up, taking to waiting out the storm by sleeping on the ground. The universe has my back today.

As we near the exit, lightning flashes outside, followed by a loud crack of thunder overhead. We make a quick stop at the rental car desk—this time I insist we have a newer car, one that looks reliable, and the rental clerk gives me a *duh* expression. Of course, they have better cars here than at the Heartwood airport. We secure the keys and continue to the parkade, making our way to our assigned car.

"Where to?" Spencer asks as we climb into a boring silver compact sedan. Boring is good. Boring is reliable. We had stopped by Spencer's apartment only long enough to collect some toiletries and a change of clothes, so we only have our two bags to throw into the back seat.

I pause. I don't know. It was a snap decision that made me hop on a flight to find Mason in Calgary, and now I realize I don't have a clue where he might be. He could already be on his way back to Heartwood. Or at a different hospital if the crash was as bad as the video made it seem. My hands shake as I fumble around, trying to open Google Maps on my phone. *Focus Ally.*

"Uh, good question." My eyes dart around as I try to think of how we might find Mason. He had answered none of my calls before the flight took off, and there are still no messages from him when I turn my phone back on after the flight. "Winnie said he was taking Charlie to the hospital. She must have meant the children's hospital. Charlie can't be over eight years old."

Speaking the words out loud makes the reality of the situation that much more grim. Charlie is so young. Whatever had happened to him tonight must be awful if it caused Mason to endanger his own life. It must have provoked some visceral reaction, causing all the memories that still torment Mason to come flooding back.

Maybe Mason and I are more alike than I realized. Mason was willing to put his life on the line to make sure that Charlie was okay. Maybe Mason also needs to learn which parts of his heart to keep open and which parts to guard. Perhaps we can both help each other figure it out.

"Alright, we start there." Spencer plugs in her phone before I've even gotten my app open, and punches in the directions to the children's hospital. It's another twenty-five minutes away. My knee bounces as my nerves buzz inside of me. I try to get a hold of Winnie once more, but there's no answer on her end either.

Rain sluices down the windshield, making the road impossible to see, especially in the dark. Eyes fixed on the road, Spencer grips the steering wheel until we round the corner and she pulls into the loading zone in front of the colourful building. In the daylight I'm sure it looks cheerful, but at night in the red glowing light of the emergency department sign, the looming building feels ominous.

"You run in, and I'll park the car," Spencer says, pulling the sedan up in front of the emergency room entrance.

Don't jump to conclusions, I remind myself as I step out of the car and into the pouring rain.

There are a million different scenarios I could walk into. All the possibilities play through my mind as I try to prepare myself. What if Mason isn't even here? My hair is already stuck to my face as I enter the waiting room.

I approach the triage nurse and my voice shakes, trying to get out the words. The hospital doesn't faze me; I've been working in one for years. It's the impending news from the nurse that makes my hands tremble.

"Is there a Mason Landry here? He came in with the little boy from Heartwood," I squeak out. I'm breathless even though I've only walked ten feet from the car inside the building. The triage nurse blinks back at me for a second before she turns to her computer and types a few things into her keyboard. She seems too calm and unbothered considering the circumstances. I want to scream at her that the man I love might be in danger, that I need to see him now, and if she doesn't let me in, I'm going to ... I don't know what I'll do. I've never felt so determined, so *aggressive*.

"Ah, you mean the man-child that's been eating all our popsicles?" Relief floods over me and a shaky laugh escapes from my mouth. Mason is here. He's alive. He's alive, and he's well enough to be eating popsicles and annoying the hell out of the nurses. Just as Mason Landry would. "He's in fast-track."

The nurse gestures towards the double doors leading to the treatment area and smacks a button on the wall that causes the doors to swing open, letting me through.

"Thank you." My voice catches, tears threatening to spill.

I push through the doors and search the bustling department for those chestnut brown waves and the plaid flannel that I would bet Mason is wearing. It doesn't take me long to spot him. He's outstretched on a hospital bed that he is far too big for, holding a bright orange popsicle. He looks up just in time to see me walking through the door, and my gaze meets his deep brown eyes.

The sight of him stops me in my tracks. For a moment, Mason looks stunned, as if I'm the last person he expected to walk through those doors. Then he closes his eyes, shoulders slumping with relief. I have about five seconds to reconcile the simultaneous overwhelming love and the burning rage. He rises from the stretcher as I close the gap between us.

"Don't get up," I say, noticing the sling on his arm, but Mason doesn't sit back down. We regard each other, and I absorb every detail of his face, wanting to etch this moment into memory.

"Of course I'm getting up for you." He says as he makes his

way to standing. His mouth opens, but I interrupt him before he can say anything else.

"What the fuck is wrong with you?" I shove the shoulder that isn't being supported by the sling, but he still winces slightly. Good. Mason can endure some discomfort for the absolute terror he just put me and everyone else who loves him through. My voice is harsh and the words land, making Mason take a small step backwards.

"Me? What about you, future Mrs. Nate Winslow?" Mason reaches down and picks up my hand, expecting to find what, I'm not sure. An engagement ring? He must have seen the video circulating of the party. That sure made its way around quickly.

"How dare you, Mason Landry? You think I would show up here with a ring on my finger? *Nate's* ring on my finger?" Mason's chest falls as he lets out the breath he had been holding.

His voice lowers an octave as his expression goes serious as he says, "The only ring I want to see on your finger is mine, Honeybee." Mason lifts his functional hand to cup my cheek, and I let my eyes flutter closed at his touch. His thumb brushes my cheek, calloused but still soft, and I soak in the feeling of it on my face.

Until I remember that I'm still mad at him.

"So what made you decide that you had a death wish? I mean, no rationally thinking person would have gotten on that helicopter if they didn't have to." There's still a soft wobble in my voice. I've been terrified for him, and now, admitting that fact feels like I'm opening my chest and exposing my heart.

His smile disappears, and his gaze darkens.

"The fact that I lost you." I wasn't expecting an actual response, but I can tell by his tone that he isn't really joking. "I'm so sorry, Ally." His cracked voice giving away the emotions overtaking him.

"I just," I stammer. The last three hours are hard to fathom enough to put into words. "I thought something happened to you.

I saw that video, and I kept thinking that the last time we spoke it was ... we were angry with each other."

"I'm not angry with you, Honeybee. Never with you. Even when I thought you had gone back to that scumbag, I was never angry at you. I beat myself up thinking that I was the one who let you go. That I made you feel like you weren't the most important person in the world to me. You are the most important person in the world to me." Mason says as he slides his hand from my cheek around to the back of my head, twining his fingers through the hair at the nape of my neck. I rest my forehead against his chest, minding the arm supported by a sling between us. My tears soak into his T-shirt, and as I pull away, he holds my chin between his thumb and his finger and tips my head back so I'm looking up at him. "But it's okay if you're still angry with me. You have every right to be. You can let yourself be angry with me."

The edges of my outrage have dulled, less sharp now, less painful, but still there.

"Being back there, seeing all the people that only like me when I'm playing small, playing the part they want me to, it made sense to me. It's the intention that counts. And you, Mason Landry, don't have an ounce of ill-intent in your body." Mason's mouth turns up into a soft smile that makes me want to kiss it. "That, and the fact that Spencer gave me a well-deserved verbal spanking."

"Remind me to thank Spencer for that." Mason winks at me.

"Mason, who is Noah?" I blurt. It's the answer to the question I've been carrying around in my heart ever since I got that first glimpse at what makes Mason tick. The last puzzle piece forming a picture of his motivation for giving so much of himself to the clinic.

Mason nods. He sits down on the stretcher and pats the space next to him for me to sit beside him.

Sitting in the fluorescent light of a children's hospital emergency department, cartoon paintings of animals dancing along the walls around us, Mason bares his soul to me.

"Just after I took over the clinic, I had a patient, Noah," Mason starts. "He lived next door to Winnie and she babysat him a lot. Which meant he hung out in the clinic a lot since she was always there." I stay silent, not wanting to move, or breathe, or do anything that might interrupt him. His voice is low, a deep rumble, and the weight of this story is palpable. This talk is a long time coming for him.

"One evening, I got a call from Winnie. Several calls, all of which I missed. I was out on a date with this lovely girl that I had had a crush on since elementary school. I didn't want any interruptions. I couldn't believe I was getting a date with her. There was no way I was ruining it."

I ignore the pang of jealousy I get imagining Mason so excited to be going out with another girl and let him continue. This is Mason's story. It has made him who he is. He wouldn't be Mason without it, and whatever happened, I wouldn't change it. I wouldn't change him.

Mason continues, his eyes still fixed on his lap. "When I got to the clinic, Winnie was there with Noah and his mom. He was limp in her arms." He swallows hard, his Adam's apple bobbing in his throat, before carrying on. "He had been climbing the big oak tree in their front yard and fell from one of the higher branches. He had lost consciousness but then came to and his mother, Susan, thought he was fine. By the time he came into the clinic, the bleed in his brain had happened so fast."

My throat clenches around a hard lump. Shame and grief are written on Mason's face, the way he is staring down at his lap, refusing to meet my gaze.

"He died that night, and there was nothing I could do to help him." Tears collect on his dark lashes and in a moment of instinct, I shift closer to Mason, taking his hand in mine.

"Hey. Look at me," I say, and he does. His eyes are glassy. "That was *not your fault*."

"If I had just gotten there sooner—" he starts.

"Then what? You don't know what would have happened, Mason. With a fall like that, there was nothing you could have done, not in Heartwood. It would have been hours for him to get to a hospital with a CT scanner and even then, there's no guarantee he would have survived."

Mason looks up at me now, pain evident in his eyes. They hold every memory of that moment.

"You are just one person, Mason. You cannot be all things to all people, and you certainly cannot hide yourself away, work yourself into the ground, because of one freak accident."

Mason's eyes flick down to my mouth. In an instant, his lips meet mine, soft but purposeful. When he pulls away, he leans his forehead against mine.

"I didn't mean to use you, Ally," he whispers, and I nod, finally understanding the tangled mess of emotions that he has been grappling with. "I didn't tell you about the funding crisis because, well, first because I was your boss, and it wasn't your problem to fix. But then I started to fall for you, and I cared about you, and I never wanted you to worry about the stability of your job. I truly believed that you could save the clinic. That *we* could save it, together, before it ever came close to shutting down."

"I see that now, Mason. My heartbreak was so fresh, and I was looking for confirmation that all men are the same. All men are like Nate. I wanted to protect myself from getting hurt again. I didn't know how to do that because I've never learned how to stand up for myself. So I chose to protect myself by running. But it wasn't fair. To you, or to me." I look up into Mason's eyes before uttering the words that I've come here to say. "Promise me this time things will be different, Mason. That you won't close yourself off to me."

"Trust me, Ally. I want things to be different, too. I'm done trying to do this on my own."

Before I can respond, Mason's hand comes up to cradle my face, and his lips meet mine. I melt as his tongue grazes my lips, needy, motivated.

"This is a children's hospital." We pull apart, startled by a voice behind us. Spencer is standing next to the curtain that barely provides any amount of privacy around the stretcher, arms folded, and laughs. "Let's keep things G-rated, shall we?"

Spencer winks at me and gives Mason a very pointed once over. I can't tell if she's checking to make sure he's okay or trying to make him feel judged for what he's put me through. I wouldn't be mad about either. I make brief introductions, still trying to wrap my head around the fact that Mason and Spencer haven't met. The two people I love most are here, with me, in the same room, and my heart is whole.

"What a waste of a perfectly good voodoo doll!" Spencer rolls her eyes.

"You made a voodoo doll of me?" Mason stammers. I give him a *don't ask* look.

To my relief, Mason laughs it off before turning back to me.

"Will you come home with me, Ally? I mean, to Heartwood?" Mason's words don't need clarification. Heartwood is my home now, and I nod, a smile taking over my face.

"What about—" I croak, turning to Spencer. I'm not about to just leave her high and dry after she had come all this way for me.

"Don't worry about me. I'm sure I'll figure something out," Spencer offers and she leans in to give me a peck on the cheek.

"Oh, shut up, *I'll figure something out.* You're coming back to Heartwood. We can find you a place to stay to wait out the storm," I insist. After everything that Spencer has done for me, it's the least I can do. I'm also hoping that she'll meet Grady and decide to stay in Heartwood a little while longer.

Spencer's mouth opens in protest, but I watch her expression change and her eyes widen, her mouth hanging ajar. Her cheeks flush, the colour almost matching her fiery hair. My head swivels, following her distracted gaze all the way back to the door.

Grady Landry, all six-and-a-half tattooed feet of him, is striding in through the double doors, a rain-soaked T-shirt showing off his muscular biceps.

I shake my head. From the moment I met Grady, I knew he would make Spencer absolutely feral. She's a sucker for men like him, tattooed and burly. Spencer is nothing but predictable.

"Ready to go?" Grady stops beside us, and I notice the brief, almost imperceptible second he takes to let his eyes roam over Spencer.

Spencer nods. She turns to me and shields her mouth with one hand as she mouths the words *Oh. My. God.* And then I watch her try to regain her composure.

"Yeah, okay. I'll come back to Heartwood with you. Wait out the storm," she says. The corner of my lift quirks up along with one of my eyebrows. *This could be dangerous*, I think to myself. But out loud, all I say is "We're ready" as I twine my fingers through Mason's. "I'm ready to go home."

CHAPTER 32
MASON

IT's NEARING midnight by the time we make it back to Heartwood. The conditions on the road were slick, and flash flooding made some sections almost impassible. The wind and rain are already easing up, a perk of fall storms in the prairies—they're fierce but swift and leave as quickly as they roll in. Still, Grady took the drive slowly, white-knuckling the wheel for an hour and a half.

We dropped off the rental car at the airport, and all crammed into his truck, Ally and I in the back seat, leaving Spencer and him up front. Ally sat close to me, not wanting to let go of my hand. She rested her head on my shoulder, quickly falling asleep once we hit the highway. The heavy feeling of Ally's head on my shoulder makes me feel like my heart will burst, and I lean down to breathe in the heady coconut smell of her hair more than once.

Spencer and my brother bicker playfully in the front seat for most of the drive until Spencer also dozes off. Grady isn't used to being around girls that can handle his teasing, let alone hand it right back. She's a firecracker if there ever was one, but she would do anything for Ally, and that makes it hard not to like her.

The cool night air is fresh after the rain and the smell of the wet earth is almost sweet when Grady drops Ally and me off at the cabin.

"You can stay at the cabin with us, Spence," Ally offers as she hops down out of the truck. She's still groggy from her nap in the car. She has a faint wrinkle along her cheek from where it rested on the seam of my shirt, but she's so beautiful I can't take my eyes off of her.

I have to blink a few times to convince myself that I wasn't imagining her standing there in the emergency department. How had I been so stubborn that I didn't see how much I need Ally in my life? There's no point in thinking about it now. Right now, I want to get Ally into the cabin and show her just how thankful I am that she came back for me.

"Thanks, but fuck no. I will not be a third wheel to your little *reunion*." Spencer laughs, her finger waving between Ally and me. "Grady can drop me off at the motel."

I don't hide the sigh of relief I let out. As much as Spencer has been an amazing friend to Ally, and I owe her everything for bringing Ally back to me, all I want right now is to have the cabin all to ourselves. Ally whacks my arm with the back of her hand, but she doesn't protest Spencer's suggestion, either.

We wave off Spencer and Grady and head inside the cabin. It's dark inside. I haven't been back here since Ally left. I couldn't bring myself to face it, the colossal mistake that I made. But tonight, coming home with Ally feels right. I used to avoid the cabin, never wanting to feel the emptiness that Dad had left behind. But Ally came into my life and filled a void, and now I can't imagine living anywhere else with her.

Sure, the cabin will need some renovations, maybe an addition out the back. It won't be big enough for a family. It was only supposed to be a vacation property. Until a month ago, I didn't think that my heart was big enough to even entertain the idea of having a love life, let alone a family, and now I want both. And I want both with Ally.

Ally frowns at her tote bag as she plops it down on the bed.

"What's wrong?" I ask, my heart skipping a beat as I consider Ally may be having second thoughts.

"I just realized I moved *all* my stuff back to the city and now I have to move it all back again. Not to mention the fact that I only brought one change of clothes with me."

I laugh, a mix of relief and unadulterated joy that this is the biggest problem between us right now. I close the space between Ally and me once again, wrapping my hand around the back of her head, twining my fingers through her hair and gently tugging on it so she's looking up at me. I bring my lips close to hers, just grazing them.

"Who says you'll need clothes?" I whisper against her mouth before letting our lips collide. Ally smiles into my mouth as she kisses me back.

"Who says you'll be doing anything wild with that arm of yours?" Right. I forgot about that.

"Minor inconvenience," I say. I'm not letting anything stop me from fucking Ally right here and right now. "You might just have to do most of the work. You think you can handle that, Honeybee?"

Ally's mouth curls into a playful grin as she places her hand on my chest, pushing me back and down onto the bed.

"I think you're the one that won't be able to handle not touching me while I ride you." I allow her to guide me back down onto the mattress, relishing watching Ally as she moves to unbuckle my belt. Ally takes an excruciatingly long time undressing me, taking extra care of removing my shirt over my broken arm. The break isn't as bad as it could have been, and the doc put it into a sling instead of a cast, but I still can't move it or put weight on it.

I shiver as Ally plants soft kisses all the way down it from my shoulder to my elbow as if her love might be the very thing that heals me. What she doesn't realize is that she already has. She's already healed me in ways she could never understand or imagine. She brought me back to life. I had hidden myself away for so long, too afraid to confront my fears, my demons. Too caught up in the stress and burden of my job.

Ally removes her own clothing sensuously, as if putting on a show for me. I take in the soft curves of her body as each piece falls to the floor. Ally is stunning. She crawls across the bed and brings herself up to straddle me, her soft flesh making contact with my cock, instantly hardening it. Ally takes her time, leaning down to run a trail of kisses up my chest. She reaches down and takes my cock in her hand, rubbing my tip in small circles around her clit.

This time feels different. This time, there are no walls between us. Everything is laid out bare. We're not in a hurry. We have all the time in the world together. This time, we savour every single moment, allowing it to stretch out before us, slow and sweet.

Ally tilts her hips back, never once letting her lips break from mine. She lowers her hips down, taking my cock inside her. She's already ready for me, for my size. I moan into Ally's mouth, the two points of contact between our bodies feeling like pure, sizzling, hot fire. And then Ally pulls her lips away from mine, sitting up tall so she can rock her hips back and forth, her firm breasts bouncing with each movement. She tilts her head back, eyes rolling upward, her lips parting in a soft moan.

She rocks on me and rides me until we both find release and collapse into each other, our breathing ragged and shallow. Ally lays her head back on the pillow next to mine, her eyes closed in sweet ecstasy, the afterglow of pleasure almost lighting her from within.

Ally is the light at the end of a long and dark tunnel. She's the bright spot that gives me hope for the future. Guilt settles in my gut, a hard knot that I'm struggling to undo. I never meant to push her away. I let my fear of failure get the better of me. The part of me that believed there was no room for her got the better of me. I'll never be able to undo that.

I brush a strand of that beautiful strawberry blond hair off her cheek.

Wrapping my good arm around Ally's petite frame, I pull her in close so her head is resting on the soft spot beneath my shoulder. She snuggles into me, trailing her fingers up and down my arm, stopping at the tattoo on my bicep.

"I meant to ask you, what does this mean?" Ally asks, one finger tracing the outline of the bear I had inked on my skin last year.

"Protector." I say, pausing for a beat before elaborating. "The bear is a symbol of protection, a leader who defends others against all threats. The mountains represent Heartwood." I feel Ally nod against my chest.

"You carry such a heavy burden, Mason, always feeling responsible for others, putting others above yourself."

"I would never hesitate to protect the people I love, Honeybee. And now you're at the top of that list." I bury my face in her hair, breathing in her sweet scent.

"I know you'll always have other priorities, Mason. I'm never going to ask you to neglect your role. I know how important that is and always will be. I just want to know that I'm important to you, too." The fact that Ally even has to question where she is on my priority list is too much.

"You're all I need, forever, Ally Wells," I whisper, placing my lips on her forehead.

"Is there room for me in there this time?" Ally leans away and points her finger at my chest, right to my heart.

"More than enough. I'm done shutting everything and everyone out. I promise." And I mean it, I will do everything in my power to make her believe me. At this moment, I think I know how I can do that.

Ally smiles and nuzzles her head into my chest.

"I never thought I'd be the kind of girl that sleeps with her boss," Ally says with a low, raspy giggle.

"What would you say about me not being your boss anymore?" I ask.

"You're not going to fire me now, are you?" Ally turns from where she is lying on my chest to look up at me. She knows I would never do anything so drastic, not in a million years. But concern still shadows her expression.

"Never, Honeybee. I don't want to be your boss anymore. I want to be your partner, your equal." I lift my hand to tuck a stray lock of hair behind Ally's ear. "I want to put your name on the clinic license."

A smile spreads across Ally's face. Her eyes glimmer as they become dewy, making my insides quiver. Just her gaze alone has me coming undone, powerless against her.

"Are you sure? You'd do that for me?" Ally has never felt appreciated for what she brings to the table. People have always found some way of using her willingness and drive, but they've never seen her for the unstoppable force that she is. Not the way I do, now.

"Positive. I'm not just doing it for you, either. You bring out the best in me, Ally. And I am happy to relinquish some control over the clinic to you. Your first order of business as a partner will be to find another nurse to hire."

Ally stretches herself up so she can plant a warm kiss on my mouth, delicious and sweet. Ally is mine, and I am Ally's, and as our lips move together in unison, I can't help but think that we'll make an unstoppable team.

"I love you, Mason Landry," Ally whispers into my mouth. And that's what does it.

From now on, the only person I'm on call for 24/7, is Ally Wells.

ONE YEAR LATER

"The swaddle should be nice and snug, tighter than you think. Babies love to feel safe and secure," I explain, demonstrating the optimal technique for swaddling a newborn. The group of women sitting in a semi-circle in the clinic's waiting room watch with rapt attention. "Try it out."

I hand out a swaddling blanket to each of the mothers-to-be and observe as their hands fumble and shake as they wrap their baby dolls.

"I feel like I'm going to squish him." One woman laughs from the back of the room. It wasn't challenging getting the prenatal program up and running. What was challenging was finding the physical space for everyone who wanted to attend.

Heartwood has seen a massive influx of newcomers over the last year, and an even bigger influx of new families, or couples hoping to start their families. The interest in the group is more than I ever could have imagined, and now I spend my evenings three days a week, here, teaching everything from swaddling to breastfeeding tips to administering Tylenol for teething.

And *I love it.*

There's something about watching a woman walk through

those doors, their anxiety palpable, and helping them develop actual skills that will empower them as they go through their transition to motherhood. It makes me downright giddy.

I encourage each one of them to bring their partners, those who have them. Occasionally they do, though many of them work long hours as loggers, leaving the women to care for their families on their own. I don't judge though. It just fuels my passion for making this program a safe space, a supportive community.

"Amazing job today, ladies. We'll see each other next week. Except for Faye, who will hopefully not be joining us, as she'll be too busy welcoming her little one." Everyone turns in their seats towards Faye, who looks about two years pregnant. She places a tender hand on her swollen belly, and the gesture sends a pang through my chest. *Longing.*

"At this rate, I think I'm going to give birth to a teenager." Faye chuckles.

The women all gather around her to give her their well wishes as I wander around the waiting room, collecting all the baby dolls.

"Will you be joining us at Thistle + Thorne tonight?" Eva, a brunette with just a hint of a baby bump, asks as she gathers up her purse. Appetizers and tea is the Friday group's ritual, and the invite is always open to me, too.

"Not tonight, Eva. My parents are visiting from out of town, and we're having dinner with them. You enjoy!"

I finish tidying up the clinic and lock the front door as my phone *pings* in my pocket. I know it's Mason texting from the ringtone.

Mason: Coming home soon? Dinner is almost ready. xo

Home. *Our* home. He moved into the cabin a couple weeks after I came back to Heartwood, and he's slept there with me every night since. It wasn't easy for him to loosen the tight grip he had on the daily and nightly operations of the clinic. But packing up the cot in his office and moving it back to the shed with the rest of the camping gear was a necessary step and one that slowly brought life back to him.

Therapy is also playing a part in Mason's return to his life outside of work. Though it wasn't an easy go at first, once Mason accepted that his reaction to what happened with Noah was a symptom of a larger problem, he sought out a therapist who diagnosed him with post-traumatic stress disorder. The first few weeks were the hardest, as he had to relive the events of that day, the blame that he placed on himself. But he was able to process it in a much healthier way. Slowly but surely, the cracks in Mason's heart healed, and the light returned to his eyes, his laugh becoming even more infectious than before.

I quicken my pace as I close up the clinic. Thinking about Mason's smile makes me want to be with him now. Not a day goes by where I don't see Mason, and I wouldn't have it any other way. He proposed to me once, eager to solidify our relationship with official vows. I don't need official vows to feel secure with him, though. After one catastrophic engagement, I am more than content taking my time before jumping into another. Neither of us are going anywhere, and to me, that reassurance counts for more than a ring on my finger would.

The gravel of the driveway crunches beneath my feet as I near the cabin. I wrap my wool coat tight around me as a shiver runs through me. Dusk is blanketing the valley now, and the glow from the front window of the cabin is inviting, the smoke rising from the chimney beckoning me inside to warm myself by the fire.

As I open the front door, I'm greeted by the warm smell of herbs and spices, saliva pooling in my mouth.

"Hi, sweetheart." My mother greets me at the door, planting a kiss on my cheek.

"Hi, Mom."

A pit forms in my stomach as I recall the way I avoided talking to her for the last year, all because I was too afraid to tell them I was forging my own path. I push the feeling away, bringing her into a tight hug instead. There's no sense in dwelling on the past. All I can do is move forward, start owning my truth, and allow the people around me to either accept me or walk away.

My parents would never walk away. Despite the disappointment they felt when I told them I would stay in Heartwood for good, they did their best to support me. Dad had to throw in a few snide comments about the fact that I would officially be an *Albertan*. The rivalry between British Columbians and Albertans is unmatched. He came around eventually.

It helped that they came to visit during one of the most stunning seasons: larch season, when all the trees in the Rockies change to a gorgeous, vivid yellow.

Mason and my dad erupt into laughter, clinking their beer glasses together in the kitchen. Mason turns back to the mushroom risotto he's stirring on the stove. The sight of him cooking, wearing an apron around his waist, hugging his hips where his snug fitted T-shirt meets his jeans, makes me salivate more than the smell of the food cooking. My eyes dart to a vase of peonies sitting on the counter that weren't there this morning. Mason must have clipped them from the bush he planted in our yard.

My dad swivels in his seat at the island as he hears my voice and doesn't hesitate to envelop me in a bear hug. I breathe in the familiar earthy scent of him. A year away from my parents was too long. For a split second, a stabbing feeling pricks at my chest as I remember how long it's been since Mason hugged his parents this way. A soothing sense of gratitude replaces it as my dad pulls out of our hug and wanders into the kitchen to place a firm, fatherly hand between Mason's shoulder blades. My parents took Mason in, no questions asked. If I love him, they love him, they said.

"Hi, Honeybee," Mason says, handing me a glass of wine.

"None for me, thanks." I place a hand on his muscular back as I stretch up to kiss him. He leans down to meet me, our lips meeting in a more comfortable way now, but the feeling of his mouth on mine still ripples through me from the tips of my fingers to the tips of my toes.

"How was your class?" my dad asks.

"Amazing. It's so special watching how the women come together and support each other. I'll never get tired of it," I say, thinking about the way they all offered words of encouragement as Faye got up to leave.

"We are so proud of you, honey," my mom chimes in. "You've created such a beautiful community, a beautiful life, for yourself here in Heartwood."

I fight back the tears that are stinging my eyes. As much as I have tried to not seek validation from my parents, from anyone, the words touch something deep inside me. To be loved for your true self is a thousand times better than being liked for someone you're not.

"Thanks, Mom," I say past the lump in my throat.

"I know it took us some time to come around, but we see now that Heartwood is a special place, and we're so happy you feel at home here," my dad says, wrapping an arm around my shoulder and giving it a squeeze.

"I'm proud of her, too," Mason pipes up. "Ally has done a phenomenal job at the clinic. It would not be what it is today without her. Hell, I would not be where I am without her. She saw potential in me when I couldn't see it myself."

"Here, here." My dad lifts his glass, prompting everyone else to do the same. Except my hand is empty.

"It's just too bad I won't be able to teach the prenatal class much longer," I blurt. Mason looks at me with a furrowed brow, trying to comprehend. "I'll have to join as a member soon."

My mom is the first to realize the meaning behind my words and her eyes go wide before she throws her arms up to wrap them around me. A moment later, I see it dawn on Mason, too.

"Wait, is this real? Are you pregnant, Ally?" He asks, shock sweeping across his features. I nod, unable to hide my joy. The very first moment I had helped a mother through birth, had witnessed the flood of emotions when I placed her baby on her chest, I knew that I was meant to be in her place one day, too.

"Sure am, Papa Bear." I say, waiting for Mason's response as nerves flicker in my belly. Ever since that day at the hospital, Mason has talked about wanting to get married, and have kids of our own. I'm just hoping he's not tied to that specific order.

His eyes shift back and forth between mine as he processes the news, and then suddenly his arms are around my waist, and he's lifting me off the ground. He twirls me around once, before setting me gently on the floor, and pulling me into a kiss that says all that I need to hear.

A family. It's all I've ever wanted, and now I get to have one with Mason. The man who jumped at the chance to play pretend doctor with Annabelle, the man whose identity as a protector is tattooed on his skin. This is all I've ever wanted, and so much more.

WANT A BONUS SPICY SCENE
WITH ALLY AND MASON?

Sign up for my newsletter and receive your spicy bonus scene. Go to www.megrileyauthor.com or scan the QR code below:

I send out e-mails once a month with sneak peeks, updates about upcoming books, and some lifestyle content! I never share your information and you can unsubscribe any time.

EXCERPT FROM THE BOYFRIEND BOYCOTT

SPENCER

There's a six-and-a-half-foot wall of muscle and tattoos climbing off the motorcycle on the gravel drive outside the cabin, and I can't breathe. Whatever Ally has just said to me has gone in one ear and out the other. My eyes dart around the kitchen where we're sitting at the island, trying to look anywhere but towards *him*. Grady Landry.

Grady Landry, whose t-shirt is creeping up his waist, showing a sliver of his tanned skin, as he lifts his helmet off. His dark brown hair is perfectly mussed in a way that makes me want to run my fingers through it. God he's hot. I thought so the very moment I saw him, but who wouldn't? With his thick arms covered in matching inked sleeves, his short, groomed beard, and the almost child-like way he's smiling at Mason, he looks as if he came out of the same mold they used to make all my other boyfriends. I give my head a shake. I'm strictly off men for now. Especially men like Grady.

It was stupid of me not to expect to see him here, my best friend is having his brother's baby after all, I just didn't expect it to happen the night I arrived in Heartwood. Something Ally says sneaks its way past the all-consuming thoughts swirling around my mind, and I hear her repeat the question she just asked me.

"How's your mom?" Ally asks. It's a loaded question, and she knows enough not to even bother asking about my dad. Not that I would know how to answer anyways, given that we haven't spoken in over six months.

My mother is a different story. Marla Sinclair likes to make me very aware of everything that is going on in her life. It has always been that way. She flits around, generally only caring about herself and whatever boyfriend or husband she has on the go, while I have been the stable one in our relationship.

"She's Marla." I offer. She is like no other. My eyes flick over to the large front windows of the a-frame cabin, out to where Grady is pulling Mason into a quick hug before moving out of sight around the side of the house. A muffled *whoop* from one of the Landry brothers that already arrived and is probably a couple beers deep drifts through the front door. "Living her best life in wine country, you know how she is."

"Still with Roy?" Ally asks. She moved to the Okanagan after her second marriage fell apart, found herself a house by the lake that she loves. I really thought she was getting her life together, finding herself, thriving in her own independence. And then she met Roy, and he gave her attention, and her pattern repeated.

"Yup. Still with Roy." I don't elaborate. Ally knows that Marla's relationship with Roy is her longest one yet, at three years out from their nuptials. But the clock is ticking. Roy isn't a bad guy per se. He is just another replica of the men my mother has dated, and married, in the past. Their love feels lukewarm, and a by-product of the fact that Roy tells my mother that she's pretty. All her past relationships have been the same. She is so easily swayed at first, but then the honeymoon period ends, and the butterflies fade, and the man she thought was so charming moves on to the next best thing.

The Sinclair women have whatever is the opposite of a green thumb when it comes to dating. Any long-term relationship just withers and dies under our care, no matter how well we think we water it. I think we subconsciously pick men who are like orchids —pretty to look at, but a bitch to keep them that way. I've seemed to inherit this trait from my mother.

That's why I stick to casual flings, 'situationships' if you will. Different city, different guy. Some of them have been just memorable enough that I've kept them around for more than a night, but they all end the same way; a half-hearted "we'll keep in touch" as I head for the airport. But none of the assholes I choose to date are around for the long haul, so it's better for everyone if I stay detached.

"She's nothing if not consistent at least." Ally says, rounding the small kitchen island with a plate of burger patties in one hand and placing her free one on my shoulder as she passes by. "I'm going to take these out so Mason can fire up the grill, can you bring that tray of condiments?"

I nod and set down my wine so I can prep the tray of containing various sauces, when I realize Ally forgot the ketchup. She's already gone out the front door with her plate of burgers, but it only takes me a second to locate the bottle in the door of the fridge. When I pick it up, the liquid inside is separated. *I'll just give it a good shake, we'll be good to go.*

Putting some necessary force into it, I lift the bottle and shake, but the lid must have been ajar, not fully tightened, and it pops off almost instantly. Bright red ketchup *bloops* out, right onto the centre of my camisole. It's my favourite one, too. A silky jade green camisole with cream coloured lace trim around the bust.

"Fuck, fuck, fuck," I mutter, turning to the sink to grab whatever kind of cloth or towel to clean the front of my shirt. Whatever I do, the blob of red only gets bigger as it smears around and soaks into the smooth satin fabric. "Fuckity fuck!" It comes out as a shout, but I get cut off from the rest of the string of curse words I want to scream when I hear heavy footsteps on the porch.

I swivel around to see Grady on the steps up to the cabin and I have the sudden feeling that I would love to just disappear into thin air. He's the type of attractive where I can't picture him doing anything embarrassing, so I'm not ready to face him with half a bottle of ketchup on my shirt. Scrambling, I look for anywhere to hide. Bathroom? No, maybe he's coming inside to use it. *Jesus, why is this cabin so small?*

With nowhere else to go in the tiny, open concept cabin, I decide the pantry cupboard is my only option. It's a fair size, with enough room for one, if not two people. I slink inside quickly and quietly, and slide the accordion door shut behind me.

The slats in the old wooden closet door are parted just enough that I can see Grady stalk into the kitchen and crouch at the open fridge to find a beer. His broad shoulders curve around as he reaches down to grab a bottle, the muscles in his back rippling under his shirt.

I am such a creep. This is one secret that I will take with me to my grave.

The beer bottle lets out a *pffth* sound as Grady pops the cap on the handle of one of the kitchen drawers. He takes a sip—okay, more than a sip—and rolls his shoulders. Something about him seems tense, and he cranes his neck to look around the corner. He's scanning the cabin, almost like he's looking for someone.

As he turns around, I realize the slats in the door might just be big enough for him to see me. I slowly back away, into the shadow of the pantry cupboard, my breathing shallow and quick. My gut roils when I realize I'm going to have to explain my sudden appearance at the barbecue.

My elbow bumps something behind me, that lets out a puff of dust on the impact. I turn to find a bag of flour leaning precariously on the shelf. *Shit.* Moving as silently as I can, I push the bag back to a secure spot, but it's too late. The cloud of powder has made its way to my nostrils, which are now flaring as I wrinkle my nose in a desperate attempt to stifle my sneeze. No luck.

I sneeze, and I sneeze *loud*. Like the kind of sneeze that I would imagine only your middle-aged father is physically capable of, and one that rattles the house. I cover my face with my elbow, hoping the sound was muffled enough that Grady assumed it came from outside. The heavy footsteps I hear across the kitchen tell me that it didn't work, and I squint in the sudden bright light as Grady opens the closet door.

The way his hazel eyes scan my body makes me very aware that I'm still covered in ketchup, and now have a fine layer of flour adorning every inch of me. Grady's jaw flicks as the corner of his mouth quirks up into a playful, lopsided grin. His expression is amused, but not mocking.

"This isn't-" I start, but I'm interrupted.

"Nice place you've got here," Grady says with a casual nod, as if assessing the pantry cupboard, the way he would if I was showing him around my home. "Ally said you had a...unique living situation now but this isn't quite what I pictured."

And then, as if I've casually invited Grady in for coffee after a date, he squeezes himself in next to me and slides the door closed. His broad chest takes up the vast majority of my field of vision, being so close to him, and I have to crane my neck to look up at him. There's a playful smile on his lips, as he waits for me to respond, to play along with the little scenario he's made up to ease the sting of my embarrassment. Colour rises to my cheeks as I realize what he's doing. I can't tell if it's even more humiliating this way, or if I'm grateful for him making light of me spying on him from the closet, but I decide on the latter as I consider a quippy response.

"Yeah, the rent is killing me though." I answer. *Lame*. But Grady goes along with it. He lifts his chin as he looks around the closet once more, exposing the column of his neck to me. I can just make out the outline of his adam's apple in the dark, bobbing as he swallows.

"What does a stunning zero bed, zero bath, studio like this go for nowadays?"

"Ally is charging me my first-born child. Didn't you know? She isn't pregnant with Mason's baby, it's mine."

"Wow, that's steep. But I guess there's a ton of storage in here." Even in the dark, I can tell that Grady's eyes are roaming over my face, and my mind stalls under the weight of his gaze. I'd be lying if I said I haven't thought about wanting to be this close to Grady, and my heart pounds as we stand here breathing each other's air. He's tempting in a way that wars with my resolve not to get involved with anyone.

I chew my bottom lip, my tell when I'm thinking, but I've run out of witty comebacks. Grady must register that the role play has come to an end because he says "should we join the rest of the crew out back? Or would you prefer it if I closed the blinds, and you can just spy from the window."

I give him a playful shove on his shoulder and the solidness of the muscle under his t-shirt catches me off guard. Emerging from the closet, the light reveals the stain on the front of my shirt once again. Grady's warm honey-brown eyes flick down to my chest ever so briefly, in an obvious attempt to only take in the ketchup and nothing else.

"I look like I've been through the Texas Chainsaw Massacre. I don't know if I can go outside." I joke, but heat rises to my cheeks.

"It might be slightly alarming, especially for the medical professionals," Grady says, referring to Ally and Mason, both with years of experience looking at real blood. "But no one here is judging you, Spencer."

The way my name rolls off Grady's tongue, it doesn't sound like a word that he's said for the first time. I know he hasn't, we've interacted before.

Goodnight, Spencer. It was the only time he said my name,

when he lingered in the doorway to his guest bedroom that night I stayed at his place. It had come out with a slight shake then. But as he says it now, it sounds as though he's practiced it. The word is familiar in his mouth. As familiar as saying the word *hello.*

"That's easy for you to say, this is your family," I point out. And now they're my best friend's family, too. "You forget that I'm meeting half of them for the first time."

"Tell you what," Grady says, crossing the kitchen and reaching for the bottle of ketchup on the counter. He picks it up, and before I can say anything at all, he flicks open the lid and squirts a blob down the front of his shirt, the crisp white cotton now marred with a streak of red.

"Grady! What did you-" I cry out, half shriek, half laugh. Grady just looks up at me and grins, that lopsided grin.

"There. Now we both look like the walking dead." His eyes sparkle behind thick dark lashes as they linger on me, making my skin prickle. I wonder how long we would have stood there, staring at each other, if Ally didn't come back into the cabin at that exact moment.

"Spence, people are wondering where the condiments are," she says, and she stops in her tracks as she comes through the front door. "Oh. All over the two of you, by the looks of it."

"Yeah, we had a bit of an... incident." Grady explains, tossing me a playful wink, an acknowledgement that we now share a secret, an inside joke. Something that's just ours.

"Well, I see you've beat me to the re-introduction. Grady, you remember Spencer, don't you?" Ally says, gesturing between us before picking up the tray of sauces I was supposed to take out ages ago. Grady's eyes are on me once again, and my skin is hot, feverish.

"Of course, I remember Spencer," he admits. "She's not easy to forget."

ACKNOWLEDGMENTS

So, I sort of wrote a book? It still feels extremely weird to say that out loud (or on paper). Stories and books have always been a major part of my life, ever since I was young. But I never allowed myself to dream about writing my own one day.

First of all, thank you, my readers, for picking up Ally and Mason's book! If you enjoyed it, please leave a review online or share this book on socials!

Second, I would like to thank the Canadian healthcare system, for making my job as a nurse just unbearable enough that I started to dream about bigger and better things for myself. Don't get me wrong, I love being a nurse. Not to mention, without my experiences in medicine I never would have dreamt up Ally and Mason. Life is all about trusting the path you're on, regardless of whether or not you can see where it's taking you in the moment.

I also need to thank the people who worked with me to make my big dream a reality.

My beta readers, Priscilla and Liv, who were the first to lay eyes on my very rough manuscript and hype me up to the point where I was downright giddy about my story (and maybe a little delusional). Liv, your patience with me through my inevitable panic spirals was unmatched, and I'm so thankful to have you in my corner.

Melissa (my lovely editor at Dark Grove Press), thank you for sticking with me from the early days, the inception of this story, getting me to the end of my first draft, and then helping me polish up the final product.

Thank you, thank you, thank you, Chloe Quinn for bringing Ally and Mason and the town of Heartwood to life on the cover of my little book. I feel like the luckiest author in the world to have your art represent my work.

Jessie (the woman behind the fun and quippy blurb you see on the back), you knocked it out of the park! You took my very mediocre blurb and turned it into something truly magical!

Okay, phew! Onto the people who supported me behind the scenes as I navigated this new chapter of my life as an author.

Brandon—my book boyfriend IRL. My husband. My partner. I love you and everything you do for me to see to it that all my dreams come true. You believe in me wholeheartedly, never wavering. You allow me to grow into new versions of myself, loving each one more than the last. You never question me when I decide on a whim to pick up a new hobby, whether that be knitting, sewing, or now, writing. Words are not enough to describe how grateful I am for you.

Kat, Ashleigh, Molly & Kelsey—your friendships are so deeply valuable to me. I will never not write books with strong female friendships because of you. Everyone needs a Spencer Sinclair in their life, and you all are mine.

Stephanie—you inspire me every single day to learn and grow more as an author. I feel almost spoiled to have you as a role model, someone to learn from, someone who has shown me what is possible.

My therapist, Jennifer—as a certified Ally Wells myself (what *Love on Call* character are you?), I know how hard it is to fully recover from being a people pleaser. This book is everything I have learned about myself over the last two years, thanks to you. I hope it's right. If not, we can discuss it in our next session, I guess.

Mom and Dad—you jumped on board with zero hesitation when I told you that I was pursuing being a romance author. Your support and belief in me throughout my whole life is what has allowed me to try new things without fear of failure. I hope you never read this book, but if you do, I'm sorry (not really, I love smutty romance and I don't care who knows it).

Next in the Heartwood series is Spencer & Grady's book! Brainstorming their book has gotten me through some major creative slumps while I was editing and I'm excited to share it with you soon!

XO,
Meg Riley

ABOUT THE AUTHOR

Meg Riley is a Canadian romance author, who writes sweet, spicy, and swoony romantic comedies set in the heart of the Rocky Mountains. Originally from a little town called White Rock, B.C., Meg moved to Calgary, AB, where she currently lives with her husband and dog.

Website: www.megrileyauthor.com
Instagram: @megrileyauthor
TikTok: @megrileyauthor